LETHAL DECREE

Dr. Trent W. Smallwood

The Reading Glass Books
1-888-420-3050
www.readingglassbooks.com
fulfillment@readingglassbooks.com

To order additional copies of this book, kindly visit Amazon.

DEDICATION

Above all, I wish to thank my daughters, Brielle and Berlin, who have always believed in me and have consistently been my two poles of inspiration. From their humor, their wit, sarcasm, and most of all, their understanding, these two young ladies emulate my creative extremes and have reliably been my effervescent beacon. Thank you two for being the highlight of my life. I would not change one thing about you or the role you have had in my journey. There is not a prouder father than me.

I also want to thank my Godfather Thor S and my most faithful friends Jim A, Jason C, Sherry S, Eric H, and Mary V for being such vital references and advisors, always quietly hovering over my shoulder as I navigated through this project.

Many others were involved, and I wish to thank you also for your hand in this first book. Hopefully, there will be many more stories to follow.

Lastly, I wish to thank my mom. A remarkable woman who has always been there for me and provided me the humor and advice in the years leading up to this endeavor and well after.

CONTENTS

DESCRIPTION

Growing up in the spacious hills of Virginia, Sebastian Storm's destiny was mapped out at an early age. Tragically losing both of his parents as he entered adolescence, Sebastian's fate was set in motion as an unexpectedly adventurous new path lay before him. Through the destined guidance of a remarkable mentor and his son, Sebastian studied and developed the prowess of advanced military combative style. It was quickly realized that Sebastian possessed the gifts necessary to become a soldier elite. The United States government honed his skills further and, in the process, crafted a supersoldier.

Storm was called in when all others had failed. Channeling his turbulent childhood, Sebastian concentrated his focus on those that wronged the weak, his vengeance swift and calculated, a virtual modern-day champion for those who couldn't defend themselves.

As a new, destructive breed of terrorism enters the global arena, Storm's self-reflection surrounding his own vulnerability is realized. But, when he learns that the leader of this auspicious organization has set his focus on Storm specifically, he is compelled to meet this new threat head-on. The leader of this group, Tobias Teague, and Sebastian Storm, have long been rival entities bred by the same training early in their careers with a bitter tragedy that defined their emergent animosity for one another. For over a decade, they have avoided each other; but now, Teague has planned a horrific terrorist event that will warrant the fear of the world, giving him the respect he demands.

On the off chance of meeting a unique and stimulating woman, Sebastian's path whorls into a tailspin of emotions he has never experienced and forces him to reevaluate where his priorities lie and what his future may bring, questioning his vulnerability even further. Duty being paramount, Storm's focus concentrates on Teague. Sebastian Storm is Teague's only obstacle, and he will stop at nothing to achieve his goal. Two soldiers, the best in the game, their bond strong, defined by hate, by history, and by their lethal decree.

Prologue

Keiko's Requite

Tokyo, Japan
2019

With the darkness came a sense of calmness and tranquility, peaceful even. It was late in the evening, just before midnight. The steady echoes of the bustling city streets below were all that one could hear in the distance but muted in his mind as he focused on the task at hand.

He had received vital information earlier in the week from his mysterious source, an anonymous contact he had relied upon for years. Recounting the specifics of this mission, his attention to detail was beyond reproach.

His informant had never let him down. For fifteen years, the information was flawless, arriving anonymously without demands. Each tip was precise and invaluable, creating an unspoken bond of trust. The source's motives remained a mystery, adding to the intrigue. This clandestine partnership was his greatest asset, a thrilling game of reliance and intuition. Encompassing within its own form. . . a measure of justice and balance.

He is attired in all-black, his combative outfit furtive and covert, blending flawlessly within the dark and elusive landscape of the night.

The residence, known as the Park Mansion Akasaka Hikawazaka, was remarkable in its presence and stature. Many of Tokyo's most affluent people lived within the aesthetically pleasing fourteen-story building. Among them, Hiroshi Mikatani resided in the penthouse on the fourteenth floor with his wife Keiko and was the wealthiest and most influential of all the residents living in the building and, by far, the most revered.

Hiroshi Mikatani was considered to be a ruthless and uncompromising man, openly arrogant about his blatant disregard for human life and business acumen. He had initially built his fortune in illegal drug distribution, then expanded into human trafficking and prostitution. His elaborate ventures were well protected under seemingly legitimate textile shell companies he had organized years before, giving him the appearance of developing a lawful empire, but those who knew him feared his reputation, above all.

In addition to profiting from his illegal enterprises, he had numerous child-driven sweatshops he covertly operated throughout Asia, exploiting human life in a multitude of pathways. Mikatani was an intelligent and callous businessman, calculated and cunning to a fault but malevolent to the core. A virtuoso in pressuring individuals of influence, Mikatani took advantage of the Japanese political system and manipulated the nuances of governmental officials to benefit his various business initiatives and exploits.

His young wife, Keiko Kitagawa, was a considerate and nurturing woman coerced into marrying Hiroshi when she was only sixteen years of age. An exquisitely beautiful yet innocent young lady, Keiko was making a name for herself in print and modeling in the prestigious Tokyo fashion market when she caught the wandering eye of Hiroshi Mikatani, and she became the object of his distorted obsession and desire. He quickly became obsessed with Keiko and obtaining her had become his only fascination.

Her life changed and forever altered the moment Mikatani made her his primary focus. Mikatani's leverage came when he learned that Keiko's father was a small business owner and owed a substantial debt to an associate of Mikatani.

Upon obtaining this information, it was arranged the debt would be forgiven if Keiko agreed to marry Mikatani. As expected, Keiko's father reluctantly consented to the proposal, thus absolving his debt and obliging Mikatani's good graces all in the same stroke.

Within days of the wedding, Hiroshi Mikatani forced Keiko to forfeit her career to satisfy his own insecurities, as he feared other men would desire his young bride if she continued to pursue her modeling endeavor.

They had been married for ten years, and she never loved her husband for forbidding her that dream, but as a virtuous wife, she was obligated to tolerate Hiroshi for nearly a decade before giving birth to their only son, Akira, only eighteen months before. When she found out she was pregnant, she feared her husband's reaction as he gave up on her bearing children years before, blaming her for her inability to conceive a child. Akira had become her small miracle.

The young boy was a shining beacon and a blessing for her in an otherwise dismal spiral of despair for Keiko. Akira enabled her focus to become reignited while raising her only child. Hiroshi Mikatani was happy she had produced a son and a Mikatani heir, but Hiroshi determined he possessed little tolerance for the needs and demands of an infant.

Keiko's dire situation ultimately came to light, provided by Sebastian's mysterious source. The month before, a frightful incident occurred where Mikatani had become enraged over Akira's incessant sobbing and crying. The poor boy suffered from a fever and wailing profusely as a result, igniting Mikatani's fury as he was far from a paternal or sympathetic man.

In an effort to avoid upsetting Hiroshi, Keiko attempted to comfort Akira's suffering, afraid of what Mikatani was capable of doing if he was angered beyond his limits. In his rage, Hiroshi grasped the young toddler from her arms in desperation and forcefully held his hand over Akira's mouth, suppressing the boy's cries and whimpers only to satisfy his own baseless irritability.

Keiko attempted to regain control and pull Akira from Hiroshi's grasp. Still, he resisted, and his guards held her fast as he went into the living room, unsympathetically stifling the crying child as he unknowingly smothered the child's nose and mouth in the process. A few minutes went by as Keiko cried, though thankful Akira's whimpering had ceased, hoping Hiroshi had grown tired of holding the boy.

When Hiroshi was finally satisfied that his son had stopped crying, he released his hand from his son's face. Only then did he observe that Akira's skin had become blue and pallid from the lack of oxygen.

Attempting to revive him, Hiroshi gave up after only a few seconds, handing his unmoving, asphyxiated son's body to the nearest guard and walked out of their apartment, unwilling to accept any responsibility for what had just transpired. In his rage, Hiroshi had smothered his only son, and he perished in that moment.

Hiroshi displayed no remorse or sadness over causing his son's needless death. The bewildered guard simply held the unresponsive boy and looked blankly at Keiko from across the room, unsure what to do or say.

From the bedroom doorway, held at a distance from the guard, Keiko witnessed her son's lifeless body held within the guard's arms, knowing he was gone. Her hands instinctively went to her mouth, screaming out as she collapsed to the floor over the pain and shock that overwhelmed her over the loss of her son, paired with the renewed hatred she had for Hiroshi.

Such a senseless death, all caused by her husband, a selfish monster. She knew that she could no longer be a part of her husband's life or his world. She reviled Hiroshi, and after her son's passing, she would never look him in the eye again.

Several weeks passed, and still mourning the loss of her son, Keiko was always closely monitored by Hiroshi's bodyguards, for Hiroshi feared she may attempt to take her own life. Keiko had certainly considered the option, but her greater wish and hope was that Hiroshi would someday face his own demons and answer for all his terrible deeds.

In an attempt to get out of the apartment and keep herself occupied; Keiko forced herself to visit the local market daily to focus on more positive distractions.

While touring the market, a middle-aged man on a bike clumsily ran into the guard assigned to her, causing a slight commotion in the area. At that moment, a young Japanese girl posing as a student cautiously approached Keiko and whispered, "Please remain looking forward. Someone is watching over you; look for him to contact you soon. Open this alone, destroy it, and tell no one of this meeting. Be very careful."

The young woman softly reached Keiko's hand, gently placed a folded note in her palm, and closed it before blending into the crowd before Keiko made sense of what was happening.

By then, the guard had helped the man up on the bike, pushed him away, and rushed to Keiko, looking for any suspicious people or anything out of place around them. The guard, noticing nothing irregular, as Keiko gripped the note tightly within her hand, eager to get home and understand the situation better while playing back in her mind what the young girl had said to her at the fish stand, still puzzled by what had transpired in those few seconds.

She was confused and frightened but eager to know more. She told the guard she wasn't feeling well and wanted to return home. The guard escorted her back to the penthouse.

When home, aware her husband was not in the penthouse, she immediately headed to their master bathroom, where she wouldn't be disturbed by the bodyguards or residence staff.

She closed the door gently for privacy, sat upon the commode, and slowly unfolded the note, sweaty and creased from her clutching it for the past hour. Upon opening the small message, Keiko read,

> *Please follow instructions carefully: You will soon hear from someone who will make your husband answer for his actions. A burner phone was placed into your right jacket pocket. Secure it in a safe place. Someone will contact you soon, authenticating with the word Pegasus. Please destroy this note.*

It was all she could do not to cry at that moment after reading the note. Had her prayers been answered? Who was this person who wished to help her, and what was their interest in her or motivation for doing so? What did they stand to gain from all of this? She had so many unanswered questions and just as many fears running through her mind.

At that moment, a deep sense of dread overcame her; how would anyone get near her husband? His enemies considered him as an *"antatchaburu"* or an untouchable. Harming him seemed an overwhelming impossibility. Keiko felt It was a hopeless notion at best.

Her husband was far too shrewd a man, and paired with all his paranoia, one man, let alone a small army, could never get close enough to Hiroshi Mikatani, who spared no expense in ensuring his own protection.

She tore the note into several pieces and flushed it down the toilet, retrieved the phone and hid it well, and went into her bedroom and wept over the loss of her innocent son and for her own misery and cursed the name Hiroshi Mikatani until she cried herself to asleep.

Finally quiet and settled, Keiko rarely slept, but when she did, it was the only time she experienced any peace.

Sebastian Storm was no stranger to the night. It was where he did his best work. With the darkness came so many more tactical advantages and options, consistently exploiting its obscurity to his benefit in some form or fashion.

The Park Mansion, Akasaka Hikawazaka, where Hiroshi Mikatani resided, posed little concern for him.

His more immediate challenge included the highly trained bodyguards positioned strategically upon the premises and the advanced security system Hiroshi Mikatani had chosen to protect his penthouse.

The United States government had always provided invaluable resources to Sebastian, which were at his disposal, unofficially, as they were not entirely aware of his personal clandestine operations. These resources were vital as they tipped the scales in his favor during these unsanctioned undertakings, yet careful never to perform while on the company's clock.

He was on his own: no backup, no outside surveillance or aid by any means. A lone wolf, and Sebastian preferred it that way in these instances.

Each mission presented a different set of circumstances and perils for him to navigate. With his attention focused on every detail, he calculated most contingencies. Still, there were those unforeseeable anomalies that may ensue at any given moment, yet the risk was always present, always looming.

Strangely, he embraced those capricious moments when a new variable would often materialize and assess and test his abilities further, keeping his senses acute and focused, challenging his nature and, above all, his resolve.

With this specific encounter, Sebastian's best approach for the penthouse was by way of the roof. He had found the building adjacent to the Akasaka Hikawazaka building was the Ottohuro Hotel, which has thirty-four floors, giving him roughly 225 feet of elevation over Mikatani's Penthouse and his intended target. Carefully scouting the Akasaka Building from his higher vantage point, he located three of the guards from his current position atop the roof. He had studied the floorplan and guard patrols for three days and ensured he had their routines well documented.

Using his silenced Bergara B-14 HMR sniper rifle, Sebastian calculated the wind, timing, and ammunition needed for the 250-yard targets. He was familiar with marks ten times the distance, but his trial wasn't the distance in this instance but rather in terminating all three guards within seconds of one another.

His timing would also be essential in taking out the remaining bodyguards after landing on the roof, where there was a small putting green, ideal for an aerial landing. He noted their ten-minute routine radio check-ins between the guards so he would have a short window to eliminate the three outside guards, travel the 220 yards to the rooftop, terminate the remaining four guards, and pray none of his victims were discovered in that short period.

Sebastian smiled at the challenge set before him. This was his craft, and he knew it. These moments made him feel alive, and he cherished any opportunities presented to eliminate oppressors or those associated with them.

Sebastian had reached out to Keiko several days prior with the burn phone provided to her. He had been observing her from his Ottohuro Hotel vantage point to authenticate receipt of the instructions given to her by the female student at the market.

He was about to contact her directly via text to confirm her response visually because they had never met; he had only reviewed pictures of her in the file provided to him. Confirming the woman's appearance from his photos of her to that of the striking woman standing in the window, he verified that she was, in fact, Keiko Kitagawa.

Carefully studying her through his binoculars as she stood with one leg somewhat bent forward. Wearing only a robe, opened slightly, revealing her lean body and sumptuous curves beneath, unknowingly exposing herself in the expansive window while Sebastian examined her from afar.

She gazed out through the full-length window and stepped backward three steps to a chaise lounge chair positioned in front of the window, allowing the breathtaking view before her to be fully appreciated. Beauty such as this paled to her after the loss of her son.

x

She thought of Akira throughout the day, and his memory reminded her of her hatred for Hiroshi. She sighed, pushing his image from her mind.

She elegantly lay down upon the oversized chaise, leaning back, enjoying the picturesque view before her. She held the burn phone in one hand as she thought in silence, waiting in the spacious penthouse bathroom. This quiet place was her sanctuary, her only place to think and reflect.

She would periodically check the new phone for any word from the stranger she was promised would contact her, yet two full days had gone by without so much as a word, which saddened her.

Sebastian used the days to observe her, dissect her habits, and study her and her husband's daily regimen. He couldn't help but establish that Keiko was a physically exquisite woman in all forms. Tall for an Asian woman at five feet seven, thin but curvy with high cheekbones and soft, succulent lips. He saw why she was desired to bless the covers of fashion magazines.

Hallowed with striking long hair, she wore down well below her waist, full and thick. She was nearly a perfect physical specimen, humble, natural, and vibrant in every way.

While Sebastian watched her through the large bathroom window, he noted and reveled in her beauty, humility, and pain. He noted the suffering in her eyes and how she carried herself; he felt her sadness as he experienced it well himself. Keiko seemed dejected and somber, most likely from the life she was trapped within and having just lost her only child at the hands of her frightful husband.

She so desperately sought a way out, witnessed within her eyes and how she moved, her burden significant. Feeling her anguish, Sebastian closed his eyes hard, understanding her pain. He mourned for her and her torment. Sebastian thought of how such a striking woman could live such a wretched and sorrowful life, being swept up into her husband's existence simply to possess her, his greatest trophy.

Alluring as she was, Sebastian had an objective, and the mission was always his focus . . . . *always.*

While he intently observed her through his binoculars, he decided the moment was favorable to reach out to her, knowing she was holding the phone at that instant. He texted her, "Hello Keiko, code word Pegasus. I know you have been waiting for me to reach out, but I needed to ensure you were safe and not compromised. There are some questions I wish to ask you. Is that permissible? I'm here to help with your situation. . . . *a friend*."

He studied her as she looked down at the incoming message and observed her somber expression suddenly brighten. Startled by the incoming message, she sat up upon the chaise lounge chair; in doing so, the right shoulder of her robe dropped, revealing her breast and the splendor of her figure even further.

Unfazed by her nakedness, she began to read the incoming text diligently. She hesitated and responded, "Yes. Of course, but please tell me who you are. And why do you want to help me?" She is cautious and untrusting of the situation or fears that her husband may well be behind the interaction, testing her loyalties. That possibility always loomed over her.

Sebastian thought about her question for a moment but chose to avoid her inquiry, then typed his response, "Thank you, Keiko. I'm here to help. How many guards are in the apartment at night? What is the alarm code and verification?" She sat more erect, now more attentive to the task and eager to please this mysterious man.

She wasn't entirely trusting of him, but at this point, she was desperate for anything to change her current circumstances. "Eight to ten guards normally. We do not sleep in the same room. He often has other women over at night or sleeps alone. The security alarm code is 12112003, and the verification password is 'B-R-I-E-L-L-E', which will disarm the alarm. If I may, what is your name?" she asked again as Sebastian considered the question for a moment. He replied, "It's not important. Call me . . *S*. . . for now. Is there anything else I should know?"

Keiko pondered the question further for a moment when she received this subsequent text. As if sensing his gaze from the adjacent building, she looked up from the bathroom window directly in Sebastian's general direction as if she felt his presence while he watched her. Instinctively flinching, Sebastian corrected himself and looked directly at her, reminding himself that she couldn't see him from his distance but observing the eerie notion from her intuition, knowing he was only a few hundred yards away from her.

She hesitated momentarily and replied, "Are you close . . . S? I sense you are, somehow . . . . Regardless, tonight or tomorrow, there should be fewer guards. This morning, my husband mumbled something about some of his men being gone collecting debts owed to him tonight and tomorrow. There are also infrared sensors outside of the master bedroom. My husband is a paranoid man."

Considering all the information Keiko had provided, he replied, "Understood. I want you to stay in your room and lock the door when you go to sleep tonight, and no matter what you hear, don't come out until the following morning. I will deal personally with your husband. Is there anything you want me to say to him?"

Sending the text, he peered through his binoculars; he watched her wipe a tear away from her face as she wrote, "Tell him that this is all for Akira, . . . and thank you for doing this for my son and me, S. I'm not sure who you are, but I am so thankful for you and being such a blessing. Good luck and be careful; his men are killers and protective of my husband."

Sebastian continued looking at her through his binoculars as he received her text. Keiko was standing again in front of the window and looked out over the city that lay before her with one hand flat against the glass, steadying herself, the other resting on her exposed thigh, phone in hand.

Her robe opened fully now, revealing her sensual and curvaceous figure underneath. The bareness of her skin and smooth mound was fully exposed, and he noted she was comfortable in her nakedness, confident in her sexuality, and basking in her femininity. Her breasts were heaving slightly from the exhilaration derived from the exchanges she had with Sebastian, as well as the excitement of the possibilities Sebastian had expressed about her husband.

She embraced her tension and fantasized in anticipation as her anticipation was building, not in a sexual manner necessarily but rather intertwined with the nervousness surrounding her current situation that may well change for the better if this man possessed the ability to make it so.

Her smooth skin glistened as she slowly rubbed her stomach, her beautiful femininity entirely bare, perfect, and revealed to Sebastian watching from afar. There was something about this man, his confidence and strength, that she strangely sensed and empathized with him.

She wondered if he was observing her at this moment. She secretly desired that he was keeping a watchful eye on her and appreciating the image of her before him. She fantasized about what Sebastian looked like in person. Keiko imagined him tall and strong and brought her hand to her mouth, embarrassed for thinking of such thoughts. How could she consider such possibilities at a time like this? She thought, but she also became intrigued at the thought of the unknown and the excitement of it all. Keiko looked out over the city. Was he out there? She found herself wondering and hoping his focus was on her.

Reveling in her beauty, Sebastian couldn't help thinking if she sensed he was observing her every move. He also wondered if she was aware she and her son were just two of the victims in a sea of countless others who suffered because of her tyrannical husband.

She continued to look at the phone, hoping he would text again. Keiko was indeed a stunning woman, despondent, beaten, and trapped within this extravagant jail, a twenty-eight million dollar prison atop the Akasaka Hikawazaka building, fourteen floors above the ground.

His final response was, "Destroy the phone and erase the messages, Keiko. You will have your life back soon. I promise you this." Sebastian looked for her reaction from afar. She smiled for the first time at hearing this as she typed, "Please tell me who you are." But Sebastian never responded. It was midmorning; she had to wait several hours until nightfall, but she would have her vengeance later that evening, or so she hoped. She sensed the energy around her changing.

Bringing himself back to the moment, Sebastian narrowed his sights on the farthest and most isolated guard from his current position and vantage point. He noted the guards had just completed their ten-minute radio check-in; the clock was now starting. He pressed the timer on his Garmin Fenix 8 sports watch and set te timer for nine minutes, allowing himself a minimal cushion.

Honing his silenced Bergara sniper rifle at the farthest target, he took a half breath and gently squeezed the trigger, letting go the single silenced round as it landed squarely at the back of the soldier's head, dropping him where he stood. His second and third shots had the same result, with the final guard taking the round through his right eye. Neither of the guards were aware of what hit him.

After the final shot, Sebastian quickly broke down his sniper rifle within a few seconds, placed it into his specially designed backpack, and immediately began sprinting toward the northeast corner of the building and leaped off the edge without any hesitation or fear.

Soaring into the darkness, immediately deploying his parachute and, within seconds, landed upon the putting green on the roof and dropped to one knee, pulling the parachute up quickly and into his pack, leaving no trace of his presence nor entrance other than the dead guards surrounding him on three corners of the building's rooftop.

Checking his watch, Sebastian noted he had seven minutes remaining before the next radio check would commence, so he needed to keep up his pace. Pulling his silenced Heckler & Koch (H&K) 9mm from his jacket, he began to concentrate on his next objective.

Slowly walking down the exterior stairs from the putting green to the large outdoor pool, Sebastian had an optimum vantage point of the interior of the elaborate living quarters. He assumed the glass was bulletproof and needed to breach the outer perimeter of the building quietly.

He located two additional guard positions, one being outside by the pool and the other in the kitchen area within the residence.

He paused until the guard by the pool approached the retaining wall, firing a well-placed silenced bullet at the soldier's head, dropping him with a soft thud, then slipped through an open side door into the living room. Careless and lazy, he thought, in leaving the exterior door unlocked. Before entering, he found the security pad to disarm the security for the residence and erased all security footage for the previous hour using the security credentials Keiko had given him.

This operation never existed, possessing no footprint.

He was certain there were two to three additional guards to contend with, and he needed to eliminate those threats before dealing with Hiroshi himself.

Sebastian eased into the kitchen, noticing the guard watching television with his back to him. Slowly approaching the guard from behind, Sebastian had his gun trained on the back of the guard's head in the event he turned before he was upon him.

Once positioned just behind the guard, Sebastian placed his gun into his specialized magnetic breast pocket holster. With his left hand, he applied pressure to the side of the man's temple, simultaneously placing his right hand at the base of the guard's neck, snapping it, killing the man instantly, leaving the guard's body upright in the chair, head slumped slightly forward. He reached over and turned the television set off.

At that moment, a sixth guard casually walked into the kitchen holding two Italian 'take out' bags of food, catching Sebastian by surprise. He instinctively dropped the bags he was carrying in an effort to grasp his own gun, but Sebastian was far more intuitive and agile. Already reaching for his silenced 9mm, Sebastian took aim and put a single round between the man's eyes. The guard slumped to the floor with a soft thump.

Sebastian crouched low and hid behind the island within the kitchen, listening for any footsteps from the clattering of the dropped bags onto the hard stone floor. From what Keiko had mentioned, there were often up to ten guards in the apartment during most evenings.

He had eliminated six of the guards effortlessly. Sebastian had to assume there may be up to four more guards within the home.

He may have trusted Keiko's information, but he would be foolish to depend on it entirely.

He took the earpiece from the last guard and placed it within his ear as he began to approach Hiroshi's master bedroom, taking notice of the infrared silent alarm Keiko mentioned to him. It had been seven minutes since he had taken out the guards on top of the building, so he only had two minutes to inspect the rest of the apartment. He cleared the rest of the main areas and made his way to the front door.

Looking through the peephole, he saw the left shoulder of the guard standing just to the right of the front door that led to the hallway. Sebastian opened the door; the guard turned his head as the bullet entered through his left eye and tore through skull bone and brain matter, spraying dark crimson across the wall behind him. As the guard began to collapse, Sebastian grabbed him by the back of his suit jacket, dragged him inside the penthouse, and closed the door gently when the guard's feet were clear.

He paused for a moment to listen for any chatter coming over the earpiece, but all was silent. Seven guards accounted for by his count. Sebastian made his way to the dimly lit hallway to the master bedroom.

He was approaching the nine-minute mark, but the mission was progressing without complications. He waited for the check-in of all the guards, but the radio remained silent. The residence was clear.

Something awakened Keiko from her light sleep. She quietly lay in bed, staring at the ceiling, thinking of her life and the loss of her son Akira, and sadness came over her. She missed him dearly and detested her husband for what he had done to their child. Akira didn't deserve his fate, nor did she. The house seemed so quiet, more than usual; something seemed different, but she remained where she was told, as instructed by the stranger she called *S*. Keiko again noticed an intense energy around her at that moment, and it made her heart beat faster.

She had sensed the same thing when she exchanged words with *S* earlier that day. Keiko was acutely aware of her aura and the energy within and with others, and she sensed a strong presence, or energy, close by.

Lock the door and do not come out for any reason, the stranger had said. She would obey his wishes, although Keiko was a curious young woman. She would respect his instruction for now; at least she would try, for the time being, she thought.

Sebastian located the two distinct infrared sensors Keiko had warned him about and disarmed them before approaching the master bedroom. He looked at his watch as it reached his ten-minute timetable, but there was no chatter over the earpieces confirming that only Hiroshi and Keiko were left within the dwelling.

Drawing his gun, Sebastian cautiously opened one of the two large French doors leading into the master bedroom. He immediately located Hiroshi Mikatani sitting upon his large king bed, fixated on the television, not yet noticing that Sebastian had entered the large room.

Severely overweight, unkept, and grotesque in appearance, he sat upon his bed wearing only white boxers and an open white robe, engrossed with the pornography showing on his large screen television.

Two Asian women were partaking in the mutual oral pleasure of one another on the screen as the heavy man was intently absorbed, unaware of anything else, engrossed in the images before him.

Sebastian put a bullet through the television, abruptly terminating the noise, making the room immediately quiet. Startling Hiroshi, he glanced to the side, noticing Sebastian by the side of the bed, and cowered to the back of the headboard, glaring at him.

"Who are you, and do you have any idea who I am? You have made a grave mistake in coming here. My men will rush in here any minute," shouted Hiroshi in Japanese. Sebastian responded in semi-broken yet effective Japanese, "I'm aware of who you are, Mr. Mikatani, and that is precisely why I am here this evening. Your *men* will not be coming in, sir. That said, this is for Akira and Keiko," raising his gun in the process.

Hiroshi Mikatani blankly looked at Sebastian when the bullet penetrated his forehead, blowing out the back of his head and splattering blood and brain matter all over the headboard. Sebastian looked at him unphased.

Mikatani expression was frozen in place as Sebastian cocked his head and fired two additional rounds into his heart. There was no reason for Sebastian to prolong the inevitable with small talk or eventual groveling; Mikatani was a terrible human being, and he deserved the fate that befell him.

Sebastian was hopeful that Keiko would finally be able to move on and have closure to this part of her life. With Hiroshi's Mikatani death, she would be free of his control and consequently a wealthy woman in the process.

Sebastian turned and began to quietly exit the master bedroom, cautiously stepping into the large hallway and slowly closing the door behind him, turning to see Keiko standing before him down the hallway, not twenty feet away in front of her own bedroom door.

She looked so innocent and vulnerable in the dim light, simply dressed in cotton panties and a tank top. Her beauty was soft and delicate but perfect. She was even more captivating in person. Seeing Sebastian come from her husband's room, in her heart, she knew it was done, completed, and finally finished for her, and Akira's poor, innocent soul was now avenged.

Keiko looked blankly and naïvely at Sebastian, taking in this figure before her, the man that vindicated her, awarding her a sense of relief, allowing her pain to now diminish though knowing it would take time. She hadn't anticipated how handsome he was, rugged and edgy, but his face was strong and determined, his presence commanding.

She sensed the goodness within him, his energy and . . . *his power*. Keiko was drawn to Sebastian's strength, and it excited her, which surprised her in light of what had transpired in the adjacent room just moments before, death exuding from the room behind him.

She fantasized at that moment about being with such a man. He was a resilient and dominant force that was, in fact, kind and understanding—she sensed it. Keiko felt Sebastian's suffering, and it awkwardly comforted her somehow. She was strangely drawn to him and fascinated by his talents. He had bested all of Hiroshi's men and that was no easy feat. He had somehow given her freedom, releasing her of her bonds, allowing her safe passage from this prison.

Without a word, she sauntered up to him and put her arms around him, holding him tight, in her way, so thankful for what he had done for her. Sebastian knew she needed this moment, the physical contact, the first step in her own personal healing. It was her way of thanking him, but he was also acutely aware he had to leave the apartment soon. He was vulnerable and compromised while in the home, and he was putting them both at risk of being there any longer than necessary.

After a moment, he gently separated from her, looking down into her beautiful large almond-brown eyes, he whispered in Japanese, "Keiko, you must return to your room and lock the door behind you and in the morning call the police and report what you awakened to here."

She looked at him impassively and quizzically, refocused beyond him to the door of the master bedroom, knowing her husband lay inside. Without saying a word, she walked around Sebastian and continued to the bedroom door, opening it as Sebastian turned and observed her and simply waited, understanding the closure she sought.

Quietly walking to the bed, she looked at Hiroshi Mikatani, lying there, deformed, silent, eyes open and lifeless. She noticed that Sebastian had shot him three times and knew that even Hiroshi Mikatani, the untouchable, the antatchaburu, was not invincible at all.

He was just a man, but to her and many others, a monster.

After allowing the moment she needed, Sebastian walked up to her and put his hand on the small of her back, and she turned, looking up and into his eyes. Keiko replied in broken English, "I will do as you say, but please tell me your name."

Sebastian hesitated yet was impressed with her English. Even with an accent, her words were angelic, pure, and possessed such a soft genuineness, compelling him to abide by her wishes. He couldn't resist her and validated why Hiroshi Mikatani had obsessed over this woman.

"My name is Sebastian," he replied reluctantly. "Will I see you again, Sebastian?" asked Keiko. "That's not advisable, Keiko. You can't be seen with me, I'm a ghost, I live in the shadows, I . . . " explained Sebastian. But as he spoke, she put two fingers up to his lips to stop him from resisting and said, "Well, I wish to when the time is right. I'm drawn to your energy, Sebastian, and I'm resourceful and have my ways." And with that, she turned and walked back to her room, turning one last time to look at him and smiling, placing her hands together and bowing in true Japanese fashion before entering her room and locking the door behind her as he had instructed her to do.

An exciting and captivating woman thought Sebastian and yet remained relaxed and unwavering despite her husband's gruesome demise. Sebastian cautiously slipped into the hallway, careful to avoid camera placements, then crept into the stairwell, descended the fourteen floors, and snuck out of the rear exit unnoticed.

The authorities would never be able to connect Sebastian to what happened at the Park Mansion Akasaka Hikawazaka that evening, nor would he ever be a suspect, and Keiko would be a fortunate victim in its aftermath and somehow spared or unnoticed by the wrath that was bestowed by that of her husband.

The fact that Keiko was unhurt came into question by the police the following day but was eventually cast aside; it hypothesized that either the assailants simply overlooked her as she slept in the spare room or was not the object or their focus and only her husband was the intended target.

The authorities suspected that Mikatani's business dealings had finally caught up to him or one of his many enemies had been scorned one too many times. Otherwise, it was deemed an open-and-shut case, and few people were upset over the loss of the tyrant.

Sebastian left for a flight later that afternoon to Athens, Greece, to investigate an arms dealer outfitting several formally identified ISIS factions of the now Islamic State (IS), the radical Islamist group that had seized territory in Syria and Iraq.

Sebastian had a particular talent for instilling trouble into various organizations, causing disarray and eventual collapse, and his superiors were looking to him to perform that same task in Athens. This mission would take months of work with his team, but it was these challenges that Sebastian Storm was bred to do, and he thrived on the chaos he created in his wake.

Chapter 1

Sebastian's Turmoil

New York, New York
2020

He cautiously entered his large suite at the Waldorf Astoria Hotel, immediately picking up the aroma of perfume in the air. He couldn't place it, but the scent was familiar as he drew his gun, inspecting the entryway and living room per his regimented protocol. He was frustrated at not being able to place the bouquet of the aroma subtly filling the air until he came before the bedroom door; then, it struck him, and he smiled.

Keiko.

It had been nine months since Sebastian executed Hiroshi Mikatani in Tokyo, and he had often thought of how Keiko was adjusting to her new life. A life without the abuse and suffering she had endured. Sebastian had vindicated many such victims over the years, and he often thought of all of them from time to time. It was his unusual burden he chose to carry, but it also fulfilled his destiny, as well as his purpose, or so he thought, to help justify the death that lay in his wake.

He slowly opened the French doors to the master bedroom. There, atop the bed, Keiko was lying seductively facing him, exquisite and pure, not wearing any clothing but a sheer light blanket only partially covering her legs, most of her body fully exposed.

Sebastian had to capture the moment in his mind observing her skin as light as silk, sunless but supple, smooth, youthful, yet flawless and alluring as if she were a porcelain doll. The impeccable curve of her hips was enthralling and seductive as she supported her head cupped in her hand, with her folded arm lying on the bed. He wondered how long she had been waiting for him.

She smiled invitingly but didn't move as he opened the doors fully as she lay on the bed. Her perfectly contoured breasts were exposed, gently rising, and falling with each breath. Her legs together, resting atop one another but outlining her figure, bare as baby's skin. Sebastian drank in her beauty, walked over to the bed, and sat upon the corner, gun still in hand, appreciating her magnificence and contours. He smiled but shook his head, bewildered at how she could have found him. As if reading his mind, "The front desk called up when you entered the property, and I wanted to be ready for your arrival. Please don't be angry with me for being here, Sebastian," as she smiled, melting away any annoyance he may have harbored.

He grinned and said in Japanese, "Oh Keiko, curiously, I wondered if we would ever meet again. I can tell you are more than capable of somehow locating me. That is no easy task, and you already impressed me when we met that you are an amazing and ingenious woman as well. I am most curious how you found me?"

His question was genuine as he was both concerned and intrigued by her ingenuity as she successfully located him in New York. He prided himself in moving within obscurities and darkness. People, whether with good or malicious intent, had tremendous difficulty in locating Sebastian Storm at any given time, especially if he didn't wish to be found.

She smiled back at the question and replied, "You may remember, Sebastian, I mentioned that I am resourceful, and my husband's money affords me certain luxuries . . . . or valuable information otherwise unattainable to most people. It took me a long time and considerable resources to find you, though I will admit. But in the end, I did just that. I found you, and I'm glad I did." Her smile was disarming and seductive.

As Sebastian listened to her speak, still holding his gun, he brushed her hair back over her ear, appreciating her beauty as he gazed into her alluring eyes.

She closes her eyes, enjoying the sensuality of his touch, bearing the steel's coldness upon her skin. Her hand begins to touch his hand as she takes the gun from him and places it on the bed, "You won't need this tonight, I promise, Sebastian," says Keiko as she enticingly winks at him.

Keiko then guides his hand to her hip as he brushes over her skin with his hand, appreciating the contours of her feminine curves. She seemed flawless in body, instilling the desire for him to merely touch her, to verify this wasn't some pensive dream he didn't want to wake from.

"You are the very definition of perfection, Keiko." Keiko put her hand on his cheek and replied, "Oh, I'm more than flawed, Sebastian. Broken even, much like you, I sense. From the first time we met in my home, I could sense your pain, your turmoil. But, when I first saw you in the hallway and felt your essence and strength, I knew I must see you again."

She eased her hips gently onto her back, looking into his eyes the entire time as his hand drifted from her hips to her stomach as she continued to hold his gaze. She bent one knee, inviting him and his touch to torture her further, and strangely welcomed it. His hand further explores her body, wandering now over her breasts as her nipples became erect by his contact. Her hand came to rest on his thigh as he explored her further.

Never losing eye contact, her large, striking brown eyes drink him in as he squeezes her ample breasts, watching the effect it is having on her, and she bites her lower lip softly in anticipation while looking at him intently. His tanned hand contrasted with her pale, smooth skin beneath his touch.

Her husband had never touched her as Sebastian did, and it excited her beyond any other experience she had ever felt. Hiroshi had been rough, vulgar, and selfish, but he was no more, and she had to keep reminding herself of that fact. This man was her champion. She owed him any desire he wished, for, giving her the gift of . . . . . *freedom.*

Her inviting spirit was her gift to him for saving her life. Supple and beautiful, her exposed body before him, he couldn't help but appreciate her elegance as he continued to caress her. Subtly, her hand came up to his again and began to guide him lower to the place where she desired.

She tenderly urged his hand to her abdomen and then urged him lower still, easing him to her mound, waiting and wanting him to experience the allures of her femininity.

He gently touched her mons as she eased her legs open further, beckoning him in, nudging his hand with slight firmness as he mildly resisted further exploring more of her. Sebastian felt the moistness of her skin between her legs, arousing him in the process. Keiko enjoyed his soft touch as she opened her legs further for him, inviting him and welcoming his caress. Her own hand drifted further down his own thigh, enjoying his strong legs.

She wanted him to know his effect on her, though she was confident he was more than aware already. Feeling her moisture on his fingers, Sebastian began delicately stroking her sensitive button, watching her writhe as he teased her spot as she had never experienced before. Sebastian knew his way around a woman, how to excite her and make her ache for him.

Keiko enjoyed his exploring for a time, arousing her further, before she slowly eased over onto her stomach, keeping her legs apart as he lightly squeezed her rear now, enjoying its petite plumpness as two of his fingers again found her moistened folds as she lifts her tight rear end to meet his fingers and pulls him in deeper. She watches him intently as the stroke with his hand is sensual and erotic, methodical and igniting a fiery heat deep within her that she had never experienced.

He begins touching her faster, pulsating further, and gently introduces the third finger, pushing her limits as she is about to let loose what she was hoping he would release within her, her climax imminent as he increases his cadence and rhythm with his fingers as she licks and bites her lips, clenching the sheets, watching him as she begins to orgasm.

Her lips parted, trying to hold her moans back, drenching his fingers, enjoying her spasms as they dissipated. He slows his intensity as she starts to ease her rear and come to rest and relax within a normal position, still lying upon her back as she recovers, but she is far from finished. She rubs his arm as Sebastian relaxes upon his back, a brief interlude, enjoying the tranquility for a time.

After a moment, Keiko sits up and positions herself atop him, straddling him, exposed and vulnerable. She leans down, kissing his neck. She smells of lavender as her hair falls forward, covering his face and neck, arousing him with just her simplicity and purity.

As she caresses him, she begins to undo the buttons of his shirt, then pulls it off him completely as her bare body slides over his chest. Then she comes to rest her torso on top of him, straddling him still as their lips meet, and kisses him more passionately, massaging the back of his head, lightly pulling his hair.

She feels him growing more aroused beneath her and continues embracing and kissing him sensually as her hand moves downward, and she unzips his pants, wanting more of him exposed and available to her and her desires. She will not accept any denial of this pleasure she has anticipated for so long.

Sebastian is amazed at the sexual prowess with which Keiko operates around him. His carnal desire escalates with each passing second as she slides her petite body down below now, between his legs, her naked figure resting upon her knees on the end of the bed in one fluid motion. She eases his pants off, looks at him approvingly, and whispers, "I want to please you, Sebastian."

She takes all of her long, thick black hair and wraps it several times with her hands in almost an artistic display and then knots it above and behind her head, exposing the beautiful curves of her face now. Having him in a vulnerable position, never taking her gaze from his, mesmerizing him in the process, she places her hands on each of his toned thighs and comes up to him. Her large, sensual lips graze his own as her scent consumes Sebastian, heightening his senses further.

Keiko, though innocent in many ways, is well versed in the lascivious fulfillment of a man, and Sebastian's desires became the object of her own in releasing her from her literal prison—free of the chains that bound her; she was captive as far back as her adolescence. Free of the torment and fear that her husband instilled each and every day, she suffered with him.

She kisses him, deeply thankful that their lives somehow crossed paths and fell within their given fate. Sebastian was the first man that she had ever desired, as intimacy with her husband was forced and repulsive in every form to her. This moment was . . . . different in every way, knowing it would be. She wanted Sebastian, implored him, and needed him. Keiko had chosen him to fulfill her, as she was certain he would not disappoint any expectation she may have; she was certain of it. Keiko yearned for him the moment she saw him in the dark that evening, exiting her husband's tomb within her home that night all those months ago.

As she softly kissed, tasting him, her right hand drifted downward, enjoying his flat, contoured stomach until she found her prize. Keiko's large eyes opened wider as she attentively looked into Sebastian's own, validating that she was pleased with what he provided. She touched his face with her own and began to stroke him. She enjoyed the effect she was having on him.

Keiko looked into his eyes as she touched him, seducing him physically and emotionally, knowing its effect was welcomed. She wanted more of him; she kissed him again, then broke her lips from his, peering deep into his eyes, looking for what made Sebastian the man he had become and wanting to know more of who he was. She could see his pain, his focus, and his power. She not only saw it from the scars that covered his body but felt it as well, and she only craved more of it, feeding off his force and quintessence as they touched.

There was something exceptional about him as she could sense it and pull from the energy that emanated from his center. She wanted to please him and eased back down between his legs, taking hold of him, and stroking him tenderly and deliberately to enhance his pleasure from her.

On her knees now, she takes his tip upon her tongue, running it along its ridges, feeling him tense somewhat yet enjoying his reaction. She takes his head into her mouth and savors him, exploring and enjoying yet fantasizing about their union and connection. Her only sexual experience had been with her late husband; she has never experienced anything as sensual and erotic with him, but it excites her at the thought of Sebastian ultimately taking her.

She will have him, she thought, but not yet. Taking him a little deeper between her lips, he tenses his upper body, gifted in her abilities, giving her the space she needs to fulfill and pleasure him. She strokes softly, and her sucking begins to quicken, looking up at him and knowing she pleases him with her womanly talents. She has him erect, but her impatience begins to overwhelm her, and she slowly takes him out of her mouth but continues to fondle him as she rises from her knees, opens her legs, and gently straddles him once again.

Her left hand touches the side of his face, still looking attentively into his eyes as she slowly and deliberately eases him into her, just the tip at first, gyrating to get her fluids to saturate him, aiding in his entry. He slides deeper until all of him is immersed within her. Her femininity grips him tightly, and she begins to move her hips in slow yet controlled movements as her pelvis maximizes how much he enters and exits her. She brings both arms up to rest upon his chest as she enjoys the rhythm she has set for them as he thrusts in and out of her. Her pallid skin is soft as her breasts heave and bounce above him in a controlled, sensual pace, erotic in her cadence and movement.

He places his hands on her curvy hips, taking him in very deep now and enjoying her control the speed and tempo of their lovemaking. She is satisfied just in this, in pleasing him and making her feel protected and secure. Hitting just the right spot and being fully aroused, she finally takes him in altogether now, in just the correct position, angle, and stride, stimulating both of them equally. Keiko responds in such a way that he senses she is close to reaching orgasm again, exciting him further. Her tempo increases as she looks at him again, holding his gaze, and whispers, "I can't hold on, Sebastian, I can't." As she gushes, clamping like a vice around him, enjoying the convulsions as they erupt fully.

She tightens her muscles and spasms, gasps, and moans, heightening Sebastian's stimulation. She notices her reaction elicits his own, and he follows her in ecstasy and unloads inside her full and deep, skin glistening from their combined perspiration, both relishing the moment of elation, appreciating one another's physical chemistry and synchronicity for a few seconds before settling into normalcy after their intensified moment.

Their bodies begin to quiet as their heartbeats begin to stabilize, yet they appreciate the closeness and admiration for each other. Her leg now draped over his as he lay on his back, her head on his chest, enjoying her desire to keep him close to her. He smiles and brushes some of the loose strands of hair from her face behind her ear so he can visualize more of her exquisite facial features. Her beauty is intoxicating, and he winks at her and appreciates the woman that she is as well as the resolve she has had to endure in her previous life she left only months before.

She looks deeply into his eyes, witnessing a part of his soul, and says softly, almost in a whisper, "Sebastian, I sense your suffering and sadness. Your eyes tell the story; it's in your spirit and heart. I can see it all and feel it within your energy. There is no denying it." He smiles at her and wonders how she can understand so much and yet not know him at all. Keiko continues, "A man's eyes never lie.

You carry a lot in your heart, in your . . . . *being*. Many people have hurt you. Yet, you have saved many people, too. I can feel it. You have grieved for people close to you and even for people you barely know." How does she know such truths, he wonders.

A sadness comes over her face, hoping for some response from Sebastian, but he has learned to disguise his pain. Her instincts were correct, but he neither affirmed nor denied her observations, and she could sense his resistance to sharing them with her. She understood as she realized she had not earned his trust. He has perfected this defense, and she realized his reluctance to share his agony with anyone.

Sebastian Storm was an elite combative instrument, bred for one intention, a purpose that was clouding him recently, and he didn't know why the doubts had begun to set in as of late. Keiko realized his conflict but didn't want to press him either; he had already done so much for her. No more words, she determined.

She smiled again, "I want you again, Sebastian." he winked, obliging. Their sexual energy dynamic pleasuring one another for hours before falling back onto the bed, drenched and weathered but content.

After a few minutes, she shifted her weight and turned so as to face away from him but still touching intimately. He turned with her, his toned frame pressed up against and behind hers firmly, fitting into the contours of her body, protecting her once again. He was what she desired, and he cherished her being with him at that moment.

She nuzzles her body up into his as they fell asleep content and relaxed, and for the first time in her life, she felt . . . . safe.

Hours later, Keiko rests her head upon Sebastian's chest, satisfied and content, deep in slumber as he listens to her gentle, methodical breathing, its pace and rhythmic beat putting him into a trance-like state. Sebastian's eyes were open, staring at the ceiling fan above, twirling as his mind was immersed in reflections of his past and present.

Thoughts of his father, his mother, James, Hillary, and Sean flood his head: all key players within his life and instrumental in his own journey. The sliver of time with Keiko, he was aware, was a perfect mistake, but now, his resistance to her charm and beauty diminished, and he also recognized that she needed this for her own closure.

He was to leave that morning for London, as he had business with the South African Ambassador Zuma the following week. He needed to prepare thoroughly for his operation, as he had always done with every mission.

It was the middle of the night; Sebastian turned to appreciate Keiko's angelic face, content and quiet as she lay upon the pillow, facing him. He cherished her beauty one final time, taking a mental image of the extraordinary woman lying beside him. She deserved a better life and hoped she would be happy in the years to come; she deserved that much.

Touching her cheek with the side of his hand, he didn't want to disturb her as she slept. She was magnificent and extraordinary, a woman that any man would long to have, but there was no place for that in his life. He sacrificed that part of his existence a long time ago.

Sebastian gently eased out of bed, sat on its side, and quietly stood, knowing he had to escape into the night and not look back. He had no regrets or hesitation in his resolve; his tenacity was what kept him alive for all these years.

He wasn't designed for the normalcy of life that most people enjoyed; no, he was on a far different path. He was confident she would empathize at least on some level, knowing more than most of what he indeed was . . . .

. . . . *A killer.*

She, above all, understood his role, his place, and his determination to right the wrongs of others. Sebastian stood bare, watched Keiko a moment longer, and then headed to the bathroom in the outer room so as not to disrupt her slumber. He showered, quietly packed his things, and slid out of the front door, but not before hesitating and placing a single rose from the center table ingress next to her on the bed.

A few hours later, Keiko looked at the clock; it read 6:12 am. As she opened her eyes further and noticed the single flower, she realized Sebastian was gone, and a sense of sadness came over her, realizing at the exact moment he was not going to return. He was a wanderer, a soldier, a nomad, and a slave to a greater calling. His mission was more significant than both of them, and she accepted her moment with him, though brief, was what she needed to cleanse her of her past.

Sebastian saved her and absolved her from her tragic life with Hiroshi Mikatani; because of that, he was more of a fantasy or an enchanting delusion to her than anything else. If only for just one night, he fulfilled her in so many ways, and she was grateful for the small moment of time with him.

She accepted she would likely never see Sebastian again, and she forced herself to be content in valuing the short time he allowed them to have together. She smiled at the contemplation, and her last thought was the single rose that he left, pulling it to her nose, taking in its floral fragrance as she began to drift back to sleep, relaxed and emotionally and physically nourished.

A sense of contentment overwhelmed her, and a gladness was sensed deep within as if a large weight had been lifted from her. Keiko could still detect his scent upon her, and she was at ease with that simple gift he left for her.

Her eyes closed as she faded off to happier memories and the simple smile of her son, Akira's face filling her dreams.

Roanoke, Virginia
1991

He lay perfectly quiet, unmoving, and controlled within his manipulated lifelessness. The young boy was already well versed and practiced within his discipline of achieving absolute tranquility and stillness for hours if needed within any environment. Maintaining a sniper's stance, his position was poised and deliberate as he studied the animals and insects as they freely roamed within the lush landscape, navigating through the rugged terrain blanketing the Virginian mountainside.

He studied and examined, acutely aware of his surroundings. Expertly maintaining his sense of calm, the unsuspecting wildlife would often happen upon him, curious yet unafraid because of the child's strict adherence to complete stasis and silence within the surrounding environment. He respected their world. He was a stranger, a mere guest within their habitat.

He valued nature completely, in all of its beauty, as he skillfully blended within the forested backdrop he had come to revere, becoming one with the earthly topography encircling and engulfing him.

How comfortable he had become at merging with his environment, enough to even dupe the inquisitive creatures slithering upon him, over or around him, on their continual quest for food or water.

They were all one and the same in the setting. He was proud of himself for mastering his dedication to maintaining complete stillness for hours, if need be, an ability he had nurtured and developed over the years. Achieving this feat so well, the wildlife mistook him for the terrain in which they thrived, which had always been his goal.

Unfazed in his concentration, the young boy found himself sharing the ecosystem with all creatures equally.

It was in these moments of solitude and harmony he would often think of his mother, back at home, alone with his father. In these minutes and hours of quietude, a sense of guilt would occasionally come over him, and he often became overwhelmed at the thought he was failing her in some way. Yet he thrived in these solitary moments, away from his father, his own sadness, and his mother's unhappiness.

The young man, barely in his early teens, was already surmounting the nuances nature presented. Why was he unable to have the same harmony at home, he thought? He had already conquered the symbiotic arrangement rarely experienced between man and nature. Still, he had much to learn concerning the nature of man to man, which was a far more complicated animal.

These mountains provided for him, his peace, and his sense of calm. He often wished he experienced the same peacefulness at home as he experienced there in the wilderness but sadly aware it would never occur, not while his father was in their lives.

It was there in the forest he would discover more about himself and his understanding of life, and the incidents that defined and cultivated what he would someday become. Life had a plan for him, and although he was unsure and uncertain of what it was at that point, he knew he was destined to make the world a better place, safer in some idealistic way.

He desperately wanted to see his mother, his greatest supporter, content on some level, and he harbored deep in his heart she would never achieve it until his father was finally severed from their lives completely.

They would never be genuinely fulfilled until his father was gone, responsible as the sole source of their misery. The boy would often think and fantasize about his father being far away from the two of them. He dreamt of a life without him, a faraway existence where he and his mother could live in serenity. This was a fantasy for young Sebastian, one he would contemplate and play in his mind almost every day, hopeful someday for his prayers to be answered.

He thought the temporary void of his father's absence would be easily filled and replenished quickly. They would never miss him as he wasn't an additive part of their lives.

Initially, he experienced enormous shame in the notion and thinking so ill of his father. Over time, the remorse gave way to a subdued ecstasy at the belief his father would someday be out of their lives forever.

His father was cancerous, and it pleased the young boy at the thought of how his life, his mother's life, could be without all their pain.

These images would pervade Sebastian's young mind while lying upon the woodland floor of the timberland, visualizing a happier time, full of color and vibrancy and the potential to discover his true self and destiny.

He would have it someday, maybe not that day, but it would happen, and he and his mother would be blissful and content in a world devoid of his father, his darkness, and the cloud raging violently above them.

Snap . . . . he heard the familiar sound in the distance, and it startled him as he refocused his gaze some fifty yards in front and to the right of him.

He smiled as he softly said to himself, "Got another one." He stood up after waiting in the bush for hours for the familiar sound. A sound he enjoyed every time it broke the silence of the forest, the sound of one of his traps being activated by an animal he had ensnared.

Once standing, he wiped the dirt from his grimy jeans, looking down, knowing his mother would be angry with him for always coming home filthy, but that was a stress he would deal with later. He would try to explain to her each time being dirty is what boys do, but she never seemed satisfied with his explanation.

Now, he would get to enjoy the fruits of his labor as he sauntered down the hill toward his trap.

Chapter 2

Retribution

London, England
Present Day

He made his way down the dimly lit alleyway, the same he had emerged from a few hours before, now retracing his steps and organizing his escape. He occasionally crouched to take inventory of his environment. He had an acute awareness of everything around him, one of his superpowers, he thought to himself with a little smirk. He trusted his intuitions, emphatically even relied on them as they rarely failed him and even on this rain-drenched night, proved no exception.

He immediately noticed the two police officers at the end of the alley and well before there was a chance of detection. They were clad in raincoats, standing and talking to one another, oblivious to their surroundings.

Though not present when he had crossed this path earlier, these two officers presented a new variable to his escape. He crept closer to them along the brick stone wall, his steps masked by the torrential rain as the heavy drops pounded the pavement. The officers lacked any proper awareness of their surroundings, paired with the idle and insignificant banter between them, allowing Sebastian some degree of latitude within his maneuvering.

In a world where sluggishness seemed the norm, he had the opportunity to know where others were incompetent. Like a master strategist on a chessboard, he deftly utilized the lethargy of the policemen to his advantage. Their languid demeanor became his cloak of invisibility, a shroud of complacency shielding his every move.

With the finesse of a seasoned infiltrator, he danced through the shadows, exploiting their lackadaisical watch with the grace of a cat stalking its prey. Each step was calculated, each movement a testament to his skillful manipulation of their apathy. This was no mere stroke of luck; it was a calculated gambit, honed through countless trials and perfected through experience.

As he slipped past them, unnoticed and unhindered, he couldn't help but smirk at his ability to navigate around those preoccupied. It was a game of wits, and he was the grandmaster, orchestrating every move with precision and finesse. In the end, it wasn't mere luck favoring him—it was his mastery over the art of exploiting people's weaknesses and complacency. All the while turning indolence into his greatest ally.

These scenarios were often unsettling for most, but Sebastian never wavered or hesitated. Instead, he capitalized on the opportunities in which he was presented and often used them to his benefit. His movements were calculated and surgical in their execution as he navigated through the concrete jungle of London, concentrating on his objective.

He always lingered within the shadows. As a result, everyone was unaware of his presence. Sebastian Storm certainly did possess exceptional powers on many levels, some would say, but he would also argue this was both his blessing and a curse. His abilities forced him to hyper-focus on all details, whether great or small. He had to process data exponentially as a result, and it would often prove tiresome, yet necessary. The upside was it kept him alive, and he preferred it that way not to mention fostering his need for control of the scenarios he was able to influence.

The rain remained unbearable and monotonous, making his exodus far more predictable, uncomplicated, and effortless in his fortitude. He always recognized and respected the risks, the importance of what he did, and the greater good. All factors summed up were what influenced the benefit of his efforts. Above all, he was mindful of all the circumstances of his assignment and calculated the consequences his failure might create. It was not an option, nor had it ever been.

Soaked to the core, Sebastian Storm moved with grace between the shadows, utilizing an intermittent lapse in light, nowhere near observable by the mere commoners, unmindful and bustling about, consumed with themselves and their agendas at the late hour.

His movements were a display of elegance, with the utmost in stealth and swiftness, if one ever cared to notice. His gait was confident and trustworthy. He was deliberate and unwavering in his execution. There was a reason why he was considered the best in his profession. He darted across a narrow road, heading east into the dense tree line of a small neighboring park. The woodlands would provide cover, reminding him of his childhood and the forest for the second time that evening.

He could hear the sirens in the distance. He took a moment to take stock and estimated the wailing horns to be blocks away, opposite his predetermined path.

As the moon cast its eerie glow over the silent city streets, Sebastian moved with the agility of a predator on the hunt. Each step was deliberate, each breath calculated, as he closed in on his target with the determination of a lone wolf on a mission.

No one would stumble upon the scene until the veil of night began to lift, granting Sebastian the precious gift of time. He seized it with both hands, his heart pounding in his chest as he pushed himself forward, driven by a relentless sense of purpose.

Crouching in the shadows, he took a moment to steady himself, his senses alert and attuned to every sound, every movement. Time was of the essence, and Sebastian realized he couldn't afford to linger. With a silent prayer to the darkness, he pressed on, covering ground at a pace that would make even the most seasoned athlete envious.

His target, the ambassador of South Africa, loomed large in his mind, a symbol of everything he despised in the world. This mission was no ordinary task—it was a crusade, a battle against injustice and oppression. And tonight, Sebastian was the avenging angel, determined to mete out justice in the dead of night.

As he neared his zone of safety, his pulse quickened with anticipation. The end was in sight, the culmination of weeks of meticulous planning and preparation. With every fiber of his being, Sebastian was ready to bring his mission to its dramatic conclusion, to rid the world of one more perpetrator of suffering and pain. Reginald Zuma may have thought himself untouchable, but tonight, he would come face to face with the wrath of a man on a mission to cleanse the world of its sins.

The ambassador had a particular affinity for young boys, but the Zuma's appetite would never be satisfied again once Sebastian had completed his mission. The particular charge was not unlike his mission in Tokyo several months prior. Sebastian made it his mission to protect those who struggled to protect themselves.

Like Hiroshi Mikatani, no other victims would ever suffer the same fate again, not by this man's hand. The target, as with all his selected marks, deserved Sebastian's level of justice. If Sebastian Storm selected one, then their destiny or doom was sealed.

His sentencing was immediate, and not one of his victims had ever escaped or set free from Sebastian. He determined all his target's present and future and held himself accountable to be their self-appointed judge and jury, executing their fate as he saw fit.

He closed his eyes for a moment, recounting the hours of the evening. Three hours prior, the rain had just begun; a cool but constant sprinkle canvased the streets and buildings. The darkness of night settled in, and all was quiet within the South African embassy. He had been patient, remaining still and cautious for what felt like hours in the delivery foyer, waiting for the embassy shift to change, which it did at precisely 11 pm.

He had been observing the embassy for the past several days, studied the guards' routines, and even appointed creative names for each guard as he monitored them in an effort to pass the time. When the shift ultimately changed, he used the pause in protocol to pick the security lock to the basement door, taking advantage of the thirty seconds it took to reboot the security cameras.

In an instant, he was in the basement package delivery room, quickly maneuvering into the air duct system and stairs where needed and waiting for enough time to calculate the guards' intervals and tendencies. He logged ten guards were in the building and another six guards outside the property's perimeter.

This group of guards was moderately trained, with no one exceptional soldiers within their ranks except for the chief security specialist, Cornelius Randor, a retired decorated special forces soldier with the South African Army and now assigned as Ambassador Reginald Zuma's primary bodyguard.

In delving into the depths of Randor's background, Sebastian unearthed a trove of intriguing revelations. Randor, it appeared, possessed a mastery of combat techniques bordering on the legendary, coupled with a keen awareness of the ambassador's clandestine activities. But what caught Sebastian's attention was the unsettling revelation Randor willingly turned a blind eye to the ambassador's insatiable appetites, ones he himself often orchestrated with meticulous precision.

Despite being privy to the ambassador's questionable pursuits, Randor shrugged off any moral obligation, rationalizing that it was not his place to intervene in the private affairs of his superior. To him, it was merely a facet of the ambassador's persona fell beyond the scope of his duties. However, for Sebastian Storm, this complacency was not only a misstep; it was a grave error demanding retribution.

With a fire burning in his veins, Sebastian resolved to confront Randor and challenge his indifference. For Sebastian, loyalty was not synonymous with turning a blind eye to wrongdoing; it meant holding oneself and others accountable, regardless of rank or position. The stage was set for a clash of wills, where Sebastian Storm would emerge as the harbinger of justice, refusing to let any transgression slide unchecked.

Randor's mandate seemed straightforward: safeguard the ambassador's well-being at all costs and cater to his every whim, no matter how peculiar or unethical. Among the unspoken rules of their arrangement, it was firmly established only Randor was permitted to linger in the ambassador's presence after dusk—a testament to the ambassador's disdain for the ineptitude of the evening shift guards, whose mere presence grated on his nerves and fostered annoyance.

Yet, there was more to this nocturnal arrangement than met the eye. Behind closed doors, the ambassador harbored a web of secrets, particularly concerning his after-hours escapades of a more intimate nature.

It was a delicate dance of discretion, one in which the ambassador placed unwavering trust in Cornelius, relying on his unwavering loyalty and professional decorum to safeguard his reputation from prying eyes and wagging tongues.

For Randor, this duty morphed into a relentless routine of vigilance and begrudging acquiescence. Night after night, he found himself stationed in the ambassador's opulent chambers, his gaze fixed upon the flickering glow of the television screen as his charge indulged in his evening rituals.

Though Randor harbored a simmering resentment towards the ambassador—fueled by a cocktail of disdain and professional obligation—he understood the stakes all too well. He might loathe the man he served, but he was a consummate professional, committed to executing his duties with precision and efficiency. The ambassador's private life was his own and Randor believed his employer alone would have to ultimately answer for the ambassador's indiscretions.

Thus, Randor navigated the labyrinth of his conflicting emotions with the finesse of a seasoned diplomat, his outward demeanor a mask of stoicism concealing the tempest raging within. He might not harbor any affection for his charge, but he recognized the importance of his role, bound by the unspoken contract of duty and discretion. And as the shadows lengthened with each passing evening, Randor braced himself for the next act in this intricate drama, knowing in the murky world of diplomacy, loyalty often came at a steep price.

Knowing the complete layout of the building, schedules, routines, camera positions, and protocol, Sebastian maneuvered undetected until he reached the floor above the ambassador's private residence. He recalled from intelligence briefings and his extensive research that the ambassador enjoyed his evening brandy followed by an evening bath and was not to be disturbed unless necessary.

He selected this particular evening to enter the embassy because he knew, with some disgust, the night before, Randor had arranged for the ambassador to be entertained by a young boy, no more than eleven years old, for the entire night. He also was aware the ambassador would enjoy the evening off and be solely in the company of his beloved brandy and experience his habitual hot bath and steam.

In an office space directly above Ambassador Zuma's chambers, Sebastian eased the exterior window open, searching for any activity below, noting the two soldiers in view, roughly four hundred yards away, on the south side of the building.

He was inconspicuous and blended well with his surroundings, a skill he had developed at a very early age. In addition, he determined the part of the wall on the side of the building was well shadowed, courtesy of the .22 caliber silenced handgun he used to extinguish the surrounding lights the evening prior.

Sebastian, with an unwavering eye for the minutiae, orchestrated every facet of his covert operations with unmatched precision. That evening, he edged himself out over the precipice, his existence hanging by a mere thread—a sophisticated wire and pulley system anchored securely to the window's upper frame. Positioned on the sill, his feet jutted outward, poised as if on the brink of a deliberate plunge into the abyss below.

With a calculated motion, he gently loosened the clamp holding the wire, initiating a slow descent. His feet, still anchored on the sill, served as a pivotal axis, enabling his body to lower in a meticulously controlled arc. Suspended in a ballet of gravity and engineering, his form aligned perpendicular to the imposing structure and parallel to the unforgiving ground beneath.

This precarious arrangement was not merely a test of physical endurance but a strategic maneuver. It minimized his exposure, cloaking his movements in the shadows cast by the building itself. With each deliberate step, Sebastian made his descent, navigating down the cold, unyielding surface of the building's exterior, from the window to a point thirty feet above the ground—a silent specter in the night, master of his secretive craft.

He began his controlled descent several inches per second and, from his unique vantage point, could faintly make out the top of Randor's head as it came into view through the window on the floor below. As expected, Randor was facing away from him, toward the television, relaxing within a sofa chair.

Perched precariously on a window ledge, Sebastian had ingeniously converted the unusual spot into a strategic vantage point, one that would cunningly outmaneuver Cornelius Randor, the veteran head of security, or any other security threat. Comfortably ensconced inside the chamber, Randor was primed for threats that might breach the main doorway, yet he overlooked the potential for an incursion from the seemingly innocuous window.

In a masterstroke of timing and technique, Sebastian deftly triggered a remote device, setting off a charge he had artfully installed in the air duct earlier. This device was specifically designed to emit a mere whisper of a burning scent—subtle yet distinct enough to engage the senses of an observant security chief. This faint but deliberate aroma was designed to simulate danger, stirring Randor from his end-of-shift complacency.

The unexpected scent cut through the fatigue that clouded Randor's senses, snapping his focus back into sharp clarity. The day's length had dulled his alertness, but this peculiar olfactory cue reignited his vigilance. He methodically retrieved his Glock 9mm from the nearby table, where it lay within easy grasp. With a measured blend of prudence and readiness, he rose and cautiously opened the chamber door a sliver, peering into the shadowy, quiet hallway.

Poised at the threshold, weapon at the ready, he listened intently, his strategic mind evaluating every possible scenario that might unfold from this unexpected alert.

As anticipated, through the exterior window, Sebastian studied Randor as he cautiously made his way to the door leading to the hallway. Nothing appeared out of place or askew other than the faint aroma that initially alerted him. Randor determined that all was quiet within the embassy, a typical night and nothing out of the ordinary.

He opened the door further, his gun pointed and aimed before him, and he deliberately made his way down the hall, following the subtle scent of smoke. He inspected the area for several minutes, opening doors and clearing various rooms and common areas in the vicinity before he either lost the scent, it had diminished, or he became desensitized to its potency.

Either way, he suddenly panicked, realizing he had foolishly left the ambassador unattended the entire time he had investigated the surrounding area.

He quickly made his way back to the living quarters. he reluctantly made his way over to the bathroom door, knowing fully he was about to annoy the ambassador with the interruption, but the dignitary's security was Randor's chief concern. He quickly returned to the ambassador's chambers.

He knocked lightly upon the bathroom door and grudgingly asked, "Ambassador, sir, I wanted to check on you. Are you okay?" After a hesitation, the Ambassador responded: "Of course I am, you imbecile, give me some peace!"

Shaking his head, Randor calmed his beating heart, confirming proof of life his employer had given him, and returned to the outside chamber door, closed and locked it. He settled back in his chair and laid his gun into its familiar place upon the table adjacent to his chair. A false alarm, apparently, and made to look like a fool in front of the ambassador. A perfect end to a long day, he thought.

At that moment, Sebastian slowly rose behind Randor 's sofa chair and, with one sweep, pushed Randor 's gun off the table and placed him in a chokehold with his right arm.

Randor fought and squirmed, but Sebastian held him fast and whispered into his ear, "You should have defended those boys, Cornelius. Easy targets to be exploited by men like your boss. That was a foolish and costly mistake." Randor's eyes opened wider as the oxygen in his lungs left him.

Placing his left palm flat against Randor's left temple, Sebastian snapped Randor's neck with little effort. When he felt Randor's fate was sealed, he gently eased him fully into the chair, gradually resting his head against the back of the headrest, placing his arms upon the armrests and nudging Randor's gun with his foot underneath the chair and out of the way. It would appear he was simply sleeping, which was all too common most nights.

Sebastian then stood up and within a few seconds, was standing outside the ambassador's bathroom door, cautiously listening, and evaluating the situation and determining if there was any activity from within the bathroom.

He recalled the bathroom layout down to the detail of where the tub was situated, along with where the ambassador would most likely be positioned within the tub. Before opening the bathroom door, he could see the steam billowing from the space at the bottom of the door and illuminated by the room within as he softly eased the door open, only to be met with a wave of haze and humid mist saturating the bathroom.

He took a moment to allow his eyes to adjust to the moist and hazy environment. After a few seconds, he made out the silhouette of the ambassador's head resting on the side of the tub, slightly facing forward, away from the opened door Sebastian had emerged.

He cautiously crept closer, thankful the ambassador was unmindful of any presence within the vicinity. As Sebastian carefully approached, he withdrew a small metal instrument, sharp, thin, almost surgical in nature, and roughly six inches in length, resembling a small thin icepick.

He knelt and, with his left hand, embraced the ambassador's head firmly, lodging it against the hard porcelain of the tub, covering his mouth like a vice grip.

The ambassador's eyes widened in fear, as he kicked and thrashed the water within the tub. Sebastian whispered, "Remain still, Ambassador," and in a controlled, soft and cryptic voice said, "You will never hurt anyone again. It is time you answer for your sins."

In that instant and in one fluid motion, with his gloved right hand, he inserted the syringe-like instrument at the base of the ambassador's skull an inch within the hairline, upward and forward, and extended the entire length, killing the ambassador instantly, leaving no blood trail or synovial brain fluid—a perfect kill by Sebastian's estimation.

When the victim would later be given an autopsy, in many cases, this small lethal, but effective weapon and the wound it created was most often overlooked and mistaken for a brain aneurysm. Simple, clean, and perfect. Surgical stealth was Storm's signature, and this mission was no exception.

Holding the ambassador steady until Sebastian was confident his life had drained completely, he gently loosened his grip and eased the man's head against the edge of the tub, stood up, and walked to the front of the man, looking at the ambassador's motionless corpse lying in the bath, arms draped over the side, naked and exposed.

It was simply the method he chose for his victim. With Randor dead in the next room, the homicide detectives would be frenzied but Sebastian planned to leave no mark of his existence.

As he stood silently, Sebastian's thoughts momentarily drifted to the harrowing plight of the young boys who had fallen victim to the man's cruel indulgences. Each one had endured unimaginable abuse, their innocence exploited for fleeting gratification, leaving behind deep psychological scars that would likely mar their souls for life. The weight of their collective suffering pressed heavily on his conscience, a somber reminder of the dark depths of human depravity and the predator's infecting humanity.

However, amidst this reflective sorrow, there was a burgeoning sense of resolve within Sebastian on some level. He was acutely aware of the gravity of his current mission and its irreversible consequences.

Looking at the man before him, now subdued and eerily serene, Sebastian experienced a complex mixture of emotions. There was a palpable relief that this man's reign of terror was conclusively over, that no more innocent lives would be shattered by his actions.

It was not only a moment of retribution but a solemn vow of protection. As Sebastian steeled himself for the next phase of his operation, he carried both the burden of the past atrocities and the solace of preventing any future ones.

The duality fueled his determination, anchoring his resolve in the grim but necessary reality of his actions.

Sebastian's mind was clouded by the haunting images of the young boys irreversibly marred by the ambassador's egregious acts. Now, the ambassador lay before him, his life extinguished, his form vulnerable and exposed—stripped of all dignity in death as his victims had been in life. The starkness of the scene, with the man's body devoid of any shield or covering, seemed a starkly appropriate end for one who had perpetrated such ruin.

In this quiet, decisive moment, Sebastian felt a deep, grim satisfaction. He had engineered an irony was not lost on him—the once powerful man reduced to nothing, his lineage of cruelty ending here in this nondescript bathroom. By ending the ambassador's life, Sebastian had put a stop to his abhorrent abuses, ensuring no more young lives would be shattered by this man's twisted desires.

Surveying the bathroom with meticulous care, Sebastian moved with precision. He was acutely aware of the forensic traces that could link him to this scene. His movements were calculated, ensuring minimal contact with his surroundings. He methodically turned off the tap, the sound of running water halting abruptly, and sealed the drain, leaving the ambassador's body submerged in the still water of the tub—a chilling tableau of finality.

With every step, Sebastian covered his tracks, leaving the room just as he had found it, save for the lifeless figure now laying in eternal repose. His actions were not just about retribution but also about erasing his presence, leaving behind a crime scene that whispered of dark deeds but shouted no names.

Before departing, Sebastian paused to appreciate the grotesque position in which he left the ambassador, and how he would be discovered when ultimately found, just as Sebastian wished: exposed and humiliated, a riotous and suitable spectacle as he had left so many boys feeling the same.

This act was for them, and all that symbolized what those poor victims went through, a living legacy this wretched man instilled within so many souls he had demoralized over the years. Sebastian was content in his endeavor and satisfied with his artistic setting and the image he had crafted before him.

Upon leaving the bathroom, Sebastian quietly closed the door and returned to where Randor sat undisturbed and still within the chair where he had been left. Both men had paid the ultimate price for their roles in the ambassador's transgressions, and their victims will now certainly enjoy some legitimacy for the ambassador's demise. He went to the window and exited the room the same way he had entered—undetected.

For years, and with hundreds of missions completed, ever meticulous in his preparation, Sebastian was fortunate enough to have a secret and anonymous contact had continuously supplied him with the information he needed for the given mission, much like what had occurred in Tokyo several months before.

Those auspicious dossiers would arrive encrypted upon his laptop several times a year. From where was unknown but always the same method of delivery. Sebastian accepted most of the files and targets and rarely denied any targets supplied to him.

These pursuits were off the books and of a unique and private nature, not sanctioned by the United States government but fed Sebastian's sense of purpose and justice.

For years, Sebastian had pondered who his reliable Source was but eventually became more consumed with the quality of the information his contact frequently provided him than the provider themselves.

The government or its superiors did not sanction these covert missions. Still, these cases had come before them on some level but usually lacked national importance and were dismissed or forgotten by his division. A perfect opportunity for Sebastian to exercise his need to balance society in the way he justified its end. He was confident his unknown source echoed his sentiment and was also why they provided the dossiers from time to time for Storm to peruse.

Though his Source and Sebastian had never met, Sebastian still trusted the information to be reliable after all the years and the reoccurring receipt of the "special" missions being completed consistently and without issue or compromise.

A few years into his career, Sebastian received some anonymous information about a private school registrar abusing children. It was where Sebastian's drive for justice was introduced by his Source through an encrypted email he received.

During the first few missions, Sebastian was hesitant; but as the intel was proving solid in nature repeatedly, he began to rely on it without question.

He sensed his Source was also driven by the need for balance, much like Sebastian did and proved to be a valuable tool to implement his vengeance against wretched individuals that society spewed out.

Sebastian had a few very effective resources on his side and used them effectively as assets when necessary: his efficient machine of retribution, he thought of it. These special assignments never interfered with the critical missions the American government often involved him in. The protection of the American people was always his priority.

He appreciated life's challenges as far back as childhood. They were often where his most significant lessons were derived. He welcomed those moments, but tonight, none had transpired, save the brief interlude with Randor. But that barely counted, and he was almost disappointed that all had gone according to plan. It was a true rarity in his business.

But the rain, the heaviest he could ever remember, posed some difficulty in visibility as he approached the safehouse, yet the positive, masked his movements beautifully. Sebastian had almost reached his oasis, his inevitable escape from this evening's events. His objective was nearly complete; he needed to get to his safe house and only then would he be marginally protected, at least for the moment.

He made his way through the trees of the sprawling park, slowing around the bushes to take stock of his surroundings, honing his awareness, and prepared for any unforeseen disruptions that may arise. He approached the end of the tree line on the fringe of the park and found the direct line of sight to his safe house.

Sebastian, stopped, then slowly stooped and gently lay upon his chest on a grassy section, appreciating the final leg to this evening's escapades.

It had been a long night.

Sebastian examined every person, fixture, shadow, car, step, tree, and window, anything he could find that was out of the ordinary or could prove a threat to him and his immediate directives.

He never took any situation for granted, and although the evening had gone without issue, he was not going to diminish his efforts now, not when he was so close. He needed to get to the safe house, shower, eliminate any evidence of his presence, and escape on the first flight to Vienna, Austria, at 5:34 am the next morning.

He was so close now as he lay for what appeared like minutes scanning and studying until his hair suddenly stood up on the back of his neck.

Not two hundred feet in front of him, in a dark shadow, beyond the wall of heavy rain, a glimmer from the edge of a man's glasses appeared and seemed out of place. He studied and watched him for a moment, seemingly hidden but not as well as he could have been. To Sebastian, he stuck out and determined something was amiss.

The man's mistake was his eyeglass lenses reflecting from the streetlights above. His head darting in all directions once identified further confirmed Sebastian's assumptions.

The soldier attempted to remain undetected, but Sebastian found him. Unlikely the only one lurking about, Sebastian assumed he was the first one of potentially many. Sebastian knew from experience mercenaries were rarely alone and if there was one, he would expect two to three more close by and most likely ready to hop into a potential entanglement.

Once he had a lock on the first perpetrator, he quickly found the other two, one attempting to be inconspicuous in a stairwell window three flights up, the other also in the tree line, like himself, not sixty feet east of Sebastian's current position. He counted three but aware that might only be a part of his welcoming party, making the next few minutes critical in his execution.

The men weren't there to talk; they had a far different agenda. They appeared to be well-trained operatives, and they had only one objective, one goal—to see Sebastian removed from the equation . . . *permanently.*

In the next several minutes, Sebastian maneuvered closer to the third subject in the tree line, watching him, using the downpour as cover, studying his movements and the others intermittently to determine if they had changed or modified their positions or if there were additional players to contend with. Still, they had not, remaining foolishly idle, easily trackable. Sebastian planned patiently, capitalizing on their complacency.

He wondered then, how had they found him? They were waiting in ambush for Sebastian's return to his safe house. As he approached the third soldier in the tree line, Sebastian drew his military Ka-bar blade in anticipation of any impulsive or sudden movements from the soldier.

Sebastian hesitated for a moment as the soldier's neck microphone chirped, and he replied, "Negative, area clear, two out." Sebastian was in a vulnerable position but had no other option. This was his only opportunity, and he couldn't risk the soldier potentially alerting the others.

He crept closer, low and from behind, thankful he had the rain to mask any noise, glancing at the other two mercenaries' positions before progressing. Observing no change, he dug into the rain-soaked earth, carefully positioned his stance and posture, ready to employ his abilities upon the unknowing victim.

He rose directly behind the assailant. There was no contest. With remarkable reflexes and agility, Sebastian lunged and placed his left hand on the soldier's jaw, simultaneously covering his mouth. His right hand sliced deep through his throat and severing through muscle and vocal cords until he met the bone of the spinal column to stifle any sound.

He then delivered two quick well-placed jabs from behind directly into the soldier's right kidney with the K-bar, dropping him gently into a dead heap. Sebastian eased the soldier's lifeless body to the ground softly and quietly, dragging him deeper into the thick bushes and out of view, already maneuvering toward his next target.

One down, he took the soldier's earpiece to listen for any communication between the remaining mercenaries. All was silent. He held his position, hoping they didn't communicate via their headsets until he could eliminate at least one of the other two soldiers, which would bolster his odds considerably. He then relocated his position inside the tree line and crossed the street out of the line of sight of the other men.

He expertly maneuvered through parked cars and utilized the shadows to his advantage as the original mercenary with glasses came into focus, looking in the opposite direction searching for his prey. Sebastian drew his silenced Heckler & Koch (H&K) 9mm, engaging a light run toward the unassuming assailant, his footsteps masked by the sound of falling rain he advanced towards the entrance.

In one fluid motion, Sebastian fixed his sight on his target while in motion and fired one silenced round at the man with the glasses as he made a subtle turn of his head toward Sebastian in that moment. The man's eyes began to widen, shocked by the sheer confidence in Sebastian rushing his position. The impact of the bullet struck the soldier's forehead squarely, which was Sebastian's intent, using the glimmer of the glasses as a reference for a headshot, liquefying the soldier's brain instantly, dropping him where he stood.

As anticipated, the third mercenary sensed something was amiss within his ranks and broke radio silence to confirm.

"Radio check, call confirm," asked the third mercenary as Sebastian simply listened. With no response from the rest of the team, it confirmed he was the only soldier left and dismissed his post from the window to descend the three flights.

Sebastian assumed he had only a few seconds to beat his adversary to his position to intercept and maximize his advantage. Promptly moving toward the exit door, Sebastian could hear the final soldier's clambering boots as he began running frantically down the stairs to bear down on his mark.

As the soldier cautiously came through the door, Sebastian grabbed the muzzle of the soldier's assault rifle and slammed it hard against the man in a violent but methodical fashion. In the struggle, three silenced rounds emerged, wildly missing their mark as Sebastian dominated the scuffle, forcing the muzzle to smash into the soldier's face, causing the bones in his nose to shatter, stunning him.

With a solid upward force to his face a second time using the stock of the man's own assault rifle, Sebastian dealt a death blow, splintering the bone of his nose into the man's frontal lobe, killing him instantly. He, too, dropped to the ground, another lifeless mass falling by Storm's hand. Not surprised, Sebastian had amassed quite the body count that evening, he realized.

His tactics were efficient, deliberate, and almost ruthless in execution; Sebastian's focus was unrelenting and controlled. There was no second place in this game and reading his adversaries he had learned at a young age. He studied them, learned then used their weaknesses against them.

It had been an eventful evening for him, bringing the body count to five in a mere few hours.

Sebastian harbored no burden or guilt over their loss of life; the world was just a little safer with all of these men taking no additional breath, and he was content with that outcome.

Sebastian thrived in the meticulously orchestrated chaos of his dark craft, a maestro of mortality, commanding each scene with chilling precision. In the sterile silence of the bathroom, with the lifeless ambassador before him, Sebastian reveled in the tension pulsing through the air. It was here, on the razor's edge of peril, where he felt most alive, his senses sharpened by the proximity of death—a dance with danger electrified his very being.

This stark, calculated environment was where Sebastian's skills shone brightest. It was as if he were born for these moments, his instincts honed to navigate the shadowy corridors of human frailty and malevolence. The ambassador's demise and Randor's incapacitation were pieces of a larger puzzle, meticulously placed by Sebastian's hand to ensure the narrative unfolded on his terms.

The quiet of the night enveloped him, yet his mind raced forward, always one step ahead. He relied on the fact the bodies would remain undiscovered until morning, granting him the cover of darkness to make his escape. Despite the victory of tonight's operation, the lingering knowledge his previous safe house had been compromised gnawed at him. The sense of exposure was acute, heightening his awareness that every second counted, every movement could tilt the scales between escape and entrapment.

Sebastian then deferred to his secondary location, a small apartment eight blocks away, and in short order arrived only minutes later. He again scanned the area for any threat or compromise to minimize his risk and exposure. Sebastian wondered how those soldiers were privy to the fact he would return to the location and, more importantly, who had sent them. Someone would answer for this, he vowed.

He despised loose ends and realized the mystery would take some unraveling to find out who had betrayed him. Neither seeing nor feeling any sense of peril, Sebastian remained more at ease as he approached his alternative location and guardedly inspected the apartment door for any tampering but detected none. Seeing no sign of a manipulated or forced entry, he entered and cleared the rooms one at a time, his gun at the ready.

Not letting down his guard, Sebastian collected himself and realized, and equally, hoped he was out of harm's way, if only for a brief period. As he focused on the quiet surrounding him, he became acutely aware of the all too familiar pitter-patter upon the roof, the sound that had beset him the entire night . . . *the cursed rain.*

Exhausted and chilled to the bone, Sebastian peeled off his drenched clothing, which clung to his skin with a cold, clammy grip. Each piece fell to the ground with a wet thud, forming a sodden mound on the bathroom floor. He stood fully exposed but comfortable, content in being free of the wet garments.

Moving with a weary deliberateness, he ambled into the bathroom, where the air felt as frigid as the water had soaked him through.

There, he placed his silenced 9mm on the sink ledge—a constant companion in his line of work, an extension of his own lethal capability. While he didn't need the gun for protection per se, it was his tool of choice, a precise implement in his arsenal of mortality.

Sebastian was a man whose very presence could be menacing; his hands, his surroundings, anything within reach could serve as an instrument of fatal consequence. The reality that he was more an agent of death than a harbinger of life. This image often shadowed his thoughts, casting a solemn tone over his moments of solitude. This acknowledgment brought with it a complex mixture of pride and regret, a dichotomy that he bore as both a shield and a burden.

Seeking some semblance of comfort, Sebastian reached out to twist the hot water faucet, anticipating the soothing embrace of warmth. However, the initial surge of water was shockingly cold, tinged with brown—a stark reminder of the harshness of his environment.

His hand reacted instinctively as the icy liquid bit into his skin, a sharp contrast to the heat he so desperately sought. The cold droplets ran down his fingers, each one a tiny echo of the grim realities he faced, reinforcing the stark divide between the warmth of life and the coldness of the path he walked.

After a few moments, the cold water transitioned to warm and clearer as the pipes flowed from being sedentary for weeks in Sebastian's absence. Eventually, the hot water stream emanated from the old rusty faucet. The steam rose and began filling the room, fogging a portion of the broken mirror before him.

Sebastian dipped his hand into the water once more, feeling the inviting heat wash over his fingers. He cupped the semi-clear liquid, allowing it to pool in his palm before lifting it to his face. The warmth cascaded over his skin, its sensation a sensual embrace that melted away the tension. He closed his eyes, savoring the moment as the heat seeped into his pores, rejuvenating and calming him.

The sensation was intoxicating, a brief respite from the storm of his thoughts, grounding him in the here and now. Grabbing a towel, Sebastian's movements remained mechanical as he dried his face and glanced up at his reflection in the cracked mirror before him.

The fractured glass splintered his image into segments, each piece reflecting a different facet of his complex persona. Despite his resilience, the man looking back at him was visibly worn—his expression etched with fatigue, anger, and a deep-seated disillusionment with the society surrounding him.

The scars mapping his skin throughout his body were not only physical reminders of his tumultuous past; they were emblematic of his inner turmoil, making him feel akin to a modern-day Frankenstein, stitched together from the battles he had endured and survived and others . . . . . *perished.* He was the product of their deaths, and he wore those scars like a badge.

Sebastian's life was marked by a profound struggle with the darker aspects of human nature—the capacity for cruelty, the ease with which harm was inflicted upon others. Now in his late 30's, he had been a direct witness and participant in considerable acts of death and suffering.

His hands, while often the instruments of such deeds, were not the only ones; the world teemed with others who sowed pain with reckless abandon. This constant exposure left him grappling with the blurred lines between his actions and those of the individuals he hunted. Sometimes, in the quiet solitude of moments like these, he pondered the true distinction between them—were they reflections of one another, different only in justification and motive?

This existential quandary hung heavily over Sebastian, feeding into the anger and dismay he directed towards a society perpetually on the brink of moral decay. Yet, each glance in the mirror, each scar, and each reflection served as a reminder of his purpose, however fraught with contradiction it might be. It propelled him forward, fueling his resolve to navigate the murky waters of right and wrong, even if it meant being both judge and executioner in a world rarely witnessed beyond the surface.

Sebastian's acquaintance with death and pain was neither brief nor incidental; it was a profound education beginning early in his life. The loss of those close to him, often in senseless, needless circumstances, wove a grim tapestry that framed his every action and thought. These early experiences, steeped in sorrow and loss, were not just memories—they were the chisel and hammer that sculpted him into the man he had become in both good and bad ways.

This historical framework of death haunted him, a relentless shadow shaping his worldview and his identity. Each loss, each unnecessary departure of a soul he cared for, added depth to his understanding of life's fragility and the indiscriminate nature of loss. It forged him into a figure who could confront mortality with a grim familiarity, yet not without the personal toll such confrontations invariably exacted.

The agony of these experiences was a constant companion in Sebastian's life, vividly replaying in his thoughts and invading his memories.

Good, decent people he had known and loved were snatched away, most of them claimed by tragedy. The cumulative weight of these losses lingered heavily in his psyche, often resurfacing in his dreams which were now frequent and disturbed.

Visions of the deaths he had witnessed—and those he had orchestrated—merged into a haunting montage that clouded his sleep and further, into his dreams. These nocturnal visions were a stark reminder of the duality of his existence: both as a witness to death's random cruelty and as an agent of calculated violence he, himself inflicted. The line between passive observer and active participant blurred, imbuing his nights with a restless, uneasy energy he struggled to balance.

Sebastian lived in a world where the specters of past experiences loomed large, informing his every decision and haunting his every step. The continuous interplay of past atrocities and the ongoing struggle with his role in such scenarios created a complex inner dialogue, challenging his notions of justice, retribution, and redemption. As he navigated this dark terrain, the memories of those he lost—and the faces of those he eliminated—formed a haunting mosaic of his life's painful and poignant journey.

Sebastian was always able to maintain a stoic demeanor, but deep down in his core, he still suffered and tortured himself for those lost close to him, those he could not save. That was the weight he carried daily in his reflections of his past. They constantly reminded and tormented him.

The glass was steamed fully now as he wiped the frosty mirror with the palm of his hand, exposing the image of a man standing before him . . . in his prime, dark, tall, standing just short of 6'3" and athletic, toned and chiseled after years of meticulous attention to his body, his mind, and his polished abilities.

All those attributes were respected, honed, and acutely developed through his dedication. His stature was commanding.

He was a menacing presence and imposed it confidently. Dark stubble, with a hint of gray peppered along the sides, covered his tanned skin, distinguished, attractive even, but downplayed and restrained. Despite his best efforts, when Sebastian Storm walked into a room, males and females alike sensed his presence and inner strength.

Sebastian's mastery of his craft was rooted in a profound ability to vanish into the fabric of any environment. From an early age, he learned the art of blending in, a skill he honed with relentless dedication. Anonymity was his cloak, simplicity his armor. Whether in the bustling streets of a foreign city or the quiet corridors of a secured building, he could adjust his presence to be as noticeable as a shadow at dusk—seen, yet unremarkable, and difficult to grasp.

This ability wasn't merely intuitive; it was the product of meticulous study and practice. Sebastian understood the nuances of his surroundings—the way light fell in a room, the typical behaviors of people in various settings, and how slight deviations from the norm could draw unwanted attention. He absorbed these details, using them to craft a version of himself that was perfectly suited to each unique backdrop, seamlessly integrating into the very essence of wherever he found himself.

Sebastian Storm was more than just a skilled operative; he was a symphony of discipline and precision. Each movement, each decision was calibrated with the precision of a finely tuned instrument. His training was not a part of his routine; it was a doctrine he lived by, elevating him to the pinnacle of his field. Lithe and agile, he moved with an ease that belied the potential violence he was capable of unleashing when necessary.

In his line of work, defeat was not an option—Storm didn't lose. He was sculpted by his experiences and training for one purpose: to incapacitate, maim, or kill. His existence was dedicated to this end, making him not only a master of survival but a formidable force, a ghost in the world of espionage and covert operations.

In short, Sebastian was a perfect killing machine with no equal. He looked into his hazel green eyes and deeper still into his soul and could see he felt cold, burdened, fearless and dedicated, yet still desolate and isolated. He sensed it within his eyes they contained a story few people were aware of.

He turned off the faucet, and once more, wiped the fogged-up fractured mirror with his hand, pausing as he considered the face before him, drinking in his image and hearing with a vengeance the never-ending thunder and rain outside, still relentless, still unwavering it been his intonation for the entire night.

He could now feel the heaviness in his eyes, the real conflict between what was good and just and what was evil and abysmal, constantly pulled by conflicting paths, driven by an intensity he could not fully comprehend nor completely adjourn either. He looked deep into his vibrant eyes and reflected upon his past, his childhood, specifically . . . *his beginning.*

From a tender age, Sebastian was heralded as a protagonist by some, destined for a singular, formidable purpose. Yet, as he matured and delved deeper into the shadows of his profession, he found himself increasingly haunted by existential quandaries about his true role and the moral implications of his actions.

His journey into this clandestine world began in childhood, under the tutelage of a cadre of uniquely skilled mentors. These individuals recognized the raw potential within him and meticulously sculpted it, shaping Sebastian into a weapon of precise efficacy. They instilled in him not only the skills, but also the belief he was a shield against chaos, protecting those who could not defend themselves.

However, as his career advanced and the complexity of his missions grew, so too did his doubts. The very people he believed he was protecting—were they truly safer because of his actions? Or did his interventions merely replace one threat with another, possibly darker one? These questions began to erode the clarity with which he once viewed his mission.

This internal conflict was not merely about identity but about the impact of his actions on the broader tapestry of human life. Each operation, each life altered or extinguished by his hand, added weight to this introspective burden. Sebastian Storm, once a clear-eyed warrior, now found himself wrestling with the shadows within, questioning whether the path he walked was one of justice or destruction.

This duality of purpose—protector or destroyer—became the central struggle of his existence, challenging the very foundations of his being.

Sebastian found himself at a moral crossroads, pondering the essence of his existence. Was he truly a savior, a lone sentinel guarding against the night? Or was he, perhaps unwittingly, the very darkness he strove to vanquish?

The question he would constantly ask himself, a troubling notion began to gnaw at his conscience. Despite those around him often comparing him to that of a hero, he had realized the possibility he might be more akin . . .

. . . . to the very monster he had vowed to protect them from.

Chapter 3

Sebastian Storm

London, England
Present Day

At 6:30 am, the American Ambassador, Frederic Rinaldi, was awakened by his head of security and informed the ambassador to South Africa, Reginald Zuma, and his chief of security, Cornelius Randor, had been killed sometime in the middle of the night. They were discovered at 5:06 am by their internal security patrol.

The assassination was presumed to be a professional operation, but details were still being compiled and forthcoming. Scattered and inconsistent information had been disclosed as of the morning. It appeared the Ambassador was the intended target, and his head of security was simply in the wrong place at the wrong time.

In addition, two Americans and one German mercenary were found dead roughly a mile from the South African embassy several hours before the Ambassador was found.

At the time, the authorities didn't know if the two incidences were related but hadn't ruled it out. Authorities suspected they were connected in some form based on geographical proximity, cause of death, and closeness in time of occurrence. The authorities had no leads nor motive for the ambassador's demise and were not relating the two in the media. No one had come forward claiming any responsibility for the deaths.

Vienna, Austria
Present Day

Sebastian arrived in Austria later that morning and found a café a few miles from the airport to refresh after his flight. Having departed from London early that morning, he was craving a late breakfast and needed to unwind after the prior evening's events.

After walking up to the host table, Sebastian was greeted by a tall, thin Austrian man in a suit. Sebastian specifically requested a particular table along the brick wall toward the rear of the café and took the seat facing the majority of the crowd.

Following the host to his specifically requested table, Sebastian was now preoccupied with the colorful picture of organized chaos strewn about the large café. With hurried patrons milling about him, the environment catered to the mid-morning crowd and their caffeinated addictions and social essentials.

Sebastian mastered the art of becoming one with his surroundings, his presence often as inconspicuous as the air itself. He thrived in the background, a silent observer of the frenetic pace of life swirling around him.

His fascination wasn't merely casual; it was strategic, a critical component of his operational toolkit. Positioning himself in bustling environments, Sebastian absorbed the rhythm and pulse of the places he infiltrated. He studied the flow of people and the energy of the space, analyzing the layout with a tactician's eye. Each venue was a new puzzle to solve, from identifying potential exits to noting security weak points, readying himself for any scenario that might unfold.

In the covert landscape of his profession, intimate knowledge of his environment was paramount. Sebastian's heightened sense of awareness extended well beyond mere physical layouts; it encompassed a deep understanding of human behavior and potential threats. He remained ever vigilant, always tuned to the slightest disturbance signifying danger or a threat to himself or those around him.

His concern for security extended beyond his personal positioning. Whenever possible, Sebastian chose seats that afforded him a solid wall behind his back, avoiding the vulnerability of open or blind spaces. This was not just a preference but a strategic choice, providing him with a constant, unyielding barrier—one that protected him from unseen threats and allowed him to maintain focus on the dynamics of the field of view before him. Every environment was an arena to Sebastian Storm.

Seated quietly, his presence muted and unremarkable, Sebastian studied the world as if watching a play where every actor and every move meant something more than met the eye.

Here, in these crowded spaces filled with unsuspecting individuals, he was in his element, wielding his observant nature as both shield and sword. This was how he navigated the world—an unseen guardian navigating within plain sight, his mind always mapping the next move, his senses always searching for the slightest hint of the extraordinary contained within . . . . *the ordinary.*

Observing the news story blaring on the large flat-screen television mounted above the windows, Sebastian nonchalantly focuses as the 'Special Report' narrating the specifics of the unexplained deaths in London, surrounding the Ambassador to South Africa and his head of security. Few details were disclosed, but he haphazardly noted from the coffee shop table, feigning little interest like most of the other patrons sitting about the café. However, he did have a trivial interest in what the media had to say about the altercation to the public.

Strangely, there was no mention in the news piece of the three men he eliminated at the safe house. He was confident the London authorities had difficulty determining the specifics of those five deaths the prior evening. Sebastian smiled to himself, as he knew they would never find their killer. His attention to detail assured it.

A waiter hurriedly approached and asked Sebastian for his desired beverage. A plate of fruit and coffee, always black, the purest form, simple, unremarkable, a constant with Sebastian was the order he politely put in.

He didn't consume anything artificial or manipulated. Such was the same with Sebastian in all forms: pure, uncut, and, in ways, unrefined. He glanced up at the television, the news story of the Ambassador's demise carried on, speckled with the myriad of details the media thought essential to enhance the narrative, but nothing of any substance was ever mentioned.

Also seemingly fixed upon the television, the waiter viewed the news story until reality nudged him, and his attention was broken after a moment.

Glancing at Sebastian, noting the shared interest in the story, the waiter finally revealed in passing, "Shame that Ambassador was killed. He appeared to be such a good man. Sounds like he did so much for his country. It's amazing the crazy people out there today would end someone's life for no apparent reason." He politely listened but Sebastian Storm reflected on one of his hard and fast rules: No small talk in public places unless he initiated it. Small talk would make an individual more memorable.

He shook his head sadly over the misfortune of the poor, unassuming ambassador and his bodyguard as the waiter picked up on Sebastian not up for idle chit-chat and walked away.

Despite Sebastian politely nodding his agreement with the statement before he left, secretly thinking, "Well, except for the part where the Ambassador had sexually abused numerous young boys for years . . . what about those victims?" But of course, nothing was mentioned to the waiter. Sebastian was content in knowing the real story despite how the media portrayed the man. He possessed the Ambassador's entire sordid dossier.

The world around them lived in obliviousness, sheltered from its realities and ugliness. The waiter was simply voicing an opinion based on the information given, nothing more. Sebastian couldn't condemn the young man for his ignorance. He would never know the absolute truth.

Considering the waiter's unfamiliarity with the ambassador's true malice, Sebastian dismissed the thought. He accepted the waiter's perspective, however oblivious it may be, tolerating that he only partially understood the circumstances surrounding the South African ambassador.

The world was better without those five men, and Sebastian understood the greater significance. He felt a small amount of remorse for Randor, though, a dedicated soldier, but also validated his part in the ambassador's secret life, allowed it, and in many cases fed the ambassador's appetite for pedophilia.

No, Sebastian thought, Randor deserved his demise as well. He should not have permitted it or, at the very least, dismissed his part in the evil escapade, but he chose to disregard his Boss's unsavory hunger for those unable to defend themselves.

Randor was satisfied with merely following orders, turning a blind eye. Unfortunately for him, that was not a sin Sebastian would dismiss, and Randor and the ambassador paid dearly for those transgressions.

The news quickly moved to the developing moment for a young Governor, who was shaking up the state of Wyoming. Sebastian did have an interest in the story as Governor Damian West was the up-and-coming son of the highly respected Senator, Samuel West, who also happened to be Sebastian's boss's boss. The West family was making a name and dynasty for themselves, and their story always interested Sebastian.

The story moved on to tumultuous weather hitting the Hawaiian Islands. His attention trailed off.

He refocused his efforts on the occupants within the café. He scoured the premises for a moment, taking in the multitude of consumers sitting or passing through the establishment, most conversing between themselves.

Sebastian's methodical approach to observation was akin to a sophisticated algorithm in human form, continually processing and analyzing the myriad variables presented by everyone in his vicinity.

Size, gender, stature, and more subtle cues like energy, fluidity of movement, and even the rhythm of their gait were all data points that he meticulously cataloged. Each person, whether an employee, a customer, or a casual passerby, was assessed for their potential threat level—anyone could be the vector of an unanticipated danger.

In his line of work, the ability to discern subtle shifts in a crowd's mood or an individual's demeanor may mean the difference between safety and peril.

Sebastian's vigilance was unyielding. His eyes moved discreetly but decisively, capturing and analyzing every interaction, every movement. This wasn't just surveillance; it was an acute psychological assessment, a dynamic reading of human behavior that allowed him to anticipate and react before a threat manifested.

This continuous evaluation was both a discipline and a craft. Sebastian had honed his skills to the degree that he quickly compartmentalized and prioritized the information he gathered, sifting through the noise to pinpoint genuine risks. This wasn't paranoia but prudence, a survival strategy perfected through years of navigating dangerous waters.

Each analysis, while swift, was thorough, a process Sebastian regarded not just as necessary but as a skill of paramount importance—one that he both respected and relished. These abilities were not merely professional assets; they were lifelines. Over the years, his adeptness at reading a room had extracted him from the jaws of death more times than he could count.

For Sebastian, complacency was the enemy, and his relentless pursuit of awareness was his greatest ally in staying one step ahead of chaos, always alert, always alive.

Sebastian recalled several years before, his attention to detail was paramount and saved countless lives in an airport in Germany. In that instance, he was progressing through the menial task of airport security in Frankfurt, Germany, and a suspicious man positioned several spots ahead of him in the security line quietly displayed numerous signs of physical anxiety and anxiousness not usually observed in those types of settings. Sebastian focused on him and his actions a little more carefully for several minutes.

The man's attention was constantly diverted, traveling alone, apparent nervousness, perspiration, and trembling were all attributes recognized by Sebastian as an individual with less than honorable intent.

His experience had taught him that historically, the man's characteristics were more than peculiar within the large group of people surrounding him. The man's apprehension was subtle, not evident to airport security or any other passengers traveling, but Sebastian knew better. He had been trained to identify such questionable individuals.

Trained to notice even the most minor deviations in people, he studied the man closely for the following few minutes. Sebastian suspected there might be more to this man than being a mere weary traveler.

The individual was darker skinned, in his mid-forties, most likely Afghani, Pashtun specifically, thought Sebastian.

He had two identical medium-sized carry-on bags that he was maneuvering clumsily around the X-ray/security bench. One of his bags remained on the floor, and he subtly and inconspicuously pushed it under the preparation table as he managed the other bag and the various items he carried, blending well with the other passengers.

The dubious individual had placed his first bag on the table, opening only one of two suitcases, and removed his toiletries per standard protocol before feeding it inconspicuously through the X-ray scanning belt. Interestingly, the second bag he had left upright upon its wheels on the floor and pushed it further under the table, ensuring his bag remained generally hidden or overlooked.

Sebastian immediately determined the man took advantage of the disarray of passengers trying to get through the line, cutting in and even upsetting those around him with his aggressive and pushy behavior.

Many passengers were dealing with upset children, luggage, and airport security and didn't have the time to monitor those around them. He appeared to capitalize on the customary distractions and general bedlam one experiences while enduring airport checkpoints. The individual used the chaos to his advantage and advanced through the line quickly.

As the man pushed his first bag through, the second of his bags remained obscured and hidden under the security table, seemingly abandoned and unnoticed by anyone—except for Sebastian, who was fully aware of the overlooked baggage. Something appeared vaguely familiar about this man, but Sebastian couldn't place him, but he did feel like he had seen a likeness of him somewhere.

Also in line, a young female German student stood ahead of Sebastian in line. As the group remained stagnant, he lightly touched her arm, and in a light conversational manner and slightly flirtatious, he quietly said, "Look at this guy."

He gestured toward the suspicious man at the X-ray table. The woman initially looked at Sebastian, smiled, then turned to the man he referenced. Sebastian added, "He is all over the place, and look, he's even forgetting his other bag. We should tell security so they can tell the man he may have forgotten it. These inexperienced travelers," Sebastian shook his head paired with a light laugh, seeming more entertained by it all instead of concerned.

The young woman, intrigued now, began watching the man more intently, fixed upon the figure, and said, "He looks frightening! And how could he forget his bag? It's so far under the table like he almost pushed it away. Did you see that?"

She looked at Sebastian for validation as he nodded and replied, "Yes, yes, you are correct. Very observant of you." The man hurriedly forced himself through to the body scanner, eager to get his jacket he had run through the X-ray but neglecting his first bag as they both watched now as well and began impatiently making his way with the general flow of passengers, collecting their baggage leading outside of security.

It was then the woman became more concerned and said, "He didn't even grab his first bag . . . or either of his belongings. Wait, this isn't right. We need to say something to the police."

Sebastian's guidance affirmed as she immediately motioned the nearest Polizei guard, clad in assault gear and brandishing his rifle, saying in German while gesturing to the solitary bag, "Officer, that bag was left by that man in the blue top and tan pants. And his other bag as well. He looks like he intentionally left them there." She pointed at the man and again at the bags he had allegedly left behind.

The officer looked at the bag, walked a few steps toward the bag's location, and asked the people nearby if it was theirs. When they replied or shrugged, it wasn't, he instantly got on his radio to apprehend the individual matching the young woman's description who was attempting to make his way out of the controlled security arena.

Three Polizei and two plain-clothed customs officers reacted quickly and approached the man and asked if the bags located on the table, were his property. The man shrugged and was hastily ushered back to the preparation table, denying the hidden bag was his but appearing more nervous at that point. Multiple surrounding passengers, hearing his denial, exclaimed they had seen him with both bags just minutes earlier, yet the man denied their accusations vehemently.

The man was then thoroughly searched, and a detonating device that somehow eluded the X-ray was found in the left breast pocket of his jacket. He was immediately taken down, cuffed, and carried away with his arms outstretched to ensure he had no possible way of alternatively detonating the potential explosives.

The two bags in question were also quickly confiscated, placed into explosion-proof boxes, and hurriedly carried off along with the man now in custody.

Sebastian later learned from his division the man was, in fact, Afghan terrorist Sayed Hussain Jawad, the twelfth on the *Most Wanted List*, who had been in disguise while at the airport in Frankfurt. Jawad was part of the semiautonomous Haqqani network, a subsidiary of the Taliban.

Formed in 1994, the Taliban were the predominant umbrella group for the Afghan insurgency, controlling over one-third of the Afghanistan nation. This was a substantial break and a fortunate occurrence Sebastian had been present as Jawad's first bag appeared to be the decoy. Still, the second suitcase contained enough explosives to destroy a large part of Terminal A at the Frankfurt airport and would have led to an estimated 300–400 deaths when detonated.

The irony in this debacle was the Jawad's leader, Aaqel Abdul-Alim, had been assassinated by Sebastian only seven weeks before, while he quietly lay sleeping in his home in Jalalabad, Afghanistan. It was why Sebastian recalled Sayed Hussain Jawad, though in disguise, he simply couldn't place him. He identified Jawad as one of Abdul-Alim's radicals and top lieutenants.

They were all fortunate Sebastian had been in the security line at the time, and his quick thinking changed the outcome of that fateful day.

The young German female student was interviewed, following the apprehension, on the local Frankfurt television station as well as CNN and took no shame in accepting her heroic role in the apprehension of Jawad and spelling out to the news crew every detail of what had led her to suspect the known terrorist. She never mentioned Sebastian's suggestion to involve the Polizei.

———

She was commended for saving countless people's lives, for if she had not warned the police, Jawad would have ensured he was at a safe distance from the blast radius. After a few hundred feet from the explosive placed within the piece of luggage, he would have detonated the weapon, killing many innocent people as a result, and escaping amid the pandemonium that would have likely ensued. The young lady was deemed a hero and proudly accepted the distinction. The media never mentioning Sebastian in the interview, but he was more than happy with the outcome and maintaining his anonymity.

Sebastian interpreted people well and tended to understand how the human brain would often perform. He considered humans a fairly basic instrument.

It was one of his many gifts and talents, and every situation drew on those abilities. He didn't desire praise or acclaim; it wasn't his fashion. He relished in his capacity to manipulate any given situation only slightly nudge people into doing what human nature dictates. The young woman didn't disappoint him in the least. A terrorist threat had been averted due to his ability to get her involved, and the rest was set into motion.

His concentration returned to his reality within the café. With the exception of two individuals, the grouping of people within the establishment proved essentially benevolent in nature.

As Sebastian's gaze narrowed to two particular individuals, the first—an attractive brunette woman—demanded his attention. Seated at the café bar with her laptop opened, she was not only within his line of sight but seemed to have strategically chosen her position to maintain her perspective. Appearing to be in her early thirties, she was graced with a poised and professional air, her confidence palpable even from a distance. Yet, it was her curiosity towards him, perhaps unintentional, perhaps calculated, that intrigued him most.

The woman's choice of seating was a tactical one, Sebastian surmised. Why face him, a seemingly unremarkable spectator in this urban tableau, when the café offered a panorama teeming with more vibrant scenes then the one she had chosen?

Her decision struck him as deliberately orchestrated, her body language subtly evocative, suggesting an awareness far beyond casual interest. It wasn't just her physical appeal that drew his eye but the cerebral challenge she posed. Was she merely another café-goer, or was there a deeper game afoot?

As she occasionally glanced up from her screen under the guise of casual observation, her eyes flickered with a recognition of his scrutiny, adding layers to the mystery. Sebastian's instincts, honed by years of reading subtle cues in perilous environments, tingled with the thrill of this cerebral cat-and-mouse. He decided to study her a while longer, noting the finesse with which she balanced her professional demeanor with an almost imperceptible hint of intrigue.

This kind of puzzle invigorated Sebastian—intelligent, subtle, and undeniably engaging. Her presence commanded his analytical prowess, challenging him to decipher her intentions, all while keeping the interaction wrapped in the sophisticated allure of a potential covert dance.

Sebastian's keen observation of the café's patrons might have inadvertently drawn the brunette's attention. In an environment bustling with casual chatter and the clink of coffee cups, his intense focus on the crowd was an anomaly, a ripple in the otherwise smooth flow of mundane activity. To the discerning observer, his behavior signaled something beyond ordinary interest, perhaps hinting at a deeper, more strategic examination of those around him.

This heightened awareness was not easy to camouflage, especially not to someone as observant as the woman with the laptop. Every so often, Sebastian caught her stealing glances at him, her curiosity piqued by his meticulous survey of the room. Yet, whenever he shifted his attention directly towards her, she would quickly avert her gaze, her eyes snapping back to the digital display before her as if she were deeply engrossed in her work.

Her reactions intrigued Sebastian further. She was not behaving like a typical patron absorbed in her own world. Instead, there was a cat-like caution to her movements, a strategic redirection of attention whenever she caught him glancing at her. This was not the behavior of a professional in the conventional sense—her demeanor lacked the overt polish of someone trained for surveillance or intelligence work. Yet, she was undeniably skilled at maintaining an aura of nonchalance while clearly remaining alert to her surroundings.

Sebastian sensed a complex puzzle in her presence. She was unclassifiable—a person whose role and purpose remained shrouded in ambiguity. Determined to unravel this enigma, he resolved to keep a discreet but unwavering watch over her. The dynamic between them, charged with a mix of intrigue and covert recognition, added a layer of intellectual excitement to his surveillance. Here was a challenge that stimulated both his professional instincts and his personal interest, setting the stage for a subtle game of observation and strategy within the lively backdrop of the café.

The second individual who captured Sebastian's analytical gaze presented a contrast yet a parallel to the enigmatic woman. This man, in his mid-forties and exuding an unmistakable military bearing, navigated the café space with a purposeful stride. Upon retrieving his order, he chose a strategic position at a table that, like Sebastian's, allowed for a protective view with his back against the wall. His posture was upright, his movements, measured hallmarks of someone trained to remain vigilant.

From the way the man scanned the environment—subtle yet systematic—it was evident to Sebastian that he possessed a background in the military. His eyes flicked from person to person, not with curiosity, but as if he were running a silent drill, continually mapping exits, and noting faces without seeming to look too hard. He carried the relaxed readiness of someone trained to be perpetually aware, yet his demeanor suggested he was off duty, not actively engaged in any operational role at that moment.

Sebastian's mind catalogued these observations, slotting the man into a mental file marked for further scrutiny. The café, a microcosm of society, had become his temporary field of analysis, each patron a variable in the complex calculus of security and threat assessment.

As he continued to focus, Sebastian felt the familiar thrill of the hunt, the cerebral challenge of piecing together snippets of behavior into coherent profiles. The world around him was indeed an ever-evolving arena, each individual's actions rippling across the surface of his strategic considerations. His ability to blend his personal acuity with professional necessity meant that he was never truly off duty, his life a perpetual balance of observation and action.

Momentarily, his focus shifted to the television broadcasting the news. The screen flickered to a story about an NFL player accused of domestic violence. It was a jarring reminder of the outside world's dramas, which, while distant, mirrored the smaller, more intimate plays of power and vulnerability he witnessed in the café. Such stories, though removed, were part of the broader societal narrative that shaped his understanding of human behavior—a narrative that, no matter how distant, fed into his continuous assessment of the human condition. Sebastian absorbed it all, every detail contributing to the tapestry of knowledge he relied on to navigate the dangerous waters of his profession.

Enjoying his coffee for a few more minutes, Sebastian continued studying the people as they were arriving and departing the busy café. He noticed the attractive woman in front of her laptop once again, sitting at the table several yards away, punching keys on her keyboard.

She smiled at him when their eyes met, catching his attention this time. She was writing something down at that moment. Looking at her, he returned the gesture and then glanced at the younger fellow, enthralled with his opened book, and appreciating his moment of solitude. He was simply there for the benefits and amenities the café provided and nothing more.

Sebastian cleared him as a nonthreat, but this woman, what was her story, he wondered?

At this moment, in the corner of his eye, he noted the attractive brunette began shifting her position. She closed her laptop, stood up, and collected her items, hesitating as she straightened and pulled her skirt down, ensuring she was more than presentable. Once she gathered herself, she slowly walked toward Sebastian's direction.

As Sebastian's eyes scanned the room, they were unexpectedly caught in the direct and steady gaze of the brunette. Her eyes, previously darting and discreet, now held a bold, unyielding intensity that pierced through the casual ambiance of the café. The shift was startling and more direct now, and for a moment, Sebastian allowed himself to truly evaluate her—as she stood and began to move toward him, her movement fluid and assured.

She navigated the space between them with an elegance that commanded the air around her. As she approached, her physical presence became undeniably striking. Standing at an arresting five feet five inches, her stature was accentuated by the heels she wore, which lent her a sleek, imposing form. Her body moved with a lithe grace that belied the casual setting, each step measured and potent with an almost feline quality.

Sebastian, ever the strategist, felt a twinge of heightened awareness mix with his initial appraisal. Her approach was unexpected, and her intentions unclear, igniting a spark of intrigue tinged with wariness. His hand subtly tightened around the dinner knife he'd been idly toying with, his body tensing in readiness beneath the surface of his calm exterior.

Though armed with more lethal means, Sebastian preferred to keep the encounter as clean as possible, prepared to defend but reluctant to escalate without necessity. He cautiously examined her as she approached.

As she drew closer, the air was charged with a palpable tension, a mix of danger and allure. Sebastian's mind raced with possibilities—was this a confrontation, a challenge, or something entirely different? Her confident approach, her unwavering gaze, they spoke of a purpose he couldn't yet decipher.

This mystery woman, with her enigmatic intent and undeniable allure, had turned the café into a chessboard, and Sebastian found himself both a player and a piece in whatever game she was playing.

She stopped abruptly in front of his table, gave an innocent but seductive smile, and said, "I don't normally approach strange men I don't know, but something about you compelled me to do exactly that . . . *this time*, and throw caution to the wind, I suppose. I have also always trusted my instincts. So here I am." He smiled but she wasn't finished.

The woman gently brought forth a piece of paper, folded, laid it on the table and managed to touch his hand slightly, and softly whispered, "I hope you can make it." Not expecting a response, or worse, a rejection, she followed with a slight wink and a smile, she sensually turned slowly and eloquently walked away, without giving him a chance to respond or react in any way. As she walked away, he thought her breathtaking, suggestive, confident, and mysterious, knowing he was watching her as she left which was exactly her intention.

She never expected a response to her statement. She simply wanted to deliver her intended note. Resisting the temptation, Sebastian studied her as she walked away toward the entrance, confirming her thoughts of observing her as she left.

When she got to the exit door, she turned once more, catching him observing her. He knew he had been caught, and she liked it as she smiled and winked at him before turning again and leaving the café and was out of the door and gone. Rarely was Sebastian ever nervous, but at that moment, he felt genuine surprise and excitement. There was something unique about the mysterious woman.

Once she left, he quickly scanned his environment; disappointed, he allowed his attentiveness to lapse and become diverted by a beautiful woman. Once content, he slowly unfolded the piece of personal stationery she had given to him, and along the top of the page in embossed letters, her name, "Adriana Mercer," was the first thing he noted.

The handwritten note said, "Hello, I'm Adriana and would love to meet for a drink this evening, in the lounge within the Hotel Sans Souci here in Vienna, if you would be so inclined, at 8 pm. I would very much like to get to know you better and what better way than over a drink. Don't be late." Simply signed, "A" at the end.

He looked up again, if only to steal one last glimpse of her, but she was already out of view. He smiled to himself. Even in his humility, he still attracted attention from men and women alike. The female persuasion, especially, seemed to be drawn to his presence and energy, or so he had been told in the past.

With his travels being somewhat random, obscure, and erratic, he occasionally entertained a woman if the opportunity arose. Still, he was cautious about such engagements and rarely participated in them. He was unsure if he would take her up on her proposal, but he had most of the day to think about it.

While considering that brief exchange, he couldn't help but overhear a rude and boisterous heavyset man a few tables away, oppressing the young server waiting on Sebastian earlier.

Sebastian reoriented his focus to the individual and studied the abhorrent man who appeared seemingly disgusted with the waiter and his service while standing, upset over some trivial oversight concerning his order.

"What do you mean you don't have sour dill pickles? What kind of place is this? Quit looking at me like an idiot and find some! I'm not going to wait forever . . . *Move!*" said the man as the server floundered and scrambled, running into a chair as he hurried away in desperation to please the disgruntled customer. The man scoffed and swore under his breath, stomping about like it would positively affect the situation.

As Sebastian's attention shifted to the boisterous American man, his observation became a study in human character and the darker facets of power dynamics. This man, with his unruly demeanor and unrefined manners, thriving in exerting his dominance over others through public displays of intimidation and cruelty. His behavior was a textbook example of the type Sebastian found most contemptible—those who wield power not with respect and responsibility but through oppression and spectacle.

The café had become an unwilling stage for the man's performance. With every unreasonable demand and harsh word, he bulldozed through the server's attempts to placate him, his voice growing louder and his gestures more exaggerated. It was as though he relished the disruption he caused, feeding off the discomfort and attention of those around him. His actions resonated with a deliberate intensity, turning what could have been a minor inconvenience into a full-blown public display.

This spectacle was not merely annoying—it was a calculated assertion of his perceived superiority. As the scenario escalated, the man swelled with a grotesque kind of pride, basking in the role of the antagonist. He was now fully immersed in what would only be described as the second act of his distressing drama, seemingly oblivious to the distress he was causing others, or perhaps, more accurately, delighting in it.

Sebastian reluctantly observes the situation unfold with a cold analytical detachment, yet beneath that, a simmering disdain brewed. He understood this type of behavior all too well—the bully masquerading his insecurities as strength, who uses public spaces as arenas for asserting dominance.

Observing the effect this man had on the environment—the way the server hurried with a mix of fear and frustration, the way other patrons shifted uncomfortably in their seats—Sebastian's disdain was tinged with a resolve. Such individuals not only disrupted peace but eroded the civility that binds social interactions, making them a peculiar focus of Sebastian's broad assessments of threat and human behavior.

The young server returned. "Sir, I am truly sorry, but we do not have sour dill pickles. We would like to take care of your bill for you . . . It's the least we can do," explained the waiter with a faint smile crossing his face. The heavy man, sweating profusely now, glared at the server, and screamed, "The least you can do? Unacceptable!" He slammed his fist on the table, knocking over his water as nearby patrons and the server gasped.

Having had enough, Sebastian needed to end this spectacle. He then stood up, quietly put the note from Adriana into his pocket as he made his way toward the man swiftly, displaying a soft smile, and said, "Sir, there is no—" The man turned his head to Sebastian and bellowed, "Don't get involved, mister, if you have any idea what's good for you." He opened his mouth and turned back to the server to give him round number three of his diatribe.

Sebastian had positioned himself alongside the man now and gently put his left hand upon the overweight man's lower back from behind, finding a point six inches above his belt line, slightly to the right of center, and pressed firmly on the single point as he whispered in the man's right ear, "As a matter of fact, I'm well aware of what's good for me."

The man turned as he heard what Sebastian said and felt the pressure on his back at the specific point at the same time, puzzling him, paired with the sensation something was overcoming him. At the moment following, his vision dimmed, and the large man saw only darkness seizing him and weightlessness as his large frame slumped and crashed into his table, spilling water, cups, and sugar about the area.

Sebastian had already stepped several feet aside in the wake of the man's collapse. The confusion and chaos didn't appear to involve the man's immediate paralysis and inevitable plummet to the ground. People rushed to the collapsed man, flashing water at his face, and shaking him as he slowly regained consciousness, dazed, disoriented, and confused, but . . . *quiet and silent.*

The intended result accomplished, Sebastian walked out of the front door of the café, slid his sunglasses over his eyes, still watchful of his surroundings as he departed. Sebastian always appreciated the simplicity of trigger points and their use localized to the involuntary small yet specific spot in the contracted muscle of choice.

Specific pressure on an area creating instantaneous pain and dysfunction within the specific muscle group. The pressure points are in precise locations of the muscle where there is decreased circulation, increased muscle contraction, spasm, and increased nerve sensitivity, causing a sharp pain or a constant ache, and often immediate short-term paralysis ensued in most individuals. In essence, pressure to the point would cause a deliberate and immediate short circuit of the human central nervous system, causing an abrupt short-term shutdown of the human body.

The man would recover fully without issue but ceased his unfitting behavior abruptly and gave the unfortunate server some delight in thinking the man may have been served some portion of karma in the moment for his appalling behavior.

Two blocks farther down the street, Sebastian heard the sirens as they approached the café. He smiled inwardly, knowing the man would be inundated with medical tests and expenses for the next day or so, all to come up with no explanation as to why he experienced this acute paralytic episode, and all would be stumped.

It was Sebastian's good deed for the day.

Chapter 4

The Conflict Within

Vienna, Austria
Present Day

Sebastian's career was deeply interwoven with a specialized task force dedicated to combating terrorism—a field requiring precision, stealth, and an acute psychological acumen. The Anti-Terrorist Special Division (ATS Division), a brainchild of Division Chief Hillary Bastini, was his professional domain. Chief Bastini was not just a superior; she had been a pivotal figure in Sebastian's life since his adolescence, guiding his transformation from a raw talent into a master of counter-terrorism tactics.

Hillary Bastini, or HB, had crafted the ATS Division with meticulous care to address rising global threats. Under her leadership, the division evolved into a formidable force renowned for its innovative strategies and the exceptional caliber of its operatives. Sebastian, one of her earliest protégés, embodied the division's ethos—highly trained, focused, and supremely efficient.

He was their best, without equal.

Each operation Sebastian undertook was executed with a comprehensive set of protocols he had internalized over his years of service. Approaching any unsecured area—be it a hotel room, a safe house, or an operational site—required a rigorous mental checklist Sebastian adhered to without fail. His preparation was exhaustive, covering both mental readiness and physical gear. This included electronic surveillance countermeasures, communication devices set to secure channels, and personal defense weapons, all chosen based on the specific demands of the mission.

Moreover, Sebastian's approach extended beyond mere equipment. His psychological preparation involved scenario planning, risk assessment, and contingency strategizing, allowing him to maintain control in unpredictable environments. He trained to anticipate and neutralize threats, often before they materialized, ensuring he was never caught off guard.

This deep integration of mental acuity and physical preparedness was what made Sebastian a quintessential operative in the ATS Division. Under the shadow of Hillary Bastini's mentorship, he not only learned the tools of the trade but also the underlying philosophies that shaped their application in the field. His role was critical, his responsibilities vast, and his commitment unwavering, all forged in the crucible of one of the most elite anti-terrorist units in the world.

In his customary fashion, he made his way toward his safe house, scanning, searching for anything amiss or irregular in any way. He always had premises with more than one entry and would often enter or depart at any of those entry/exit points. The safe house, fortunately, included a rear entrance accessing a back flight of stairs. The access was rarely used, and Sebastian felt this was most suitable personally because his vantage was more controlled, being on the second floor. Few people, save the tenants, were aware of this entry point.

Sebastian made his way up the narrow stairway, carefully stepping slowly on the fourth and twelfth stairs purposely as he had loosened the wooden steps slightly in the past to make them creak when stepped on. The familiar *creaking* could be heard from his loft, alerting him to anyone's presence: another simple yet effective security measure of Sebastian's. In addition, as another critical and inconspicuous security alarm, he would always meticulously and strategically place a simple strand of his own hair, measuring 1–2 inches in length, upon his door frame.

He found if he "wet" the single strand of hair with glycerin, then precisely and strategically placed it, usually above or on either side, with half the strand on a closed door with the other half against the doorframe. The strand was barely noticeable, if at all. The single strand connected the door to its frame.

When he would return to the flat, if the single blade of hair was no longer there or torn from the door or frame, it meant that an intruder had breached the particular door, alerting Sebastian and allowing him to determine and adjust accordingly to the situation often without the invader ever being aware of Sebastian's presence.

On this inspection of the rear door, he found the single fiber of hair was pulled loose from the door frame, alarming him slightly. The piece of useful information alerted Sebastian and let him know there was someone inside his safe house or had been inside during his absence.

As an additional precautionary measure, if Sebastian could ever have two adjoining lofts, he did so, one simply outfitted with the simplicities of living and the other having more of life's lavish amenities he enjoyed.

The smaller loft of the two acted as more of a panic room. It was always secured with two different aliases, methods of payment, and hidden compartments containing an arsenal of weapons, two-way mirrors, varying currencies, passports, and any necessary items in the event he was in an immediate departure.

All the precautions were exceptionally private; he didn't even disclose the details to his superiors. Sebastian had many such secrets, but these anticipatory measures were what kept him alive.

He approached the adjacent loft's door and found his entry measures intact, therefore secured, and cautiously and quietly entered the secondary unit to observe his main loft.

When looking through the simple yet effective two-way mirror, he could see some minimal movement in the dimly lit room within the adjacent apartment but noticed the intruder sat somewhat still and controlled, keeping their position out of the line of sight of Sebastian's perspective despite the lights being off. The intruder was fixed on the two entry points of the main loft, obviously aware of the back entrance but unaware of the adjacent loft where Sebastian was observing him.

By way of a small trap access door, Sebastian cautiously drew his silenced 9mm and entered the room adjoining the living room where the perpetrator was patiently waiting. He was certain they were likely confident they had the edge on Sebastian when he entered because they had only two exits/entrances covered.

Sebastian positioned his gun higher, aiming at the estimated height of the intruder but still out of his line of sight. Then, he quickly burst into view, startling the figure sitting quietly, waiting. Before Sebastian could put a single slug into their head, he immediately recognized the assailant as the ATS Deputy Director for counterterrorism, Hillary Bastini.

His boss.

In the dimly lit corridor of the safe house, the tension was palpable as Bastini, momentarily caught off-guard by Sebastian's rapid response, regained her composure. Her breath hitched, her muscles tensed, then relaxed when she recognized Sebastian's familiar, albeit intense, gaze.

His eyes, sharp and discerning, briefly swept over her before his body language subtly shifted, indicating his recognition not just of her identity but of her unarmed state. They did not have a sanctioned appointment, breaking protocol.

Sebastian's voice, low and controlled, broke the tense silence, delivering a chilling reminder of the razor-thin line between life and death in their profession. "This was almost the day you met your maker, Deputy Director. There was no meeting scheduled today," he murmured, the words laced with the gravity of the near miss. His hand remained steady, the gun still aimed at a critical point on her forehead, underscoring the severity of their protocol and the ever-present danger of their operations.

"Are you alone?" he asked sharply, his tone carrying an edge of suspicion and the unyielded readiness to act should the answer dissatisfy him. The question wasn't merely procedural; it was a vital assessment of risk, necessary in the shadowy realms in which they operated.

HB, understanding the stakes and the necessity of clarity in such moments, responded quickly and firmly. "Yes, Sebastian, just me. Promise. Sorry for the intrusion. I should have scheduled, but I have my reasons." Her words were designed to reassure, to diffuse the immediate threat posed by Sebastian's poised weapon.

Her affirmation brought a momentary pause as Sebastian processed her words, his expression unreadable. The gun, however, remained aimed for a beat longer, a silent testament to the seriousness with which Sebastian took every encounter, even with a trusted superior. The atmosphere was charged with a mix of professional respect and the intrinsic tension of their dangerous world, where trust was both a necessity and a luxury, sometimes hanging in the balance of each charged encounter.

He took an additional moment to listen, evaluate, process, and determine if there was any other threat, but there was none he could detect. He relaxed for a moment.

He was always on high alert despite knowing the woman for nearly twenty-three years. His instincts always came first and foremost. She broke the silence after a moment. "Jeez, Sebastian, I didn't even hear you. Were you here all the time?" He replied with a simple "No," and then Hillary asked, "How did you get in here? What door did you come through? Oh wait, never mind, I don't want to know."

She waved off the urge to understand. "Good," he said with a sly smile, "because I wouldn't have told you anyway." She quickly quipped, "There is no one like you, Sebastian, not even close. You are a true rarity, the best of the best. It's like you have spy superpowers."

Here we go again, Sebastian thought and winked at the gesture he had heard many times before from her and many others. "I'd offer you coffee, boss, but I'm a minimalist and only sleep here—with one eye open, of course."

She looked around as she stood and said, "You know I hate coffee, Sebastian. I'm married to the bathroom when I drink that stuff, though whiskey rocks would be a nice offer after the day I have had." She then looked around the flat as he prepared the drink.

"You know, if the spy business didn't work out, you could always be an interior decorator. You have impeccable taste, Sebastian, more than anyone I know. This loft is a true work of art." She appreciated the high ceilings, modern furniture, and the artistic decor. He handed her a glass of Kentucky's Best Bourbon, I.W. Harper's, with a large ice ball, having one himself, knowing full well it was her favorite. It was a little early in the day for a drink, but he could tell she had a lot on her mind.

She quickly added, "Ahh, my favorite, you remembered. Cheers to you, Sebastian, and your decorating skills." She smiled at the remembrance and was reminded of how she was always amazed at Sebastian's attention to every detail. He was a true master in all forms.

"There must be some real trouble in paradise if you showed up here personally, in Vienna no less, unannounced, HB. This is an unexpected surprise . . . Hit me with it," he said. she took a big pull from the bourbon and pondered the question for a moment, forming her thoughts.

She looked at him intently for a delayed moment without diverting her gaze, always the professional she thought and always about the business at hand. Taking another sip of her drink, she softly said, "It's a real clusterfuck, Sebastian, and honestly, it's got my superiors all bunched up because a few agents have lost their lives in this tangle. And we suspect . . . your old friend, Tobias, is at the bottom of it. Back from the dead."

Sebastian slowly sat down and closed his eyes, then laid back in the chair and squeezed them hard in thought, bringing to the surface painful memories he had buried well into his past.

Tobias Teague.

There was so much history in that name. A name he had not thought of in some time. Where it all began flashed before him, bittersweet in his recollection of those days and the infamy associated with the man mentioned.

Agent Hillary Bastini had been with the FBI for the better part of four years when it all started, Homeland for several more in the early 1990s, and finally, spending the last twenty-four years with the ATS Division. She was recruited by the FBI while in college at Duke University.

She escalated up the ranks quickly, initially as an astute field operative, before being approached by the CIA for counterterrorism for a position as team commander following the first World Trade Center attack in 1993 by Ramzi Yousef and Eyad Ismoil. When the 1995 Oklahoma City bombing occurred, Hillary Bastini was called in, and ultimately, her group apprehended Timothy McVeigh, who was later executed in 2001, and the Department of Homeland Security (DHS) was formed in that same year.

Agent Hillary Bastini, known among her peers simply as HB, was a master tactician renowned for her strategic acumen and relentless pursuit of national security while with the FBI. Later, she was recruited as the Secretary of the Department of Homeland Security(DHS) for a time, as its own entity separate from the CIA or FBI.

HB quickly distinguished herself with her sharp intellect and innate ability to navigate complex anti-terrorism operations. Her early career saw her spearheading daring infiltrations that disrupted terrorist networks from within, saving countless lives and preventing untold destruction.

Recognizing the need for a more targeted approach to neutralizing global threats, HB engineered the formation of a clandestine squad. This elite team, operating off the official records, was assembled to engage and eliminate high-level adversaries silently, efficiently blending into the background post-mission to maintain plausible deniability. Her leadership in these critical early missions laid the groundwork for a new paradigm in covert operations.

The success of her team did not go unnoticed, and soon, the DHS sought to harness her expertise in a more specialized Division called the Anti-Terrorist Division that dealt with terrorism on a global scale.

With the creation of the new covert Anti-Terrorist Division in 2003, HB brought her specialized unit along, integrating their unique skillset into the broader intelligence framework. At the DHS, her role expanded, allowing her to safeguard American and Global interests in even more complex and nuanced ways.

Her operations, often cloaked in the guise of natural events or unfortunate accidents, were masterclasses in subtlety and effectiveness, maintaining international stability while keeping the true nature of the interventions hidden.

Despite the critical nature of her work, HB often found herself wrestling with bureaucratic constraints. Resources were scarce in the early days of her division, and she frequently had to achieve her objectives through sheer resourcefulness and strategic ingenuity. Yet, through it all, HB and her team remained the unsung guardians of the nation, their anonymity a cloak that allowed them to carry out missions essential to national and international security.

HB's leadership not only kept countless American lives safe but also solidified her legacy as one of the most effective yet understated figures in modern counterterrorism. Her ability to do so much with so little, to navigate the shadowy corridors of international politics while keeping the U.S. safe from unseen threats, marked her as a true, albeit hidden, hero of her time.

———

HB was the team commander who got the call to clean up a mission when the usual traditional and customary practices came up short, or worse, failed, or were derailed enough that the operation could become a potential international embarrassment for Homeland.

HB answered to the counterterrorism director himself, (retired) Commander J. T. Brigham, who served under President Bill Clinton. He was a decorated navy commander, hardcore and dedicated when they brought him over to direct the counterterrorism division. His missions were legendary but invariably, by the book.

Under Brigham's leadership, his division was responsible for terminating 39/42 of the highest-ranking terrorists most wanted. His record was spotless, and he worked to keep it that way. He gave HB a very short leash but with the strict policy of maintaining "plausible deniability" to protect his spotless record. He feared ever being another Oliver North and fending off Senators like North had to in the Iran-Contra affairs.

Brigham just wanted the "wins," so he let her operate as she saw fit with how they went about getting them, strictly on a need-to-know basis. Brigham always required assurance his division would always come out clean if scrutinized, and HB was a master of maintaining that sensitive challenge.

When her special division was created in 1997, it had no official name at the time but worked under the veil of the evolving Department of Homeland Security (DHS).

HB spent the next five years and a limited budget profiling and training potential operatives meeting her specific criteria. HB and Brigham often argued over the lack of governmental support and resources for her project. With George W. Bush winning the 2000 election, the climate then began to evolve.

On September 11, 2001, the world stage forever changed as the Al-Qaeda attacks of Osama Bin Laden on the World Trade Centers, Pentagon, and United States Capital brought the world, especially the United States, to its knees. When President Bush asked what could be done in response to the attack, the same name kept coming up . . . Hillary Bastini. The Department of Homeland Security was officially recognized the same year.

HB was immediately summoned to the Oval Office, and after lengthy discussions, President George W. Bush created in 2003 the Anti-Terrorist Special Division (ATS Division) and gave HB full reign and unlimited resources to protect the United States from domestic and international terrorist threats.

She set out straightaway on her mission to formulate and organize the best team she could compile and begin setting up her command in Quantico, Virginia. With the change in administration also came the departure of Commander J. T. Brigham. The 9/11 attacks proved too much for his stomach lining, and he realized he wasn't designed for the new brand of terrorism.

A progressive Congressman from Wyoming, Senator Sam West, stepped in and proved to be the saving angel HB needed to perform her job adequately. Later, President Bush organized with HB and Senator West to take the division to an entirely new level.

West endorsed her completely and extended her full authority and autonomy to create the team she needed to combat this new global threat. Together, the trio became a virtual wrecking ball for all terrorist organizations, large and small.

Her long, arduous selection process, building and developing her ATS Division, began to take shape. She felt the preeminent operatives possessed primary attributes proving essential for her highly covert operations.

Her "discovery team" consisted of masters within the organization, the finest in their craft, who helped her narrow down the daunting task of finding her specialized team. She felt that along with the solid physical element any soldier should possess, they also required the mental wherewithal, adaptive nature and abilities, subdued personality, and the capacity and desire to be unsurpassed in performance.

This final aspect was paramount as HB's intent was to capitalize on these soldiers' inherent nature to excel and be exemplary in execution above all and frame their young minds to become the weapons, she intended them to become.

The recruitment strategy devised by HB presented a formidable challenge in the formation of her elite counterterrorism unit. Her approach was unconventional and stringent: she deliberately excluded candidates with prior sanctioned military training, which immediately disqualified a vast majority of the typical applicant pool. This deliberate filtering process was rooted in her visionary strategy, aiming to mold operatives whose skills and instincts were not predefined by standard military doctrines.

HB's recruitment philosophy emphasized raw potential over refined skill. She sought individuals untainted by conventional training paradigms, who could be sculpted into operatives with a unique set of capabilities tailored specifically to the covert nature of their missions. This approach was not merely about training efficiency but about creating a breed of soldier whose thinking and tactics were innovative and unpredictable to adversaries accustomed to conventional military strategies.

Exceptions to this rule were rare and only considered under extraordinary circumstances, highlighting the rigidity and clarity of her vision. The ideal candidates were those unversed in the traditional arts of warfare, providing a clean slate upon which HB could imprint her sophisticated tactics and strategies.

Her end goal was audacious yet clear: to forge not just soldiers but master craftsmen of warfare, honed to perform with lethal precision under her guidance. These operatives were to be the epitome of organic development in the field of combat, evolving from untrained civilians to supremely effective agents of their country's silent wars. Under HB's tutelage, they would transform into what she envisioned as the perfect instruments of defense and attack, capable of executing missions with a level of finesse and discretion not typically found in regular military personnel.

This radical approach to building a covert unit was not without its challenges, but it was a testament to HB's innovative leadership and her commitment to redefining the boundaries of what an anti-terrorism operative could be.

She had no place or tolerance for the traditional soldiering habits to be "unlearned" as that inefficiency would not be abided. She desired her team to learn with only one form, one vision, and one outcome, and she was determined to find the most elite, train them, test them, then . . .

Unleash them. Tobias Teague and Sebastian Storm were both products of the indoctrination.

HB spent months considering and eliminating subjects that came before her desk. She would find a hopeful candidate only to be rejected for some obscure reason: psychological concern, addictive personality traits, a prior arrest, DUIs, abusive tendencies, drug history, etc.

The screening process was rigorous and took months to sift through the potential candidates, but slowly, a working list was assembled, and the individuals were vetted. Additional candidates were eliminated after the vetting process because of some black marks in their history, but all were looked at and evaluated closely.

After several months, HB's team narrowed their list to 44 potential candidates from the 39,234 initial profiles they had compiled.

Tobias Teague was at the top of their list, fitting their desired profile on each and every requirement almost perfectly, except for one . . . . .

He was married.

San Francisco, California
1996

It was a crisp, cool morning, with light rain falling upon his dampened skin. He was one with his body and focused always on maintaining himself. Tobias Teague continually enjoyed running in the city, which gave him the peace he desired. The tumultuous hills and concrete landscape proved a worthy course for his industrious, rigorous circadian excursions, with each daily ritual rarely repeating itself.

Growing up in Sausalito, nestled just beyond the Golden Gate Bridge, Tobias was born in Marin County before his parents moved him closer to the city. He was an only child growing up with a stern father who didn't put up with any mediocrity from his son and instilled a strong work ethic into young Tobias at an early age.

He loved the variety the city of San Francisco continually provided him. This trek tested his endurance more than most of his tours, and as he sprinted the last hill off Jackson Street, finishing strong, he was proud of his ten-mile jaunt, timed at just under an hour.

The rest of his day would be dedicated to scholastics. He needed to study for his clinical psychology exam set for the following morning, and he was fortunate to get a good run in before a full day of studies. An Olympic hopeful, martial artist, and triathlete, he sacrificed the dream to go to college and make something more of his life for himself and his wife, Emily.

With just one year left before finishing graduate school, he was excited to begin a new challenge post-college.

Tobias approached the stairs to his home and climbed them two at a time, eager to see his adoring wife, who always welcomed him upon his return.

She would be proud of his run that day, which was his single most significant inspiration. She grounded him, stabilized him, and kept him balanced. He adored and cherished her for providing her support to him.

As he opened the door, Emily patiently waited and kissed him, and he immediately sensed someone else was in the home.

Tobias's intuition was honed well above most people.

A striking older woman stood up from the couch, extended her hand, and said, "Hello, Tobias, a pleasure to meet you. My name is Hillary Bastini. We should talk."

———

Vienna, Austria
Present Day

Sebastian thought of the man for a moment. If evil had a face, it would be the image of Tobias Teague, a changed and disturbed man. He was a tremendous talent, the young man who would later become a tormentor of the weak and oppressed. Possessing no conscience or remorse, cold, calculated, and without feeling, Tobias Teague became a hardened shell of a man with no concern for anything except money and power, all fueled by hatred . . . *and loss.*

He harbored a hatred for Sebastian Storm above all.

Tobias was now fueled by a volatile cocktail of anger, revenge, insurmountable loss, and inner pain. He hadn't always been this way, and Sebastian couldn't shake the guilt that gnawed at him, knowing he played a part in Tobias's irreversible transformation years ago. The man Tobias had become was a direct result of their shared past, a dark shadow cast over both their lives, and Sebastian felt the weight of that shadow with every step they took closer to their inevitable confrontation.

Tobias and Sebastian had trained together in their early years and recruited in 1998 while developing the Department of Homeland Security. Tobias was HB's first choice while developing her Anti-terrorist division. Sebastian was recruited a few years later, in his late teens, the year the 9/11 attacks occurred. Tobias had been recruited several years before Sebastian and had always questioned HB's intention of bringing Sebastian on at such a young age.

They both possessed immeasurable talents in all facets of espionage, surveillance, explosives, close-quarter combat, weaponry, long-range weapons, counterterrorism, and advanced combat tactics. There had always been a competitive element between the two that was never resolved.

If Sebastian had an equal, Tobias was certainly that individual, possibly even the more gifted of the two arguably. They were similar in so many ways but also very different. Sebastian possessed a clear and stable aptitude, whereas Tobias often enabled his emotions to creep into his decision-making and execution of his responsibilities.

Sebastian, though conflicted and flawed, had goodness within him, at least at times. Tobias had a heart as black as onyx, hardened, toughened, and without mercy, remorse, or loyalty, especially since the loss of his wife.

The event changed him profoundly. This, the zenith for Tobias and his abhorrence for Sebastian, was the unforgivable fate of his beloved wife, Emily.

Sebastian was the focus of his aversion. Tobias held Sebastian responsible for Emily's death, who was the only woman Tobias had ever loved. She was his entire world and was snuffed out in an instant, transforming his existence into a twisted tangle, forever altering him. All those years ago, Sebastian was forced to make a difficult decision for the greater good and the benefit of the United States . . . *and his morality.*

Storm was forced to make an impossible decision.

Panama, Central America
2009

The fateful mission forever altering Tobias's psyche had been dismantling the Santiago cartel in Central America. Eliminating key cartel figures, in addition to their leader, ensured the organization's collapse and flooding of various contraband into the United States and all North and South America.

The American government, specifically the DEA, had been attempting to overthrow the cartel leader for several years with the hope of dismantling it. Still, the assassination of the American ambassador in Central America by members of the Santiago cartel forced more desperate measures. Considered by many a terrorist act, the call was made, and Bastini was brought in to end the conflict—

surgically. The world was watching, and they needed her precision in this matter.

HB assigned Tobias as the lead in the operation and Sebastian as the primary on the ground. The operation had gone sideways once Tobias and Sebastian had captured the cartel's leader, Rafael Santiago, but had not terminated him yet to gain intelligence on the mechanics of his organization.

During that time, the cartel managed to obtain intelligence on Tobias and that he had a wife back in San Francisco, California, and determined with her capture, they could potentially leverage her to bargain for the release of their revered leader, Rafael Santiago.

The cartel infiltrated Tobias's San Francisco home and took Emily hostage, demanding the immediate release of their leader, or she would be executed. Tobias was beside himself and angry he didn't see the cartel making that play.

HB instantly took Tobias off point and replaced him with Sebastian due to the sensitivity of the situation, taking a turn to more of a personal nature.

Tobias was outraged at being relieved of command and replaced with Sebastian. As a result, Sebastian was given the lead, but the mission had changed to sparing Rafael's life, at least for the moment, until Emily could be recovered.

It was a critical mission as Rafael Santiago was known as a tyrant, often engaging in killing sprees out of paranoia or false accusations created within his group or instigated by rival cartels. He had the most production and distribution of cocaine in the Western Hemisphere. Still, the DEA and the CIA couldn't get close to him as he was dug in well, and his organization protected the infrastructure expertly.

When the United States government realized they were losing the war with the cartels in the Central and South Americas, they called in Bastini's outfit to clean up the mess that had escalated to a global level, deeming the cartel as a form of terrorism.

The United States was on center stage, being watched closely on the global front, examining meticulously how the United States would deal with this immediate threat. HB was unsure how Santiago's cartel could obtain personal information on any of her unit, but sadly, the stakes were escalating with one of her own agent's families in the mix, and she knew these situations rarely ended well.

HB was highly concerned with this instance, not just the well-being of Emily Teague but also the repercussions for Tobias if this went sideways. If they didn't recover Emily, Tobias may never be the same, and the last thing she needed was him going rogue and killing everyone in his way.

Tobias was acting on emotion, becoming increasingly disruptive, and ultimately had to be placed under guard in solitary confinement so as not to disrupt the ongoing fluidity of the mission.

It was established both parties would exchange their respective prisoners at a mutually agreed upon location. The exchange between Rafael and Emily was to occur on an obscure bridge on the outskirts of Panama. Both parties were to set each other's captives free, simultaneously, from their separate ends of the bridge, passing each other until each group had their respective cargo secure.

Sebastian took an observatory position higher up the mountain ridge above the bridge to maintain a better vantage point of the entire transaction.

Both prisoners had black bags placed over their heads, obstructing their faces, and were escorted by a guard from each side of the bridge. Sebastian informed his group to take off Santiago's bag to confirm his identity. The cartel members pushed Emily forward, her face still obscured, angering Sebastian for disregarding his request. As a result, he was unable to see her face.

Observing the cartel's bagged captive and not liking the situation, Sebastian was immediately on the radio and demanded of the cartel members holding Emily, "Remove the bag over her head. We need to see her face! I need proof of identity. . . *Now!!!*"

However, the lieutenant on the cartel's side barked back in broken English, "She is already on her way, and not until we know Rafael is safe and not in harm's way, or we kill her right here; we do not negotiate this with you."

"Fuck," muttered Sebastian as he was at the mercy of these thugs and hated the predicament. They were savages and unpredictable at best and certainly could not be trusted, but his hands were tied as the fluidity of the situation commenced.

Sebastian had his best sniper, Rob Maven, trained on Rafael's head if the situation worsened. He had instructions to eliminate the target if given the signal. Reluctantly agreeing to proceed, Sebastian approved the exchange already set in motion as Rafael and Emily walked toward each other on opposite ends of the bridge. Emily was unaware of Rafael's proximity, as she stumbled forward.

The situation angered Sebastian, but all he could do at this point was play it out, "There is no fucking reason to have their faces obscured. . . no reason!" thought Sebastian. What was he missing, he thought?

Reaching his destination first, Rafael was quickly ushered toward their awaiting black Mercedes G-Wagon as Emily arrived a few seconds following. Sebastian watched the entire transaction through binoculars, telling his lead sniper, "Keep a bead of Rafael's head, Maven; do not take your eye off the ball!"

"Copy that, sir," responded Maven.

The soldier accepting Emily on the ground was more concerned about receiving her and ushering her to safety, paired with unfastening her wrists, than removing the bag over her head as Sebastian yelled into the radio, "Get her bag off, dammit! We need validation of her identity!"

The soldier handling Emily fumbled with his earpiece, taking several additional seconds to execute the order, losing precious time, but eventually pulled off the bag covering her face and immediately realized their captive was not Emily! The woman was a young Panamanian woman, roughly Emily's age and build, but they used a decoy to impersonate her. The operation was beginning to fall apart.

Sebastian glared through his binoculars, eyes widening in disgust and surprise upon realizing they had been duped. At this point, Rafael's soldiers had the door open to the Mercedes, tearing off his hood and stuffing him inside before their ruse was discovered.

Sebastian shouted to his sniper, Maven, "Green on the shot, take the shot, Maven, take the shot!"

Rob Maven had Rafael within his sights, tracking him the entire time. "Sayonara motherfucker," whispered Rob as he took in a half breath and lightly squeezed the trigger as Rafael was just being seated within the SUV, the door beginning to close. The silenced round sped its 506 yards directly into the left temple of Rafael Santiago while he was looking over the bridge and smiling in Sebastian's direction.

His head slumped as the door slammed, and the driver sped out of the area. Sebastian threw the binoculars against a nearby tree, shattering them. "Get HB on the phone," Sebastian softly said to his lieutenant. "Nice shot, Maven, good work. . . . We are fucked!" said Sebastian while patting Maven on the shoulder and quietly acknowledging the group of five agents next to him.

Later that day, HB entered the holding cell where Tobias was being detained, sitting at the aluminum table, shackled with padded wrist restraints to protect himself and anyone in his proximity.

She sat down at the table as he looked up. "Tell me she is safe, HB, and Sebastian didn't fail. *Tell me!*" HB sighed at the question. "They used a decoy for Emily, and Tobias, we took the shot on Rafael. It was the only call. We will find Emily," she answered faintly.

Slamming the table and shaking his head, Tobias was furious. "Why, HB, why didn't you reclaim Santiago to save Emily? You killed her only chance, her only bargaining chip. You know what they will do to her now. Because he is dead, she is dead, fucking dead! They don't need her any longer. Was it Sebastian's call, HB? Was it?!?!" He was right, and she knew it, but it was the call they had to take.

HB stood up, ignoring his question. "We will find her, Tobias." Knowing the cartel's response would be an eye for an eye. She knew how barbaric they were and how they operated. Hillary Bastini knew all too well that the odds were that this would not end well for Emily unless some miracle occurred.

"Was it Sebastian's call, HB? Answer me. Was it his call?" He was now straining on the chains that bound him, tearing the skin from his wrists in the struggle as he labored against the restraints. Blood was beginning to spill as even the padded cuffs began to cut into his skin, but he didn't care, his rage intensifying with each passing moment.

Tobias yelled as HB walked through the door, "Was it Sebastian? Goddamn you, Sebastian! Tell me, HB. I will kill you, all of you!" As he spits those words, the door closes, muffling his screams. Blood dropped to the ground from where the handcuffs held him fast. The door closed behind her.

His pain was fully realized now; he knew how this would end, and he held them all responsible. "Fucking Sebastian . . .," he slowly and quietly muttered with both bloodied, cuffed hands over the table, his head down, his face and hair sweaty from his rage. He was defeated and helpless.

In the following week, HB's team meticulously eliminated each remaining cell of Santiago's cartel, feverishly searching for any sign of Emily, but with each mission, their hopes diminished.

They began fearing the worst as each cell came up empty, and no information was obtained in any of their raids and searches. On the eighth day following the termination of Rafael, Tobias was released and took personal leave in Emily's absence and spent every waking moment in the following weeks scouring Panama looking for her or searching for any information, but the efforts proved fruitless. Dead bodies followed in his wake, but HB had to let him have his peace.

After several weeks, it was time to return to their home in San Francisco.

The cab pulled up to his home nearly three weeks following the incident in Panama. He looked out the window for a few moments before leaving the cab, staring at the front of his home, knowing and feeling the emptiness inside.

From within the cab, he looked at what was his and Emily's residence, summoning the courage to return to their home without her by his side. It was the most fear he had endured in simply looking at his docile home, knowing it was empty.

The impatient cab driver cleared his throat and said, "Sir, is this the address?" Breaking from his trance, Tobias blankly looked at the driver and nodded. Tobias exited the taxicab and closed the door as the car sped off. He turned back toward his home and sluggishly climbed the steps outside his front door.

Approaching the front door, he noticed the package set before the threshold atop the porch on this cool and rainy morning. The packaging slip showed it had been delivered five days before.

He glanced at the tattered box for a moment before unlocking the front door. Looking down at the box again, he squeezed his eyes shut to hold back the tears, blinked, and regained himself. Pushing open the front door of his home, he set down his suitcase, left it, slowly knelt, and picked up the weathered and ragged cardboard box that had been laid on his doorstep, warily carrying it with both hands.

As he walked through the living room to the kitchen, he gently placed the box on the table, pulled a chair, and sat down, facing it. He stared at the box for minutes, knowing what lay inside. His emotions raged within, his heart turning to stone as he sat silently, gazing at the box shabby and torn before him.

A single tear fell from his eye, the drop of salted water following the track within the crease of his face. He wiped his face dry and sat up. Finally, he pulled the tape from atop the box and opened the flaps on the top portion of the box.

The stench was what he noticed first, knowing what lay within. He waited, basking in quietness and solitude for a few more moments, unable to force himself to consider what he would find, but he was certain what lay within the confines of the brown container.

He slowly turned and tipped the open carton toward him, revealing a blood-soaked towel. He pushed the towel away to reveal his adored Emily before him.

The parting gift from the Santiago cartel. Their eye for an eye.

———

Her severed head lay still, lifeless and silent, her skin ashen from the time that had passed, but her beautiful green eyes stared out of the package directly at him. Her face was bloated, but it was his Emily, always lovely to him. He gently settled back into the chair, never tearing his eyes from hers.

After a time, his sadness overwhelming, he closed his eyes, focusing his wrath paired with all his rage, fixated on the disgust that overcame him. He welcomed and embraced his indignation. He wanted and thrived for it now; it fueled the fire emerging within. Any good in him was forever gone, replaced with his hate and resentment. Transformed was all that was virtuous and pure in his life and was forfeit now as Emily was his stability. His balance now gone forever.

She was his equilibrium, the rock that held him fast, tethered Tobias from falling into that dark place he yearned to be. She was the key, the lever maintaining him at his truest. She brought what little good was in his heart to the surface. Without her, he just wanted to wither back into the black, the abyss that fueled his heart the most.

His thoughts shifted while still staring into her eyes, but his vision changed to the image of the man he blamed for all this and his suffering.

Sebastian Storm was the cause of her loss; his decision set forth a motion that could not be reversed. Sebastian's choice was what killed Emily. She must have agonized at the hands of the cartel.

Beaten, tortured, raped, he couldn't imagine what she endured before the end, and Sebastian would taste her pain someday. Tobias remained fixated on Emily's lifeless eyes. Nothing he could do would bring her back, but now he must feed his vengeance; he must set out to be what he was meant to become. Everyone will suffer for his loss.

Everyone.

He slowly stood up from the chair, a broken man filled with animosity and indignation. Tobias was consumed by it now. He stared at the box a moment more as it lay upon the kitchen table where he and Emily had spent so much time.

His gaze turned away finally from the face of his wife's image, grotesquely lying there, peering out at him from within the container. Her image pleading with him to avenge her. To make those who caused this have to answer for it.

Tobias stood up, then turned and walked beyond their living room where they had laughed so many times over the years, continued through the front door, leaving it open to the front porch, past his waiting suitcase, and proceeded down the outside stairway, and continued down the street . . . . he never looked back and never returned.

Her vision would be the last vision he would ever have of Emily: bloodied, bloated, and distorted. The grotesque image was his lifelong moniker and never faded for him in the years that followed.

His heart was eternally shattered and fragmented, forever tormented, and indignant, and the loss of Emily altered him permanently. He no longer felt for anyone or anything; his motives and emotions were now alternatively set and concentrated on only feeding his loathing and his determination.

He would never make room for anyone else; that portion of him died with Emily, and the core piece of his life was over now, historical, and completed in some way. He would revel in his pain, fueling what he was to become.

He had a new mission now as he walked down Jackson Street, never to return to their home ever again. Sebastian could possibly have saved Emily had he eliminated Rafael's receiving team, recaptured Rafael, obtained him once again, and renegotiated terms, but he chose the mission over her, which was the termination of Rafael Santiago above all. He knew it was the mission objective, but Emily could have been saved.

Storm was unwilling to risk losing Rafael Santiago, and Emily paid the ultimate price for his decision. Had Rafael escaped, it would have enabled him to go deep into hiding and change the entire landscape of the operation. Despite Sebastian's decision to sacrifice Emily for the greater good, Tobias would never forgive him for the betrayal and for leveraging Emily's safety. The scenario was winless by any count; Sebastian had to make the impossible choice and he did exactly what protocol dictated, but it didn't matter to Tobias.

<hr>

There was no guarantee that Emily would be located or even alive when the exchange occurred. Tobias should have considered this, but he was far too emotionally invested to see the actual warfare for what it was, and the consequences had Santiago lived.

It wasn't personal; it was an impossible call on every level. But Sebastian chose the option he felt was best, and HB and the team supported his decision.

As a result of that tragic day, Tobias had become the epitome of evil in every sense, thriving on people's fear of him and what he was capable of in his chaos. He had become an empty vessel, devoid of emotion and empathy.

He wreaked global havoc and prospered in that endeavor and profited from it in various forms of terrorism on both a macro level with multiple casualties to special precise "single termination" exercises. His precision flawless in its execution.

With his astute insight of explosives, he could set undetectable charges terminating only a specific target or isolated group. His organization slowly grew in reputation, but all the while, he maintained complete animosity for over an entire decade.

Several years prior, Tobias was contracted to eliminate a rival CEO of a technology company that retained his group and their set of talents. For this specific mission, the individual was reasonably well guarded and somewhat of a recluse, making it difficult to get close to him. Tobias chose a more explicit and strategic method to accomplish this particular task.

Researching his targets extensively, Tobias utilized a hand-selected team, profiled the subject, and exploited any angles they could find on the given individual.

Spending nearly three months planning, Tobias uniquely orchestrated the elimination of this target by ultimately deciding to dose the CEO with several skin-contact scenarios using an element called thallium.

A low-dose absorbable chemical, thallium competes with potassium absorption and is odorless and tasteless, making it generally undetectable, especially in low doses. Tobias coordinated multiple trace doses through skin contact while the target dined at restaurants, valeted his vehicle, or boarded his private jet. All the dose transfers were spread out over multiple weeks, inconspicuous, and masked within everyday occurrences that most people took for granted.

Tobias's people would serve the CEO in various restaurant locales and strategically place the thallium on their protected fingers, subtly grazing the top of his hand, placed upon his keys after he valeted his car, or the flight attendant lightly touching his forearm in a flirtatious manner. All effective means to deliver the drug to its intended target over time.

These small doses eventually led to massive cardiac arrest and death, thus fulfilling Tobias's contract, eliminating the target, and making the cause of death nearly impossible to trace.

Tobias had spent years in hiding following his wife's death, planning and developing his organization to the point of being a strategic global player in worldwide target assassinations, espionage, and various organized terrorist contract work.

He spared no expense in maintaining his anonymity while he secretly rose in power and stature. Well, insulated and deeply embedded within the fabric of his organization, he was able to remain out of the watchful eye of HB and her illustrious Machine as she valiantly referred to her division.

Tobias Teague was masterful in the art of the strategic kill. Still, Sebastian had thwarted many of Tobias's planned missions, and those deviations cost Tobias a tremendous amount of money and inconvenience. Tobias had sent kill squads to eliminate Sebastian over the years, but every time, Sebastian prevailed, eliminating them with relative ease.

Sebastian, among all his many talents, was the maestro of elusiveness and would continually remain a step ahead of Tobias's teams of "would-be" assassins. However, Sebastian was unaware that Tobias was behind any of these efforts and often wondered who was pulling the strings. Tobias detested Sebastian in every sense, and he vowed to have his vengeance at some point.

Over the years, Sebastian developed the unique ability to ignore all fear. He determined it was simply an emotion, a fabricated reaction based on socialized conditioning from parents, instinct, culture, and society.

He felt all people had an expiration date, so he had learned to accept his own fate, for when it finally caught up with him, he would face it head-on and welcome his inevitable demise. Sebastian Storm accepted he could not change or alter that fact.

That said, he did, however, fear only one thing, or rather one person—*Tobias Teague*. He feared the man because Tobias possessed no limits, no moral fortitude with which to weigh like other humans. And like Sebastian, he too was fearless, and that was dangerous. Sebastian knew if Tobias were to ever acquire Sebastian, or anyone close to him, in any fashion, there was no question his mortality and potential suffering if up to Tobias, would be most assured.

Sebastian's fear was not in dying as he would accept this honor when fate came knocking. His trepidation was Tobias would torture Sebastian to no end, and his torment would be long, painful, and purposeful. Essentially, this would be a response to what he felt his wife, Emily, most likely went through, and so Sebastian Storm would suffer the same.

Tobias would want to see him agonize for days, if not weeks, before he was even remotely satisfied. Even then, ultimately, in Sebastian's annihilation, Tobias would remain disappointed Sebastian hadn't been distressed and anguished enough to allow his wife to be tortured at the hands of the Santiago cartel.

Sebastian felt there was no question Tobias would make anyone who was meaningful to Sebastian a target as well. This was Tobias's methodology and religion, and he practiced it devoutly.

On that fateful day in Panama, Sebastian was dealt an impossible decision, and Tobias should have understood his plight but felt Sebastian was to blame for the cartel's retaliation. Someday soon, he would make him pay for it. It all made sense now. The man who had been once a mentor had now become his greatest adversary.

Tobias . . . *Risen from the dead.*

Sebastian had often wondered what had ever happened to Tobias after Emily's death was confirmed, and now, he knew he had spent the last decade fostering his hatred and resentment and turning its focus on destruction and death. The reports of his death so many years before were a farce.

Sebastian slowly opened his eyes and asked HB to give him the details of this mission and how he could be of service. HB spelled out the nuances of how Homeland had been tracking multiple terrorist explosive experts, and all indications were Tobias appeared to be behind the plot. ATS Division had been given the file because of the sensitivity of one of their own planning an attack.

HB explained, "Homeland felt they needed our team directly involved in this operation. After all these years, it appears Tobias's voice was recognized in some transmission a few weeks ago, which surprised me and made my skin crawl, frankly, when I heard it. They wanted confirmation of his voice. It was definitely him, no question. We had lost all tabs on Tobias some time ago. Simmons confirmed his body in Florida." Sebastian nodded.

"We have watched him over the years, and he has led an otherwise docile life often found on a beach somewhere until he eventually fell off the grid. We assumed he drowned in a bottle or drugs, alcohol, or both, in all honesty. It seems careless to me he would resurface like this, or was it his intention all along, a trap possibly? Although he did seem agitated when I heard the recording," HB added.

"He is more than capable of manipulating intel to throw us off track. You and the APS Division trained him after all," Sebastian responded subtly. "Where do you think he was when you intercepted the audio?"

HB responded, "The recording's location was in London, Sebastian. He had dropped off the grid after the Santiago debacle, as you know. Just . . . disappeared, went completely dark. Nonexistent for many years, but our intel suggests he may have been there, working covertly, in the shadows, recruiting the last of his team, and we believe he also may be there to plan an attempt on you as well.

It would explain many of the attempts on your life in the past we could not explain," she sheepishly stated.

Sebastian contemplated this as his would-be attackers in London may very well have been part of Tobias's crew. They were trained reasonably well. A three-person team would prove effective against a single target, but Sebastian wasn't just any target, not by a long shot. Unfortunately, Sebastian had not been able to question any of them.

"This changes things substantially, HB, but I do take every precaution, as you are well aware," Sebastian said with a cunning smile, assuring her he would be ready, as always.

Changing the subject, probing as she did so well, HB asked, "Did you see the news about the South African Ambassador being assassinated as well as his chief of security at the consulate in London late last night?"

Sebastian narrowed his gaze as he hesitated for a moment and then replied, "Yes, I did. Tragic, wasn't it?"

With a wry smile, she responded, "Our intel suggests he had a . . . eh, a not so savory appetite for young boys, I guess. Not such a wonderful man, after all. We all have our deep, dark secrets, don't we, Sebastian?"

Sebastian again contemplated this information, already knowing full well the insatiable "appetites" the ambassador craved, the intel provided by his silent "informer" weeks before, and then stated, "Well then, maybe he got what he deserved, HB. Karma, you know? And yes, some of those secrets are forgivable, but some are not. I guess the ambassador got what he ultimately deserved. Maybe those poor young boys can have some closure and healing knowing the man died a gruesome death." He gave a slight shrug.

"Yes, karma, that must be it, Sebastian, 'gruesome'? I didn't know they disclosed how he died, only that he did," replied HB. With her vast resources, paired with the deep and thorough understanding of her operative's diverse and complicated psychological profiles, HB knew her operatives intimately, understanding the modus operandi of all her agents equally well.

She was aware of Sebastian's need for world balance and righteousness. She afforded him substantial latitude, knowing he needed to satisfy his personal balance—and who was she to question his motives?

She knew much more about him than she let on and preferred it that way. HB was well aware of Sebastian's thirst for justice on behalf of the weak and the innocent after some of his experiences as a young man. She also knew when not to press any subject for fear of driving these complex personalities farther away or to a darker habitation than they already dwelled.

"Yes," replied Sebastian, "I'm sure it was fitting for his sins, is all I'm saying. Anyway, what's the next step, HB?"

Avoiding her inquiry and probe, HB would let it go and not push the issue. HB's inner struggle with this predicament was derived from Tobias's loss of his wife, Emily. The incident changed him forever and pushed him to the brink of despair.

She knew many of her top agents dwelled on the precipice of a delicate spiral if triggered in a particular fashion. Sebastian offered nothing in light of her probing, and she would have to be content with that notion and accept no additional clarification or explanation, as it would never come over the death of the ambassador. He would tell her if he felt she needed to know, but she knew better than to provoke him.

She was more than aware Sebastian was in London as early as the night before finishing up business from a prior mission. She didn't believe in the slightest the perception or assumption he wasn't involved with the incident surrounding the ambassador, but frankly, she didn't care.

One less dreadful pedophile on the streets made her sleep just a little better at night. Her concern was these extracurricular escapades put her best and brightest agent at some additional risk. Still, she held her tongue, understanding the outlet was needed, and his desire realized.

Sebastian's profile has always been interesting to her. This sense of morality was evoked in protecting the vulnerable and those who couldn't defend themselves. Where did it come from, she often thought? Her questions were never fully answered or realized in all her research, but she had learned to accept her lack of complete understanding. She allowed a measure of range and latitude in that regard, especially when it came to Sebastian.

She knew from his dossier that Sebastian's childhood was murky at best, and of course, he would never offer up any explanation of his early years when probed. She knew both parents were deceased, the details of their untimely fatalities somewhat of a mystery. His mother had died while he was young, twelve to thirteen years old, and in some fashion, was strange and unexplainable.

So, too, had his father passed, shortly after his mother, in some bizarre hunting accident was equally peculiar in that Sebastian's father rarely hunted. But both parents' cases had been opened and shut, almost immediately and with little to no evidence on either of the deceased, obviously collected twenty-five years prior with a small-town mentality ever present in Roanoke, Virginia.

Sebastian was an enigma, an anomaly, but also a well-oiled machine, precise, and very nearly a perfect weapon. Years before, an old friend, James Woodford, had brought Sebastian's talents to her attention and heavily promoted them.

Unwavering, calculating, and destructive in his precision, Sebastian respected and honed his skills, which were already well developed when she recruited and trained him and Tobias so many years before.

HB agreed to send Sebastian the formal file in its entirety, fully classified information in the typical encrypted manner and emphasized that she was looking for a full report and strategy from him by the end of the week. Sebastian always came through, and she had no doubt this issue would be an exception.

HB sensed Sebastian was a little more serious than usual and asked, "Are you okay, Sebastian? You seem . . . different today."

He smiled at her and replied, "Of course, HB, just considering my fate and relevance, like anyone, I suppose. I'll be okay." She wasn't convinced but didn't want to push the issue.

She said goodbye and quietly left through the rear entry, but not before Sebastian ran an efficient reconnaissance departure protocol before he would let her leave. When he felt secure, he allowed HB to depart, calling her driver to pick her up outside. He watched her through the window from his loft until she got into her SUV, waved, and drove off, slipping out of sight. His gaze lingered for a few minutes, following her departure to see if any questionable cars emerged from where HB had left his sight. Nothing.

Sebastian thought to himself, impressed with how well HB knew him and sensed his inner turmoil.

He had been thinking of late of his own mortality and value within his tactical domain, as he had come to know it well, its nuances as well as its challenges, and how much was still left to understand about himself and people in general.

The list of people who knew Sebastian Storm on the deepest level was concise and was a short list.

He liked it that way.

Chapter 5

The Beginning

Roanoke, Virginia
1994

Sebastian lay quietly waiting and watching, burrowed within the shrubs and thickets at the base of the mountains outside the small city of Roanoke, Virginia. The city's population was roughly sixty-two thousand.

The town was small, simple, and unrefined but a wholesome place to grow up. He was born on a Tuesday morning at Carilion Roanoke Memorial Hospital in March of 1982.

Coming from a long line of Storms, Sebastian's family lived just outside of town. Both parents were born and raised in Virginia, but Sebastian was the last of the lineage for both the Storm and Britton surnames.

Positioned within the Blue Ridge Mountains of southwest Virginia, Roanoke was a peaceful and quiet town recognized for the Roanoke Star. Also referred to as the Mill Mountain Star, a neon landmark overlooking the city from the summit of Mill Mountain, observable from Sebastian's small home.

The surrounding state park area was home to trails, segregated hunting regions for control of overpopulated animals, picnic areas, and the Mill Mountain Zoo within the vicinity as well. This area was where Sebastian liked to test his rabbit traps the most. His ingenuity was exceptional, his designs flawless; Sebastian enjoyed the engineering behind the mechanisms and their design, determining the best mechanisms to ensnare the rodents, as his father referred to them.

Occasionally, Sebastian delved into the intricate world of animal psychology, seeking to understand the cunning instincts and adaptive behaviors of the elusive creatures that regularly evaded his traps. His fascination with nature was a blend of awe for its straightforwardness and a deep curiosity about its complexities. He marveled at the rapid adaptability of animals, a testament to the dynamic interplay of life and environment.

His father, however, dismissively referred to all such creatures as mere rodents, though technically, they were not. In fact, rabbits, which often fell under his father's broad and incorrect classification, distinctly differ from rodents. Unlike the Rodentia family, which does not include rabbits, these animals boast an additional pair of incisors and several skeletal differences that set them apart.

Sebastian was well-versed in these nuances and repeatedly tried imparting this knowledge to his father. However, his attempts were often met with indifference. His father, set in his ways, displayed a marked disinterest in being corrected, particularly by his son. To Sebastian, who was keenly observant even at a young age, his father's stubborn ignorance bordered on foolishness, painting him as a man unwilling to embrace the subtleties and wonders of the natural world he so casually dismissed.

Rabbits, hares, and a few other species comprise the Lagomorpha family of animals. Shrews, moles, and hedgehogs are also not considered rodents. Sebastian would also trap these animals and later release them without intending any harm to them.

He often thought his father a dupe for not desiring to understand this fact, but he also didn't care what his father's opinions were on anything, possessing little respect for the man. He enjoyed the thrill of the hunt, and the mechanics behind ensnaring the animals intrigued him, but he never intended to hurt or kill them.

Sebastian was an only child, never fortunate to have a sibling, and thus learned to entertain himself at an early age. His parents were simple people, requiring few of life's comforts. His mother worked downtown at the Taubman Museum of Art, highlighting works by American artists such as Thomas Eakins and John Singer Sargent.

She worked at the museum mornings and was employed five days a week. Sebastian enjoyed touring the museum and attempted to culture himself as best he could within the institution, realizing there was so much more to the world than what he experienced in Roanoke. Sebastian's interest pleased his mother immensely regarding her young son's pursuit of educating himself and learning about new things.

His father's current vocation was a steel worker at the foundry, a blue-collar employee since high school, but he was often between jobs because of his temper and habitual lousy attitude. He was never meant to rise up the ladder, nor did he seem to possess the interest to do so.

Sebastian couldn't remember his father holding down a job for more than a few months at a time and recalled numerous instances where he would return home from work complaining about his superior's focus on his father's attitude and issues he had with other employees, which was an all-too-common theme in the Storm household.

Sebastian remained quiet, unmoving, and still, watching his most recent trap design from a distance, attempting to lure its prey. During these times, he would often think about life, specifically his parents, the wilderness, school, and most of all, his future.

He despised his father on every level and considered him selfish, aggressive, abusive, and degrading to all of those people he possessed any kind of relationship. His father didn't appear to be liked by anyone.

Sebastian detested how his father treated both he and his mother, but he was just a child; what options did he possess and what could be done about it, he often thought. Sebastian's mother was affectionate, submissive, and . . . *weak*. Taking advantage of those qualities, his father never treated his mother respectfully.

Sebastian yearned for the day when he might protect her better, but he wasn't strong enough. Not yet. He often fantasized about being much older and stronger so he might care for and protect her more from the monster his father had become.

Sebastian's home life was tumultuous and fraught with discord. His return from school was often met with the cacophony of his parents' voices raised in heated arguments. The atmosphere was thick with tension, and his father's anger would sometimes escalate into shouting matches, reverberating through the house like thunder. On the darkest days, these verbal assaults turned physical, leaving scars both seen and unseen.

In the aftermath of these confrontations, Sebastian would hear the muffled sobs of his mother from her room. Each sob was a sharp stab to his heart, intensifying his resentment towards his father. The silence that followed his father's abrupt departures, sometimes lasting days, was a bittersweet relief. In his absence, the house transformed into a sanctuary of peace, allowing Sebastian and his mother moments of fragile happiness, a stark contrast to the oppressive atmosphere of his presence.

However, the cycle of arguments and violence appeared unending. During the explosive episodes, Sebastian witnessed his father's uncontrolled fury, helplessly observing as his mother bore the brunt of the aggression. The sight of his mother in pain was devastating; it left Sebastian feeling powerless, fueling a deep-seated desire to protect her but finding himself constrained by his youthful helplessness and the complexities of their family dynamics.

He feared his father would take her life at some point, and the thought scared him the most. The thought of living his life without his mother often caused him to become anxious and desolate.

When the tempest of his father's fury erupted, especially when fueled by alcohol, it often swept Sebastian into its destructive path after Jonathan grew tired of his mother.

Jonathan Storm's anger, intensified by inebriation, found a regrettable outlet in his son. The domestic environment would crackle with the tension of raised voices and, all too often, devolve into physical altercations.

Overwhelmed by the turbulence, Sebastian found sanctuary in the rugged solace of the mountains. There, amid the ancient stillness of stone and sky, he could release his emotions and gather his thoughts far from the chaos of his volatile home life.

Sebastian's thirteenth birthday dawned under the shadow of his father's wrath. That morning, Jonathan's voice boomed through the confines of their kitchen, laced with an unusual venom. The night before, he had begun his descent into aggression with a half-bottle of vodka, and the morning found him resuming his bender. The alcohol stripped away any remnants of restraint, leaving behind a man rife with hostility.

This outburst was not just another echo of frequent disputes; it was sharper, more biting. Sebastian, newly thirteen, lay in bed listening to the familiar yet increasingly severe cacophony of his father's rage colliding with the quiet despair of his mother's responses.

The harsh reality of his home life on what should have been a celebratory day painted a somber picture of his adolescence. It underscored a poignant truth: on this milestone, instead of joy and presents, Sebastian was gifted with the stark reminder of his need for the peace only the mountains could provide.

Jonathan had lost his job the previous day, and in those low times, he tended to take it out on her the most. Jonathan was a disappointment to everyone, but primarily to himself. Like so many arrogant men, he was entitled to greatness and success, though he had been largely idle and unreliable his entire life. Life didn't owe Jonathan Storm, but he felt far differently about it.

Sebastian had always observed his father and his actions and was old enough to understand his father wasn't a victim as he claimed but instead created his own misery and wanted anyone close to him to suffer as well.

He may not have wanted this life, but he never strived to make it better for any of them. He took solace in abusing Sebastian's mother and having a child to take his frustrations out on, most often verbally, but the physical element was increasing by the month.

Early struggles with his emotions and self-esteem, Sebastian blamed his father's lack of affection and love for either of them to be the cause of some of his childhood anxiety. Sebastian felt the immanent void every day of his youth.

His mother, however, instilled a softer, more emotional, and expressive side within Sebastian, and he appreciated her for her genuine attentiveness and counseling during those difficult times.

Sebastian vowed never to emulate his father in any form, especially the hateful and abusive side of him. No one deserved his cruelty, least of all his affectionate and caring mother.

She was crying now and asked Jonathan why he was so angry. She reminded him it was Sebastian's birthday and that they should do something special for him, being a new teenager. His father said, "Today, today is his birthday? Well, he needs to man up and realize birthdays and parties are for babies, and those days end today!"

Sebastian's mother was gradually unraveling under the relentless onslaught of Jonathan's ferocity and selfishness. Each outburst, each venomous tirade, chipped away at her resilience, pushing her to the brink of despair.

The household air was thick with tension, almost palpable as if the very walls were saturated with the distress emanating from the ongoing conflict. In these moments, Jonathan's anger seemed to target her almost exclusively, his words like arrows finding their mark with cruel precision.

From behind the slightly ajar door of his room, Sebastian was an unwilling eavesdropper to the tempest in the kitchen. His heart pounded in his chest as his mother's voice, filled with pain and confusion, cut through the cacophony. "Why do you hate Sebastian and me so much, Jonathan?" Her question, raw and loaded with emotion, hung in the air—a poignant encapsulation of their fractured family dynamics.

Sebastian felt a mix of anger and helplessness as he listened. The voices, though muffled, carried a clear message of the pain his mother endured and the complexity of emotions she navigated: love for her husband, protectiveness over her son, and a desperate longing for peace. The distress in her voice resonated deeply with Sebastian, echoing his own feelings of abandonment and sorrow in the face of his father's inexplicable resentment.

He turned to her slowly, "Really, why? Honestly, why? Because I didn't ask for any of this, Samantha. . . . You, him, none of it. He was a mistake, and come to think of it, you were too, but you got pregnant and screwed it all up. I should have left long ago—you aren't what I want. I didn't want any of this, and I sure as hell don't want a thirteen-year-old kid!" he screamed as he threw his glass across the room, shattering it against the wall, startling Samantha. Her hands instinctively rose to her face, terrified of her husband and of what he was capable of.

Alarmed, Samantha emerged from her chair, wailing, and proceeded up the stairs and slammed the door behind her. Sebastian felt tremendous dread and despair over his father's words and his animosity for the two of them.

When given a chance, he had no shame in expressing his distaste for Samantha and Sebastian.

Quietly dressing so as not to alarm his father, Sebastian quietly put on his jacket, crept into the hall adjacent to the living room, slipped out the front door without being noticed, and ran for what felt like miles, deep into the forest, to his sanctuary, his safe haven of freedom. No one would find him there; it was his domain.

Fueled by sadness and trepidation, he feared for his mother and desperately hoped when she went to her room, the fighting was done—no more anguish, no more yelling, no more of him.

Sebastian hoped he would just leave her alone. It was moments like those when he wished his father was dead. He yearned for him to leave the home and return to an empty house. A desire that his father did just that: leave, at least for a few days. It always helped when he wasn't around.

The hours passed quickly, keeping his mind focused on more pleasant things around his campsite. Dusk was setting it, getting chilly as the sunlight was diminishing. Sebastian had been in the forest for over twelve hours, tweaking his snares and inspecting the countryside for more locations to place his traps.

He thought of his mother and pondered whether enough time had passed to return home, hoping the dust had settled, but still, he was weary of the notion.

He didn't want to return to his father aggravated or angry for being gone so long. The sun had just set, and the remaining light swiftly faded as Sebastian reached the outskirts of the property of his home. Feeling cold now, he was hesitant, warming his hands with his breath, searching for any sign that would indicate the landscape within the house was more docile and peaceful.

He made the few steps up the porch and opened the door, already ajar. As he cautiously pushed the door further, he listened for anything out of place. No lights were on, which appeared strange to him at this late hour. He knew the home well, but with no light came an eerie atmosphere of trepidation and anxiety he identified all too well under his family's roof.

"Hello?" he weakly muttered, not entirely certain if he anticipated any response or desired one. When no one replied, he made his way to the kitchen and flipped the light switch.

The intense illumination occurring all at once was slightly blinding as his eyes adjusted. Once they were focused, he scanned the kitchen and noticed the eggs and bacon his mother had been cooking that morning on the stove had burned, although the stove was off. The milk was still out and warm to the touch. It appeared as though nothing had changed since he had left earlier in the morning. "Mom? Mom are you there?" he attempted again. Still, no response. The house was peculiarly quiet.

He felt immediately saddened by the lack of vivacity within the home. His mom possessed an energy he always felt around him, encircling, and protecting him. That comforting feeling had subsided, leaving him with a cold, frigid sensation, and he began to shiver for a moment at the thought of her absence and where she could have possibly gone.

He then realized that the moment before he had walked up the driveway, his father's car was not in the front driveway of the home, so he suspected his father had left, which made him instantly feel better in some strange way.

But where was his mother, and did she leave with his father? Maybe to look for him within the forest as they feared he had run away since he had been gone for the better part of the day. He would have passed them on his way back home if they had been searching.

Sebastian slowly made his way down the hall to try her room upstairs; maybe she was sleeping, far too distraught after the strenuous day she had experienced.

The stairs lay beyond the kitchen, and the hall was dark and unlit, but the light switch was located at the foot of the stairway. Though difficult to see, he made his way down the hall, mumbling again, "Mom? Mom, are you there?" Still, with no answer, he approached the stairs, reaching for the railing, but his foot struck something soft on the floor.

As Sebastian's hand trembled, reaching for the light switch, a profound sense of dread overwhelmed him. He hesitated for a moment before gently flicking the switch, casting a dim glow down the staircase. His eyes darted downwards, and his heart sank at the sight that greeted him. There, at the foot of the stairs, lay his mother, her body twisted into an unnatural position, a silent figure draped in the pale fabric of her nightgown from the night before.

The stark, eerie stillness of the scene pierced Sebastian's soul. He crouched to his knees, his mind racing with fear and confusion. Her body curled into itself, her hair falling chaotically over her face, obscuring her features. Her neck was bent at an agonizing angle, suggesting the grim reality of the situation.

Kneeling beside her, Sebastian's hands hovered hesitantly, afraid to touch, afraid to confirm his worst fears. The cold, hard truth was etching itself into his heart, yet part of him clung desperately to a sliver of hope—that this was just a terrible misunderstanding, that somehow, she would stir, and the nightmare would end.

But the oppressive silence in the air, broken only by his shallow, trembling breaths, spoke volumes. Sebastian was confronted with a reality he had dreaded most yet never was truly prepared for, and it threatened to engulf him in its dark depths.

Sebastian cautiously whispered, "Mom . . . Mom, are you okay? Mom, speak to me! Please, mom. Say something. . . . ." He shook her shoulder. Sebastian hesitated, pulled his hand back as she felt stiff to the touch, then extended his hand again to brush her hair back from her beautiful face. As he softly touched her striking brown hair and eased it back from her face, he caressed her skin—it was cold to the touch.

As Sebastian tentatively reached out, his fingers trembling, he gently swept her hair back from her face, revealing more of the grim tableau before him. Her eye, open and unseeing, stared blankly, a haunting gloss over it that spoke of profound stillness. It was the vacant stare of the comatose, devoid of the warmth and recognition that had once greeted him every day.

Her body lay limp, a stark contrast to the gentle, animated gestures she once made. As he observed more closely, he noticed a thin trickle of blood that had begun its slow descent from her nose, meandering down her cheek in a delicate, sorrowful path. The blood, a stark red against her pale skin, collected in a small, dark pool on the polished wooden floor, no larger than the size of his hand.

This small, poignant detail—the blood, so minimal yet so profound—struck a deep chord within Sebastian. It was a visceral reminder of the fragility of life, how swiftly and silently it could be altered. The sight rooted him to the spot, a mix of shock, sorrow, and an acute sense of helplessness washing over him as he knelt beside her, enveloped in the harsh reality of the moment.

Sebastian's eyes closed slowly as he sank to the floor next to her, the cold reality setting in with a heavy, suffocating weight. She was gone—the mother who had caressed him, whose gentle touch had so often chased away the shadows of his world.

He would never again see her smile that could light up a room or feel the comforting warmth of her hands as she rubbed his arms during their quiet evenings together, sometimes while watching television, sometimes as he drifted into sleep. Her presence had always been a haven, a soft echo of peace in the turmoil of their lives.

Now, that sanctuary was shattered. Forever. In a moment, everything had changed. Sebastian's heart clenched with the gnawing certainty that his father was somehow linked to this tragic endpoint. The suspicion rooted deep within him, coloring his grief with a tinge of bitter anger.

He remained there on the floor, time slipping by unnoticed as he gazed at her still face. A single tear escaped, carving a wet trail down his cheek before dropping silently onto the floor. Each blink brought another wave of sorrow, enveloping him, drowning him in the profound depth of his loss.

Gradually, he shifted, lying down on the hardwood floor to nestle against her one last time. He draped his arm gently over hers, the familiarity of her scent—a poignant mixture of her essence and a faint trace of her perfume—washing over him.

It evoked a montage of happier memories, a cruel contrast to the present. Despite the sharp sting of his grief, there was a strange solace in believing she was now in a place free from pain and suffering, a place devoid of the misery that had clouded her final days.

In this heartbreaking moment of proximity, Sebastian found a bitter comfort, clinging to the thought that she was at peace, even as his own world became irreparably broken.

The day changed him forever.

Vienna, Austria
Present Day

Sebastian felt the frosty bitterness on his face, reminding him of that fateful day on his thirteenth birthday when he found his mother at the bottom of the stairs. He opened his eyes, appreciating the view from his balcony overlooking the south side of the Volksgarten Park in Vienna.

He enjoyed his coffee on the cool morning, appreciating the solitude and quiet surrounding him. Frigid weather always made him think of his mother. He could never forget the feeling of her cold skin on his fingertips as he pulled back her hair, revealing her face so many years ago.

He always thought a child should never bear witness to such a tragedy, to have to find his parent in that condition. A far too extreme and traumatic life experience for someone so young to have to face. It did, however, teach him much about life, its harshness, and its difficult lessons. Life was unforgiving and unfair, discovered Sebastian far too early in childhood.

His mother should never have suffered as she did, but in the end, he hoped she found peace. Peace for her but vengeance and anger for Sebastian. That day flipped a twitch for him in many ways and began his long journey, an expedition he would never truly return from. It set him on a forever quest for justice and fairness for all, and he was determined to see it through.

The haunting image of his mother's lifeless form was indelibly etched in Sebastian's mind, a chilling snapshot that resurfaced relentlessly each day since that icy evening. It was more than a memory—it was a vivid, persistent echo that grew sharper with each passing moment. In his deepest pain, there was a peculiar longing, a paradoxical craving for the sharp sting of that agony. It was the very fuel that ignited his daily resolve, a harsh reminder that spurred him onwards.

Sebastian detested this addiction to his grief, yet he recognized its necessity, its grim purpose. The intensity of his sorrow was like a drug, a necessary dose of dark inspiration that he needed to sustain his mission and hone his craft. This mission had not been a choice but rather a destiny thrust upon him, sculpted by his profound loathing for the man who had robbed him of his only true source of joy.

He did not welcome this burden, yet it had been bequeathed to him as if fate had chosen him to bear this cross. It was a mission forged in the crucible of his hatred, a relentless drive to confront and perhaps dismantle the legacy of a father who had shattered his world. This pain, this relentless replay of his darkest moment, had become the signature of his calling, the defining force of his existence.

He shook off the vision and turned to more pressing issues. For the better part of the day, Sebastian studied the voluminous file HB had given him and came to the same conclusion Tobias was involved, at least on some level. How had he eluded them for all those years? The question remained.

Still, he had far more to investigate to determine the level of depth his old adversary was involved and realized he might never understand completely.

Among his many skills and talents, Sebastian possessed a photographic memory. He scanned each document, committing them to his subconscious, cross-referencing all the information in his mind to produce any clue or item missed that might help them determine what angle or intention Tobias may be maneuvering.

Several times throughout the day, the beautiful stranger, Adriana, from the café, had emerged from deep within his thoughts. Her confidence, poise, voice, and elegance intrigued him. He cursed himself for his weakness in letting her consume his thoughts, but he could not resist.

Glancing at the clock, he noted the time had crept up on him. Almost 6 pm. Her requested meeting time was now upon him.

8 pm, Sharp, don't be late, he recalled the note saying.

Chapter 6

Adriana

Vienna, Austria
Present Day

Despite the whisperings of caution in his mind, Sebastian found himself stepping into the grand lobby of the San Souci, a gem nestled in the bustling heart of Vienna. The hotel was no stranger to him; its corridors and quiet nooks were as familiar as the back of his hand, having been both a sanctuary and a stage for earlier chapters of his life. On this day, he crossed the threshold not merely as a guest but as a man on a mission, cloaked in the subtle elegance that his circumstances demanded.

Sebastian exuded a blend of sophistication and determination, dressed impeccably in a fashionable black tweed jacket and perfectly fitted slacks, complemented by a crisp white shirt left casually unbuttoned at the collar. Each step through the opulent lobby was measured, his sharp eyes scanning the surroundings with an air of tenacity and intrigue. He was a portrait of modern elegance, his attire, not only a statement of style but an armor of confidence as he navigated the familiar yet unpredictable terrain of the San Souci. This return was fueled by more than nostalgia; it was charged with a purpose that thrummed quietly beneath his calm exterior, a blend of personal resolve and the haunting drive that shadowed his every move.

Sebastian was still marveling at the cleverness and audacity of the woman who had approached him in the café. Her directness had been refreshing, a bold gesture that piqued his interest immediately. Captivated by her ingenuity, he found himself unable to refuse her intriguing offer, drawn in by the allure of the unknown that she represented.

As he walked through the foyer of the building, his presence commanded attention. Women turned their heads, drawn to his distinguished appearance and the confident, purposeful air with which he moved. Sebastian's attire, meticulously chosen, complemented his handsome features and the natural charisma that radiated from him. Each step was measured and deliberate, echoing the inner focus and intensity that guided him.

This was a man who understood the power of an impression. His gaze was steady, his posture poised, suggesting a narrative of a life lived fully and deliberately. Those in the foyer couldn't help but speculate about the man behind the compelling exterior—what adventures he might have experienced and what compelling destinations lay ahead for him on this day.

Commanding an audience as he entered the lounge, Sebastian always attracted the attention of women and men alike. He entered the dim area and quickly scanned the room for the mysterious woman he had met only hours before, the woman he couldn't seem to keep off his mind the entire day.

It wasn't like Sebastian to behave in such a cavalier manner, but something inside of him was craving some semblance of a simpler life, an existence with some form of normalcy. A reality not hurried or controlled but rather a hint of regularity and elation the rest of the world experienced each and every day. He was beginning to long for the simplicity, the type a normal life could offer.

Sebastian had arrived fifteen minutes early. He made his way through the lounge toward the direction of the bar top. To be on time was late for him.

The area was dimly lit, a strategic nightmare, but only one primary access into the premises and easily monitored as people entered and exited. Perusing the patrons colonizing the lounge as he entered, he quickly ascertained she had not yet arrived, which he appreciated.

He settled on a table in the corner, a stone wall to his back, easily observing the entire establishment with little effort. The lounge appeared secure, putting him more at ease as he waited for his mysterious guest to arrive.

A striking waitress appeared before Sebastian, sporting a casual but alluring smile, and asked if he would like a drink. Sebastian hesitated, considered the question, and replied with a subtle smirk, "I'm waiting for someone. Please check back when they arrive. And my name is Storm."

"But, of course, Mr. Storm. What a fortunate lady she is," she said with a wink, turning on her heels and diverting her attention toward another customer in the distance.

At precisely 8:00 pm, the atmosphere in the lounge shifted palpably as Adriana Mercer made her entrance. She was a vision in a sleek, all-black ensemble—a form-fitting mid-thigh skirt paired with towering four-inch Jimmy Choo heels accentuated her poised, statuesque figure. Her walk was a study in controlled elegance, each step a deliberate testament to her unrivaled confidence.

Adriana paused just inside the doorway, her sharp eyes scanning the room with a strategic intent. She searched for Sebastian, eager to gauge the impact of the succinct note she had slipped him earlier. Her arrival had the intended effect; the lounge momentarily paused in collective admiration. Like Sebastian, both sexes alike couldn't help but take in her striking presence, captivated by her aura of sophistication and allure.

Her appearance wasn't just visually stunning; it was a dynamic expression of her personality—bold, intelligent, and undeniably sexy. As Adriana's gaze swept over the lounge, a subtle smile played at the corners of her lips, hinting at her satisfaction in knowing she commanded the room, her presence almost tangibly drawing the attention and intrigue of everyone present.

Describing Adriana Mercer as merely stunning would have been a disservice. She exuded an air of elegance and effortlessly a pure confidence, embodying a presence that was as intriguing as it was commanding. Adriana was a blend of intelligence, allure, and poise, striking a perfect balance between self-assuredness and an approachable charisma that steered clear of arrogance.

Adriana captivated the room from the moment she entered, but her focus was singular. She quickly spotted Sebastian secluded in a dimly lit corner of the lounge. A knowing smile curved her lips—a silent acknowledgment of the game they found themselves woven into. With the grace of a seasoned seductress and the precision of a chess master, she began her approach. Each step was a measured, seductive dance, echoing the fluid, confident strides he had admired in the café that morning. She knew what she wanted and she had no qualms going after it.

Her approach was not just a walk; it was a deliberate, mesmerizing display of allure and intellect, a magnetic force pulling Sebastian into her orbit even before exchanging a single word.

He drank in all of her image in full, as if time had slowed down for him to truly appreciate this stunning woman. She moved exquisitely, controlled, edgy yet refined, all in the same breath, her gaze and focus confined to Sebastian, which was almost hypnotic.

She concentrated on nothing else and relished knowing she was holding his attention as she walked toward him. She sensed him watching her posture, elegance, and magic in merely her movement and his energy as she advanced.

He began to rise from his chair to greet her as she approached and, with a soft smile, took her soft hand within his own, expertly kissed the back of it in a gentlemanly fashion, and gently uttered, "You are simply . . . *delectable*. My name is Sebastian. Sebastian Storm."

He held her gaze for a moment longer than appropriate, making her blush ever so slightly as she put her opposite hand to her chest and said quietly, "Well, hello there, Sebastian Storm, and thank you. As you well know, I am Adriana. And may I add, you are quite palatable yourself. And quite tall," as she looked up into his hazel eyes.

She regained her composure quickly. He hastily repositioned himself beside her and pulled her chair back as she gently sat down, holding his attention the entire time. He effortlessly slid to his chair, where he sat before her arrival, and smiled again as he positioned himself alongside her at the small table.

Adriana was eased closer to the table by Sebastian, drawing her closer to him. Her eyes took in the intimate ambiance he had chosen. The setting was quintessentially romantic—shadows danced on the walls from the dim, muted lighting, and their secluded corner offered a cocoon of privacy away from the rest of the world. It was the perfect backdrop for whispered secrets and discreet conversations. Sebastian had chosen well, and Adriana appreciated the thoughtfulness behind his selection, recognizing the promise of the privacy they both desired.

As she settled into her seat, her presence drawing the shadows closer, enhancing the allure of the moment. She carefully appreciated the surroundings and the man who had intrigued her enough to warrant this meeting. Her eyes, sharp and discerning, flickered with a hint of curiosity and excitement at unraveling the enigma that was Sebastian.

Leaning slightly forward, the soft fabric of her dress whispering with the movement, Adriana's voice was a melodic whisper, imbued with warmth and a touch of anticipation. "I'm so glad you could make it this evening, Sebastian," she said, her words flowing smoothly, accompanied by a subtle, inviting smile that softened her features yet hinted at the layers of complexity she held within. Her tone was gentle yet confident, a perfect match for the seductive serenity of their surroundings, setting the stage for an evening filled with intriguing possibilities.

In that moment, she appreciated the elaborate attributes of the attractive man sitting next to her. He was far more physically attractive that evening than he was that day, but obviously, what she had seen in the café prompted her to approach him regardless.

She had a good feeling about him and followed her intuition. Adriana inwardly smiled, pleasantly surprised and delighted he had taken her up on her bold offer from the morning. He returned the smile, "There was no chance I would miss this after such a tremendous introduction today."

Tall and dark, with a hint of gray within his stubble and hair, distinguished with a presence strong and commanding of a room, no doubt a resilient characteristic he possessed in abundance. In the brief moment of the meeting, she sensed his energy and magnetism, yet he possessed humility and softness as well.

She instantly assumed women must gravitate toward him and his mystery, but it didn't bother or intimidate her in the least. It's part of what excited her, and she sensed it in the café that morning, which motivated her to approach him with her invitation. She believed it was what attracted her initially to him in the café. Not only strong and imposing but surprisingly soft and with an approachable and alluring voice, no less. When he had initially greeted her, she was anxious to hear more.

Adriana, once settled, said, "I was very curious about whether I would actually see you tonight, Sebastian." With a wry smile, she was eager just to hear him speak; uttering any semblance of words he strung together stimulated her. It energized her and fulfilled some primal desire, and she found herself fascinated by him instantly.

After a moment, he smiled and replied, "With such an auspicious and unique delivery of your ahhh. . . invitation, how could I ever decline such a request? And in all honesty, I surmised what I witnessed in the café was only a surface layer of anything and everything that is . . . Adriana Mercer." She couldn't help but smile at his subtle wit and mildly flirtatious manner as if to say, "There is far more below the surface, Mr. Storm."

He grinned softly and gave her a chance to absorb his words. She considered what he said, and with her own mischievous smile and subtly placing her hand over his in an equally coy manner coupled with a slight pat of his hand, she replied, "Oh, Sebastian, you really have no idea. Wait, so you only appeared tonight because of my impressive enticement and memorable delivery of said invitation?"

Maintaining his gaze and grabbing her hand a little more firmly, not letting go, he said in a soft voice, "Firstly, I have a pretty good idea, Adriana, more than you may think. I'm fairly intuitive myself, and second, you captivated me well before you delivered your invitation," he lied.

After a few moments of candid conversation, the waitress again returned and, upon seeing Adriana, exclaimed, "Well, Mr. Storm, your young lady has arrived, and I must say, the two of you make the most dashing couple. I'm Sofia; what can I get for the two of you this evening?"

Adriana pondered the question for a moment and responded, "I'll have a Belvedere Vodka on the rocks, please, with a double lime twist." She then glanced at Sebastian, and he said, "Sofia, I'd like a Port Ellen thirty-four-year-old over a single large ball of ice, no garnish, thank you.

He smiled at Sofia, and she melodiously uttered, "Not only attractive are you two, but sophisticated selections as well. À votre santé (cheers in French) to you." "Merci," Sebastian responded as Sofia's brow rose as she turned to fulfill their order. Sebastian turned to Adriana and said, "I think she likes us."

Adriana smiled and said, "What's not to like? Look at the two of us! We make a handsome couple." With a suggestive smile, she continued, "She might be fun—another time. And Storm, huh, that's a strong name, Sebastian. Impressive." Sebastian, not thinking, said, "Well, thank you. My current focus is all on you. So, tell me more about you, Adriana. I can imagine you have quite a story."

She responded with a humble yet assured disposition, "Oh, not so much. I'm just a simple small-town girl from the Midwest, military brat, educated in the big city, a flair for international business and pharmaceuticals, and making things happen, I suppose. Detailed to a fault, dedicated and determined, Sebastian, as you have witnessed already." She winked and then continued, "I believe in being straightforward and honest, and I go after what I want and unwavering in my conviction of that notion."

He asked the question because he simply wanted a moment to watch her speak, selfishly and sensually; she satisfied him on all levels. He was fascinated by simply observing those supple lips moving as they touched and parted, revealing a beautiful smile underneath.

He appreciated her intelligence exude in her expression and dialogue and maintained her form of using her body to tell her story. She had an alluring confidence, pulling him in and making him devour every word she uttered.

"You strike me as the type of woman used to always getting what you want, and I'd imagine quite unsettled if you don't," he assumed. "Hmmm, I don't really know; it's never happened. That part about not getting what I want, I mean." She smiled. "And in all honesty, Sebastian, you wouldn't be able to tell if I were at all 'unsettled' because I can keep those emotions well under wraps." She laughed lightly, but he concluded she was probably telling the truth and rarely experienced disappointment.

Sebastian genuinely laughed and focused on Adriana's eyes before saying, "Well then, that makes two of us. I guess we are both a little unfamiliar with disappointment, aren't we?"

He enjoyed testing and teasing her. Her quick responses and quips made her light on her feet, and she enjoyed displaying her humorous side in their dialogue. "Yes, we are, and suits me just fine, Sebastian," she replied.

"So, *Mr. Never Disappointed*, what are you doing here in Vienna? Wait, don't tell me . . . Are you an oil baron or an international spy, maybe? Ahhh yes, that must be it?"

Little did she know, thought Sebastian. "Huh, an International Spy, interesting. Would that excite you if I was so fortunate, Adriana?"

"Oh, most definitely!" she cooed, "The whole James Bond thing is really so alluring. Black tuxedo, unique drinks, exotic tropical and metropolitan locales, fast cars, and even faster women. It's all a bit of a whimsical fantasy, don't you think?" She was baiting him now, teasing and stimulating his curiosity and torturing him to a degree.

Adriana reveled in the art of playful banter and subtle teasing as she engaged Sebastian across the dimly lit table. Each exchange was a delicate dance of words, a test of wits designed to probe the depths of his intellect and resilience. She delivered her remarks with a sharpness cloaked in charm, her eyes twinkling with mischief as she pushed him further, eager to discover the limits of his tenacity.

Sebastian, for his part, accepted her challenges and returned them with equal finesse. His responses were clever and considered, laced with humor and a hint of audacity that suggested he was more than capable of holding his own in this intricate game of verbal sparring. His enjoyment was palpable, his engagement in their dialogue seamless and spirited.

As the evening unfolded, with each witty repartee and intellectual parry, Adriana found herself increasingly intrigued. It was a revelation that came with a rush of exhilaration—here was someone who danced the dance of minds with her, who matched her stride for stride in the complex choreography of conversation. The realization that she might have finally met her match added a thrilling new dimension to their encounter, sparking a dynamic interplay charged with allure and the electric pulse of mutual recognition.

He responded, "All the erotic and scandalous women became so tiresome and daunting over time, you know, but those sports cars, how could one ever fault those beautiful works of art? How they handle their voluptuous contours and curves, acceleration, vibration, and thrill. It's almost . . . carnal in nature, and to experience its engine's smoothness, the fondling of the gearshift, the roar and purr, the elevated beating of the heart, and the tightness of the seat all around you, almost gripping you, even. It stimulates and heightens you and every nerve ending. Truly exhilarating, don't you think?" He decided to push his limits with her, curious if she picked up his subtle metaphor. She did not disappoint.

Adriana's eyes twinkled as she replied, "For a moment, I thought you might be describing me, Sebastian." She became slightly flushed but had to keep up with him even though she was caught marvelously off guard by his illustrative description, even becoming aroused when she heard him speak.

Sebastian asked, "Oh, was I, Adriana? Do tell me which part."

Adriana responded, "Well, all of it, frankly, but if you are asking which specifically . . . the tightness of the seat and smoothness of my engine, err, I mean the car's engine, and how did you know I purr? And the visual of you 'fondling the gearshift' had me more than a little flushed, I'll admit . . . and excited! Honestly, you appear to be the alluring James Bond type. I am guessing you know your way around a nice car and the performance of its engine?"

He was hitting all of her hot buttons as the banter was making her heart beat faster by the minute. Was she getting ahead of herself? Adriana then had to adjust her position in the chair, and she thought, "Damn. Now he knows he has me all flustered."

Sebastian smiled when she shifted her beautiful hips in the chair and realized instantly she was somewhat baffled by him. "My mind wanders a little on what the excitement might possibly entail. There are a lot of nice visuals and contemplations in that simple word, certainly, Adriana," countered Sebastian. He needed to slow the progression of the conversation.

He then began switching gears. He said, "As exciting and arousing the notion of an occupation in international espionage sounds, unfortunately, I regretfully admit I'm a mere businessman from New York, mortal and flawed at its fullest." Possessing a passport, address, and a deep profile which was fully verifiable, he thought. "I deal in rare and lavish exotic stones. I'm essentially a specialized diamond broker." His explanation is somewhat anticlimactic intentionally but also deliberate in every regard.

Sebastian thought for a moment. He wondered why he was so intrigued by this woman. In general, women rarely interested him on any large scale. It wasn't because of his lack of respect or conventional attraction for women but because he was honed and concentrated on his craft, and women would tend to be far too distracting in that endeavor.

He never let his heart and emotions become affected or influenced by anything save his family. A small part of his paranoia made him wonder if this was her angle, or was she just a woman who proved to be fascinating, fluid, sarcastic, and enthralling all in one? He laughed at himself as to why he was even considering this at the moment. He was more intrigued she was able to thoroughly secure his attention more than anything else.

In some ways, he longed for a far more modest life, ordinary and consistent, possibly even mundane to some. It was the notion of simplicity he alluded to with HB earlier that morning. Deep down, he desired more regularity in his otherwise busy life.

Sebastian had thought of it often in the past few weeks and wondered if he would be tolerant of the humble and routine existence; he found his thoughts drifting with increasing frequency.

Sebastian had been meticulously chosen for a role that was tailored to his very essence, a destiny into which he had delved with unreserved commitment. The realities of this existence came naturally to him, so deeply ingrained in his being that any alternative life occasionally seemed enticing, a brief allure on the edge of his consciousness. Yet, each time such thoughts surfaced—sparked perhaps by the echo of a conversation, the aftermath of a world-altering event, or a fleeting connection with someone transformative—he swiftly quashed them as mere whimsical distractions.

These fleeting diversions were momentarily forgotten, relegated to the back of his mind until the next inevitable trigger brought them bubbling to the surface. But Sebastian's resolve remained unshaken; he was bound by what he perceived as a higher calling, a duty that transcended personal desires or the immediate needs of any singular group.

He found his true solace and purpose in navigating and mitigating the chaos that perennially threatened to engulf the world. In this realm—on the very brink of potential disaster—Sebastian thrived, wielding his influence and skills in a delicate ballet of cause and effect. It was here, in the dance with danger and the strategic defusing of crises, that Sebastian felt most at home, most alive. His life was a testament to the belief that one could, indeed make a significant difference, steering the course of events away from the abyss of catastrophic collapse toward a semblance of order and stability.

The world's instability is precisely what added to steadying his own balance. He hoped his small contribution helped keep humankind, at least, partially equalized, although not in an egotistical or narcissistic way.

It was simply . . . . *his duty.*

He considered himself an instrument to "neutralize" a portion of the world's anarchy and turmoil. At least, this was what reassured him, believing that it was all for something more worthwhile, something far more significant. He had to believe in the higher calling that beckoned him and developed his acute sense of purpose and worth.

The chaotic nature of humans and their destructive nature was precisely the drug Sebastian required to stabilize his own inner struggles. Eliminating the world's bedlam and malevolence only made Sebastian stronger and more whole as a man, at least on some level.

Bringing himself back to his reality, he smiled as he appreciated the beautiful woman sitting next to him as she spoke, enjoying the banter as it flowed effortlessly between them.

Sebastian's life was an intricate tapestry of half-truths and expertly maintained facades. Ostensibly a diamond broker, his profile boasted of legitimate transactions and a list of high-profile clients. However, this was merely a veneer, a plausible cover for his more clandestine activities. Despite not actively brokering for anyone, his acumen in the exotic gem trade was not just for show. He had mastered the nuances of the industry, leveraging this expertise to amass wealth far exceeding the salary his official government position provided,

Sebastian Storm's entire annual governmental salary was graciously donated to the orphanage he spent time in during his adolescence in Roanoke, Virginia.

This financial perspicacity provided him with independence that few could claim. Sebastian's business ventures—discreet yet incredibly lucrative—generated tens of millions of dollars each year in income. Yet, for all his wealth, his lifestyle remained deceptively simple to the casual observer. He preferred understatement and modesty in his public persona, a strategic choice that kept prying eyes at bay.

Despite this outward simplicity, there was another side to Sebastian, known only to himself—a life of unbridled luxury that he indulged in privately. His most cherished escape was a luxurious villa nestled on the shores of Lake Como and his cabin in Montana. These properties were where Sebastian's true lavishness unfolded away from the world's eyes. Here, in this secluded haven, he allowed himself the full extent of his desires, sparing no expense in creating a sanctuary that was as opulent as it was hidden.

In these moments, free from the constraints of his double life, Sebastian truly reveled in the fruits of his labor, surrounded by the breathtaking beauty of Lake Como and the mountains of Montana, both of which were far removed from the chaos of his professional endeavors.

Lake Como, Italy, was his unique and special sanctuary hidden in a cove on one of the world's most beautiful bodies of water particularly in Northern Italy. Sebastian had paid handsomely to keep it a covert asset, and he had every intention of keeping it that way. He was certain not even HB was aware of his secluded lake residence. He affectionately called this little secret castle he kept in northern Italy his "Game Room."

There, he kept all life's pleasures and validations of his personal successes. A mystic and spiritual locale for Sebastian comprised of all his worldly possessions and pretentious trophies he had acquired over the years. He would take refuge at either property between missions or when HB would let him slip away for a week or two.

The waitress returned with a second round for both of them, and Sebastian found himself thinking he rarely entertained a second cocktail. It dulled the senses, slowed him, and fostered an undesired lethargy that could prove fatal if an ill-timed consequence stepped in his way.

There was something uniquely captivating about this woman that drew Sebastian into uncharted emotional territory. Her presence stirred something deep within him, a sensation he hadn't experienced in years. It was both exhilarating and unsettling, jolting his well-guarded persona while simultaneously softening his usually sharp and calculated thinking. For the first time in a long stretch, Sebastian found himself willingly shedding the armor of detachment that he habitually wore.

The emotions she evoked in him were surprisingly simple, reminiscent of the basic, unguarded pleasures that those leading regular, habitual lives might encounter daily. This newfound sense of normalcy was alien to Sebastian, leaving him both confused and curiously enchanted. He was unaccustomed to this type of vulnerability, to the openness that came with ordinary human connections.

However, at that moment, he found himself embracing the sensation, allowing it to wash over him like a soothing balm. It was intoxicating, like a potent drug coursing through his veins, compelling him to lean into the experience rather than retreat.

Sebastian wanted to explore this sensation further, to immerse himself fully in the commonality and simplicity of it, and to savor the unexpected joy it brought. It was a stark departure from his usual world of calculated moves and hidden agendas, offering a tantalizing sample of something genuine and unscripted.

He twitched slightly in his chair at the feeling he was experiencing. But somehow, with the haughty sensation he was facing, he didn't push away, didn't mind, and almost welcomed it, which was a departure from his nature.

Always disciplined, always poised, always . . . *consistent,* this was Sebastian Storm's personal decree. His life had afforded him few substantial relationships. The loss of his mother early in life aged Sebastian instantly and made him question how close he would let people get to him. Her death changed something deep within him and permanently altered his outlook on life and the people he encountered.

Sebastian's childhood was built with enormous trust in his mother, but he couldn't help but think both she and his father had failed him in some way at a young age in different ways, stripping him of his entitled childhood. Sebastian felt betrayed by his parents for not being there when he needed them most.

He quickly determined relationships and people were fragile and might be taken away without warning. The bitter lesson had been taught to him early in life. He detested the hurt, the grief of loss and disappointment; therefore, he would just avoid it altogether when anyone got close to him.

Sebastian had long harbored the conviction that vulnerability was synonymous with weakness. From a young age, he learned to fortify his heart against the world, a protective measure against the inevitable pain and loss that shadowed his every relationship. This philosophy was painfully reinforced in the wake of his parents' deaths, events that thrust him into the cold, uncertain world of foster care.

Initially placed in a foster home, he was starkly reminded of his undesirable status as an older child—too old, as his temporary guardians bluntly stated, to be appealing to prospective adoptive families. This cruel assertion cast a shadow over his already fragile sense of self-worth and belonging. Eventually, he was moved to an orphanage, a place teeming with children, each vying for the elusive promise of a "forever family." But as the days turned into months, no family came forward to claim him as their own, and Sebastian's hope gradually eroded into resignation.

This procession of rejections and transient relationships with indifferent caretakers led Sebastian to a profound emotional detachment. He became desensitized, building a formidable barrier around himself, becoming impervious to the well-meaning but ultimately superficial attempts of adults who passed through his life, purporting to understand and help him.

Over time, this protective detachment evolved into a sophisticated defense mechanism, shaping a young man who was exceedingly self-reliant, deeply introspective, and wary of emotional entanglements. His experiences hardened him, not just against the pain of unfulfilled connections but also against the very notion of vulnerability as anything other than a liability.

All the people in his young life failed him . . . all except one, the one man who viewed Sebastian and all his potential and devoted the time to make him the man he was today—feeling rejected and discarded while at the orphanage. Sebastian was lost until this man, in particular, recognized the remarkable capabilities Sebastian possessed.

His mentor unknowingly became his savior in the process, making all the difference to Sebastian, identifying the abilities Sebastian had buried deep within. Their time together, productive and wholesome, was sadly cut far too short years later, taken well before his time, adding yet another substantial loss for Sebastian. This man and his son instilled beliefs and fostered training so significantly that it eventually crafted Sebastian into the ultimate soldier he has become today, a warrior without equal.

Eventually, his mentor's tragic and untimely passing sent Sebastian into a vortex of self-doubt and inner disturbance, far too early for his young years. This trauma caused him to rely chiefly on himself, depending on his own resolve and distinctive abilities but left him calloused to letting anyone into his inner circle.

Sometime later, the men who extinguished his mentor's life would suffer greatly at the hands of Sebastian for what they had done. The three men paid dearly for taking away the only person who ever cared for Sebastian in his youth, save for his mother.

In some ways, it was Sebastian's christening of sorts, his emergence as a champion of those ill-fated quarries that came into his life.

It all began with the loss of his parents. He was the first victim, the first of many to be requited. But now, he was no longer the casualty—he was the vindicator for those hapless souls. In his pain and anguish, Sebastian focused his rage, having been created from those ashes, and emerged as their hero.

"Are you all right, Sebastian?" asked Adriana, snapping Sebastian back into his current reality. "You seem a little distracted," she continued.

He quickly rallied and saved the moment. "Yes, I am so sorry, Adriana. I just remembered I had forgotten to call a business associate today, and I usually never forget such small things . . . It was an important oversight. Please forgive me."

She said, "Of course, love, I do that all the time. Do you need to call him?"

Sebastian considered the question, then quickly replied, "That may be a good idea. I just made a mental note to make sure I do it first thing tomorrow. Now, where were we? I can assure you that won't happen again."

Laughing cautiously, she replied, "It had better not!" She continued to smile, reassuring him.

They talked extensively and candidly for over an hour, exchanging information about each other, both enthralled and interested in one another's stories and adventures, the conversation never tedious or dreary.

Adriana Mercer, a senior account executive for a major pharmaceutical company, visited Vienna to close a large deal with an Austrian healthcare syndicate. Adriana impressed Sebastian with her dedication, passion for her career, and sophistication.

In turn, Adriana admired Sebastian and observed him in thought for a moment before saying softly, "You are a fascinating and complex man, Sebastian, and a simple diamond broker, I surmise, is only the beginning of what and who Sebastian Storm truly is. I venture to guess there is much more to you than just what you told me tonight. Like you, darling, I can read people quite well, and that talent had rarely failed me in the past. But I respect your prudence.

There is much, it seems, similar about us." He recognized her developed intuition and feared she might see right through him if he was not careful.

He looked at her, slightly preoccupied, sensing the effects of the cocktail. He purposely avoided her observation, "Would you excuse me for a moment?" "Of course. Are you okay?" she asked, placing her hand on top of his for a moment.

He turned his hand and squeezed hers for affirmation. He gently stood up, turning to Adriana. "I'm tremendous. We will continue this in a moment. Those drinks have gone right through me, it seems . . . I'll be just a minute. Hold your thought, promise me?"

She smiled and said, "Okay. I will be waiting here with bated breath. Don't make me wait long." And with a wink, he was gone.

As Sebastian excused himself from the table and made his discreet way towards the washroom, his mind churned with a tumult of thoughts. He was simultaneously critical of and captivated by his own reactions that evening. He chastised himself for what he perceived as a lapse in judgment regarding Adriana. Typically, he maintained an ironclad control over his emotions, but Adriana's presence had effortlessly breached his defenses. Her allure was magnetic, irresistible—something he found himself helplessly addicted to, yet something he ardently desired to explore further.

Adriana represented a rare escape from the relentless pressures of his occupation, a profession that demanded constant vigilance and emotional detachment. In her company, Sebastian found a semblance of relief, a welcome respite that he felt he not only needed but deserved. She was like a balm to the weariness that often shadowed his soul, offering him moments of unadulterated joy and exhilaration.

As he navigated the quiet of the dark corridor, his footsteps echoing softly, Sebastian realized that he was not inclined to dissect the nuances of their connection just yet. The reasons behind their intense chemistry seemed inconsequential now.

He was more interested in surrendering to the experience, allowing himself to relish the present engagement without the usual burden of analysis and caution. This rare relinquishment of control was both thrilling and liberating, and he was determined to immerse himself fully in the intoxicating now.

The second and more immediate and vital issue was the subtlety of the man in all black at the opposite corner of the bar who had been fixed on them for the better part of the evening. He had attempted to hide his interest in him and Adriana, but the notion simply underestimated Sebastian and his abilities.

Miscalculating Sebastian's talents and capabilities was imprudent and reckless; his track record proved as much.

Elusive, restrained, and patient, the man's fortitude struck Sebastian like an iron fist when he realized this individual had marked him. The man's intention was a far different matter. The sensation of being watched had only crept into his subconscious while with Adriana. The man was a seasoned professional and not a simple patron enjoying the leisurely benefits of an evening at the hotel lounge.

There was something far more valuable to him.

Sebastian's acute instincts, finely honed over years of navigating perilous environments, flared to life as he noticed the man at the bar. The individual is inconspicuously sipping water, positioning himself strategically with a clear view of Sebastian's movements yet making a show of disinterest.

Adriana was out of his direct line of sight, a detail that didn't escape Sebastian's awareness. Despite his initial oversight, Sebastian quickly pieced together that this man had not been present when he first arrived. He must have slipped in quietly after Sebastian and Adriana were served their first drink—a detail that nagged at Sebastian for not observing sooner.

Chiding himself for this rare lapse in vigilance, Sebastian felt a twinge of professional embarrassment. It was unlike him to let down his guard, especially in unfamiliar or potentially compromised settings. This moment of realization sharpened his senses, reinforcing the need to remain alert.

Turning into the dimly lit corridor leading to the washroom, Sebastian's thoughts were momentarily interrupted as another man exited the washroom. They exchanged brief nods—before continuing in opposite directions. Once inside the stark, clinically white washroom, Sebastian conducted a swift, thorough check of the space, confirming he was alone. He knew all too well that he had very little time.

His reflection in the mirror stared back at him, a stark reminder of the dual life he led—a world where every interaction masked hidden threats and every casual observer might be an adversary.

Regaining his composure, Sebastian used the solitude of the washroom to realign his thoughts and strategies, thankful he was alone. The quiet clink of his belt buckle echoed slightly as he adjusted his clothing, each movement calculated and precise.

He was now fully back in control; the old, calculated, and meticulous Sebastian Storm was back in top form. The brief flicker of doubt washed away as he prepared to re-enter the lounge with renewed focus and an imperceptible increase in his defensive posture. This unexpected element at the bar had changed the dynamics of the evening, and Sebastian was ready to face whatever challenges that might entail.

He quickly turned off one of the two lights, dimming the room further, and immediately entered a toilet stall. He positioned himself seemingly awkwardly, leaning to the side of the stall to avoid a straight frontal assault. His feet were positioned visually in the normal position for anyone looking underneath the stall door, yet he was standing so the washroom as a whole was observable through the crack in the hinge side of the door. He then watched for anyone entering the bathroom doorway. He maintained this posture for a particular reason. He was well aware of what was coming.

As expected, the man in black cautiously entered the bathroom a few moments later, immediately drawing his Beretta 9mm from his breast pocket, screwing on the silencer as he made his way toward the stalls and quietly crouched down to get a visual of which stall was occupied, taking notice of Sebastian's lower legs identified beneath two stalls from the end. The man identified they were alone and that he had Sebastian right where he wanted him.

Observing his position through the thin stall door seam, Sebastian estimated the moment as soon as the man rose again to stand. It altered the man's visual perspective, sacrificing his line of sight, all to Sebastian's favor as the assailant was now unable to detect Sebastian's position change.

Putting his feet soundlessly to the left of the toilet and drawing his own silenced weapon, Sebastian hugged the left side wall as he anticipated what would follow. His instincts proved correct, as usual.

The man stopped before the stall, standing just two feet in front of the door, and smiled over the ease of the operation. He was told not to underestimate Sebastian Storm, but he was proving to be an easy mark.

He slowly raised his weapon to the height of a man sitting on a toilet and put three slugs through the door, center mass, professional placement, the bullets ripping through the door and into the wall behind. He shook his head over what an easy payday this contract had been.

The assailant then cautiously stepped forward to open the door to appreciate his handiwork as Sebastian forcefully kicked the door outward with all his strength, smashing it into the attacker's face and body, stunning the man and knocking him backward to the ground, his gun falling from his grasp and sliding across the floor.

Sebastian was atop of him instantly, pinning him with his legs and body, his silenced muzzle pointed right at the man's forehead, pressing into his skin firmly, and asked him softly, "I will ask you only once, and your answer will determine whether you die peacefully or painfully, so consider this question very carefully. Who sent you?"

With a bloody face and broken nose, the man coughed, considered the question, then said in a strained whisper, "Fuck you!" With that, Sebastian responded, "Fair enough."

In response, Sebastian forcefully thrusts his left fist into the man's throat, instantly crushing his windpipe as he begins to suffocate on his own blood and lack of oxygen in a matter of moments. The man clutched his trachea in desperation and sheer pain, unable to take enough air into his lungs as Sebastian fended off the man's flailing arms.

His eyes began to bulge and burst red from the erupting capillaries within the whites of his eyes. His thrashing diminished until he was calm. His heart experienced its last beat. The assaulter's final breath slowly left his body as he looked at Sebastian until his last living moment.

Sebastian quickly got up, walked to where the man's gun lay, and kicked it as it slid across the room, under one of the stalls, and out of sight.

Clutching the man's collar, Sebastian lifted his body from behind and placed him into the same stall he had burst from moments before and closed the door. On the adjacent stall, he saw a sign dangling with the words printed, "Out of Order." Sebastian smiled to himself and thought the sign fitting as he removed it from the door and hung it over the bullet holes now in the center of the stall door.

Calmly striding to the mirror, Sebastian adjusted his jacket and shirt, ran a hand through his hair, and seemed satisfied before departing the washroom, flipping both light switches on before leaving, using his knuckle to open the door so as not to leave any fingerprints.

Finally, he looked around, ensuring he returned the washroom and surrounding areas to its original form. Besides the small blood spatters on the floor, barely noticeable, the bathroom remained clean, unremarkable, and sterile of his existence.

Sebastian did not experience even a mere elevation of his heart rate after the encounter, which proved to be both a testament to his stern resolve, talents, and abilities but also dejected in claiming yet another life with little remorse or shame.

Sebastian understood the brutal reality of his life; each skirmish was a stark reminder of the *survival of the fittest* ethos that governed his shadowy world. The latest challenge to his survival came starkly into focus when a would-be assassin followed him into the washroom, a place where confrontations were stripped down to their most primal.

The assassin, a man with cold determination, knew the stakes as he silently stepped across the tiled floor and drew his gun. His intent was clear—elimination. Sebastian, ever vigilant, sensed the looming threat before the first shot was fired.

Sebastian was not merely a target; he was a formidable adversary, seasoned and cunning. He thrived on underestimation, using it as a weapon against those who dared to think they could best him. This assassin, dressed in the nondescript black of his trade, was no different. He didn't seek dialogue or negotiation; his actions spoke of definitive and deadly intent.

Sebastian maneuvered with practiced ease as the gunfire silently echoed in the confined space. He was a step ahead, his responses honed by countless encounters just as lethal as this one. The man's superiors would indeed be disappointed. In a world where every day might be his last, Sebastian was not just a survivor but a master of the game, always ready to turn the tables on those who sought his demise. The dance of death in the washroom was a testament to his lethal prowess and unwavering resolve.

Sebastian loathed situations like this for two reasons. The first was the man didn't confess when given the opportunity, which would have given Sebastian some insight as to why he was marked for a contract kill. The second reason is the exposure had a third party entered the washroom by happenstance. Luck was on his side, for if another person had entered the washroom, it would have complicated the scenario significantly.

The assailant could be discovered at any time within the stall, and it would be best for Sebastian not to be in the area when it inevitably occurred, as they would most likely detain all within the lounge for questioning.

There was no reason to torture or coerce the man into giving information. Sebastian respected the type of soldier and how he operated; the attempt would have proved futile in its efforts and would have taken far too much time. The assailant would unlikely divulge any important information under duress. If the man knew anything about Sebastian and his reputation, he would also know Sebastian never asked a question twice.

More than likely, the man realized his life was forfeit. Why would he give up his employer, loyalty, and honor unless he could leverage his own life? Sebastian surmised it was an impossibility. The soldier was more than aware Sebastian would never allow him to live. Professionals like him wouldn't allow a loose end as significant to be left unresolved. Sebastian was aware of this code, and the assassin would have performed similarly had the situation been reversed.

Carefully departing the washroom, Sebastian eased into the hallway, knowing cameras did not monitor the corridor. He re-entered the lounge and quickly scanned the room for any adversaries the man in black may have had in his company. Sebastian assumed that had there been more than one soldier, they would have remained together to reduce any risk of eliminating Sebastian.

He looked at the chair at the bar where the assailant had been sitting, his glass of water still present; no one was aware the man would not be returning to his seat again. It would take far more than one man to bring down Sebastian Storm. He was almost . . . offended in the attempt.

He then remembered the beautiful woman at the table still waiting for him to return, and he thought it impolite he took as long as he did. His absence had been just under three minutes.

The lounge scanned clear from what he determined as he quickly made his way to the table while not in view of Adriana and then slowed his pace halfway to the table so as to not announce unnecessarily to her that there was any sense of apprehension or urgency.

Sebastian had just killed a man in the washroom only a moment before, so the timing was essential in the following minutes. He stopped short of the table, smiled at Adriana, and said, "I have an idea; let's get out of here. I'd love some fresh air. Maybe take a walk and see some city lights. I mean, as long as you are enjoying your evening and not yet ready for it to end?"

"Oh, Sebastian, you completely read my mind; I'm in," she replied with a wink as she stood, elegant even in that simple gesture. Seemingly unaffected by his brief departure. Sebastian pulled out his money clip from his inside breast jacket, peeled off five one-hundred euro bills, and laid them on the table for the waitress, knowing this would more than cover the tab.

He took Adriana's hand in his and with a swift, yet efficient purpose, led her out of the lounge by way of the hotel's foyer, down the stairs, and out a side entrance. Sebastian needed to distance himself from the lounge as soon as possible.

Sebastian considered exiting the hotel immediately, abandoning Adriana, but then dismissed the thought. He reasoned it might be a clever consideration to include Adriana, both because it would add to any cover and because this woman excited him in a way he hadn't known in a long time. He needed to get into an open, less confining atmosphere, and outside of the hotel gave him far more strategic options.

Exiting the hotel's side door, the night was crisp and cold but comfortable, even exhilarating, and Sebastian's hand felt warm in hers. Without Adriana noticing, Sebastian fed on the environment, remained close to walls and defensible positions during their walk, feeling at ease in not detecting any threat or being followed.

They walked for a bit, silent for a while before stopping along a canal, coming across a bridge above them as they paused within the shadows to get a glimpse of the city lights before them. Adriana looked at Sebastian as they walked, clutching his arm, and examining his intensity and concentration as they moved, wondering what his thoughts were at the moment, but then quickly dismissed the notion.

Beautiful and bright, the Vienna skyline shone exquisitely in its green, white, and blue lights emanating, draping along the vast cityscape. The scenery was beautiful, perfect even, and tranquil in its essence. The cool, crisp breeze nipped at their skin but invigorating simultaneously.

They stood very close to one another, savoring their connection and ease of simply. . . . being together. She felt his energy and magnetism and was immensely attracted to his essence as she sensed he was to her as well.

No words were necessary, just the closeness of the moment, and it was mutually satisfying in and of itself. Even his scent was distinctive, masculine, and tremendously captivating to her. She wanted more of him, craving him in any form he offered. Over four hours had passed since they first met, the time flying and passing quickly.

They took some time to enjoy and appreciate the visual magnificence laid out before them, making small talk about the city's beauty. After a moment, she slowly turned, looked into Sebastian's eyes, hesitated, and then said, "Tonight, Sebastian, this was . . ."

She stopped as his lips touched hers softly, her eyes closed, embracing the moment. He paused, feeling comfortable and safe in that instant, then took more of her in passionately. Tasting her lip and their softness upon his, Sebastian pulled her closer to him.

He held her gently but with an aggressive edge that she had been longing for. Her knees became weak, and she struggled to stay upright. He sensed her shift in weight, towering above her in mere stature alone.

Her lips tasted of strawberry and vanilla, soft, supple, and impassioned. His kiss was erotic and spontaneous, commanding yet gentle, leaving them both wanting more and anticipating what was to follow. Their embrace became intertwined, sensing her sexual tension as her body conformed to his within the chilly yet idealistic atmosphere that surrounded them.

Her warmth was apparent, her femininity emanating her allure, and the fascination abound as their excitement in each other grew exponentially with each passing moment. Sebastian had his arms around her now, protective and attentive. She placed her hands inside his jacket upon his firm chest, and she discerned his masculinity and dominance building with even the hint of his maleness provoked by their bodies pressed together. It excited her to have that effect on him.

The entire evening excited her greatly and made her womanliness billow, and she was aroused in knowing he was also aware of the effect he was having on her. Sabastian brought more of her raw primal urges out in her intrigue. Adriana craved more of him, needed more, and desired to know this man on a much deeper level, both emotionally and physically.

She craved desperately to explore every part of him. Despite having only just met, the hours together seemed like months of understanding and adoration for each other. She smiled at the thought, but her pragmatic side yearned to understand why she intuited this so quickly for someone in such a short amount of time.

Adriana struggled with the conflict but was captivated by the moment and the fantasy of it all. His words startled her for a moment, pulling her back to the cold of the evening.

"You look positively freezing, Adriana. Let me get you back indoors. So unfair for me to drag you outside like this." he said and smiled. He grabbed her hand, squeezing it, and escorted her back down the street toward the hotel. True to form, he remained hidden within the shadows the entire way. She was dazed and mildly disoriented, her lips partially numb now from the cold, yet she still tasted him upon them as they began to walk.

Briskly strolling down the shadowy sidewalk, Adriana brought her fingers to her lips in acknowledgment of the flavor that lingered, enjoying the sensation that he had left behind. She was intoxicated, not necessarily by the cocktails they had in the lounge but rather by Sebastian as a whole and his effect on her. She followed her hand in his, trailing him without question or argument. She rather enjoyed his bravado and initiative. She trusted his charge, conviction, and purpose in everything he did.

She wanted him.

After nearly forty-five minutes out in the cold environment, they entered the hotel once again, immediately feeling the building's warmth thawing their faces upon entering the dwelling as they left behind the evening bitterness outside. He paused to inspect the hotel lobby, seemingly searching for something or someone, preoccupied, but she didn't care. His victim had not yet been discovered.

Adriana couldn't wait any longer, her frustration apparent yet subdued. Captive to her primal instinct, she desired more of him in any form. She knew she shouldn't give in, but it was all too much for her. She was aching for him; anything he would allow her to have, she would take willingly. She was not ready for the evening to end.

She seized the moment to pull him close to her and whispered in his ear, "Come up to my room, Sebastian. Have a nightcap with me?" She smiled in her amatory fashion. It was not her custom to throw herself at any man, but she sensed Sebastian Storm was far from anything ordinary. She hoped her comment wouldn't be taken as overly forward, but she had to test the energy welling inside her, fighting to get out.

Not noticing anything out of place upon their return, Sebastian was anticipating Adriana's invitation and was about to propose the notion himself had she not outmaneuvered him with her pre-emptive suggestion. "I would enjoy that, Adriana," he smiled at her.

He needed a safe haven, and her hotel room would be the best option for the short term. As the man in the lounge washroom had obviously not been discovered as yet, he needed to get out of plain sight, and likely no one was aware of Adriana's existence or connection to him despite her being the most beautiful woman in the entire establishment.

Those that were out to destroy him were completely aware of his presence. Still, they would be unsuspecting of her involvement with him, which proved a positive factor in his immediate yearning to become invisible at that given moment. The hour was growing late, and few hotel guests and employees were ambling about the lobby.

They immediately entered the vacant lift; she pressed the button to the eighteenth floor and turned to him as the doors closed. Holding his hand in hers, he took in her scent and noticed the sensual combination of her perfume and body chemistry, making her even more the object of his desire.

She looked into his green eyes, mesmerized by his substance. He looked down at her as his hand touched the side of her face and kissed her again, gently this time, yet still savoring, tasting the vanilla from her lips. They reached the 18th floor as the chime alerted them to their arrival. The elevator doors opened before them.

They exited the elevator and walked the short distance down the hall, coming before her door halfway down the hall. She opened the door to room 1802 and proceeded in with Sebastian in tow.

Passing beyond the threshold, she was already sliding off her jacket in the entrance hallway of the suite, letting it drop to the floor as Sebastian caught it in midair and laid it on the hall table. She is oblivious to his gesture as he smiles to himself. Adriana had a carefree and robust way about her, and he fed on her energy.

Remembering he was armed, Sebastian quickly adjusted as he slid his gun into the breast pocket of his jacket, slipped it off, and tossed it to the table as well. She abruptly turned back towards him, catching him off guard. He grabbed her hand and pulled her to him firmly. She softly collided with his body, fitting perfectly into his mass, falling victim to him and his strength.

Seductively and softly, his hand drifted to the small of her back while the other hand softly outlined her cheek and throat. He fervidly engulfed her lips with his own, and she was drawn closer to him in the heat of the moment. His left hand gently surrounded her throat, and as his affections escalated, his hand tightened slightly around her neck while his other hand pulled her tighter toward him. She was melting into him, desiring and wanting him more with every passing second.

She loved his aggressiveness and the power he possessed over her. She was his to do as he pleased, but she didn't care about the consequences nor whether he respected her for her decision to give herself to him. All she wanted was him at the moment, and nothing else mattered to her.

Sensing her excitement swelling, it fueled him further as he peered into her eyes, anticipating what was to follow. She was certain he would not disappoint her, certain of it, in fact. He tightened his grip around her neck slightly more, and she felt his arousal climbing further as he pressed against her body firmly. Loving him against her, she pulled him closer.

She thirsted for his control over her as she senses the awakening mounting between them and longed for where this encounter was heading. Adriana wanted it, needed it, desired it—all of it. She cared only for the moment and thought of nothing else.

Feeling him growing more fiercely below, Adriana was enjoying the effect she was having on him, caressing her leg, which excited her far more, only adding to her torment. She hoped she would have all of him inside her before long, and she was eager to take him. All of him.

Placing her hand on his stomach, appreciating his succinctly carved abdominal muscles flexing beneath her fingertips. Drifting lower after a time, reaching his belt, Adriana pressed more firmly against him, her fingers finding their mark, and she smiled slightly as she approved of what lay beneath.

He was perfect and precisely what she needed this evening. Throwing caution to the wind, her evening was perfect with Sebastian Storm, but all she concentrated on now was the icing on her cake.

She teased him, wanted it all, but found herself delicately stroking, enjoying the increased, arousing effect she was having on him. He was responding exactly in the fashion she desired and only wanted to escalate it further. He reacted to her touch almost instinctively, seductively moving together as they explored one another.

He slowly unbuttoned her sweater, her breasts ample and heaving, erogenous and irresistible. Adriana's thighs were bare now, cold beneath her short dress as she instantly felt exposed but welcomed his eyes as they fell upon her and what she offered to him.

She was proud of her body, her vessel, and well aware the effect she had on men, in general, but all she wanted to do was please him. Sebastian was the only thing on her mind at the moment, as her sole objective was to seduce and please him in any way he desired.

While still firmly grasping her neck, his opposite hand drifted from her back to her toned rear as he squeezed her cheek sensually yet firmly, kissing fervently and adoring the aroma upon her neck and response to his touch.

He wanted to touch her skin, her bareness, pulling up her skirt slowly with his hand. Sebastian longed to feel her stark smoothness, taking note that she omitted panties that evening, which excited him all the more at the thought of her being exposed, open, and inviting to him the entire evening. Sebastian had not had a yearning like this since he could remember, and all he wanted to do was feed into his desire and impulse. He tightened his grip slightly more around her neck as she groaned, enjoying his strength and power over her.

She loved his large hands on her, welcomed his exploring, open to all of it and everything as she began to unbuckle his pants, slowly sliding down the zipper of his trousers, easing his pants off to get better access. Their kisses were more intense now, enjoying each other in all facets as their anticipation heightened further.

Sebastian took both hands now and gripped each side of Adriana's rear end, pulling her up to straddle him while grinding her pelvis into his, making her feel her effect on him directly. She gently brought both hands to his face, caressing intently as she moved her lips to his neck, nibbling and lightly licking below his ear.

He deliberately meandered to the bedroom, supporting her thin, toned, and athletic frame, and tenderly laid her atop the bed and snuggled her neck, easing off her bra.

Her breasts were supple and firm, with nipples erect and sensitive. He took her breast onto his lips and tongue, savoring and teasing her with his tongue. He loved her scent, her skin sweet to his tongue, inviting him to value all of her.

Sebastian's weight now rested between her legs as she rubbed his thighs with her knees, partly to validate his strength, but also because her femininity was eager, dripping with anticipation, and hungry for what was most certainly to follow.

He moved slowly to her flat, hard stomach, tasting her as he went, stimulating all senses. With only her skirt on now, he kissed her stomach, slowly unbuttoning her skirt from the front, opening it completely, revealing that alluring mound tucked in and smooth with a scent of vanilla combined that he couldn't resist.

Her legs began to open slightly, inviting him further and tempting every part of his senses. He licked the top of her mons as her legs opened further, tasting her diminutive button, and savoring more of her with every pass.

Her flavor was succulent and alluring, saturated, dripping down her inner thigh and inviting all he had to give as she removed her skirt completely, opening herself up fully to him, entirely bare and exposed, offering herself for him to savor.

Knees bent, her legs open wide, taking every lap of his tongue in stride, his abilities extraordinary, thinking to herself she had never been so aroused. She was intoxicated by him and wanted more but enjoyed the moment, not wanting it to end.

He was hitting his groove now but wanted to stimulate her further. He slowly teased her with his finger, then slowly slid his middle finger in fully while increasing the intensity of his tongue. The sensation drove her wild as her pleasure intensity escalated, arching her back as the second finger found its way deep inside of her, bringing her to the point of ecstasy as he tickled and teased her swollen, awaiting cervix.

As she began to reach her orgasm, her back bowed further, inviting him, enticing him to her inner sanctum. Adriana was now moaning and seemingly euphoric from the pleasure he was blessing her with in every way. She began to gyrate and spasm as she let herself go, reveling in the moment and letting the sensation take its full effect.

Sebastian held her thighs fast as he sampled her erogenous folds, riding her rhythmic contractions along with her. Her explosion of senses was fierce and erotic as Sebastian held her firmly yet lessened his stimulation of her, allowing her to enjoy her spasms. He watched her, following and anticipating her motion as she rode the intense tremors that followed and peaked, then began its decline in intensity in the following seconds.

After a moment, she relaxed as Sebastian began to move upward to her stomach, breasts, and lips, kissing her, relishing her essence upon all her sensitive points. He repositioned himself softly beside her, caressing her gently and then quietly escalating as the attraction and arousing trembles were still very apparent to her.

She desired any remaining part of him, to welcome every aspect of his core and welcome the burst she knew he had held back thus far.

As she kissed him, her hand drifted to the part of him she had been fantasizing about since the moment she walked into the lounge several hours before. He was erect, and she smiled inwardly, knowing what was to come and starting to sense the heat again rise between them.

She strangely felt inebriated, enthralled, and irresistible simultaneously, the flood of sensations cascading over her body and his equally.

She eased his pants off, fully exposing him as she repositions herself to sample him this time; Sebastian had earned that right. Adriana desperately wanted to feel him, mesmerize him with her own talents, and return the gratification he had so thoroughly given her just moments before. She also desired to seductively torture him in the moment.

Adriana was no stranger to the wiles of a man's desires in addition to her own, but she also knew that sexual chemistry was essential to satisfy both of them. She slowly stroked him, feeling him growing still further within her grasp. She was unable to get her entire hand around him, and she loved the thought of how it would feel inside her.

Clearly aroused at the thought of him with his fingers and tongue just moments before, she fantasized more about how he would feel once he filled her with all of him. All Adriana could concentrate on was her desire to devour, pleasure, and captivate him.

She began to test his tip with her lips, teasing him just long enough to torment him, slowly and deliberately taking him in deep and sucking while twisting her fist around his generous member.

Her technique, methodical and sensual, pushing his limits of control. Adriana sensed she was bringing him close as he responded positively and without hesitation to her intended erogenous stimulation.

Continuing for a few more minutes, she continually brought him to the brink of eruption, only to bring him down again, making him ache in the process. Adriana enjoyed looking up at him as she tasted him, knowing she had his appreciation for her faculties.

She then intentionally slowed her pace until she stopped, repositioned her body, and came up to him until their lips touched once again in passion and excitement. Still tasting her upon his lips, she whispered in his ear, "I want all of that inside me. Give it to me deep, Sebastian . . . Make me appreciate my feminine wiles. Please me." Sebastian smiled, more than satisfied as he responded, "Your wish is my desire, love."

He then threw her onto her back, a simple task given her petite features. Her legs immediately opened for him, her femininity gushing, beckoning him with anticipation as she gripped him firmly. She then tantalized her outer folds with his tip, dripping from her wetness as she teased still further. At this moment, they both wanted it and needed it to happen, to feel their closeness merge, a confirmation of their connection and union.

She adjusted herself. Her domain welcomed, holding him, then steadying it long enough for him to slowly but deliberately ease just inside of her, only enough to make his tip creamy from the physical response of her own arousal.

Now he tortured her; the tables turned as he teased her for a time. She looked into his eyes as if to say, "fuck me!" but she didn't have to utter the words. He knew what she wanted.

He slowly entered further, her hand no longer needed as it fell away. She peered into his eyes, their union complete. Adriana's eyes widened as she felt him fill her. He then firmly thrust deeper inside her as he grabbed her hands and pinned her down. Pushing his full length completely now, he wanted her to feel all of him at one time. She enjoyed the helplessness coming over her but welcomed the slight pain she experienced as he began to stuff her erogenous folds completely.

Adriana appreciated his healthy curve, anatomically idyllic, hitting her deep within, perfectly lighting up all her senses as she enjoyed watching him pleasure both of them as he thrust, slowly yet firmly. She couldn't believe how deep he was, long and thick, stuffing her entirely, the slight pain diminishing but his pulse invigorating, nonetheless.

Raw and hard, he penetrated her with precise firmness and cadence as she quickly orgasmed again, enjoying it as it engulfed her once more. She put her hands upon his muscular chest to slow him for a moment to regain her breath. She certainly was not done with him by any means but needed to take a moment to collect herself.

As she enjoyed him, she noticed the first scar on his upper right shoulder and touched it as he now gently penetrated her. Then she observed another on the oblique muscle of his left abdomen. His forearm and bicep, still more of them.

Then another.

Sebastian had several healed wounds covering his near-perfect physique. Adriana counted the staggering number and made a mental note to ask him about those at some point. But now was not that time as she closed her eyes, relishing the moment and equally impressed with him as he brought out all her sensations passionately and without indecision.

Adriana enjoyed all of him with every long stroke until she gently pulled him closer to her and said, "I want to ride you," as she pushed Sebastian off and onto his back.

Adriana climbed atop him, appreciating his hardness, and slid him slowly into her again as she took him all the way in, looking into his deep green eyes, mesmerized as she felt him fill her fully, seeming like so much more in this position.

When she had him entirely inside of her, she realized he was even deeper now than before. Pulling her into a sensual rapture, she reactively arched her back to take in all of his length. She moved her hips back and forth and semicircular in motion, confirming all his manliness as it exited and entered her in a repeating motion.

Their merging is perfect now; she maximizes her cadence and rhythm to stimulate them both equally. She gripped his thickness tightly with her inner Kegel muscles, moaning herself as he welcomed the viselike grip her femininity brought to him.

She amazingly slid up and down upon him, taking his deep strokes in stride, easily now. Her femininity again began to intensify as she began a deep, even more intense orgasmic spasm, causing her pace to escalate, knowing he enjoyed watching her as he pleased her.

Sebastian enjoyed his view of her and the intensified fervor she emulated. Lying back, Sebastian appreciated the passion with which Adriana satisfied him, rousing his pelvis and pleasuring every part of him, as well as herself. She understood her body very well. He knew he was close now, and she could sense he was about to let her have all of him.

This was what she had been wanting and waiting for, but his pace and endurance were Olympic in form as she found the ideal tempo and intensity heightened with each moment that passed. She smiled, sensing he was close to his own orgasm, lips slightly apart then slowly bit her lower lip watching him, hands on his chest, and softly said, "Fill me up, Sebastian. I want every drop. Give it to me!"

He would not disappoint her.

He penetrated deeper, Adriana adjusting to taking in the last part of him. With a sensual fluidity, he raptured all he had within as deep as he was able, firmly and deliberately.

Sebastian wanted her to cherish all of him as they both exploded in ecstasy. The spasms are hard and arhythmic now, with erratic, varying intensity remaining for several moments after the initial spasm.

She gripped him firmly with her femininity, thirsty and wanting, accepting everything he had to give her. It fulfilled her, knowing she pleasured him.

She continued to ride him slowly now as if to massage and reward his efforts, slowing further for a job well done as she leaned down to kiss him. Their kisses were passionate despite their tremors ceasing. She enjoyed him explode within her and welcomed its effect. She took it all and relished in the moment for a time.

After a few minutes, Adriana eased herself to his side, rested her head upon his chest, and smiled, relaxing now, content and fulfilled completely. He lay on his back her head now on his chest.

Sebastian caressed the top of her head with his hand as they lay in silence for a few moments, reliving the erotic moment they had just shared. She had her left hand on him now, caressing his skin and appreciating his chiseled chest and abdominal muscles beneath her fingertips.

She ran her fingers over his scars once again.

She slowly looked up at him and whispered, "I want to hear their story someday, Sebastian," referring to the numerous marks and scars on his skin. He didn't answer right away as she pinched one of them, and he replied, "Perhaps, someday, Adriana," then continued, "Just not today," as he smiled at her, hopeful she would be satisfied with his answer for the time being.

For the moment, she reluctantly accepted his response and wanted nothing to ruin their moment. He was a mystery to her, and she imagined there was far more to this man than he had led on.

Changing the direction of the conversation, Adriana said, "Hmmm, that was nice, Sebastian," as her hand started to drift farther down, searching for her mark, and she found it wanting far more.

He smiled, and she continued, "But I'm not finished with you just yet . . ." as she gripped his member firmly for another of many rounds they would share that night..

Chapter 7

A New Threat Emerges

Vienna, Austria
Present Day

The wind howled outside, pulling Sebastian from a light sleep as he dreamed of Virginia's rolling hills. He watched her sleeping peacefully on her side, facing him.

He couldn't help but appreciate her beauty in the moment as the full moonlight shone through the window, highlighting her flawless features in the glimmering light. Above all else, he wanted to remain beside her and be the first image she saw as she awakened, but he couldn't stay.

It was early yet still dark in the morning save the shimmer of the moonlight as it danced upon the shadows on the bedroom walls. Sebastian quietly slipped out of Adriana's bed and dressed silently, still watching her as he collected his clothing strewn across the room.

Finding his jacket and gun in the adjoining room, he replaced his weapon within his specialized holster and slipped out of Adriana's room without waking her.

He inspected the hall for anything amiss, but before leaving, he wrote a short, handwritten note:

Beautiful Adriana, you fulfilled my every appetite. Thank you for a tremendous evening.

Sebastian wondered and secretly hoped he would see her again. He shouldn't even consider the notion, but he was eager their paths would cross once again.

Although he felt he always followed and respected strict protocol, he couldn't help but feel slightly amiss and reckless, even careless, while with Adriana the evening before, but he also felt alive and boundless for the first time since he could remember.

Caution to the wind came to mind, exhilarated but also thoughtless in his escapade. He hated leaving without saying something to her or gently waking her, but duty called, and he would never neglect his responsibilities, always his mistress, his commitment and obligation to his country and calling.

Sebastian calculated the latent and quiet hotel hallway and stairwell, and he pondered the evening before. It consumed his thoughts as he made his exit.

Who was the man who confronted him in the washroom, and more importantly, who had sent him to dispose of Sebastian? Was it Tobias or someone else entirely? Sebastian made his way down the series of floors carefully and cautiously. And how was he found? His whereabouts appeared to be public knowledge these days. The walk to his flat would give him time to think, realizing he had a lot of unanswered questions.

The stairwell was always Sebastian's preference over the elevator, providing far more security and exodus alternatives. An elevator afforded limited space and exit options, but the stairwell usually presented far more opportunities if the need arose.

He made his way to the street level, quietly exited the hotel's rear egress, and made his way the short distance to his flat, strictly adhering to his security protocols before entering his apartment. He located his laptop after removing it from its secure hidden vault in the living room wall.

Surprisingly, Sebastian found the ideal locations to conceal and secure his most valuable assets, which were often hidden in plain view yet imperceptible and invisible to the most discerning eye.

Most people would hide important items in seemingly creative and hidden living spaces. Still, Sebastian found those spots were easily located by the astute professional, whether behind pictures or mirrors, under floorboards, within the ceiling, or behind tables. In this regard, Sebastian's philosophy and thinking on concealability were far different from most.

A well-placed seam designed into a standard textured interior wall, or a panel activated by an indiscernible hidden fingerprint reader located yards away will often be a critical key to concealment. Once verified, the reader activates a veiled compartment essentially contained within a person's standard field of view and easily overlooked based on its simplicity of placement.

For example, beneath a cupboard, an inconspicuous finger sensor was positioned within the kitchen cabinetry, specific to Sebastian's right ring finger only. Authenticity confirmed would then prompt the subtle descent of a veiled compartment fifteen feet away, revealing a combination safe from the tiled ceiling above. The compartment held his secured and encrypted laptop and possessed an added security safeguard. If the combination fingerprint or retina scan mechanism did not verify its intended owner, the contents of the safe would be incinerated by a combustible material that would most likely injure the assailant attempting to breach the safe as well. He executed the necessary steps and retrieved his laptop.

In his modernly designed living space, he opened his laptop, which was equipped with the latest encryption technology. A priority message from HB filled his screen with the simple words, "We need to talk. Mustard Palace has the best sandwiches. Tomorrow, the usual time." The use of the word mustard was one of HB's secretive words, meaning of significant importance and priority, and the palace was a predetermined stronghold in the countryside outside of Vienna called the *Schönbrunn Palace*.

Sebastian was familiar with the summer residence of the Habsburg dynasty and set out immediately to meet her as she had sent the message the evening before. HB was an early riser, so when she mentioned the usual time, Sebastian knew she wished to meet at 6:00 am, early in the morning before most people were diligently up and around. Sebastian was aware from habit that HB was also calculated and consistent and valued this aspect of his superior tremendously.

Dublin, Ireland
Present Day

Just hanging up his secured satellite phone, Nicholas Prim narrowed his eyes and rubbed his temples. His boss would not be happy about this information, not at all.

The report that Sebastian had again eluded all attempts of elimination baffled Prim. He had never met Sebastian Storm, but his reputation was legendary.

Nicholas Prim was newly recruited as Tobias Teague's head of security. He hadn't yet proven himself and was far from an impressive start to his new position, having failed in both London and Vienna within a day of one another. The precision with which Sebastian eliminated some of his best operatives was astounding. He seemed almost . . . . *unbeatable.*

He had hoped to impress Tobias with his abilities early on with the elimination of Sebastian Storm, but he had failed. . . . .*twice.* Sebastian had proven to be most elusive on both attempts.

Prim had sent one of his best three-man teams to London to intercept Sebastian Storm, but they never returned. From what he understood, Sebastian had made short work of their attempt on his life. He then sent his most trusted lieutenant, Sanjeev Nostra, a decorated ex-paramilitary mercenary, to the Hotel Sans Souci to complete the job in Vienna.

Nostra was a legend in the clandestine world of operatives—a master of his craft whose reputation for precision and success was unmatched. Until now, failure had never marred his extensive record. Yet, in the treacherous game of espionage and covert operations, even legends could stumble, especially when they encountered a rival like Sebastian Storm.

For Nostra, Prim, and their cadre of elite soldiers, Sebastian represented just another target, albeit a high-value one. They approached the mission with their usual confidence, relying on meticulous planning and overwhelming force. However, they grossly underestimated the depth of Sebastian's skills and resourcefulness. Sebastian was not merely a player in their world; he was a formidable strategist and tactician, capable of turning apparent weaknesses into decisive advantages.

The confrontation, when it came, proved catastrophic for Nostra and the London team. Sebastian anticipated and countered each move they plotted with chilling efficiency. His agility, intellect, and sheer force of will turned what should have been a straightforward operation into a lethal trap for his pursuers.

As they fell one by one, the stark realization dawned on Prim: they had misjudged the man they sought to eliminate. Sebastian's mastery of the shadowy dance between life and death was not just about survival—it was an art form. In the end, their fatal mistake wasn't just underestimating him—it was believing they could outmaneuver a man who had transformed survival into a deadly art.

Those miscalculations and failures of his men could become the instrument of Prim's demise, depending on Tobias's mood that morning.

No stranger to the profession, Nicholas Prim had worked within the shadows of covert, black operations for various employers for years. As a recognized former British agent with MI6, he had worked for some of the most challenging and demanding employers in the past.

Equally as esteemed as Sebastian, Tobias's reputation was likewise remarkable, though Tobias was on the rise and reputed as being cunning and shrewd, if not distressing. Tobias Teague personally selected Nicholas Prim but was forewarned by him that he did not accept mediocrity or failure by his Head of Operations and security.

Prim was well aware of this warning and of his predecessor's downfall due to his operational failures, which, ironically, had often been at the hand of Sebastian Storm. He was determined not to let this happen to him, but Sebastian was now threatening his very existence at this point and achieved the feat in less than 72 hours. Sebastian could be his undoing.

The saving grace surrounding Prim's prior mission in Berlin, Germany, weeks before had proved to be fruitful in its execution and results. His mission was to obtain the architectural layout of the popular Museum Island on the River Spree, including the Pergamon and Bode Museums, respectfully. Tobias chose this venue carefully, coveted for its extravagant and long-awaited display of his organization's considerable prowess and supremacy. The Museum Island in Berlin would provide a worthy arena for such a spectacle.

The mission proved difficult as Prim and his team followed the chief architect of the island, Franz Von Sydow, who gutted and completely renovated the museums in 2016. They ultimately obtained the plan and relevant information, along with specifics of the design, from the German designer himself while under heavy duress and torment. They later terminated the gentleman in a form appearing as if he perished from natural causes.

Tobias insisted upon the method by which the architect met his fate, and the details surrounding Von Sydow's death were imperative to cover the true agenda of Tobias's intent and ensure a high success rate for the given mission.

Prim selected a precise, minuscule needle laced with a droplet of a concentrated cyanide gel directly into a small mole below the orbit of the right eye of Franz Von Sydow. With just enough liquid used, less than 1cc, it would initiate a small aneurysm, causing a slow and painful death over the following several hours. Prim extracted the information, verified its validity, and then initiated the kill order to his team to terminate Von Sydow, making his fatality look like he passed while sleeping, believable for a man in his late sixties and not in the best of health.

It was essential to obtain the necessary information and choreograph the death to appear as if it occurred from natural causes to circumvent any suspicion and suppress any doubt or attention to Von Sydow's demise or the information they had acquired.

The Mission was far from simple in any form, but Prim did appreciate the silver lining surrounding the Von Sydow mission. Despite the apparent conundrum surrounding the eradication of the elusive Sebastian Storm in both London and Vienna.

Prim organized his thoughts for a moment before making his way to the security room outside Tobias's living quarters contained within the Dublin compound. Initially cleared through Tobias's office security door, Prim progressed with both a visual check by Tobias's elite trained guards he affectionately called his *Supreme Elite Troops* or referred to as Tobias's personal *SET Force.*

This force was the icing on Tobias's defensive and offensive powerhouse. This Elite Force, an auspicious group, was limited to only twelve highly experienced and talented soldiers at any given time. A diverse faction of para-elite special force types, all from multiple countries and possessing various combative disciplines.

These troops possessed unique abilities, specialized and specific, having proven superior in all areas of combat in addition to their chosen tactical concentration.

Some of the SET Force were masters in hand-to-hand combat, others in martial arts, a few in explosives, and some in tactical logistics, but all well versed in small arms.

Each one of these soldiers was deeply vetted, and if any were ever eliminated on a given mission, Tobias had their replacements "on ready" to serve and replace if needed. This propitious group was revered within Tobias's organization, and each was hand-selected by Tobias himself.

It was rare to lose one of these elite soldiers while on a mission, but it was more common when a given soldier reached their mandatory retirement age, which Tobias set at thirty-five years of age.

No SET was allowed to serve beyond their thirty-fifth birthday, and that decision was never questioned or challenged. There was no ceremony, commendations, celebration, acknowledgment, and above all, any exceptions concerning the rules and protocols set forth.

Tobias retired them to a remote location with an offshore account servicing them for the remainder of their lives at a one million-dollar (USD) payout for every year served under him. This arrangement was a far more beneficial option than the paltry military pension most soldiers had to settle with during their military tenure.

Part of every SET soldier's service requirement, commitment, and agreement was that they were not to work again in any military capacity and never to speak of Tobias's employment, protocol, training, or missions. If they were ever caught violating any of these requirements, they were eliminated without prejudice along with anyone they were associated with or involved with, no questions asked.

No breach of the employment requirements has been violated to date, and Tobias didn't expect them ever to be challenged. He was known to be resolute in his conditions, and the flexibility of any rules was not part of Tobias's nature. These statutes proved to be most effective in preserving the integrity of the SET Force members and all the benefits included in its unique membership and engagement.

Additional conditions of this prestigious group included the team refraining from consuming alcohol except in controlled settings. They were also not to maintain any long-term relationships or have any contact with anyone outside the complex while employed. It was a lonely, specialized group, but their tenure was usually a mere five to ten-year commitment.

Beyond the dedicated time commitment, they would live their existence in abundance. Most considered it a worthwhile compromise, especially as most soldiers maintained a solitary lifestyle anyway.

The difficulty was being impressive enough to gain the attention of Tobias and his organization and then clear the rigorous selection process to become a member of Tobias's exceptional SET Force.

Many tried, but most failed, not living up to the standard that Tobias set forth to become a member of this prestigious team. Once accepted into this exclusive group, those soldiers were outfitted in military-grade bullet-resistant paramilitary uniforms, allowing them to maneuver fairly easily but allowing the complete protection of body armor accompanied with a small-profile helmet.

The development team called this specialized suit their Multifaceted All-Tactical body armor (or MAT suit). The specialized suits were matte black in their entirety with piping in dark red, their presence ominous. The MAT suit was the compound tech outfit set for military defense conditions.

It could resist most caliber munitions, severe blunt assaults, and minor explosive attacks if engaged in a full combat scenario, which is somewhat cumbersome. One drawback was the suit limited the soldier's full fluid movement. The tech developers designed a remedy because of the MAT suit's limitations. An alternative suit was then developed.

When Tobias was present within a public purview or in more covert operations, the SET force was outfitted in an alternative specialized and unique lightweight Kevlar Attack Matte black armor (KAM suit) configuration, even equipped with a tie for blending purposes and to move more freely with the encompassing civilian surroundings.

These KAM suits were state-of-the-art protective public domain bullet resistant suits that were virtually undetectable and, although not as protective as the MAT suit, equally as impressive in that they allowed more fluid movement and at far less in weight. However, head protection wasn't utilized, unlike the MAT suit.

The commanding protective aspect was superior when outfitted in the MAT suit, but the KAM suit stood its own against small-arms fire and close-quarter combat attacks. Wherever Tobias traveled, one to six of his SET force team were always present with any given mission for personal protection despite Tobias being a menacing force himself.

As Prim approached the secured anteroom adjacent to Tobias's personal office, two SET guards were standing by the entrance, one on each side of the medium-sized room. Access to Tobias's inner lair followed two strict protocols: the visual confirmation of the on-site SET guard and the second a simultaneous retina and fingerprint scan. All interaction was recorded by various cameras and audio equipment strewn about the chamber.

The SET leader acknowledged Prim with verbal confirmation. "Visual confirmation . . . Nicholas Prim. Please continue to the digital retina/print scan, Mr. Prim. Both thumbs are today, sir," prompted the guard. The selection of which fingers was changed daily as well as randomly.

Approaching the sophisticated machine, Prim placed his two thumbs as instructed upon the sensor while simultaneously looking into the blue light at eye level. Both pinging a "positive confirmation" as Prim stepped back, looking at the SET leader for authorization. The guard waved him through, having passed all security protocols.

Wondering about this group of elite soldiers, Prim often questioned why they were not under his command directly unless presented with a dire circumstance.

Tobias and his lead SET commander, referred to only by the code name Fury—a moniker evoking awe and fear within their ranks—had personally selected each elite squad member. This wasn't just any team; it was a precision-engineered unit of specialists, each handpicked for their unique skills and unwavering loyalty. Trained rigorously in the shadows, these soldiers underwent a regimen crafted by Tobias and Fury, designed to push human limits physically and mentally.

This close-knit group operated more like a tight brotherhood than a mere military unit. Bound by secrets and shared trials, their camaraderie was forged in the fires of intense, secretive training sessions and covert operations. Managed exclusively by Tobias and Fury, the group was insulated from typical military bureaucracy, allowing for swift, decisive action unhindered by external influences.

Their cohesion and private tutelage under such formidable leaders made them a menace on the field. Yet, despite their extensive preparation and the protective bubble of their insular world, nothing could fully prepare them for an adversary of Sebastian's caliber—a man whose tactical genius and instinct for survival could unravel even the most meticulously laid plans. This oversight would challenge their effectiveness and test the very bonds holding them so closely together.

Prim always thought it strange Tobias trusted him to run his entire enterprise, but he had limited involvement and command over Tobias's SET force. He understood so little about them, but he had seen them in action, and they were exceptional in their execution of orders. This force was threatening and ominous; in groups or singularly, they were absolute killing machines, as he had never witnessed before with any other organized group.

Sitting at his expansive desk, Tobias heard the knock at the door to his office, reviewing various mission proposals, purposely delaying any response for a few moments. He finally answered in a mild-mannered yet commanding voice while looking at the door, "Enter."

Nicholas Prim slowly entered the large room accompanied by the SET leader, Fury, who stood erect and at attention in front of the door like an iron statue. Prim attempted not to appear sheepish with the news he needed to disclose to his new boss as he made his way to his leader. The room was lavishly decorated, comfortable, inviting, and spacious. One could essentially get lost in such a place.

The most impressive aspect of Tobias's office was the enormous picture window encompassing the entire east wall, overlooking the picturesque view beyond. The window exhibits a beautiful scene of the Irish landscape that lay behind Tobias, encased in bulletproof glass.

Impressive, eight-inch thick reinforced glass, yet mesmerizing, nonetheless, expanded the entire width and height of the wall, roughly thirty-five feet wide and ten feet in height—a spectacle in and of itself. The window was so large and clear it appeared as if one could walk directly into the picturesque setting.

Tobias examined Prim as he entered the room and walked guardedly across the floor to one of two chairs sitting before Tobias's desk. Possessing an elaborate affinity for reading people, their nonverbal cues, and their energy, Tobias could pick up a tremendous amount of information from their posture, stance, and even the gait of their walk.

In the short trek across the floor of his office, Tobias was curious about the man before him and remained tentative about this new addition to his crew.

He assimilated Prim as he entered and immediately detected the negative energy Prim put forth. He assumed the man possessed more than somber news to share with him. Tobias did not accept failure well.

Highly recommended to Tobias for some time, Prim's short tenure with Tobias was everything short of illustrious. He had failed in London in eliminating Sebastian when his organization surprisingly came across intelligence that Sebastian was in the city and, furthermore, information on his exact location. The connection with the demise of the South African ambassador at the same time appeared more than coincidental. Tobias strongly suspected Sebastian must have been involved in the publicized incident surrounding the Ambassador to South Africa.

Sebastian . . . always the good Samaritan.

The termination of the South African Ambassador certainly matched Sebastian Storm's modus operandi. Sebastian always possessed a soft spot for people, which Tobias thought foolish. Tobias had always considered that trait of Sebastian to be a tremendous weakness, which would inevitably lead to his undoing.

After the London occurrence and losing three of Prim's best men to Sebastian, Tobias's confidence in Prim was diminishing precipitously. Time would ultimately tell, but he would not accept another failure so graciously as he did the first time. Tobias was merciful on that occasion, but he wouldn't be as sympathetic a second time.

Prim obtained information in Berlin that would satisfy Tobias for the time being, but terminating Sebastian Storm was a far more remarkable feat. Tobias was aware Prim had obtained the architectural information desired by his team before their untimely demise, but he was curious how Prim would disclose that vital piece of information to him.

Prim entered the room with a weight upon his shoulders that slowed his every movement. He approached the chair deliberately, his posture an embodiment of a seasoned operative's weary yet resolved spirit. With a heavy sigh, he sank into the chair, his movements languid from the strain of recent events. After a moment's hesitation, as if gathering the last of his resolve, Prim lifted his gaze to meet Tobias's steady stare.

In a crisp British accent, carrying the gravitas of their grim reality, Prim began, "Sir, our man in Vienna failed. He was eliminated by Storm."

The words hung in the air, charged with implications. Tobias remained outwardly impassive, yet internally, he felt a spark of intrigue. Prim's directness and the unflinching delivery of unwelcome news spoke volumes of his character and experience. It was a bold move to lay out the facts so starkly, without preamble or excuse, and Tobias found this approach refreshing and even admirable in its own right.

"Interesting," Tobias mused silently, his eyes narrowing slightly as he regarded Prim. This straightforward admission not only confirmed the mission's failure but also highlighted a rare integrity in the field of espionage—a willingness to confront unpleasant truths head-on. It was this quality, this unvarnished honesty, Tobias respected in a world often mired in deception and subterfuge.

Despite the setback, Prim's report impressed him, reinforcing the complexities and challenges of their shadowy war against a formidable adversary like Sebastian Storm.

Tobias's eyes closed for a moment to let the words sink into his thoughts. He was disappointed but not surprised.

Each time Sebastian Storm's name was uttered, the vision of his only love, Emily, filled his thoughts, reliving the pain of her tragic and grisly loss repeatedly and the day he walked away from that life thirteen years prior and the United States government.

Tobias was their best and most experienced, but the system failed him, and he made it his sole purpose to feed and foster his hate and demand the respect of the world through the fear he planned to unleash when he was ready. After his departure, Sebastian Storm became their primary, which only sickened him further.

The day the aversion reached its pinnacle, Tobias ascended like a phoenix from the ashes, reborn as a disciple of chaos. The only woman, or person, Tobias had ever cared for more than himself was Emily. Sebastian was a constant and visceral reminder of her loss and his failure to save her on the mission in Central America.

A reminder of human fragility was defined in that moment, and Emily's fate was tied directly to Sebastian and the choices he made that day on the bridge. His abhorrence for Sebastian grew each time he was faced with the mere utterance of his name, knowing her loss of life was Sebastian's decision and his alone. He could never forgive him nor forget it.

It had taken him years to build his network and maintain his anonymity . . . until now. He was now ready to let the world know who he was and what anarchy he would release upon them all.

He opened his eyes and glared at Prim for what seemed like minutes, then slowly stood from his chair, not saying a word, turned and deliberately faced his outstretched view of the rolling countryside before him, his back to Prim intentionally.

He appreciated the beauty that nature provided, its purity, and its excellence recognized within its own imperfections. Much like human beings, he thought. Tobias peered out over the countryside, never tiring of such a view. It calmed, naturally sedated, balanced, and aligned him and his energy. He needed these visual moments to balance the mediocrity of life, the people of the world, and the unfortunate realities he often had to invoke on others.

Hearing this news, Tobias needed this moment to steady himself, contemplate his response, consider the options, and cautiously form his next play.

Prim studied Tobias, appreciated the inner strength of this man, and both feared and respected his commitment and perseverance for what he believed. He possessed an unwavering commitment to his principles and dogmas.

As he took in the landscape for a moment longer, never diverting his gaze, in a soft tone, he asked, "Nicholas, how do you feel a strong organization maintains its success, discipline, and ultimately, its evolution?"

Slowly and purposefully, Prim looked up at Tobias, viewing the back of the man with the illustrious pictographic scene through the window beyond him. "I suppose, sir, it comes from the integrity of those within it, loyalty, and their efficiency in how they perform and how their effectiveness is executed."

Tobias contemplated Prim's response and said, "Yes, its effectiveness . . . ." Tobias muttered, but then his voice trailed off, not responding with anything more than that, but instead walked to the front of his desk and to the left of Prim and leaned against it, facing him looking down.

Looking at Prim directly in the eye, Tobias's arms crossed, holding the stance for a few moments. Then, without warning, in a blur of movement, Tobias shifted his weight forward, grabbing Prim's left hand firmly, twisting it severely, and driving Prim to his knees. Holding the last two fingers in a tight grasp and glaring at Prim, Tobias said, "I don't accept mediocrity or failure . . . or ANY lack of *effectiveness* as you call it. I warned you of this, Nicholas."

Prim's attempt to resist only caused Tobias to clamp down and twist more firmly, yet he managed to respond with, "I know, sir, but this Sebastian wasn't . . . wasn't human, he doesn't make mistakes . . ."

Tobias gripped his hand harder, intensifying the pain, moving his face closer to Prim's, and said in almost a low growl, "I don't accept excuses either. Are you not up to the task? Sebastian Storm is just a man like you or me, Nicholas. Is he not?"

"I am, sir. I will not let it happen again. Yes, he is only human. He can be defeated," gasped Prim. Tobias narrows his eyes and says finally, "No, it won't, Nicholas, and if it does, we won't be having another discussion. Everyone has a weakness. You need to find . . . his. As I have already found yours."

Without warning, Tobias twisted abruptly and broke both Prim's fingers instantaneously. Crying out but immediately ceasing the reaction, Prim didn't want to show any more weakness and fear than he had already displayed in the exchange.

Tobias let go of Prim's hand, stepped away, and returned to his outstretched view, once again his back facing Prim. As Prim cradled his fractured hand in silence, somehow lifting himself into the chair, Tobias softly said, "Remember this conversation, Nicholas, and remember the benevolence I extended you, as it won't be the same the next time. Go get your hand tended to and pray I chose your left hand and not your right."

Prim slowly rose from his chair and managed to utter, "I won't fail you again, sir." He sauntered out of the room, Fury in tow, and closed the door behind him, leaving Tobias in silence.

Tobias said under his breath, "No, you won't, or it will be your last mistake, Mr. Prim."

Tobias did his best thinking in front of his office window, but this day, he was clouded and distracted by just one thing: Sebastian Storm.

Successes and failures did not affect Tobias tremendously—his beliefs, his resolve, and his execution of all missions were accomplished with precision, and failures were a rarity in his world.

Nothing adversely affected Tobias, save for Sebastian Storm.

The only man Tobias had ever acknowledged to be his equal and his constant anguish. Tobias's organization rarely failed in its endeavors, but occasionally, if it did derail, it often occurred because of Sebastian's direct or indirect involvement or HB's ATS Division.

Tobias had eluded Sebastian and HB's detection for over a decade, but it was time to let them know he was back in the game and coming for them personally.

Meticulous in that endeavor, Tobias had remained socially buried, well layered, and protected over the years. He had grown more powerful in that time, and his inner circle was loyal above all, keeping his identity a mystery while he built his organization from the ground up.

Remaining patient and disciplined in his progression, Tobias was now strong enough and ready to enter the world arena and take his rightful place.

He would not enter quietly.

His crosshairs were set on a global venue, the Pergamon Museum in Berlin. He would make the world value his vigor, demanding the respect he deserved, but he wished more to become worthy of their fear.

Tobias had orchestrated several covert operations aimed at neutralizing Sebastian, yet each attempt had been artfully dodged. Sebastian's uncanny ability to anticipate and counteract Tobias's moves made him an elusive and formidable adversary, one who seemed to weave through the shadows untouched.

Sebastian's abilities had certainly improved immeasurably in the prior decade. Given this history, Tobias found it unreasonable to lay the blame solely at Nicolas Prim's feet for the latest failure.

Sitting behind his desk, his expression composed yet thoughtful, Tobias listened as Prim articulated Sebastian's near-flawless operational conduct. "He never seems to 'make mistakes,'" Prim had said, a hint of both respect and frustration in his voice. While the statement rang true and echoed Tobias's own observations, it was precisely this intractable perfection that made Sebastian such a coveted target.

If nothing else, Tobias respected Prim for his candor and for maintaining an impenetrable level of security, save for Sebastian's challenges. Prim's record was otherwise impeccable, managing to shield their operations from less formidable threats with a calculated efficiency Tobias valued highly. In this chess game of espionage and countermeasures, Prim had proven himself a reliable piece, a safeguard against the myriad dangers lurking in their clandestine world.

Therefore, while Prim's latest report was a concession of defeat, Tobias viewed it through a lens of strategic assessment rather than outright condemnation. It was Sebastian Storm, after all, who remained the enigma, a singular outlier in Tobias's otherwise meticulously controlled universe. The problem wasn't Prim's competence; it was Sebastian's exceptional knack for survival that continued to vex their plans.

It appeared eliminating Sebastian had proved to be a daunting task. He considered sending Prim personally to eliminate Sebastian but feared he would lose Prim in the process, as no one could seem to match Sebastian except for possibly Tobias himself. Tobias was far too valuable an asset within this enterprise to risk himself in that endeavor. Their next attempt would be significantly more planned and executed, and then Tobias would have his vengeance.

Over the prior decade, Tobias's organization has become well respected in espionage, assassinations, and infiltrations set forth by groups with specific agendas or goals only Tobias could achieve. His services were expensive but adequately compensated because he was effective in his execution, and his organization achieved its orders efficiently and successfully.

His reputation had grown strong in the ten years since he left HB's division, but Sebastian Storm had become a thorn in the progression of that success and needed to be handled once and for all.

One thing was certain: Storm needed to be eliminated . . . soon. If not, his operation may be compromised, or worse yet, fail, and he could not let that happen under any circumstances.

Chapter 8

Righteousness Realized

Vienna, Austria
Present Day

Sebastian had slept for an additional hour after returning from Adriana's hotel. He woke before light, as he did each day. He checked and rechecked his precautionary security measures and headed down the back stairs at 4:45 am to meet HB at the Schönbrunn Palace.

It was a frosty morning, and Sebastian was thankful he selected his long camel cashmere jacket and black leather gloves for his outing to the Vienna central train station, roughly one mile away. It was a twelve-minute brisk walk for Sebastian, and he enjoyed the morning air. Strangely, Sebastian savored the cool weather over a hot, humid climate.

The streets were lightly populated this early in the morning, and Sebastian enjoyed it that way. He knew the train to the Schönbrunn

------

Palace was leaving at 5:15 am, so he had a few minutes. The sun was beginning to rise as he made his way to the train station.

Leisurely strolling down the street, Sebastian began to approach the rear entrance of the train station two blocks away. As he made his way around the corner, he encountered an elderly homeless man who was being accosted and harassed by five ruffians.

The young men were in their twenties, teasing and bullying the older gentleman. Sebastian surmised this sorted group of vagrants was up far too early and coming off a long night of carousing and debauchery, and the elderly gentleman provided some form of twisted entertainment for an otherwise boring walk home for the heedless delinquents. The poor man was in the wrong place at the wrong time.

The weak, the poor, and the less fortunate always held a special place within Sebastian's heart, and he affectionately possessed immense empathy for those destitute individuals. A subtle but recurring image of his mother would come to mind. Anyone exploiting those poor souls would feel his wrath and pay dearly if they ever crossed Sebastian's path. He never tolerated such abuse and torment of those less protected.

These foolish hooligans didn't spot Sebastian as he approached them initially from behind as he pondered the situation before him. He shook his head, knowing he had no choice but to intervene, and he also was certain how the outcome would transpire.

He studied the young men before him for several seconds, cataloging their strengths and weaknesses before either engaging them or alerting them in some way to his presence. His mood was yet defined by the route he would take. They focused more on the destitute man than on Sebastian, using their reckless abandon to his advantage.

He stopped short of their position by roughly twenty-five feet, observing the escape areas on either side of the street, an open door for deliveries to his right, and several businesses, still closed, to his left.

After sizing each man up individually, he had determined there was little value for concern between them. He concluded he wasn't dealing with much in the way of any significant abilities or skills.

However, Sebastian always believed in a fair fight, and above all, he believed it was always best to attempt to circumvent a hostile situation before people around him got injured.

He had the feeling that people were going to get hurt in what was to follow. As much emotionally as physically. There was to be a lesson learned here today.

Sebastian began to walk toward the men, pulled his leather glove tighter on his right side, then his left as he proceeded directly toward the group. It was not a busy street, and the earliness of the hour accommodated minimal passersby.

Moving a few feet closer to the scene, unbeknownst to the motley crew, and then, with a firm conviction and a commanding voice, Sebastian bellowed, "Gentlemen, I beg you, please leave the poor man alone. He has done nothing to you! Have a sense of decency for his regretful luck. Just do the right thing in this instance and leave him alone. Please, just walk away."

Sebastian always attempted to avoid a confrontation, and he usually hoped for the good in people to prevail and was optimistic that catering to their integrity would give some people a sense of self-awareness and decency. He hoped they might see fit to adjust their actions, or at least he yearned they may see the error of their ways.

In observing the situation, Sebastian longed for the young men to simply recognize this poor soul deserved more than this taunting and provocation and to simply move on and continue their business.

Sebastian always coveted any and all virtue in people to emerge, for the good in people to be realized, to be respected, to be . . . discovered within themselves. But sadly, this was not going to be one of those times he anticipated.

"Ahhh, excuse me, mister? Your little warning was about the dumbest thing someone could say to a bunch of guys when he should be minding his own business, not messing with someone else's. Are you that dumbass, mister?" Touted off the man closest to him, glancing back at his crew for affirmation and appreciation of his bravado.

The young man was unimpressive and displayed a robust yet false sense of bravery for the sake of the other's benefit. Sebastian pegged him as the apparent leader of this gang of degenerates. So much for the good in people, thought Sebastian, slowly shaking his head again.

"Actually, far from it. I would imagine that specific word would probably be better served to describe your little band of misfits here. Why don't you reconsider where this is headed and just move along and let this poor man go about his way?" Asked Sebastian now for a second time.

Their lesson was about to embark, and it would be a long and painful one for these men in the following minutes. The five men, now clearly annoyed and aggravated, stopped pestering the man for the moment, shifting their focus, surprised by Sebastian's response, and garnering their full attention. At least he deviated from their focus; that was half of his intent. The other half was to work out a little frustration on his own, and he hadn't had his workout yet that morning.

All their attention was now transferred toward this insolent Good Samaritan questioning their intentions. Sebastian's disrespect for them couldn't go unpunished, and their pride and ego forced them to test the waters further. Sebastian knew what they had to prove, but their lesson would be an introspective one over the next few minutes.

Their leader, clad in dingy leather, grimy, edgy, and dirty, was carrying himself with an arrogant gait and demeanor. Puffing out his chest, he began walking toward Sebastian with his crew forming in behind him. "You have something smart to say, Mr. GQ? All I need is an excuse to kick some ass after the night I had . . . especially on some mouthy do-gooder."

The leader turned and laughed with all his boys. They all hissed and sneered as if he had said something funny, but Sebastian wasn't laughing. "Only an observation. Confidence without competence is simply . . . . *arrogance*. Leave the man alone, and let's go our separate ways. I won't ask again," softly muttered Sebastian for the third time. Sebastian knew any discussion after this point was gratuitous, and the entire skirmish would have to go the distance at this point. There was no turning back.

The leader was within a few feet of Sebastian at this point. "Ohhhh . . . 'won't ask again'? Maybe you would prefer . . ." The man taunted Sebastian as he attempted a blind "sucker punch" swing, but Sebastian, anticipating the predictable move, avoided it easily, the man's failed right hook missing its mark wildly.

With gloved hands, Sebastian squarely pounded the man's face with a combination of his left fist and ducks and then immediately came in with his right, much like as witnessed in a boxing match, following up with a second right. The leader went down hard, unconscious from the flurry of blows delivered by Sebastian.

The other four were startled and surprised at the blur of movements witnessed but slowly gathered their wits in response and started in on Sebastian simultaneously. Sebastian was more than ready for them. They all looked at one another as if to think how only one man could take all four of them, so they all rushed him together.

The first delinquent attempted a straight kick from the front, but Sebastian effortlessly grabbed his heel with his left hand and then crushed down on his knee with his right elbow, breaking the knee as he side-kicked the third man, knocking the wind out of him as he clutched his chest. As ribs crack and splinter, both men go down.

The third and fourth man came forward together, blindly, unorganized in their rush. Sebastian immediately lunged forward, extended his clenched fists aimed at their throats, and connected, forcing them both down, gasping for air, choking, their larynxes crushed, leaving them gasping for air. Not fatal injuries but sufferable ones.

The tattered crew was demoralized and dejected within just a few seconds. Standing fully upright, Sebastian straightened his jacket and pulled both gloves taut once again, noticing the slight amount of blood spatter on the knuckles of both gloved hands.

He then approached each man, thrashing about all along the sidewalk and street. Sebastian leaned down next to his first victim, one of the crew, and removed the man's wallet, then visited each of the remaining men, took each of their wallets and emptied them entirely of bills, removed their licenses, and threw their wallets next to them.

Sebastian held the money and licenses up in his hand as he walked up to the leader last, lying upon the concrete, semiconscious now. Though dazed and confused, the leader was holding his nose, writhing in excruciating pain, yet still managed to concentrate on Sebastian as he approached him, squirming on the ground, afraid Sebastian would potentially unleash a second wave of attacks upon him.

Sebastian knelt, wiped his bloody knuckles on the leader's shirt, held up his hand, displaying all the men's driver's licenses, and said, "If any of your group here ever taunts or antagonizes anyone on these streets like this again, none of you will be walking away. You tell the others on your ambulance ride to the hospital what I said, got it? I will make it my mission . . . to end you . . . all. You understand me, ah . . . Trevor?" As he looked at the leader's driver's license and read his name.

"Yes," replied Trevor, whimpering. "Good. Do you doubt me in any way, Trevor?" asked Sebastian. "No, sir, I do not," replied the man. Once more, Sebastian reminded him by saying: "I did try to avoid this ordeal, but you refused. You were fortunate I was in a forgiving mood this morning. Don't make me regret my decision, Trevor."

Sebastian gave him a long look to strengthen his threat, then stood up and turned, walking over to the older man abused by the degenerates, and helping the man up to his feet. Sebastian held in view of the older man's gaze the €460 in cash he had taken from the men's wallets.

Sebastian then held up the wad of folded euros in full view so the older man could see the bills and then placed them in the man's breast pocket. He gently said, "This should help you get a hot meal and a nice motel courtesy of these boys lying about. Sir, take care of yourself for a few days. These boys won't bother you any longer, and this is their gift for the inconvenience they caused you this morning." He handed the man a card and said, "Here's my number, and if you are ever bothered by these men again, you just let me know. My name is Storm."

The old man replied, "Thank you so much. You have a kind heart, Mr. Storm." Sebastian looked into the old man's eyes, smiled subtly, and said, "Not as kind as you might think, but you caught me on a good day. Now get out of here before the circus starts." The man looked at him, thankful for this Good Samaritan who blessed him that morning.

The old man started to ask, "I've never seen anything like that before. How did you take out all those boys . . . ?" But he stopped, shaking his head, then thinking better of questioning; the older man's voice trailed off. With a wink, Sebastian helped the man along then saw him off, hearing sirens in the distance, and set on his way to the station. He didn't want to be there when they arrived.

When he reached the block's end, Sebastian turned to appreciate the aftermath he alone had created. He didn't ask or look for it, nor desire it. He even attempted to avoid it, but if he was ever forced to exercise his abilities, he never harbored any guilt or remorse.

He didn't harm good people, only the ones deserving it, rigid in his execution, always. In a way, he was life's karma personified. He looked at the scene he had left in his wake with some measure of admiration. The old man was well down the street by that time, and the young men were helping one another up or on their phones; the first police car rolled up.

A police officer stepped out of his vehicle, scratching his head and wondering about the mess that lay scattered before him. Sebastian turned the corner and was gone.

Entering through a rear door of the station, which was rarely used, Sebastian avoided all cameras in the area. Being relatively early in the morning, the station was sparsely populated. Entering the station hall, he looked above at the sizeable digital schedule board and found his departure time and port for Schönbrunn Palace, leaving in only four minutes. Sebastian boarded the end train and found a seat at the very back facing forward, a perfect vantage point to observe any activity on the cars before him.

The train ride was twenty-four minutes long, so he had a moment to breathe and relax. He rested his eyes and thought of his childhood. The images and thoughts brought him to a point in his life where it felt like it was only yesterday.

Vienna, Austria
Present Day

"We both know that's not how it works, Frederic," continued Adriana. "The drug is pending with the FDA, and we know the patent isn't dependent on FDA approval. Austria isn't as stringent as the U.S. Stay on the attorneys and get it done. I don't want any more excuses."

"Yes, ma'am," replied Frederic as he left her office located at the Vienna branch in Austria.

Adriana had always thrived in the corporate man's world. She enjoyed toying with the men who underestimated her abilities and came to rely on the advantage it gave her in many instances. She wasn't always that way; it came with some maturity and understanding of the world around her.

Back in college, she was shy and timid, largely derived from the discipline of her father, a colonel in the Marines. He ran a tight ship, both professionally and personally, at home. As an only child, his attention was set on making her the best she could be and forbidding her from fraternizing with boys and participating in public events in high school, labeling them "a waste of her precious and valuable time and providing nothing more than a distraction."

She entered college at Columbia somewhat naïve and inexperienced socially, sexually, and emotionally. She had a lot of growing up to do, and despite loving her parents immensely, she welcomed the college experience and freedom it would provide far more than they knew.

Her father and mother helped her move into the college dormitory a week before school started. Carrying a large moving box, her vision was somewhat impaired as she passed through the entrance door.

She collided with a young man and began to fumble with the box, nearly dropping it as a result. The young man caught the box before it fell, and they smiled at each other over the spectacle they had created together. He introduced himself as David, and they exchanged a few pleasantries before her father came up and glared at the young man to move along.

Her father looked at her, disappointed, and said, "Adriana, don't waste your time with boys. Concentrate on your studies and focus on what's important. Young men only want one thing, and they are a distraction you don't need at this stage in your life."

"Yes, sir," she replied as she looked in David's direction, walking down the hall, smiling and hoping she would get to know him better in the following months.

For the next several years, she and David grew very close, yet nothing romantically, out of respect for what her father had instilled within her. Weeks after meeting, Adriana and David were studying together and decided to take a break and get dinner together. Their evening went on for hours, and in that time, they both laughed and teased each other until their server returned to their table and asked them to please keep the volume down as they were getting complaints from other nearby patrons. They giggled together, having been scolded by the server.

It was at that moment David looked at Adriana and said, "Adriana, someday I'm going to marry you. You will see." He smiled, but it was then Adriana, somewhat surprised by the comment, distanced herself from David even though deep down, she wondered if it may someday happen.

She trusted and adored David, but her focus needed to be concentrated on other areas, more important and relevant to her future, as instructed by her father. College came first, and relationships were just a distraction, her father would say, his voice echoing inside her head from time to time.

David was Columbia's top-scoring star soccer player and, as a sophomore, far and away, the most valuable player on the team. His abilities were exceptional, and David had an excellent chance of entering the professional sector after he graduated.

Over the years, they dated various people here and there but always sought each other's approval, often with one advising the other yet never dating one another.

As Adriana approached her final year at Columbia, David, being a year ahead, had only a month left of school remaining. It was already widely known he was heavily sought after by professional teams and was achieving his dream of becoming a professional soccer player.

Adriana and David had gone to dinner to celebrate receiving the professional contract and decided to walk back to their apartment complex that spring evening through the park. They strolled in silence before David said, "Do you remember what I said to you a few weeks after we met three years ago?"

She thought about his question for a moment, trying to recall what he was referencing as she looked the other way and said, "You mean about you marrying me someday?" She replied in a teasing taunt as she glanced to her side and didn't see him or notice he had stopped. When he didn't answer her, she stopped, looked around, and saw him on one knee behind her. Staring at him in disbelief, Adriana is slightly confused about what is transpiring until it hits her all at once.

"Adriana Mercer, will you marry me? Make me the happiest man in all the world," said David. She walked toward him until she was in front of him, gazing into his eyes with such adoration as her hands came up to her face as if she was still uncertain if this was her reality or simply a wonderful dream.

She wobbled back a few steps to stand before him as a flurry of emotions fell over her, and she became overwhelmed with her feelings for this young man.

Trapped within her thoughts, numb to everything around her, she finally hears, "Adriana? Will you? Will you marry me?" Still, on one knee, David remained hopeful, smiling but concerned over her silence, yet holding the ring in hopes of her acceptance. He had purchased the ring with the advance signing bonus he received for the professional contract.

She takes her hands from her face, looks at him, smiles, and says, "Of course I will, David. I love you and have always loved you since the day I bumped into you at the dorm entrance. Yes, David, yes, yes, yes, I will marry you!" He placed the ring on her finger, a perfect fit, and rose to his feet and kissed her passionately, it being the first time their lips had ever met, the moment magical and memorable in every possible way.

They savored their moment, all the lost time recovered in the next two days spent at her apartment getting to know each other and exploring all the ways young lovers do and, on a level they had not ever experienced with anyone else.

Continuous, deep conversations lasting late into the evening, extending to the morning as they would watch the sunlight coming through the windows and laugh at the thought of forgetting even to eat, simply engrossed in each other, and losing all track of time.

The two lovers would run down to the kitchen, sans any clothing, and laugh and tantalize each other while preparing something to eat, leaving a mess of the kitchen in the process, yet not a care in the world. They were caught in their moment, and they were the only two beings that existed at that time. They woke the next afternoon and realized they hadn't spoken with anyone in the outside world for nearly two full days.

Lying in bed, Adriana smiled at David and softly said, "We have been MIA for two days, David, and I keep realizing we are engaged. It doesn't seem real to me. So much has happened in the last forty-eight hours, but all I feel is complete happiness. And I have you to thank for that." She touched his face, realizing he was the best thing that had ever happened to her.

Their heads upon the pillow, David winked at her and softly spoke while they lay in bed, "I know, it makes my heart so excited that you will be my wife. I can't believe it's true. Tonight, a few of my team members want to take me out to celebrate my new professional status, and I thought I would also tell them about our engagement."

She smiled at him, but he could sense she was slightly saddened at the thought of him leaving her, if even for a few hours. He touched her face gently and said, "I don't have to go. I can cancel if you want me to?"

"Of course not. I don't want you to do that. You deserve your time with your friends, David, but then come right back to me."

They teased and enjoyed each other for a few more hours before David reluctantly got out of bed, kissed her, and said, "I'll be back in a few hours, and you will be all mine."

Adriana simply said, "Hurry home to me, David." Little did she know that very day, her life would change forever and become permanently altered in a twisted fate that no one could have predicted.

After David had left, it was after six o'clock that evening, and Adriana went to the kitchen, reminiscing about her time with David, when she looked at her phone and noticed that her mom had called numerous times in the last several hours.

She quickly called her back, and when her mom answered, she asked, "Mom, I'm so sorry, I was busy. Is everything okay?" There was no immediate response, and only a soft whimpering could be heard on the other end. Adriana repeated, "Mom, Mom, what's happened?"

After a moment, Adriana's mom answered, "Oh, honey, I'm sorry . . . It's your father. He suffered a heart attack, it just gave out earlier today. He passed, baby. He has left us. I'm so sorry. I tried to reach you all day." Adriana's heart sank as she sat on the floor. The man she both respected and revered was gone, and she was never able to say goodbye to him.

Always her rock, her compass, though stern and rigid with her growing up, her father emulated what was right and just in the world, and she always valued and admired him for that trait. Being a thousand miles apart, there was little she could do, so she stayed on the phone with her mother for the next few hours consoling one another as best they could.

At that time, Tyler, David's best friend, had kept trying to call through, but she disregarded the attempts in light of the issue with her father.

Adriana had not even a chance to speak with her mother concerning the news about her and David, as that announcement had to take a backseat to the loss that her family was suffering. She was still on the phone with her mother when she heard a ring at her front door.

Reluctantly coming to the door, still dressed in her robe from the last two days, she opened it to see Tyler's somber face before her. She looked at him quizzically and said into her phone, "Mom, I have to call you back." As her arm dropped to her side, Tyler quietly said, "I'm so sorry, Adriana. David has been in a terrible accident. I've been trying to reach you."

Adriana shook herself from her daydream as Frederic knocked on the door and announced, "Meeting in the conference room in five minutes, ma'am, just a reminder." She had been twisting the engagement ring that David had given to her all those years ago. It was on the opposite hand resized to her index finger a constant moment she kept in remembrance of him.

"Thanks, Frederic. I'll be there in a minute. Would you be so kind as to bring a hot tea to the meeting for me?" Adriana responded. "Of course, ma'am," replied Frederic.

The news on that fateful day hit her like a relentless storm, each revelation a devastating blow that left her reeling. That morning, she learned of her father's passing, a loss that shattered the foundation of her world. Yet barely had she begun to grapple with this grief when another cruel twist of fate struck—David, her beloved, had been killed by a drunk driver. He had been en route to celebrate with friends, eager to share the joyous news of his ascent to professional soccer and their engagement.

The timing was a cruel irony, the promise of a bright future snuffed out in an instant. David's dreams of a celebrated career and a life intertwined with hers were brutally cut short, leaving behind a void filled with unfulfilled promises and shattered hopes. As she absorbed the dual tragedies, the weight of her sorrow threatened to crush her, the enormity of the losses almost too much to bear.

The ambulance on the scene had taken David to the Columbia University Medical Center, where he, upon arriving, was pronounced dead when the ambulance pulled into the hospital.

Adriana's world collapsed that day after losing both her father and fiancé within hours of one another. The trauma of her loss altered her reality, eventually leading to a transformation that occurred deep within her, resulting from that dreadful moment almost fourteen years before.

For years, she had difficulty trusting anyone not to abandon her in some form, and just when she would let someone in, she would sabotage the relationship to avoid the pain she felt was sure to follow.

The pain was too great, but the fear of losing someone close to her was equally traumatizing. Adriana thought it best, at the time, to simply avoid attachments to people, thinking it the best way to protect herself against the heartbreak.

As she looked at his engagement ring upon her finger, she reminisced of their brief moment of happiness together. She had never felt the connection again that she had felt for David. It was unique and special, and she realized that very early.

That is until she met Sebastian. At that moment, she was able to let her historic tragedy give way to her heart, which was trying to push through, command its attention, and beckon her trust to love someone once more.

Sebastian brought a unique element out in her she had not felt since her brief interlude with David. She had matured tremendously since her time in college but had not yet had the courage to let someone in, but with Sebastian, she felt he might be worth that risk.

That is, if he was the man she hoped he was.

Chapter 9

Perils of His Past

Roanoke, Virginia
1995
8:23 AM

Sebastian was awakened in the Roanoke police station holding room, shaken by the duty officer carrying a glass of water and a powdered donut in his hand. "Best get up, boy, and eat this. The detective will be down in a minute. Oh, and happy birthday. Guess this is the closest thing you will get to a cake."

The man laughed at his own insensitive joke as he thrust the water and donut into Sebastian's hands and walked back out of the room. Sebastian stared at the donut and drink in each hand, numb, having no appetite, and set them on the chair beside him.

He felt like he was living a bad dream, but the unsettling reality of his mother's face began to fill the visions and consume his thoughts. A tear formed in the corner of his eye, and he realized it wasn't a bad dream at all, but if he was here in this room, she must be gone. He so desired his memory to simply be just a terrible dream, but he knew better.

He wished he had the day to do over again. His ending would have been far different; he was certain of it. Deep down, he knew his father had been involved with what happened to his mother, and he must answer for taking her from him, for the tragedy that befell her.

Burned within his mind was the image of her eyes open, glazed over, fixed in death. There was no life left in her any longer. Her spirit and light were extinguished forever. Despite his best efforts, he couldn't get the likeness of her face out of his head.

He so wished he would not have seen his beloved mom in that state, but he did, and it was haunting his thoughts. At that moment, Sebastian became aware of some muffled talking and rustling outside the holding room door.

Looking around, he noted the room was small and gray in color, unkept and dirty, with a table and four chairs, three of which had been strung together side by side to give Sebastian a place to sleep. The room felt cold and barren as he imagined criminals were coming in and out of this room all day long on most days.

He wondered if his dad had ever been in a room like the one he was sitting in. He imagined he had and on more than one occasion. The door opened, and a large, burly man with a gangly beard and a tie far too short, terminating above his belly, entered the holding room. "Hey, little guy. I'm Detective Todd with the Roanoke Sheriff's Department, okay?"

He pulled up the last remaining chair and positioned it right in front of Sebastian. He sat down and looked at the boy momentarily, trying to get a read on the young man and determine his emotional state. He eyed the uneaten donut and glass of water sitting on the chair.

Detective Barry Todd had been with the Roanoke police department for ten years, four of those years as a detective. It was an easy job for him and uncomplicated. He put forth little effort, and he preferred it that way. A heavyset man, untidy and muddled, his shirt and pants far too tight from years of adding weight but not increased sizes in his wardrobe. Detective Todd was the pillar of unhealthiness.

He again glanced at the untouched donut and water sitting on the chair again and cocked his head awkwardly, curious why the boy didn't eat it. "Not going to eat your donut?" asked Todd. Sebastian shook his head 'no,' so Detective Todd replied, "Suit yourself."

He anxiously grabbed the donut and consumed it in two quick bites, then wiped his mouth with his sleeve with half the powder still crusted around the sides of his lips.

"I got to ask you some questions about your mom and dad, okay?" Sebastian nodded, and Todd continued with his poor grammar and hillbilly accent. "First of all, you are probably aware by now that your mom is dead, right?" Sebastian slowly looked up into Detective Todd's face and nodded again. "Sorry, that was probably the wrong way to say that. Have any idea where your daddy is at?" Sebastian shook his head 'no' once again. Todd followed with, "Did your daddy and mommy fight a lot?" Sebastian nodded 'yes.'

Todd continued, asking, "Did your daddy ever hit your momma?" Reluctantly, Sebastian nodded 'yes.' Todd quickly asked, "Did your daddy ever run off?" Sebastian nodded 'yes' again. Todd was still curious, "When did you leave the house before finding your mom?"

Sebastian thought about the question for a moment and replied, "It was before 8:00 a.m., somewhere in that time. I ran into the mountains because of all the yelling and fighting. I couldn't stay any longer. It made me too sad." Detective Todd nodded and appeared satisfied with Sebastian's answers to his questions.

Suddenly, a young officer knocked on the door, hesitated, entered the room, and walked over to Detective Todd. Still studying Sebastian, Detective Todd abruptly looked at the rookie officer. "What, boy? Spill it!" obviously annoyed with the officer's passiveness.

The officer leaned over and whispered into Detective Todd's right ear, "We have the boy's father. He walked into the station on his own. He is in holding #3, waiting." Despite his whisper, Sebastian could overhear what the officer had said but didn't acknowledge he had heard anything. He was surprised his father wasn't in a jail cell.

Detective Todd looked immediately at the boy and said, "Wait here, son. Porter, keep an eye on the kid for me. I'll be back in a few." Detective Todd slowly stood up, stretched, and left the small holding room.

Detective Todd entered holding room #3 to a haggard Jonathan Storm. Sebastian's father was strewn out, reeking of alcohol, filthy as if he had been in a bar fight, and smelling of two-day-old clothing. He desperately needed a shower.

Unlike the holding cell where they kept Sebastian, each man sat on either side of the small table, facing each other.

Detective Todd examined Jonathan for a moment, sizing him up, attempting to determine of what he was capable. Detective Todd was not impressed with the man whatsoever. Uninterested and bored, Jonathan sat idly, looking about the room, appearing wearied from the long night, and after what seemed like a long minute, said to Detective Todd, "Am I under arrest?"

Detective Todd responded, "Not yet, Mr. Storm, but the day is still young. I need to ask you some questions, and I don't need any bullshit, capisce?"

Jonathan slurred back, "Sure, Officer. Whatever you say."

Todd states, "It's Detective, Mr. Storm. Did you fight with your wife any time in the last few days?"

Jonathan cocked his head and made a scowl, and replied, "We always fight. You know, Detective. Passionate marriage and all." He shrugged it off with a wry smile.

Todd asked, "Did you ever hit your wife, Mr. Storm?"

Jonathan asked, "Don't you think they all need a little discipline every once in a while, Detective?"

Todd demanded, "Answer the question, Mr. Storm. As I said when I sat down, I will not be taking any bullshit from you this morning. Was that a 'yes'?" Johnathan answered, "Yes, sometimes it got a little physical." He could see the Detective wasn't going to tolerate his shenanigans.

Detective Todd asked, "I'm curious, Mr. Storm. Do you have any idea where your son is now?" Jonathan replied, "Oh,

Sebastian? He's probably running around in the woods looking for his rodents, you know, rabbits and the like. He loves trapping them." Attempting to appear involved in the boy's personal and adolescent interests.

Todd said, "Rabbits aren't rodents, Mr. Storm. I think most people are aware of that." The statement would make Sebastian proud in the adjacent room.

Jonathan slurred his reply, "Yeah, yeah? That's what he always says, too. They all are the same if you ask me . . . vermin, all of them."

Todd asked, "You do realize your wife is dead, don't you?"

Jonathan replied, "Yeah, I heard. I'm devastated. I'm not sure I like or appreciate this line of questioning, and your suggestive tone has much to be desired. Now that I think of it, do I need an attorney?"

Todd continued, "I don't know Mr. Storm, do you? You don't seem to be very broken up about it." Detective Todd leered at Jonathan Storm for a moment before tiring of the entire interrogation and simply asked, "Jonathan Storm, did you kill your wife, Samantha Storm?"

Jonathan sat back in his chair, glared at the detective, and softly demanded, "I think I want my attorney."

Detective Todd stood up as Jonathan's statement ceased any and all additional questioning but added one last comment: "If you had anything to do with this, we will find out, Mr. Storm. Justice has a way of balancing itself out."

Sneering at Detective Todd and narrowing his gaze, Jonathan said slowly in a taunting manner, "Yep, you appear to be Roanoke's finest, which isn't saying much. Get. Me. An. Attorney." Detective Todd turned and left the room, the door closing firmly behind him.

Roanoke, Virginia
1995
11:03 am

Sitting at his desk, Detective Todd was finalizing reports and waiting on the public defender for Jonathan Storm to arrive when his phone rang. He picked it up and said, "Hello, Todd here," hearing a familiar voice. "Hello, Detective, it's Hernandez with Crime Scene. We are processing the Storm woman and ahhh . . . . I think you should come down here and take a look at some things."

Todd responded, "I'll be right down," as he hung up the phone and rushed out the door and to the elevator, taking it to the basement. He hoped Hernandez had information or evidence he could use to put pressure on the elusive Jonathan Storm.

A few minutes later, Detective Todd arrived at the basement level. The doors opened, and the Detective walked into the morgue and asked for Hernandez. A few moments later, still gloved up, he emerged through the double doors. "Come on back with me, Detective," ushered Hernandez.

Detective Todd followed him through the double doors and entered behind Hernandez to exam room no. #1. Lying in front of him was the naked body of Samantha Storm, exposed and cold, the display making Detective Todd feel uncomfortable.

He thought to himself, "These morgue people never seem to respect the decency of those who found their way to their tables." The detective always hated the sight of a lifeless corpse, but luckily, in Roanoke, they were relatively infrequent, making his job far more manageable.

On occasion, a geriatric "cat lady" would be found in her home, bloated after being discovered after two weeks from the smell emanating outside the home. Or, possibly, the retired widower who died in his Lazy Boy, still in golf attire after a severe heart attack from a myocardial infarction.

Most of them were from natural causes and rarely occurred, a homicide requiring Detective Todd even to lift a finger, but this was one of those rare instances.

Hernandez turned to Todd and asked, "Are you thinking the husband did it, off'd the wife, Detective?"

"Oh, I'm pretty certain of it."

"Why?" asked Detective Todd.

Gesturing toward Samantha's neck, Hernandez continued, "Well, here's the thing, Detective. Her neck was broken, no question, and it appears it came from a fall down the stairs. No doubt there either, and no bruises to speak of from choking or trauma from any blunt object, lacerations, knife, or puncture wounds of any kind. She either fell down the stairs in a freak accident or . . . *she was pushed*. Strangely, though, Detective, if she was forced down the stairs, there is really no way of confirming that theory unless you are fortunate enough to have a witness and the boy can't corroborate what happened. So, Detective, the plain and simple of it, I don't think you have a case. I estimate she died in the morning, and from the report, it said the boy estimated he left the home at around 8:00 a.m. I would put her time of death shortly after that, within two hours."

Detective Todd looked for a chair nearby and sat down, but not before he found a towel and covered the naked body of Samantha upon the table and said, "Doc, . . . Shit. This is a mess. What do you think happened?"

Hernandez said once again and shrugged, "Off the record, I think he pushed her down the stairs. She broke her neck in the process. Then, in a panic, he leaves the scene as he doesn't want to be the one to report the body. Let someone else find her, like the boy, I'm guessing. He may or may not have looked for his son, but it is not relevant, I suppose. No witnesses unless he suspects his son saw him do it, in which case, the boy could be in danger, but there is no way to prove it."

"Has the boy given you any indication he witnessed anything?" Hernandez asked.

Todd slowly replied, "No. He was pretty silent. I don't think he saw anything. I think I would know. But who knows, maybe he did see his father do it. Even if the father thinks there is a possibility that the boy saw him, he could be in danger. My hands are tied on this case." He asked again, knowing the answer, "So, Doc, can you give me anything at all?"

After a moment, Hernandez shook his head and answered, "Well, Detective, honestly, I think you are fucked. I don't think you have a case. There isn't a way to prove this one, and medically, I can't tie the husband to any of this despite my gut telling me he had everything to do with it. No jury would convict him. There is far too much *reasonable doubt*. I think you are done and done on this one, sorry Detective."

Todd muttered, "Damn, okay." Then he added, "I think I already knew the answer. I was just hoping you had come up with something. Sadly, if this is all we have, this guy is going to get away with murder, literally."

Hernandez just threw up his hands as if to say, "Oh well. The one silver lining is she did not suffer. It was quick for her. She didn't feel a thing."

Detective Todd slowly got up, stretched his legs, and said, "Okay. Thanks, Doc," as he strode out of the morgue and took the elevator back upstairs.

Detective Todd quietly entered the holding room where Sebastian was sleeping, still lying flat on the strung-together chairs. The poor boy had been at the station for over a day now. He shook him awake and said, "Hey, son, come with me. We are going to get you out of here."

Sebastian slowly got up, rubbed his eyes, and grabbed his belongings, which consisted of simply a backpack. They left the room, and the detective escorted Sebastian down the hall to holding #3.

Before opening the door, he looked at Sebastian and said, "Son, if you need me for anything, anything at all, you call me." He waved his card in front of Sebastian, then placed it into his backpack and zipped it up. "You hear me, Sebastian? And if your father ever lays a hand on you, you let me know," stated Detective Todd. "Yes, sir," Detective Todd nodded to the young boy and patted him on the head.

Reluctantly, Todd approached the entrance of holding #3, where, upon opening the door, his father was sleeping and contorted within the small chair provided to him. Detective Todd wasn't terribly concerned with Jonathan Storm's comfort.

Seeing his father before him, he was consumed with dread and remorse. Before entering the room, Sebastian looked up at Detective Todd, his eyes filled with betrayal, desperation, and sadness as he sulked into the room. "Mr. Storm, wake up, Mr. Storm . . .," Detective Todd said, using his foot a little harder than necessary to shake Jonathan awake.

As he opened his eyes, Jonathan was startled for a moment. "What, what do you want . . . Is my attorney here?"

The detective replied, "No, the attorney hasn't arrived, but it doesn't really matter at this point. But, here is your son, sir. Your wife's death was deemed to be an accident, Mr. Storm. You are both free to go."

Upon hearing the news from Detective Todd, Sebastian began to whimper as all he could think was, "Why . . . why would they let his father leave? Everyone knew his father killed his mother," as Jonathan was repeating, "Oh yeah, an accident. So tragic and sad. We will go to the mortuary tomorrow, Sebastian, so we can bury your mom properly. She deserves that much." He attempted to appear genuine for the benefit of the detective and his son, but neither believed him.

Barely acknowledging his suffering son, Jonathan Storm stood up and collected his jacket, displaying not a shred of sympathy or remorse could be read upon his face. He nudged Sebastian toward the door, eager to leave the police station before Detective Todd changed his mind.

As Sebastian walked through the doorway, he looked over his shoulder at Detective Todd as they walked down the long hall, disappointed and despondent but never letting his gaze waver.

Detective Todd watched as they both walked away, woeful for the boy, but at the same time, glad this case was closed. He gave Sebastian the option to call him if he should ever need him, but he figured he never would. Detective Todd offered all he could for the boy.

Still looking over his shoulder at Detective Todd as they neared the end of the long corridor, Sebastian finally turned toward the station's exit. He sadly glared at the detective for the last time, stopping at the turn before Detective Todd could overhear his father say, "Come on, Sebastian, let's go. I need a drink." And then, in an instant, he was out of sight and gone.

Detective Todd closed the door of holding cell #3. He was also closing the door on this young boy, closing the door on this child's unanswered questions, closing the door to what his mother deserved, and above all, closing the file on this case.

All would be forgotten and lost in the myriad of other cases stacked upon Todd's desk—uncaring, unwilling, and lost in the abyss of numerous other unsolved cases and yet just another statistic falling victim to a failed system.

But Sebastian would have his justice, his way, and in his time. Little did he fathom that he would have his retribution and his mother avenged far sooner than anyone could have imagined.

Schönbrunn Palace, Austria
Present Day

The speaker's tone signified the train was approaching the train station, waking Sebastian from his quasi-daydream. As he opened his eyes, the train was pulling into the stop for Schönbrunn Palace. He quickly looked over the other passengers as he sat in his chair to see if anything appeared irregular or threatening.

Hesitating momentarily, Sebastian stood up and walked to the train car egress but stopped short of the exit door. He let other passengers disembark to give him a moment to observe the flow and dynamic of the small crowd around him and other passenger cars. Very few got off at the stop, which helped him considerably in scanning the area and weary travelers.

Anyone potentially following him would stay on the train until his departure. If he waited until the last possible moment before disembarking, the simple measure would identify any would-be assailant(s) immediately. No one appeared suspicious entering or departing the train. He felt satisfied, at least for the moment.

When the conductor's final warning of imminent departure loomed from the dated speakers blaring above, and then the doors slowly began to close, Sebastian stood closer to the door and, at the last moment, stealthily slipped outside from between the doors on the train. He looked fervently around the area, observing anyone who may also be quickly departing the commuter train at the same moment in an effort to follow him. The train began to move.

He was the last to depart and confident he wasn't being followed. Nevertheless, he entered the small brick-and-mortar station building and paused meticulously, attempting to flush out anyone who could prove ominous to his well-being. Everyone appeared normal around the station as the train began to disembark.

Unknown to Sebastian, a man sat patiently and quietly upon the train, sporting an English cricket team–style cap, observing Sebastian from afar, watching him abruptly exit the train, but did not follow, stare, nor give Sebastian any attention or focus.

The man noted Sebastian's registered stop, yet inconspicuous, by discontinuing his pursuit. The man was patient, very calculated, and discreet. He was on the train simply for reconnaissance, watching and reporting only to Prim. His sole responsibility was observational only. This was Mueller's strict instruction from Tobias himself.

Sebastian stepped through the station to the curb and grabbed a taxi on the front curb. "Schönbrunn Palace, please," said Sebastian. "Yes, sir, about ten minutes, but you will be very early. They don't open for some time," said the driver.

"I'd like to be the first in line," replied Sebastian as the driver shrugged and said, "Suit yourself, mister," as he sped away from the train station toward the Palace entrance.

They rode in silence for a time; Sebastian drifted a bit and stared out the window, watching the Austrian countryside roll by—beautiful, majestic, and captivating in its simplicity, thought Sebastian. The rolling green hills reminded him of Roanoke, making him reminisce but also forlorn in recalling those memories.

His thoughts drifted to the altercation occurring the hour prior and his struggle to understand people's motivation. He considered those hoodlum's families, parents, friends, girlfriends, and even their children. They were lost and angry souls, but there seemed to be so many people made up of the same moral fabric these days. He struggled to understand people and their agendas as of late.

Sebastian knew at that moment, in just those few seconds, that he changed those men's lives forever in some way, whether positive or negative; he would never know. Though common criminals, people are just the same, and that moment was either a gift or not to each one of them. It all depended on what those men took from the experience that morning.

Their fate was forever changed when they met Sebastian Storm. They would never look at people the same way. A lesson was learned in those thirty seconds of time, and it would forever form and shape them. For better or worse, it all came down to what each of those young men decided to take from the experience and their decisions to become entangled with Sebastian Storm.

To a lesser degree, the old man, the victim in all this, would probably live high on life for a time, but the image of what happened would begin to fade and lose its vibrancy in the days following. Sebastian never overlooked the details; it never diminished for him, his images as vital and clear as if it all happened just the day before.

Looking back over his life, 231 people, 13 of whom were women, were directly terminated by Sebastian Storm for various nefarious reasons. He was responsible for a tremendous amount of death in his lifetime. It was a staggering number, by any measure, but he justified them all. . . . Each and every one. None were victims, all deserving of their individual outcomes.

This eased Sebastian's mind somewhat, but still, he did control each one of those people's destinies. He determined their existence, whether they lived or died, and by what method. He alone decided their fate.

The world was a safer place without them. At least, that was what Sebastian needed to believe. Their faces, in death, haunted him often, many dying violently but most quickly, painless, and humane even. Sebastian preferred things clean. He remembered each one of his victims distinctly, a collateral benefit of his photographic memory proving time and time again to be both the all too familiar blessing and a curse.

Sebastian was hallowed with an impeccable memory, recalling in vivid color and detail most of his life's experiences. The historical movies of days past would run continuously within his mind, reliving the experiences often. He blinked a few times and rubbed his temples, clearing his mind and shaking off the images filling his head.

His thoughts drifted off to something more positive. His mind wandered to Adriana, her soft skin, her inviting smile, and her captivating energy. Fantasies of a simpler life occupied his thoughts now, far more often, dreamlike in how they played out in his mind, but he wasn't deserving of that life; that wasn't his purpose. Sebastian wasn't worthy of such simplicity and had long ago accepted his fate and greater calling.

The car suddenly came to a stop, and Sebastian was shaken from his hazy thoughts as the driver turned and said with a sarcastic tone, "Schönbrunn Palace, mister. I believe they open in about two hours, so you should definitively be the first in line, as you requested, sir. Enjoy."

Sebastian paid the man, tipping generously, as he got out of the car and perused his immediate surroundings, looking for anything unusual. There appeared to be no one else around the premises. Even the Palace staff had not yet arrived. He made his way toward the entrance of the Schönbrunn Palace and onward to where he was to meet HB.

Sebastian was familiar with the Habsburg Dynasty summer residence. The estate was expansive and sprawling, with the 1,441-room mansion in the center of the property. The history of Schönbrunn and the buildings that previously stood on this site date back to the Middle Ages. From the beginning of the fourteenth century, the estate as a whole bore the initial name of Katterburg and belonged to the manor of the abbey at Klosterneuburg.

The immense estate boasted a corn mill and an arable farm and vineyards stretching over the neighboring hills surrounding the large 100-acre property. Over the subsequent centuries, numerous lessees are documented, including a reference in 1548 to one Hermann Bayer, the mayor of Vienna at the time. He extended and modified the property, transforming it into a substantial country estate.

The main palace exhibit wasn't open for another two hours, leaving little to no activity around the palace, which was precisely how HB preferred it. Sebastian proceeded cautiously along the south side of the property, where there was a large servant's quarters with horse stables adjacent, and it was where Sebastian had met HB in the past.

He arrived at 5:57 am. Sebastian was rarely late. He eased the door open to the stable and maneuvered himself in quietly. There were no longer any horses occupying the stables, and no one was around at the early hour. As Sebastian walked along the corridor between the two rows of individual stables at the end, he could see HB leaning against the wall, serious in her demeanor. She immediately stood upright and walked toward Sebastian. "Hello, Sebastian. Thank you for meeting on such short notice and so early," said HB, and Sebastian smiled.

"Of course, HB, I was up anyway. Did you secure the area?" asked Sebastian, always aware as he looked around.

"Yes, all secure. I got here about ten minutes ago." He smiled and then added, "You don't mind if I confirm while you talk, do you?" HB smiled back at him and responded, "Of course not Sebastian . I wouldn't have it any other way." Always on the job, always alert, thought HB. He proceeded to walk around the area as she spoke.

"I wanted to meet you remotely because I fear we may have a security breach, and I'm trusting few people within my employ these days. Tobias is mounting something substantial. Our intel is buzzing, but we can't figure out what his angle is as of yet, and that is what is worrying us."

"We suspect he is planning something somewhere in Germany, but there was still a lot of information unaccounted for, with our mixed and contradicting intel. He also appears to have a new head of security that came up in our search. A Nicholas Prim and his primary attack dog, Derek Allen, they refer to as 'Fury.' Are you familiar with either of them? We have very little information on either. Prim is prior MI6, dishonorably discharged, as was Derek Allen with the S.E.A.L.S., but not much else. I was hoping you may have something," explained HB.

Sebastian was heading up the stable stairs to the second level as he listened to HB speak but quickly responded, "No, I'm not aware of Prim, but if Tobias had anything to do with it, I wouldn't underestimate this Prim in the least. Derek Allen is a different story; Sean Woodford could probably shed more light on him. Interesting, they call him 'Fury' as he has quite a reputation from what I've heard of him. A hot head without question and fractured his Lieutenant's jaw, if I remember correctly, then was discharged dishonorably. A perfect disciple for Tobias's ranks."

HB responded, "Agreed on Tobias. His involvement cannot be a good thing. And as far as Fury and Prim, we have the same information." With a sense of concern on her face, HB said, "Sebastian, I'm apprehensive about this one. I think Tobias is planning something significant, possibly looking to make a statement now that he is at the forefront and no longer hiding his identity. It's almost as if he is taunting us or challenging our resolve, and we are all aware that he will most likely escalate his achievements for maximum effect. Our profilers suggest that he is mounting something significant to be recognized and prove himself as a major player to the world. Being fairly new to the scene, we haven't been able to locate Tobias's whereabouts, but we got a ping on Prim. HALO has found very little, so we are in the dark. He was last identified surfacing in Dublin, Ireland. I would like you to get there in the next week or so and stir up some trouble in that Storm kind of way." HB winked.

Sebastian looked over the top of the railing of the stable upper floor, and he responded, "My specialty, HB. I would be more than happy to." Their time was running short when HB said, "Good, I'll send you over the encrypted file we have on him and his operation and key players. Keep me updated per protocol. Be extra careful on this one, Sebastian. Until we figure out this mole, we need to practice every precaution. I have a bad sense this time, and you know I rarely feel that way about any mission, but Tobias will be more than content to have you removed from any equation and, preferably in a permanent way, I would imagine, based on your history with him. I'm fairly certain he would also prefer me out of the picture as well."

Sebastian smiled, hesitated for a moment as he descended the stairs out of view, and then said, "I know, HB. Tobias isn't good for anyone's health and is a 'new' thorn on the division's side, as well as my own. All of this explains a lot about the attempts to eliminate me in London and Vienna. I will be more careful in this case, but you know I always am, regardless." Sebastian was finally confident the area was completely secure as he approached HB.

HB nodded. "Yes, I'm aware, Sebastian, far more disciplined and methodical than any of my other agents. You never disappoint."

"You know me, HB, it's just the way I'm wired. I really don't know any other way," Sebastian shrugged and winked at HB, and she replied, "That's why I adore you, Sebastian. Your attention to detail is impeccable. Never a dull moment with you in the mix."

She started moving toward the stable door. As she opened the door, HB hesitated, then turned as if wanting to say something more. She decided against it and simply smiled and said, "I'll be in touch, Sebastian. Look for those files and be careful. You are far too important an asset for us. I don't tell you enough how much this Division needs you. How much I need you." She smiled once again and slipped out of the doorway.

Protocol dictated that all operatives never arrive and depart at the same time. Considering her last words, he realized much of why he did the work he did was for that woman. She saw the best in him, and he always appreciated it more than she would ever know.

Sebastian took a moment to think about his next step. He planned to leave for Dublin in the next week, but he had one more piece of business to take care of—Adriana.

Little did he know, he would never make it to Dublin.

Chapter 10

Captivated

Vienna, Austria
Present Day

Sebastian stepped off the train in Vienna at roughly 8:30 am after returning from Schönbrunn Palace and made his way to the street several blocks from his flat. The morning's earlier fiasco had long since been swallowed by the city's relentless rhythm, fading into a distant memory as the urban landscape transformed. With the dawn came a resurgence of energy; quiet streets awaken ed as businesses flung open their doors, ready to commence the day's endeavors.

The air buzzed with anticipation, the hustle and bustle of the city beginning anew. Shopkeepers arranged displays with meticulous care, the aroma of fresh coffee wafted through the air, and the once-still avenues now thrummed with the footsteps and chatter of people diving into their daily routines. The city's heartbeat quickened, each moment brimming with potential and the promise of new opportunities.

There was no residual aftermath from the debacle that occurred just a few hours prior. Sebastian was pleased that even the older man had seemingly taken his advice to get a warm meal and shower somewhere away from the vicinity. Sebastian speculated that by now, either the hospital staff or the police were handling the vagrants. He appreciated how life moved on, with the city transitioning smoothly from night's chaos to the structured bustle of the day. The streets were waking up, and the rhythm of daily routines reassured him. He thrived on this normalcy, finding comfort in the predictable flow of life.

Sebastian decided to take a detour and strolled the few minutes to the Hotel Sans Souci, where he and Adriana had met. He looked around in the reception area first to see if, by chance, he would catch her in the area, but she was nowhere to be found. He then made his way to the hotel's front desk and asked if he could leave a message for Adriana Mercer in suite 1802.

"But, of course, sir." The clerk handed him a pen, paper, and a small envelope. Sebastian wrote a short note, placed it within the envelope and returned it to the clerk, thanked him with a smile, and turned to leave the hotel before seeing a cluster of police by the lounge entrance with the area taped off. Sebastian hesitated, then turned back toward the clerk and leisurely asked what had happened in the lounge.

"Oh, that, tragic really, sir. We aren't advertising it, of course; it's a bit bad for business, but it seems that a gentleman was in a scuffle last night, and there was an incident of some sort. The cleaning staff found him late last night. Very peculiar, and the police are being hush-hush about it. Excuse me." He shrugged and turned back to another patron.

Far from a gentleman, thought Sebastian of his attacker as he exited the front revolving doors and headed down the street.

Later that morning, Adriana came to the lobby shortly before her business meeting and enjoyed her daily ritual, which consisted of a vanilla latte and a wheat bagel lightly toasted with a generous bowl of assorted fruit as an accompaniment.

As she basked in the tranquility of her morning, her thoughts drifted back to the previous evening with Sebastian. The memory was vivid, pulsating with the energy of their encounter. Though fleeting, their meeting had been charged with a thrilling intensity, igniting both their emotions and their bodies. The witty repartee between them had quickly transformed into a tantalizing dance of words, each exchange a spark that drew them closer. The chemistry was undeniable, an irresistible force that had carried them to the brink of surrender. Their connection was electric, leaving her eager to explore the depths of this newfound passion.

Adriana was certainly no prude, but she couldn't recall the last time she'd spent the night with someone she'd only just met. The spontaneity of her decision left her with a twinge of self-reproach. Yet, she was a woman guided by her instincts and unburdened by regrets. Each choice was a lesson, a step forward in her ever-evolving journey. She lived by a mantra that embraced boldness and introspection: decisions made were experiences to be valued, not regretted. Her life was a tapestry woven from the threads of her daring impulses and the wisdom gleaned from them, making her resilient and unapologetically herself.

Since losing her fiancé, David, back in college, she had learned to live life to the fullest, never looking back and always forging ahead. Her brief but stimulating interlude with Sebastian was no exception, and she couldn't help replaying much of the evening over and over in her head.

Sebastian Storm. Quite the enigma, thought Adriana.

Her curiosity about him was insatiable. Despite hoping that she had uncovered so much during their evening together, she sensed layers of mystery still veiled his true self, prompting even more questions as she pondered their encounter. One enigma that particularly intrigued her was his scars—each mark appeared to tell a silent story. Why were there so many? She suspected each scar carried its own tale, but the opportunity to ask had slipped away, and in hindsight, she wondered if it was for the best. She theorized he had been in the military as that would explain the injuries, yet he never mentioned serving in the hours they spent together, leaving her with even more questions than answers. If fate brought them together again, she hoped he would be willing to unveil more of his hidden past, satisfying her growing desire to understand the man behind the enigmatic facade.

Of all the magical moments that occurred the evening before, what stuck out most was how Sebastian made her feel. As she lay on his chest late into the night, she experienced an overwhelming sense of protection in his presence. This sentiment was new to her. She had never experienced the strength of it with anyone she had ever been involved with in her past. Something about Sebastian gave her an impression of contentment in knowing that she was safe with him and that nothing or no one could shatter that sensation.

"Excuse me, ma'am," a voice interrupted her reverie, snapping her back to reality. The hotel manager noticed her entrance into the foyer moments earlier and now approached with a blend of authority and courtesy. "Good morning, Ms. Mercer," he said with a polite nod, his voice tinged with urgency. "I apologize for the intrusion, but a gentleman stopped by this morning and left a note for you."

With a slight bow, he handed her the neatly folded note. Her heart quickened as she took it, curiosity piqued. "Thank you," she replied, her voice steady despite the whirlwind of thoughts racing through her mind.

The manager gave a courteous smile and excused himself, leaving her alone with the mysterious message. She unfolded the note, anticipation building as she prepared to uncover whatever secrets it held.

Once he left her table, she looked at the small envelope with the simple letter 'A' embossed upon the front. She turned it over and, opened the envelope, and unfolded the piece of paper. It read,

Dearest Adriana. Edvard Restaurant 8 pm, tonight, would like to see you again . . . if you have an interest. Don't be late. Sebastian.

The note was to the point, poignant, simple, confident, and mysterious, with a touch of arrogance and humor all at the same time. She reread the note once again and smiled. When she read his name at the end, she became slightly flushed and excited, hinting with a slight erogenous tingle at the thought of him and how he was able to stimulate all her senses and what he did to her the night before.

He ignited a flame deep within and allowed her to release all her carnal fantasies and desires. He understood her body well, and she longed to have him once again.

Adriana glanced around the bustling reception area, a flicker of unease crossing her face as she replayed the image of Sebastian in her mind. The vividness of her daydream startled her—she was fantasizing about him in the midst of a public setting. A wave of embarrassment washed over her; how could he have such an intense effect on her without even being present? Her cheeks flushed as she tried to shake off the distraction, but the allure of his memory was undeniable, leaving her both flustered and exhilarated by the unexpected power he wielded over her thoughts.

She imagined her sensation if he were standing in front of her at that moment. Adriana smiled inwardly, carefully folded the note and replaced it within its envelope, stood up, and proceeded to her meeting.

Dublin, Ireland
Present Day

Prim stared at his left hand, bandaged, and immobilized in a synthetic cast, his fingers painfully encased. The physical pain had become a dull throb, overshadowed by his frustration and self-reproach for failing Tobias. Each time he replayed the moment in his mind, he sensed a surge of anger and regret. Tobias had ruthlessly broken his fingers, and Prim had summoned every ounce of his willpower to resist the instinct to fight back. It wasn't just about self-control; it was about survival. He understood all too well that engaging in that battle would have been futile, especially with Fury, an imposing and menacing figure, lurking fervently behind Tobias that day. Prim's restraint wasn't born of cowardice but of a strategic mind understanding the broader stakes of that confrontation. The memory fueled his resolve, a reminder of the sacrifices and calculated decisions required in their treacherous world.

Prim realized his moment to prove himself was approaching. He had gravely underestimated Sebastian, a mistake that had cost him dearly. This time, his strategy had to be flawless, executed with surgical precision and unerring expertise. Failure was not an option; it would likely be his final attempt. Tobias had made it clear—there would be no tolerance for a third misstep. The stakes were higher than ever, and Prim's every move would have to be a masterstroke of cunning and skill. His survival and redemption hinged on this critical juncture, where one wrong move could spell his end.

Tobias's compound was state-of-the-art in every possible way. Planning the dwelling for over five years and taking an additional three years to build it was a sight to behold, from the expertly designed entry and exit to the layout of the compound in its entirety.

Tobias Teague's organization fell under the guise of a top international security firm, and with a vast amount of capital behind the organization,

Tobias had masterfully constructed the complex, shrouded in secrecy and precision. Every detail within the compound reflected his meticulous demands. The security was a marvel of ingenuity, seamlessly blending hidden and exposed cameras to create an impenetrable surveillance network. This web of watchful eyes was expertly positioned to thwart any infiltration attempts, rendering the fortress virtually invisible to would-be intruders. Each aspect of the dwelling's design showcased Tobias's unparalleled expertise, creating a stronghold that was as enigmatic as it was impregnable. His ability to build such a sophisticated and undetectable sanctuary underscored his prowess, leaving nothing to chance in this labyrinth of protection and secrecy.

The compound's security was unmatched, and with over a hundred men on site at any given time, it proved nearly impenetrable. The complex could withstand most aerial attacks, and a ground assault would prove difficult because of the labyrinth of halls and hidden doors along the myriad of walls and floors throughout the compound.

Tobias masterminded every aspect of his compound with impeccable precision, ensuring it was fortified against all adversaries. His offensive and defensive strategies were flawlessly integrated into the design, which he continuously updated with insights from his elite engineering team. By relying solely on his internal core designers, Tobias avoided third-party compromises, preserving the structure's integrity and its most enigmatic secrets. His relentless pursuit of perfection made the compound a fortress of ingenuity and security, impervious to outside threats.

The complex's location also proved a challenge for infiltrators, as it was difficult to approach the dwelling based on Tobias's myriad of redundant security sensors both below and above ground. In short, the complex was enigmatic in every way, and no attempt to infiltrate had ever been successful thus far, nor had any breach been suffered to date. Tobias was proud of that fact.

Prim was again cleared through Tobias's office security door accompanied by his SET force, per protocol. Tobias was copied on Prim's confirmation, and the main blast door began to open. Prim walked into the large spacious room along with his primary SET leader, Fury, and second lieutenant, Fist, who quietly took their positions at attention on either side of the door within the room.

A surge of dread came over Nicholas Prim as he entered Tobias's office, the memory of his fractured fingers still raw. Tobias stood before his expansive bulletproof window, a familiar stance. He often spent hours there, gazing out over the rolling hills, lost in contemplation. The view appeared to anchor his thoughts, allowing him to ponder the immense weight of his responsibilities. Tobias's brooding figure, backlit by the vast landscape, embodied the relentless pressure of his position, each moment spent in silent calculation.

Prim often wondered what went through Tobias's mind as he stared outward for what often seemed like minutes. After a time, without moving, Tobias said, "How are your fingers mending, Nicholas?"

Hesitating, Prim answered, "They will heal, sir." Tobias was the only person that called him Nicholas.

"Good," replied Tobias as he turned and sat in his chair before his large glass desk. Tobias fashioned a modern style, enjoying glass and stone décor. His office was primarily black-and-white with glass/acrylic furniture along with muted black/gray stone throughout. Iron accents finalized the finishing touches within the space.

Tobias studied Nicholas Prim intently, fists cupped to his mouth. "Nicholas," he began, his voice steely, "Sebastian Storm must be eliminated once and for all. He's a relentless thorn in our side, jeopardizing our operations. Our most critical mission is at stake, and I won't tolerate his interference. If he disrupts us, you'll be held personally responsible."

Tobias leaned in, eyes piercing. "You must eliminate him entirely and without fail. Can you accomplish the task?"

Prim responded, "Without question, sir," although deep down, he knew the task to be grim, at best, and that Sebastian had proven to be the most distinguished and elusive adversary he had faced to date. Nicholas Prim had a lot to prove to this auspicious group.

Tobias continued, "This mission is important enough that I am going to lend you three of my SET force guards, including Fury, behind you, my team leader. Fury, you up for the challenge?"

Fury stood tall and replied immediately, "Without hesitation, sir. Hoo-rah."

Tobias had a pet name for all of his SET force soldiers. Fury, being the leader, was where the tradition originated. Other elite soldiers within the team included Fire, Blade, Ice, Grizz, Hammer, and Nail (twins), and Fist, to name a few. Many of the names selected were based on an exacting attribute of that specific soldier.

Fist, for example, is exemplary in close-quarter combat, and Fury, when pressed or challenged, would go into a "rage" or "fury" like fighting mode, displaying talents with no equal. Tobias looked at Fury and said, "Fury, who would you select for this mission?"

Without wavering, Fury exclaimed, "The twins, sir. Hammer and Nail would be best for the sensitivity of this mission. The target will be terminated, sir. With extreme prejudice."

Tobias nodded, pleased with Fury's enthusiasm. "I appreciate the confidence, Fury. Nicholas, coordinate with Fury and complete the mission within the week. That's all. You're dismissed." He waved his hand, and Prim turned, heading for the door.

Tobias said softly, "*Gentlemen*, . . . don't fail me on this one, you hear me?"

Prim and Fury turned and in unison, and Fury said to Tobias, while at attention, "Understood, sir, we won't disappoint you." Tobias softly responded, "Failure is not an option . . . and good luck."

As Prim was exiting, Fist, standing at the door, said under his breath, "Third time's a charm there, rookie?"

Prim halted, glaring at Fist. "Care to repeat that?" he growled. Refusing to be the organization's punching bag, Prim had to make a stand. Fist had unwittingly volunteered to be his example.

With a scowl, Prim silently challenged him, daring Fist to make another comment. At this point, Tobias and Fury examined intently, curious how the situation would unfold. There was a general contempt around the compound concerning Prim's tenure and performance thus far.

"You heard me," said Fist confidently, standing a little taller. Prim had enough and lashed out with a right elbow, catching Fist by surprise, landing squarely on Fist's nose, knocking Fist backward and off balance.

Fist was sporting his MAT suit sans the helmet, thus suffering the full impact of the blow, staggering from the strike. Prim maximized the opportunity by sending an open palm into Fist's throat, stunning him further. Fist quickly recovered, though disoriented, and swung wide as Prim quickly sidestepped the assault and responded with a quick combination of his right and left jabs to Fist's face. Having the nimble advantage, Prim was all too aware that body blows would do minimal damage against Fist's armor.

Fist's specialty was close-quarter combat, but Prim held his own, eluded all of Fist's attempts, and would counter with significant damage to Fist's face, driving him to one knee.

Tobias and Fury curiously observed the display, both impressed with Prim's physical prowess against one of their more talented SET soldiers. In a last effort to turn the tide, remaining on one knee, Fist lurches upward with a powerful uppercut, but Prim is ready despite being in close proximity.

Prim dodges left, causing Fist to miss. Rotating to his left, Prim smashes his left elbow into Fist's face directly, then jumps up in a spin kick that lands directly in the middle of Fist's upper torso and sends him ten feet backward and onto his back.

Prim immediately jumped on top of him and delivered four rapid-fire punches to Fist's face while lifting him off the ground with his casted left hand holding Fist's armor collar with his exposed and uninjured fingers.

Fury viewed intently and at attention as Tobias finally said, "Enough!" as Prim's right hand was cocked and poised for yet another blow to Fist's face had Tobias not stopped the melee. Fist's head slumped, beaten severely and heavily dazed.

Rage in his eyes as if he had something to prove, Prim stared at Fist intently, just waiting for him to resist. Prim leaned down and said in Fist's ear, "Next time, be man enough to say it to my face, or don't say it at all." He dropped Fist's bloody head to the ground.

Nicholas Prim was no stranger to combative warfare or aggressive aggression of all sorts. Recruited and trained at a young age by MI6 and British intelligence, Nicholas Prim was naturally gifted when it came to mission planning. Exemplary in close-quarter combat, very few bested him in his illustrious career.

After seventeen years of distinguished service with MI6, his career came crashing down in scandal. He was dishonorably discharged, his reputation in ruins, after it was uncovered that he had brokered an illicit arms deal with the Taliban, pocketing a substantial profit. The news sent shockwaves through the intelligence community, transforming him from a respected operative to a pariah overnight. The betrayal was a stain on his legacy, a dramatic fall from grace that left him grappling with the aftermath of his actions and the shadow of his former life.

Many of the agents had taken kickbacks or bribes over the years, but his particular station chief decided to make an example of him while trying to clean up the image of their branch. Unfortunately for Prim, he was targeted as their scapegoat. Sadly, he was at the wrong place at the wrong time. It was an immediate career-ending infraction and left him with enormous talents but without an organization that appreciated his abilities until Tobias approached him and offered him a high-ranking position within his own organization.

After he was exposed, Prim found himself excommunicated and disavowed from his homeland and sought refuge in the private sector where he could fully practice his given talents.

Fist's taunting gave him the perfect opportunity to prove his worth to Tobias and Fury and hopefully buy some time to alter his performance. "Quite impressive, Prim," said Tobias as Prim simply nodded and, without hesitation, exited the room, leaving Fury to work out the specifics of this challenging mission. No need for Prim to gloat or reminisce. He simply wasn't going to take idle comments from anyone.

"Fury!" said Tobias, as Fury turned at the door to face him at attention. "Get someone to clean up this mess."

Fury responded, "Yessir." They walked out the door. Fist remained unconscious, bloodied, and motionless on the floor.

Vienna, Austria
Present Day

Sebastian stepped through the main entrance of the Edvard Restaurant at 7:50 pm, punctual as usual. The restaurant was dimly lit and possessed a tranquil and charming ambiance.

He quickly scanned the premises, cataloging each individual, recognizing no immediate threats within the area.

He gradually made his way to the restaurant lounge, dressed in a gray-black herringbone jacket, black pants, and shirt. Sebastian entered the lounge, surprisingly eager, unexpected in its rarity, at the thought of seeing Adriana again. She brought out a cavalier, almost rash sense of self in him, which he had seldom experienced in the past.

He smiled inwardly; the notion seemed like a delicious rebellion against his typically self-controlled and disciplined persona. It was a tantalizing, defiant release that he found both thrilling and necessary. Adriana had unwittingly unlocked this part of him, and the sensation was intoxicating. He craved more of this newfound freedom, this exhilarating departure from his usual restraint. Her presence had stirred something deep within him, awakening a curiosity and a hunger to explore the boundaries of his own desires and the potential of what they could share.

It wasn't only about the physical allure; it was the emotional liberation she offered, a tantalizing glimpse into a world where he could let go and embrace the raw, unfiltered parts of himself. Adriana had opened a door, and he was eager, almost desperate, to step through it and see where it led.

As he approached the lounge, he spotted her immediately at the far end of the bar. She sat with her back to him, a glass of white wine in hand. Her dark, custom-made dress, cut to midthigh, hugged her curves perfectly, highlighting her elegant silhouette. The soft lighting accentuated her form, casting a seductive glow that made her the center of attention. His pulse quickened as he drew closer, the memory of their last encounter intensifying his desire. She exuded effortless grace and powerful allure, captivating everyone around her, but it was him she had truly entranced. The sway of her hips and the confident tilt of her head stirred something deep within him, a magnetic pull he couldn't resist. Reaching her side, he marveled at her blend of sophistication and visceral sensuality, a perfect mix of mystery and allure that promised an unforgettable evening.

He paused, lingering in the shadows to study her for a minute or two. She hadn't noticed him yet, allowing him the rare opportunity to observe her unguarded. He took in the sight with a quiet intensity, appreciating every detail. Her mannerisms were graceful, her posture effortlessly elegant, and the way she carried herself exuded a captivating confidence. The gentle way she lifted her glass, the subtle tilt of her head as she listened to the bartender, and the occasional, thoughtful smile that played on her lips—all of it mesmerized him.

A waitress approached, ready to take his order, but he simply waved her off, unwilling to break the spell of the moment.

Sebastian wanted to absorb everything about her, to savor the way she commanded the room without even trying. The ambient noise of the lounge faded into the background, leaving only the visual symphony of her presence. His mind raced with thoughts of their last encounter, the electric chemistry that had sparked between them. The moment seemed more like a prelude, a tantalizing promise of what was to come. He recognized the magnetism drawing him closer, an irresistible pull that spoke of passion, mystery, and uncharted depths. As he continued to watch, he imagined the conversation they would have, the laughter they would share, and the secrets they might uncover.

Every second heightened his anticipation, making his eventual approach all the more thrilling. He wasn't just admiring her beauty; he was captivated by the essence of her, the enigmatic allure that made her unlike anyone else. And in that suspended moment, he noticed the surge of exhilaration, knowing that soon, he would step out of the shadows and into the vivid reality of her world.

It was then that he noted the intoxicated businessman serving the lines to her in hopes of something more possibly occurring between the two of them. She behaved respectfully, of course, but clearly, her tolerance for the man was diminishing, hoping to be rescued, he surmised. She was still unaware of Sebastian's presence thus far, and he enjoyed the amusement of it all.

Entertained over the thought of this inebriated buffoon attempting his advances on her without the desired result, Sebastian smiled, although impressed with the man's dedication and vigor devoted to his plight. It almost appeared admirable on some level, the diligent commitment the man was making in his attempts to win the affection of Adriana. She wasn't having any of it and, in his state, was oblivious to her disinterest.

Sebastian continued watching her carefully, enjoying her, studying her, valuing her as she reacted to this man and his foolish attempts to have his way with her. Far too intelligent and crafty, she was simply killing time, hoping the painful encounter would end soon for her.

By this time, Adriana was growing impatient, wondering why Sebastian hadn't arrived to rescue her from the increasingly belligerent businessman. Sebastian, meanwhile, was captivated by her stunning long hair, full lips, and even the smallest of her movements. Her poise and elegance mesmerized him, and she fascinated him on multiple levels.

Sitting at the bar, her legs crossed, she exuded sexual aptitude and grace without even the notion of trying to attract such attention. She possessed the epitome of control and mystery all in one.

His gaze narrows as he identifies her focusing in and out among the people entering and exiting the area, looking for Sebastian to emerge, clearly growing more wearied with the bothersome gentleman with every passing minute.

Adriana remained unaware of Sebastian's presence, as he had intentionally stayed out of her line of sight. Unable to bear her discomfort any longer, Sebastian decided to intervene. He carefully approached, moving into her blind spot with deliberate competency.

His goal was to surprise her, so he advanced from behind, each step measured and intentional.

She almost sensed him, aware of his presence, and before he could touch the small of her back as he took in her scent. She must have anticipated his touch and slightly turned to see him as he leaned over her left shoulder between her and the looming businessman.

It all seemed to unfold in slow motion. She smiled, a mix of elation and relief washing over her as she finally saw her prize standing beside her. Adriana took him in, unable to resist his charm, though she knew he had her at a disadvantage. No words had yet to be exchanged.

He acutely aware he was interrupting the conversation, which was his only objective. Adriana was vaguely engaged within the tête-à-tête but more than relieved by the intrusion Sebastian provided, and his timing was impeccable, not surprisingly.

Playing coy, Sebastian casually asked if she was there with anyone or alone, his mild interest accompanied by a soft smile. She met his gaze and replied, "Why, no, I'm not. I'm here all by my lonesome, actually." The businessman glared in disbelief at her response, trying to regain his composure to assert his claim.

The imposing businessman, desperate not to lose his opportunity, made a final, determined attempt to claim his prize. With over twenty minutes invested and his ego at stake, he turned his attention to Sebastian, his eyes flashing with horror and offense. It was as if Sebastian had breached some sacred gentleman's code.

In a feeble effort to regain his position and not lose face, the weary businessman tapped on Sebastian's shoulder and began to open his mouth to speak. With that, Sebastian raised his hand, immediately stopping him, effectively cutting him off, and said, "Save it," refraining from even looking at the man to invalidate his efforts.

Sebastian kept his hand raised and looked at Adriana, asking, "What do you think of the idea of getting out of here?" The businessman, stunned by Sebastian's audacity, began to protest. Sebastian, undeterred, tilted his head slightly towards Adriana, waiting for her confirmation while implicitly dismissing the man's objections.

Adriana politely yet firmly said with a wink, "Yes, please, I would love to go anywhere with you." Then, referencing Sebastian, she turned to the man who had been pursuing her and said, "No offense, but I don't believe you could compete with this in the slightest, but thanks for entertaining me and the drink, of course. Have a nice evening." She grabbed Sebastian's hand, leading him away from the bar, leaving the confused man angry and speechless as he simply allowed them to leave, perplexed over what had just occurred.

She guided him to a remote table in the corner, dimly lit and secluded, just what she was hoping to find for the two of them. The waitress stopped by their table, letting them know she would return for their selection in a few minutes.

They settled in next to each other this time, more intimate in proximity. Sebastian gazed upon her, and she said, "I was so glad to get your note today and even more excited once I read it. But I must say, you tortured me, forcing me to talk with that disgusting man for so long, Sebastian. How long had you been here before coming to my rescue?"

Chuckling, Sebastian said, "A few minutes, honestly. But it was so entertaining for me to watch the show. I believe he thought he had you all 'locked up' a few times there." He gave her a wink as she squeezed his hand gently, already letting him off the hook, "Oh, I was far from locked up, though tied up sounds nice," as she winked.

At that moment, the inebriated man from the bar began to approach them. Having reclaimed his composure and appreciating the full effect following the shot of bourbon, he had downed at the bar, regaining his liquid courage to its full capacity to make one final effort to claim his trophy.

Apparently, still upset and frustrated over losing his entitled reward, the man staggered up to their table and slurred, "She was with me, man." Struggling to maintain his balance, the man desperately battled to maintain his calmness and composure, but pride and ego can drive a man beyond mere reason and consequence.

As the man approached, Sebastian was already rising from his chair. Adriana placed a gentle hand on his arm, silently urging him to be gentle. In a calm, low voice, Sebastian said, "Sir, she is with me." The man, shaking his head in defiance, retorted, "No, no, no, you swooped in and took her; I'll show you." He half-heartedly swung at Sebastian. Effortlessly sidestepping the attempt, Sebastian let the man swing and miss, dismissing the feeble effort with ease.

With Sebastian's back to Adriana and partially obstructing her field of view intentionally, he responded with a short and quick pump of his knuckle into the man's sternum, causing him to lose his breath. Sebastian's left hand held the man's right hand fast while his right hand then quickly located the man's jugular vein and pressed firmly, depriving him of the oxygen he desperately needed.

All Sebastian needed was a few moments to achieve his goal. Paired with his intoxicated nature, the man became lightheaded and began to lose consciousness. Sebastian eased him into a nearby chair as his slump ensued and then eased his chair to the small table adjacent.

Adriana eyed Sebastian intently, concealed from the exchanges between the two men, but he handled the man with poise and respect. She thought it peculiar that Sebastian was so at ease in handling the more prominent man. He was effortless in his execution and seemingly unfazed by the altercation.

The businessman simply had too much to drink, and Sebastian was agreeable enough to help him as he began to pass out from her perspective. However, she still saw enough to note that Sebastian was more than comfortable with the calamity. Sebastian made eye contact and nodded to the bartender indicating they had a patron who needed assistance.

He quickly returned to his seat and assured Adriana that the man was fine but very soused and that the manager and bartender were on their way. "He will be fine, just a little too happy this evening, and well, you were just too much for him, frankly. Poor guy never had a chance. You got him all excited, Adriana." She smiled at his smooth charm and wit. He always had an answer for everything she thought.

Sebastian looked deep into her blue eyes, mesmerized at how intent she kept his gaze. She smiled at him, knowing there was so much more to this man than he let on. She guessed she had not even scratched the surface but was content in the bits and pieces he let her see of him thus far.

The waitress returned, saw the man several tables over being tended to, smiled, and asked what their selections were for the evening. Sebastian ordered a vintage bottle of Bordeaux, and they laughed and teased each other for the next hour as their sexual tension heightened. The connection intensified, their union unbroken and analogous, matching well in the wit and banter exchanged between the two of them.

She stroked his arm and was far more attentive and affectionate than he was accustomed to. Her legs were crossed, but she tingled and twitched from the excitement and electricity mounting between them. She couldn't help but speculate about the exchange between Sebastian and the drunk man who harassed them earlier.

The effects of the two glasses of wine were beginning to have their effect, and, on a whim, she asked, "Sebastian, I'm so curious. How did you handle that man so well? What did you say to him? He looked outraged. I mean, you did steal his prize from him, and that whole scenario should have gone sideways, don't you think?" She always possessed a curiousness to her.

Navigating her question with precision, he had to tread carefully around those unfamiliar with his unique abilities, which could easily perplex the unsuspecting observer. This caution was especially crucial with someone as perceptive as Adriana. "He was pretty inebriated, and I've found that those types are usually easy to persuade into non-action. The power of persuasion, when wielded correctly, can be quite compelling, Adriana." She looked at him quizzically, contemplating his answer. After a moment, she smiled, seemingly satisfied with his explanation, and thankfully moved on from the topic.

She leaned over to Sebastian and said, "That makes sense, given his current condition. I have a confession, Sebastian. I've been aroused for you since you rescued me."

At that moment, she slowly uncrossed her long tan legs. Sebastian studied her intently, eyes connecting as she took his hand in hers and gently, deliberately, slid his hand between her thighs, inching him closer to her moist inner sanctum. The secluded corner of the lounge presents a perfect position as they have an optimum vantage point of the restaurant, but few people could see them, certainly not clearly in the dim light.

The incident with the inebriated businessman had long passed; he had been escorted from the area quietly, and as a result, they were virtually alone. Her legs opened more as he explored her with his fingers and finally came to that inner moisture that she was yearning for him to feel and appreciate.

Her legs eased subtly wider as she began to sit up, allowing him better access. His fingers became sticky and slick from her wetness, damp with anticipation of feeling him deep inside her once again.

She fantasized as he subtly appreciated her smoothness, teasing her, and she whispered, "I want you again, Sebastian . . . Your fingers are nice, but you know what I want. I desire the magic of what that beautiful, well, you know . . . the excitement only you can give me . . . . and harder, please."

At that moment, her hand slid over Sebastian's thigh effortlessly yet deliberately. She appreciated the leanness of his muscles and toned body she felt under his shirt and pants as her hand drifted further between his legs just as he entered his second finger into her moist fold, knowing and fantasizing about what he wanted to do to her.

She smiled, loving the effect her body was having on him and how he made her feel physically, bringing her womanly senses to a sensual peak deep within.

Her legs were fully open at that point, and he smiled at the thought that she was once again without panties and could feel her wanting him to pleasure her fully and in every way. He could sense all of her desire, making his want for her even more.

Her hand then reached her goal as Adriana could appreciate his thickness through his slacks, making her reaction intensify at the thought of his manhood thrusting in and out of her was all she could fantasize about. They could both see the waitress making her way back to their table, so they subtly adjusted themselves so as not to be as compromised when she approached them.

Once she reached the table, the waitress could obviously see the attraction between her two guests and noticed Adriana's hand on the gentleman's lap as they said they were still looking at the menu.

The waitress left, and Adriana turned to him and said, "Sebastian, let's get out of here." She adoringly squeezed Sebastian's thigh as they began to stand up. "Perfect," he replied as they grabbed their coats, placed a few bills atop the table, and slipped quickly outside the side entrance into the alleyway with Adriana leading. The waitress later turned to see them leaving.

Once outside, Sebastian grabbed Adriana and pulled her to him firmly against the alley's brick wall. She looked up at him with her sultry eyes and once again said, "I want you . . . now, Sebastian." She grabbed Sebastian's hand and led him further down the alley.

It was a warmer evening than the night before as Adriana had exchanged Sebastian's hand for his arm, still in silence, as they stopped beside the alleyway brick wall, confronted by the rush of the evening air.

Sebastian turned to her as they stood and said, "Aren't you hungry, Adriana? They had the most well-prepared Alaskan—"

She abruptly cut him off. "No, Sebastian, honestly, I would like to skip right to dessert. I've decided . . . *you are the only thing on the menu.*" She led him into a dark, dimly lit part of the alley and pulled him to her with the brick wall to her back.

A light rain began to fall, and Sebastian was thinking to himself . . . rain. It always appeared to follow him. Dismissing the thought, he pulled her close to him decisively, powerfully, yet passionately. She remained unfazed by the sprinkles as they began to descend lightly at first upon them. They didn't have a care, as they were in their own world and reality. Their desire transcended any concern for rain, people, or geography.

She craved his energy as he kissed her abruptly and fervently, drawing her into his world and the enigmatic aura that surrounded him. Everything else faded away; all she wanted was him. As she gazed into his eyes, nothing else mattered. He ignited her deepest carnal desires, commanding her full attention and focus on that electrifying moment.

Adriana had ached for him over the last day in so many forms. She needed him like a drug, and she didn't care about the consequences, though deep down, she anticipated there would probably be many she would need to process, but at that moment, all she wanted was him, craving his male essence.

His hand drifted to her waist as he pulled her closer to him. She felt his firmness on her thigh and became further aroused at the thought of him and what he would do to her in that alleyway.

As if she needed to confirm what she already knew, Adriana began to feel him with her hand as the back of his fingers brushed the rain dropping from her cheek and came to rest lightly around her throat. She embraced his control and succumbed to his desire and strength to manage and manipulate what he wanted of her.

He kissed her again as he began to tighten his grip slightly, and she responded zealously, anticipating, and wanting more from him. She was helpless, his paramour, to have as he wished. She wanted nothing more nor expected it, his concubine to cater to his every desire. She savored his grip upon her neck, not soft but also not too firm as it held her to him, and she wanted it, and he knew it.

Feeling him still growing, she began losing control now and succumbed. She must have it, have him, all of him. She needed it. She desired it. She loosened his belt buckle and unbuttoned his pants to reveal her treasure hidden within.

Was it just the night before he took her, taking her to places she had never experienced before? It seemed so long ago. She ached for him in just those twenty-four hours. Adriana missed it and enjoyed how it felt within her hand as she encircled him and remembered his size as she stroked him, stimulating him further. She had to taste him. She had thought about it the entire day.

Adriana bent her knees and eased down, legs open, knees apart, crouching until she teased his tip with her tongue. Her dedicated hours spent at the fitness center practicing yoga and cardio were certainly paying off, allowing them to both benefit from her devotion to that endeavor. Looking up at Sebastian as she took him further within her mouth, deeper and deeper, tasting with a methodical rhythm, and, in doing so, she felt him growing still further inside her mouth, inciting her feminine essences further, knowing she was ready for him.

The rain fell upon her face as she savored him, enjoying the sensation of the cold drops pitter-pattering over her skin as she increased her cadence. Slightly moaning, Sebastian was finding it difficult to concentrate with Adriana fulfilling every sensation, and he relished in how truly pleasant she felt as she utilized all of her talents.

Adriana brought him almost to the point of climaxing before Sebastian eased her off him, bringing her up to his face, standing again, kissing her, tasting himself on her lips.

The rain began to fall heavier, but they cared even less now. In that instant, he turned her around abruptly as her body and hands were pushed against the brick exterior wall of the building within the alley. They were both saturated from the rain as her dress clung to her body, outlining her curvaceous figure, the cold making her nipples erect as he squeezed them firmly.

He kissed her neck as his right hand eased lower, drifting to her stomach, then still further down, finding the spot between her legs, roused and creamy from his touch, wet with anticipation, her left hand reaching around to stroke what she knew was still there and ready for her. She enjoyed his hot breath on her neck as he stimulated her.

Sebastian lifted her dress, again appreciating her neglect of panties that evening. She repositioned her legs, allowing them to open slightly further, and arched her back further, elevating her rear more, wanting him, inviting him.

Seeing the roundness of her firm backside, he had the urge to taste her, unable to wait. Crouching down further as his tongue followed the curvature of her exposed rear, she instinctively opened her legs, inviting him in and enjoying his tongue as she felt where it was headed as she lifted her rear higher, allowing him to savor all of her sweetness. The rain fell upon his lips as they softly met her moist folds, bare and completely smooth, tasting her warmth upon his tongue.

She loves what he does to her, bringing her ecstasy to another level and pushing her limits of control as she ultimately explodes and gyrates, her spasms intense and fulfilling. Sebastian tastes her warm vanilla wetness flowing over his tongue, enjoying her scent, and arousing him further as he takes his last savor before rising and kissing her neck again.

She feels his firmness against the back of her leg and knows what he wants next. She slowly reaches behind her and finds her target immediately, stroking his tip for a moment, then begins to rub him against her creamy sanctum, inviting him inside her. She began to guide him to her opening and enjoyed his tip as it hovered around her moist present, lubricating it entirely with the aftermath of her orgasm.

Bending over further, she was gushing now from her arousal mixed with rain as she took in a little more of his tip, moaning over how he felt. He used that moment to firmly stuff her full of all of him, making her moan as she took him in further. Her eyes widened as she accepted all of him, loving the aching she was experiencing as he slid himself all the way inside of her, his hands resting on her hips as he pulled her up and back towards him.

She curved her back slightly to take in all of him as he began to allow her to enjoy every thrust rhythmically. She closed her eyes to concentrate on all of his length as she enjoyed the pounding and collision of his hips into hers. Adriana's face was angled upward, making the moment surreal as the rain fell upon her face and exposed rear, cold and sharp as the droplets fell upon her exposed skin. She loved how her body responded to Sebastian and how it fell in sync with everything about this mysterious man.

The rain was in a full downpour at this point, and she could sense him tightening, his pace quickening, knowing he was about to fill her full with everything he had left. She was utterly wanting, needing, and desiring all he was giving her.

He pulled her away from the wall, allowing some space as she pushed the back of her head up, causing her hips to extend upward to get him as deep as possible as he let loose all his energy, filling her with his seed deep inside of her now, letting her womanliness drink up every drop as she moaned in climax a second time, finally satisfying both of their erotic urges. His own spasms were strong and forceful as she took in all of him. They enjoyed the moment until she needed to see his face again.

He turned back to face him, knowing he was totally in control now, held her close for a moment, kissed her neck, letting the rain fall in the moment, then backed up a half step, hands on her hips, putting himself back together as she stood up straight, and eased her dress back to its former self and position, wet from head to toe.

She turned and kissed him and said, "Now, I'm hungry and very, very . . . wet! How does room service sound?" He smiled, loving the idea. She looked at him intently and softly said, "We are something else, Sebastian. I just cannot get enough of you. I haven't felt, nor wanted it like this in a long time. You make me feel free, thank you for that," as she smiled at him.

He looked at her, conflicted and torn as the rain continued to fall, yet neither of them appeared to notice. He touched her face with his hand, her face and hair soaked from the rain.

Normally, hearing these words from a woman would prompt Sebastian's immediate exit strategy, but, in this case, it made him want to hear more. He wanted more from . . . *her*.

He replied after a moment. "There is something extraordinary about you, Adriana Mercer." He smiled, touching the side of her face as he looked into her eyes.

"I think we could say that about both of us, Sebastian," she said as she winked at him.

"A warm bath sounds about perfect. Plus, it's an excuse to get you out of those wet clothes," he suggested, and she nodded in agreement as they walked out of the alleyway and then raced back to the hotel several blocks away.

Adriana hung up the phone, having completed her room service order. She wore a sheer black robe that accentuated her features beautifully. She had opened the chilled bottle of champagne provided by the hotel the day before. She poured two glasses and then headed towards the bathroom, flutes in hand.

Hearing the faucet running from the tub in the large bathroom, she slowly made her way through the open French doors and saw that beautiful man before her.

He stood there with his back to her, slightly bent over, wearing only a towel around his waist. His hand tested the running water as it flowed over his fingers. She smiled at the sight of his focused yet humble stance, engrossed in his task of filling their tub to perfection. The simplicity of the moment coming full circle.

Her smile relaxed slightly as her gaze traced over the numerous and extensive array of scars scattered across his back—too many to count. Each mark told a silent story, adding layers to the enigma that was him. This part of him puzzled her, starkly contrasting his otherwise composed demeanor.

Slowly, she walked towards him, her eyes mapping the intricate landscape of his back. He was fixated on the running water, his thoughts clearly preoccupied. She sensed the depth of his internal focus, almost as if he were trying to wash away more than just the day's grime.

As she neared, her fingers lightly traced the largest scar on his shoulder, her touch soft and exploratory. The contrast between the rough texture of his scarred skin and the smoothness of the rest of his back fascinated her. The contact was electric, a silent communication passing between them.

He didn't flinch, but she observed a subtle shift in his posture, acknowledging her presence. The room appeared to shrink around them, the air thickening with unspoken emotions and curiosity. Her fingers continued their delicate exploration, a mixture of tenderness and desire fueling her movements. She wanted to know every story, every battle that had left its mark on him. The lines and scars were the pathway to his past making her realize there was so much more to Sebastian Storm.

He had only partially heard her as she approached him, but then relaxed, knowing it was her, maintaining his position realizing what she must be thinking. His scars were raised and visible, his emblem of war and death yet unknown to Adriana. She softly caressed the numerous other scars, some long and thin, several small and round, all irregular in shape. She appreciated them now with both hands as he allowed her to touch his healed wounds from behind as he continued to test the water flow over his hand. No words were exchanged but none were necessary in that moment.

He assumed she would have many questions, and she certainly knew there was a story behind them. Those scars. His badges. She came closer, her hands gently wrapping around his waist from behind. With a soft, almost mournful whisper, she said, "Tell me . . . "

His eyes closed, the weight of her words pressing heavily on him. He had anticipated this moment, knowing it would come, and sensed the sadness of the countless stories he had never wanted to share, now silently rising to the surface.

Sebastian slowly turned, looking down into her eyes, and brought his lips to hers, softly touching them with his own, enjoying her taste before letting them part, his right hand stroking the side of her face.

"I have a history, Adriana, a complicated one," he began, his voice heavy with melancholy. "There is a lot to explain, a tremendous amount of pain in my past. The pain I've endured and torment I've inflicted." He paused, his fingers grazing the scars. "These scars are my memories. Some might call them medals of valor, but to me, they are reminders of my darkest moments." His eyes met hers, filled with a sorrowful plea. "I know I owe you the truth, but please, trust me for now. I promise, in time, I'll share everything."

And that was all she required; she didn't have to understand at that moment, but his authentication of her request was enough for now, enough to know that he was something significant.

Changing the mood, she smiles, "Well, we have a little time before room service arrives. Do you have any ideas of what we can do to kill time until then, Sebastian?" He smiled back at her, lifted her with both hands, and replied, "I can think of a few things we can do, or at the very least, what I can do to you."

Carrying her as she straddled him, Sebastian walked over to the sink and sat her down on the counter. They kissed for several seconds as her cover opened up, exposing her completely. He eases the sheer garment from her shoulders as it drops to the counter.

She looks up again and smiles, putting her hands on his chest and feeling the scars for a moment before her hand eases to his waist, and she slowly undoes the knot of his towel. . . .

. . . . as it fell to the ground.

Chapter 11

A Threat Cometh

Dublin, Ireland
Present Day
8:23 AM

Standing over the tactical planning grid, Prim and Fury discussed the strategic options for best dealing with Storm. Recent intel confirmed Sebastian's last known whereabouts were in Vienna, Austria, several hours' travel from their current location.

Hammer and Nail entered the war room in their MAT suits and took their place on either side of Fury.

Observing the SET force was impressive. Their protocol and hierarchy were impeccable in form, positioned opposite Prim and Fury out of respect for the senior officer in the room.

Prim was fascinated with this group beyond words and appreciated their dedication and aptitude when it came to planning a mission. With this elite team supporting him, he had a significant chance of eliminating Sebastian Storm once and for all.

The proper names of the fraternal twins, Hammer and Nail, were Shura and Andrei, from Tayshet, in the northeast region of Russia. Prior military training included the Russian special forces, Spetsnaz, specifically for five tours before pairing with Tobias's organization over the preceding five years.

The twins only had two more years until their mandatory retirement. Tobias, so named Shura, "the Hammer," because of his sheer blunt power in combat and his large stature equaled that of only Fury. When sparring with Shura, Tobias had to outsmart the larger man tactfully, his strength well above average, and his impact truly "hammerlike" in its damage to any adversary. He was aptly named for that reason.

On the other hand, his brother earned the name "Nail" for his distinctive combat technique, characterized by short, precise, and rapid melee attacks that struck with the force and precision of a piston. Every movement Nail made was like a finely tuned machine, delivering blows that felt like piercing strikes. His mastery of martial arts was unparalleled, with a unique blend of speed and accuracy that made him a formidable opponent.

Nail's combat style contrasted sharply with his brother's but was no less effective. While his brother relied on brute strength and overpowering force, Nail's approach was about finesse and precision. His attacks were methodical, each strike calculated to exploit vulnerabilities with pinpoint accuracy. This divergence in their fighting styles made them an unpredictable and lethal duo, each complementing the other's strengths and covering their weaknesses.

Their combined prowess was a testament to their rigorous training and inherent skills, making them an indomitable force on the battlefield. Nail's agility and surgical strikes paired seamlessly with his brother's raw power, creating a dynamic that was both intriguing and terrifying to their adversaries.

Hammer was a tall man, towering an impressive six feet eight in height, whereas Nail was smaller at five feet eleven. Both ominous and formidable, respectively, especially when in combat together. They both had an intense loyalty to Tobias and Fury and were effective in executing any given strategy.

Dissecting the intel, Hammer pondered the information before him for a moment and spoke first in his thick Russian accent "This handler of Storm's, Hillary Bastini, is the key to his demise, in my opinion. If Storm is difficult to locate or terminate, we may be able to gain some benefit from his loyalty to her and capitalize on this flaw he has exposed. It appears he will protect her at any cost, and we can take advantage of the infirmity."

Shura was correct on this point, although it is generally not an easy feat to obtain Deputy Director Hillary Bastini. Sebastian does appear to have a soft spot for HB, and they could exploit this and plan to do so if the need arises. Sebastian respected HB enormously and would not allow any harm to come to her. If need be, she would be utilized to lure him to them.

It was determined the best course of action would be to take Sebastian at night or early in the morning when he would least expect it while alone and in a position to limit any of his defensive options for escape. If he were not alone, anyone with him would also be terminated—no loose ends.

Nail responded, "We could also attempt to take him straight away, but that has not gone well in the past with this man. He is an admirable and worthy opponent."

Prim added, "My man in Vienna had been watching him closely, but Storm is also elusive and difficult to keep up with for any length of time. As a result, Mueller has only obtained scattered pieces of intel suggesting his whereabouts, although he has narrowed it to 7–8 lofts within a small sector of the city.

We are closing in on him and his exact location, which we hope to have within the next few hours. We may have another player in this, a woman, an American, it seems, was seen with him as well two nights ago. Mueller happened upon this over a hunch he had in Vienna and is looking into her involvement as we speak. He simply has only a name. . . . Adriana Mercer."

"My man there was able to locate and report Storm meeting with her before my operative was terminated. He was one of my best, and Storm took him out with ease in the lounge water closet. Sebastian Storm has made this personal for me now."

"It will take a few days to track his routine further, but Mueller is preparing to receive us in Vienna. We need to act as if we have a short window or run the risk of Sebastian leaving the city at any time or Mueller being detected at any moment."

Fury then stepped forward, his tone firm and commanding, "Gentlemen, we'll be outfitted with our KAM suits for this operation. These suits will give us a technological edge, but remember, our adversary is far from ordinary. He is a combative benchmark and exemplary in skill—unpredictable, unorthodox, and extraordinarily dangerous. His methods defy convention, and he anticipates standard tactics, making him a formidable opponent.

"Underestimating him could be fatal. He doesn't just think outside the box; he operates in a realm where the box doesn't even exist. This man has evaded capture through sheer ingenuity and adaptability. His proficiency in guerrilla tactics, his mastery of covert operations, and his psychological acumen make him a unique threat.

"Every move we make must be calculated with precision. Stay vigilant, trust your training, and utilize the full capabilities of your KAM suits. This mission demands our absolute best. Do not, I repeat, do NOT underestimate this man. He has turned the tables on seasoned operatives and will not hesitate to do so again."

Fury's eyes scanned the room, ensuring the gravity of his words sank in. "We need to be one step ahead at all times. Anticipate his unpredictability. Use every ounce of your training and every resource at your disposal. This mission will test our limits, but together, we will outsmart and outmaneuver him. Stay sharp, stay focused, and above all, stay safe. Let's bring this man down."

"He is a master in all facets of combat, and if engaged in a scrap, he will quickly ascertain any of your weaknesses, you can be certain. There is no one better at determining an adversary's flaws than Sebastian Storm. "

"Whether it be from a specific combative vulnerability to exposure in any of your tech, he will use anything to exploit you and use it to his advantage. For example, when he determines your KAM suits are partially resistant to his attacks, he will quickly move to an exposed region on the body, such as the head or neck, to eliminate you."

"In short, gentlemen, we must not engage this adversary for any lengthy duration, and best if we work together to eliminate him. Make no mistake, Sebastian Storm operates at the highest level."

"He is at the technical combat level of Tobias. To be clear, we have all experienced the pain of sparring with Tobias in training, so do not underrate this opponent, or he will swiftly eliminate you."

"Hammer and Nail, you will run point on this, and I will be back up. Prim will run logistics from here, along with Mueller, our on-site contact, in Vienna. Are there any questions? No? Good, get it done and quickly. Happy hunting."

Later that evening, Fury and the twins left for Vienna in Tobias's Gulfstream.

Vienna Austria
Present Day

As the first light of dawn began to filter through the curtains, Sebastian eased himself out of bed, his movements calculated and silent. The warmth of the bed and the intoxicating allure of Adriana's presence made every step away feel like an act of defiance against his own desires. He loathed leaving her side, but the prospect of an unspoken morning conversation loomed like an impending storm. Sebastian was not one for emotional navigation; the intensity of his feelings for Adriana was uncharted territory, and he was unsure how to proceed.

Adriana, with her sharp intellect and perceptive nature, no doubt struggled to reconcile the mosaic of scars and injuries that marred Sebastian's otherwise sculpted physique. Each mark told a tale of violence and survival—knife wounds, contusions, fractures, bullet scars—stories that begged the question of why he bore them and what dark past they hinted at.

The morning sun cast a soft, golden glow on the room as Sebastian slipped out, his departure as quiet as the dawn itself. Adriana lay peaceful, her beauty undisturbed by the secrets he carried. The nights they shared were charged with an electric passion, leaving both spent and sated, yet yearning for more.

Sebastian's heart pounded with the conflict of wanting to stay and the necessity of leaving. His mind raced with thoughts of Adriana—her laugh, her touch, the way she made him feel alive in ways he hadn't felt in years. As he closed the door behind him, he couldn't shake the image of her tangled in the sheets, a vision of sultry elegance and intelligence. The memory of their night together, filled with whispered secrets and fervent embraces, stayed with him as he stepped into the cool morning air, ready to face another day with the weight of his untold stories pressing heavily on his mind.

Adriana was an enigma for Sebastian.

Sebastian knew he had to end it, as he always did—abruptly, without remorse, without looking back. But with Adriana, it was different. She made it difficult on so many levels, complicating his usual resolve.

She possessed every trait that ensnared him—keen wit, a sensual and seductive allure, an intoxicating recklessness, mischievous charm, intelligence that sparked his curiosity, and an intrigue that kept him wanting more. She was a flawless enigma, and that scared him more than he'd care to admit.

For now, he forced her from his thoughts, focusing on the more immediate issues at hand. He couldn't afford distractions, especially not from a woman. Adriana was a liability, a vulnerability that gnawed at him, but what troubled him more was his own indifference to this newfound weakness. The anger bubbled within him, directed at himself for allowing such feelings to take root. His attraction to Adriana was a betrayal of his own discipline, a crack in the armor he'd spent years fortifying.

The way she moved, the way she looked at him, her every word and gesture—they were all a part of the spell she unknowingly cast over him. And yet, despite the danger she posed to his focus, he couldn't help but be drawn to her, like a moth to a flame. The thought of severing their connection felt like a substantial personal loss, a necessary but excruciating act.

But he had no choice. He had to remain steadfast, let go of the tantalizing blend of sultry elegance and sharp intellect that Adriana embodied. His mission required it, demanded it. As he steeled himself for the inevitable, he couldn't help but feel a pang of regret. Adriana had shown him a glimpse of something he hadn't realized he craved—a genuine connection, raw and real.

Shaking off the lingering thoughts of her, he redirected his mind to the tasks ahead. Adriana might be a siren calling him to distraction, but he was determined to resist, to break free from her spell and maintain the cold, calculated distance that had always been his shield. Yet, even as he resolved to do so, the memory of her touch, her laughter, and the fire in her eyes haunted him, a constant reminder of the weakness he could no longer afford.

Revisiting the café down the street, he entered and proceeded to the same table he had occupied a few days before.

As he waited for the waiter to take his order, he couldn't help but notice the copy of Outdoor Life hunting magazine lying on the table in front of him.

He smiled, familiar with this specific publication from years past. Ruminating out of some sense of nostalgia, he opened the magazine, perusing through the pages for a moment before coming to an old, familiar, and memorable page he remembered well. The page displayed an ad specifically bringing him to the heart of his childhood.

He placed pressure on the page to open it flatter, reading the headline, "*Trapping Humanely Is the Manly Way*." This is where it all began for Sebastian so many years ago.

Roanoke, Virginia
1995

Detective Todd sat at his desk, wondering about the insignificance of the young boy, Sebastian; his mother's autopsy file opened before him. Detective Todd knew deep in his heart there was far more to this story than had come to light. Jonathan Storm had dodged a bullet, so to speak.

He eased back in his chair, staring at the folder for a minute, then closed the file, reached into his drawer, and found the rubber stamp with the words labeled "File Closed Date" on top and stamped the cover of the file.

He grabbed a pen from his top drawer and filled out the date as August 23, 1995. He returned the rubber stamp to the lower drawer where he had found it and threw the file into the "out" basket, along with the two other files he had dealt with that same day.

He preferred closed files, less work, and less to deal with, yet he felt a pang of deep-seated guilt creep into his subconscious over Samantha Storm's death. It just didn't add up, but he couldn't argue with the evidence. He didn't have a case, and he and Jonathan Storm, both knew it.

Detective Todd pushed back his chair, slowly stood up, picked up his jacket, and left for the evening. Happy hour never sounded better than at that moment, and he was eager to forget that particular day. The memory and the details of the day's events slowly faded as the sun began to set in the west.

Sebastian sat quietly in the backseat of his father's car as they drove in silence. Watching the countryside pass by outside the window as they drove, Sebastian was trance-like, numb to everything around him.

He looked briefly at his father and was painfully aware of his callousness as they meandered through the forest roads during the short ride back home. His father didn't appear upset despite having just lost his wife, yet Sebastian's world was shattered.

Finally, after nearly twenty minutes, Sebastian's father said, "Things are going to be different around here, now, son. Without your mom, you will need to do a lot more around the house. You will have less time to trap your rodents. It's time you start to grow up and become a man. The house will need tending to while I'm working, do you hear me?"

Young Sebastian slowly replied, "Yes, sir." "But they aren't rodents." He thought.

Jonathan continued, "Yesterday, boy, were you in the mountains the entire day?"

Again, the young boy replied, "Yes, sir."

Soon after, they arrived at their home. Jonathan parked the car in the driveway, got out of the car, and went inside, leaving Sebastian in the car alone. Slowly, Sebastian opened the car door, grabbed his backpack, and sauntered sheepishly up the patio stairs, but not before noticing one of his traps lying along the side of his home, which made him think of his mother, and his eyes began to tear up once again.

He ascended the porch stairs and entered the home. Almost immediately, his attention focused on the end of the hallway and the bottom of the stairs leading upstairs, where his mother had rested on the floor, immediately saddened at the thought of her lifeless body.

A small, dried bloodstain remained on the floor where she had lain. He immediately went to his room, closed the door, and lay atop his bed, staring at the ceiling, confused about the turn his life had taken so abruptly.

He could overhear his father speaking with someone on the phone and cowered as he stormed out of the house a few minutes later, slamming the front door, not saying a word to Sebastian before leaving. The car started outside with a roar as he revved the engine, and then his father drove off in the direction they had come only minutes before.

Sebastian often found himself haunted by the shadow of his father's contempt, a dark cloud that loomed over his past and bled into his present. He wondered endlessly why his father despised him with such intensity. Yet, intertwined with that confusion was a deep-seated hatred of his own—a burning resentment for the man who had cast a pall over his childhood, treating his mother and him with a cruel indifference that bordered on malevolence.

The most damning memory he couldn't shake was the image of his mother falling down the stairs. Sebastian was certain his father was behind the accident, exploiting the fact that Sebastian had fled to the mountains in a fit of rage and desperation. There had been no witnesses to the event, leaving a gaping void filled with suspicion and unresolved guilt.

His father's disdain was a relentless tormentor, whispering accusations and self-doubt into his mind. Each scar on his body was not just a mark of his battles but also a testament to his father's disdain, an unspoken message that he was never enough, never worthy of love or respect. It fueled his determination, but it also stoked the fires of his anger and resentment.

He recalled his father's cold, lifeless eyes that seemed to take pleasure in his suffering. His father's words were like poisoned darts aimed at wounding and belittlement. His mother, a beacon of warmth and love, had always tried to shield him, but her strength had its limits. The day she fell, the day her light dimmed, was the day Sebastian's heart hardened irrevocably.

As Sebastian grew older, he channeled his pain into a fierce independence, carving out a life on his terms, far removed from the toxic grasp of his father's influence. But the scars, both physical and emotional, remained. His relationships were fleeting, his connections shallow, a protective mechanism to avoid the vulnerability that had once nearly destroyed him.

He couldn't afford to let his guard down, not now, not ever. His father's lessons had been brutal, but they had forged him into a survivor, a warrior with a heart encased in steel.

Sebastian secretly abhorred the police for not arresting his father immediately and assumed he had talked his way out of it, as he did with everything else in his life. His mother needed to be avenged, and his father punished for what he had done.

Sebastian dropped his backpack on the floor and lay on his bed. His eyes were heavy now, fighting back his tears, exhausted from his plight, beginning to drift in and out of slumber. Sebastian hadn't gotten much sleep in the past two days. He began to doze off at the thought of being alone and away from his father, which brought him solace in some way as he wandered deeper into sleep.

Shortly before 8:00 p.m. on the summer night, Sebastian was startled and awakened by voices upstairs. The sun was beginning to set, the light was beginning to diminish, dusk would be coming soon, and the impending darkness would soon follow.

He slowly rose from his bed, confused and groggy from his nap, and made his way to the hall, then continued to the home's stairway, fixed on the dried blood his mother had left behind, once again a recurring reminder she was gone and would never return. He missed her voice and scent already. A calming element for him, his entire life. . . *now forever gone.*

Even though his mother's body was no longer there, the dried blood was left as a reminder for him as he stood in front of the staircase, looking at the stain and reminiscing of her agony at the foot of the stairs.

He proceeded into the kitchen to get two towels and a bucket from under the sink. He filled the pail with warm water, threw the towels in, then returned to the base of the stairs where he sat before the pool of dried blood, legs folded, and thought of her. He kept hearing voices, but it was unclear from where they originated. He suspected his parents' room.

Sebastian reached out with trembling fingertips and touched the bloodstain. It was raised and firm, coagulated into a grotesque circle the size of a softball. This blood was hers, the last physical part of her, and the realization hit him like a tidal wave. Tears welled up, each drop a silent prayer for her soul, hoping she had found peace.

His mind flashed back to that fateful moment just days before, to the lifeless body that had once been his sanctuary. He had been too late to save her, overshadowed by his father's cruelty. The bloodstain was a stubborn reminder of his failure, a testament to the violence that had scarred his life.

In his grief, a fierce determination ignited within him. He vowed to dismantle his father's legacy, piece by piece, to bring light to the darkness that had consumed them both. He would honor her memory not only with tears but with action.

With a final, lingering touch, he withdrew his hand. The path ahead was uncertain and fraught with danger, but it was a path he would walk in her name, ensuring her suffering had not been in vain.

He pulled the bucket of warm water closer to him and spilled some over the dried blood, letting it soak for a moment, then took the large towel and began to scrub the floor. Crimson began to saturate the white towel. Amazed over the amount of blood he had soaked up; Sebastian rinsed the stained towel within the bucket a few times before being satisfied all the blood had been removed from the floor.

He then reached for the unused towel to dry the area thoroughly but realized that after scrubbing for a few seconds, the towel was now fully stained, the blood seeming endless in its supply, having soaked into the underlying wood floor.

He scoured diligently until he was satisfied it was clean enough. Sebastian slowly got up, leaving the bucket at the base of the stairs, and returned the towels to the hamper by the washer, where he routinely found his mom working away cleaning up after her family. She often washed the soiled clothes from his mountainous adventures as well as his father's dirty uniforms from work. She had always taken such good care of them, but those days were gone.

He initially detected the laughing and movement of furniture in his parents' room above, confused by it all. The hall was still dimly lit by the passing day. Off in the distance, he heard his father in the bedroom upstairs, the room he used to share with his mom. This time, though, he was speaking with someone and laughing; then, he detected an unfamiliar woman's voice in response to his father's. The voices confused him. Who could possibly be visiting at this hour, he wondered.

His immediate thought was his mother was upstairs and this was all simply a terrible dream. He contemplated this, bewildered for a moment, then came the woman's laugh, different from his mothers in many ways. The wave of reality struck him hard at that moment—the woman's voice and laugh were not his mother but rather someone else entirely. He realized his parents never laughed, and this was his absolute true existence, no dreams but rather a nightmare as sad and disastrous as this scenario playing out before him.

His eyes began to fill with tears and rage again as he ambled back into his room. Without thinking, he abruptly opened his closet door, grabbed his baseball glove and bat, and closed the closet door as he had done a thousand times in the past. He stopped short of his bedroom door, hesitated, deliberating, disoriented, and thinking momentarily about his situation. He realized he didn't need the baseball glove and threw it on the bed but retained the bat as he blustered through the door, down the hall, stepping over the bucket filled with bloody water, and continued up the stairs where he came to his parent's room. It was only his father's room now, he thought peculiarly.

Hugging the bat tighter, he slowly tried the knob; it was unlocked as he gently turned the knob and pushed the door open further. Standing, his father had his back to him, shirtless, giggling and teasing a woman he had never seen before but partially obstructed by his father's body, making her unaware the door had opened.

She was straddling him, topless as well, with her arms crossed around his neck, holding a beer bottle in one hand, shifting her weight to one side, allowing her scope of vision to expand. She instantly locked eyes with Sebastian, startling her, and then he heard, "Wait, who . . ." as she let out a soft scream and hopped out of Jonathan's hands and immediately to her feet.

At that moment, Sebastian's anger neared its peak. He began running toward his father, his baseball bat lifted and ready to strike as he moved, but his father's experience and size were no match for the young boy charging with mindless rage.

Years of barroom brawls had made Jonathan aware and versed with various weapons, blunt or otherwise. Sebastian swung wildly, and Jonathan, anticipating the swing, swiftly turned and caught the bat midair, fisting the shaft of the bat and bashing it into Sebastian's face. The strike didn't catch Sebastian squarely, but enough to throw him backward onto the floor, the right side of his face slightly lacerated on the cheek from the blow.

As Sebastian backpedaled and crawled through the opened door, Jonathan gripped the bat held over his right shoulder in a baseball batter's stance while walking swiftly toward Sebastian, his expression angry and determined. Sebastian had just entered the door frame when Jonathan's wrath came full circle, and he began his downswing immediately and possessed just one intention—to kill or cripple anyone in its path.

In his anger, Jonathan misjudged the arc of his swing, catching the top of the door frame instead of his intended target, giving Sebastian a moment to gather himself and quickly hop up and run down the stairs, skipping the last two. As he hit the main floor, he sidestepped the spot out of respect, as if his mother's lifeless body still sat crumpled at the bottom. Within seconds, he was out of the door to the mountains, his safe haven, his sanctuary. . . . .

His escape . . .

Jonathan hurled the bat to the corner of the room, turned, and grabbed his shirt that had been thrown onto the bed. As he put his shirt on, the woman whimpered, "What's his deal?" Ignoring her, he reached the closet door, opened it abruptly, and grabbed his shotgun and two shells. Jonathan snatched up his jacket with his other hand as he ran toward the bedroom door.

He stopped, looked at the woman, and said, "He's going to the woods, I'm sure. It's time to end this; finish it all. I want a new life and end this one once and for all! Stay here, Paulina. I'll be back after dark. I only have about 45 minutes until I lose the light." He headed down the stairs quickly, hitting the last step, kicking the bucket, and spilling the bloody water all over the floor. He stared at the bucket, then kicked it again, sending it down the hall in frustration, and proceeded out the front door.

Jonathan began jogging down his driveway, shotgun in hand, looking for Sebastian. A quarter mile ahead, he could barely see him as he approached the tree line and disappeared into the forest a good two minutes ahead of his father.

Jonathan stopped for a moment to catch his breath and looked for any signs of the young boy, but he was already entered the tree line. He began running again, noticing the light was fading.

He arrived at the edge of the forest and began running into the thick canopy, ascending the incline, clutching his shotgun, and heading in the direction where he suspected Sebastian may have gone, but this was Sebastian's domain, his lair, and no one knew the terrain better than he.

Jonathan was now entering Sebastian's world. Stopping and slowly turning and seeing his home in the distance, Jonathan began realizing this pursuit may prove a grave mistake. It was not his arena. It was also when he realized he had forgotten a flashlight, an essential item, as the sunlight faded by the minute and the dark cover of the forest began to close upon him. He forged ahead, determined.

Sebastian understood and respected the mountains and their intricate landscape very well. Although he had several options in locations, he did not choose the obvious primary camp location in an attempt to avoid his father altogether.

He selected a spot close to his second favorite perch where his vantage point was more idyllic. He observed the expansive forest landscape along with the natural corridor formed by the terrain, funneling anyone entering into the channel, and he suspected his father would be no exception. By choosing this spot, he was able to keep an eye on him and track his progress. It also provided far more escape routes in the event his father saw him, and he was forced to evade shotgun pellets.

In the early years, Sebastian had expertly laid his traps and encountered, on occasion, a trap torn apart from the evening before by a larger animal. With blood splattered about, he surmised it was a black bear searching for food, and a "trapped" animal was nearly perfect and easy prey for larger animals. He simply had only to get him out of the box, and the trap proved little challenge for the strength of such a beast.

This frustrated Sebastian because he always caught and released any animals his traps would ensnare. It was simply the sport of the hunt for him to capture, but he was always happy to let them go. As expected, in these situations, the animal was usually killed in the process of the bear locating the trap and tearing it apart to get the animal within.

As a result, Sebastian devised an elaborate bear trap that would safely and humanely attach itself to the bear's foot upon pressure being applied, activating the trap. The apparatus was designed to be cumbersome but not injure the animal in any way, inhibiting movement substantially but confusing the animal thoroughly.

This snapping action and fixation of the heavy metal trap upon the bear's foot and ankle would deviate his attention from the trapped rabbit and meander away in frustration at having this weight firmly fixed to his foot until it was released remotely.

At one point, months before, a ranger on patrol came about the camp and questioned Sebastian about his traps, "I think the Chief would probably like to see this thing, young man. Do you mind bringing it by and discussing it with him?" Said the ranger to Sebastian, replying, "Of course, ranger, I would be happy too," Within a few days, Sebastian and his mom set up a time to meet with the Chief Park Ranger, elaborate trap in tow.

Sebastian set up an arrangement with the park service/ humane society to discuss his traps well before using them, and the agreement was set forth that it was permissible by the rangers to use, provided:

(a) The chief Ranger inspected and approved the apparatus.
(b) The trap was humane in all forms, not capable of hurting the animal.
(c) Fixate a small tracking device (activated upon the trap's movement) so the bear can be monitored, sedated, and relocate the animal to a better location before safely removing the ankle trap.
(d) The trap could be deactivated and released with a remote trigger system.

Late that afternoon, Sebastian delivered the specialized trap to the park ranger's office to inspect the apparatus. They were impressed with the design.

The Chief Ranger, James Woodford, inspected the contraption and said, "Young man, this is impressive! The remote system and locking mechanism are relatively simple to disarm with your special hex-shaped tool that won't hurt the animal. I like it. And what is the weight of this thing?" He lifted it from the table with some effort and then set it back down. "A hundred pounds or thereabouts, I'm guessing?"

Excited, Sebastian replied, "Yessir. And look, Ranger, it won't hurt the animal, even if they thrash about, and it lies just under the leaves, so they won't see it. The bear will be completely surprised until you guys sedate the animal, capture him, remote disarm it, and move him to a better place." Sebastian was beaming excitedly and was very proud of his invention as the ranger applauded his efforts.

"How old are you, son?" he asked.

"Twelve, sir." Replied Sebastian. The Ranger continued, "Your parents must be so proud of you! You remind me a lot of my son, Sean. You two could be brothers with the same drive and verve through and through. Maybe one of these days, we could patent this and sell it; what do you think? What would you call it?"

Sebastian smiled as he had already considered this and replied, "*The Bear Hugger*, sir. You think people would want to buy this ranger?"

The ranger straightened up, smiled, and patted Sebastian on the head. "Ha, great name, and yes, I believe they would, son. I have no question. There is nothing like this out there. Spot on, young man, just perfect. We have needed something like this for our bears around here. You let me know when you have made it just right, worked out all the kinks and such, and we will patent it, okay? And creative name, by the way!" The ranger left the room, and Sebastian loaded the trap onto his wagon with one of the other rangers.

Ranger Woodford saw Sebastian's mother in the reception room, walked over, and said, "You have a sharp boy, that one, ma'am. He will go a long way. I talked to him about a business deal when he is ready and has any issues worked out with his trap."

Samantha responded, "Why, thank you, Ranger, I am very proud of him. He has put a lot into that little project of his."

Ranger Woodford smiled and walked down the corridor to tend to his other duties. Sebastian emerged with his wagon and trap and brightened when he saw his mom and said gleefully, "Mom, the ranger thinks I can sell my trap and said he would help me. Isn't that awesome?"

Samantha replied, "It sure is, Sebastian. I think you should when you are ready and have it perfected. I love that it doesn't hurt the animal." Smiling, she watched her son proudly as he eased his trap out the door and to their car, navigating the wagon. She looked at him adoringly and was certain he would achieve tremendous things in his lifetime.

She simply needed to get him raised and out of Roanoke forever. That's when she would leave too, she thought and smiled inwardly; they would both finally be free of their prison.

They drove the short distance to their home late in the afternoon. "I'm so proud of you, honey," she gloated. "You are so smart. You have so many incredible things to look forward to in your life. I'm a fortunate mom to have the luck of having such a tremendous young man as a son."

Sebastian smiled when she praised him and replied, "Thank you, Mom, I am glad I have you. Thank you for always wanting the best for us and supporting me and my funny *'rodent'* traps." They laughed together with a twinge of sarcasm directed toward Jonathan.

Their conversations never involved or mentioned Sebastian's father, but it was in these moments they always cherished each other. They had a tremendous bond, the two of them. She just had to insulate Sebastian from him until he was older, and then, someday, he would protect both of them.

When they got home, Samantha pulled into the driveway and parked. Together, they eased the trap back onto the wagon from the back of the car and rolled it up to the front of the house.

Shortly after, as the evening approached, Sebastian's father returned home from the day in a particularly unpleasant mood derived from work's daily issues and stresses. He saw the trap atop the wagon in front of the house, stopped before it, shook his head, and kicked it over, disgusted. He climbed the patio stairs two at a time, yelling, "Boy! Hey boy, get that damned contraption out of the yard before I burn it!"

Sebastian's mom came to his rescue, saying to Jonathan, "Please settle down, Jonathan, he will move it. Sebastian worked on his trap for a long time. Please don't break it. You should be proud of him; the ranger thinks it's very unique and special. You should be happy for him."

"Proud of him?" Jonathan screamed as he approached Samantha. "That thoughtless hunk of metal is just a shit pile for me to clean up and deal with later! There is nothing unique about it at all."

Attempting to settle him, she softly said, "Please, Jonathan, he is only a boy—" Without any warning, he struck her with the back of his hand, sending her to the floor, her lip cut.

Sebastian heard the commotion and opened the door of his room, taking a step forward, looking down the long corridor, and seeing her bloodied face. She feared for him and waved him off with a motion to go back inside his room, attempting to protect him from his father.

Thankfully, Jonathan was looking in the other direction and wasn't aware of her warding Sebastian off. The pain Sebastian saw in her eyes broke his heart, physically hurting as if he was in the room taking the beating himself. He was certain if he were able, he would kill the man right then and there, but his age limited his understanding and strength, and he succumbed to the fear he had for his father. He remembered feeling helpless and weak as a result.

Samantha Storm was more afraid Jonathan would turn his wrath towards Sebastian. If that ever occurred, there was no telling what may follow or what Jonathan Storm was capable of doing to the young boy.

She hoped she could sway Jonathan's anger and rage to be focused solely on her and to keep Sebastian safe from him. Sebastian understood far too well and gently closed the door, knowing she sacrificed so much for both of them, her life forfeited for the sake of sparing his own. She was the most incredible woman to him, truly his champion.

Sebastian adored her for her bravery, and it was in that valor he pulled his own strength and gallantry in the years following. He knew at that moment he should not interfere, but he would have his moment someday, and the vengeance would be swift and unrelenting.

As the door closed, the yelling seemed to fade away, replaced with tears. Like so many times before, he drifted to that faraway place.

Chapter 12

His Mentors Emerge

Vienna, Austria
Present Day

"Sir? Excuse me, sir?" said the waiter to Sebastian. The waiter simply smiled, knowing everyone had those moments from time to time.

Sebastian shook his confusion off quickly, regaining his reality, smiled, and replied, "Forgive me. I would enjoy a coffee, black, simple. That's all, thank you." The thoughts of his childhood sometimes replayed like a movie within his mind, causing him to daydream far more than usual as of late.

The waiter laughed slightly, catching his patron unawares. "Looks like you could use it. That little pick-me-up is sometimes all we need to get back on track." The waiter smirked with a wink as he left to place the order. Sebastian was polite in kind but didn't need the lecture accompanying the order. The man was simply making conversation.

It was a different waiter from his prior visit, which he preferred so as not to be as easily remembered. Being predictable was a dangerous element of his craft, angry at himself for returning to the same place twice, but he enjoyed the familiarity and ambiance of the café.

Sebastian immediately scanned the premises, evaluating each individual as before. Only three other patrons were enjoying their morning ritual, giving themselves a sense of amnesty, if only for a moment. His clouded judgment provided him a momentary sense of relaxation, which he rarely afforded himself.

His focus settled back on the opened page in the copy of Outdoor Life as he finished appreciating the all-too-familiar ad. "Trapping Humanely Is The Manly Way."

The page featured a fierce, snarling bear, mouth wide open, sporting razor-sharp teeth and claws that could tear a man in two. This image draped the page, displaying the black bear's dominance and ferocity.

Shown on the same page, lower and to the right, was the same bear, docile and relaxed, emotionally sedated by the trap-like boot with the name *Bear Hugger* stamped in the middle of the page. The name he had created from his childhood for the trap had somehow stuck, and he was proud of that fact.

Little did he know at the time, but his concept created a market tipping point, developing a niche for Sebastian and James Woodford in the years following.

Sebastian smiled inwardly. His little contraption ended up paving the way to immeasurable success and financial windfall for Sebastian in his early adult years.

He exited the café and walked past the seat Adriana had occupied several days before when he first met her, after which she dropped her invitation to him.

He thought of her and smiled. He was missing her and was longing to see her again.

Roanoke, Virginia
1996

It had been roughly nine months following the death of Sebastian's parents, and Ranger James Woodford stopped into the Roanoke Orphanage as he often did several times a week and headed to the front desk. He smiled at the receptionist, who had been there for over twenty years and said, "Hey, Susan, here to see Sebastian. Is he around?"

"I'm sure he is, Ranger. Hold on. He is probably holding court somewhere around here, as usual." James Woodford laughed and waited for a minute or two as Sebastian came running up the stairs and saw James hovering around the front desk.

"Hey, James," he said as he ran up and gave him a big hug and smiled most genuinely. They had become close over the prior year, and James was fascinated by Sebastian and his maturity.

James was a widower, fifty-six years old, and had been hired as the youngest Chief Ranger in Virginia at the time, holding the post for over fifteen years. Prior to the ranger post, James Woodford was in special operations for the military for twenty years before retiring. That part of his career he always kept quiet about and didn't disclose much about those days.

He had seen a lot in his time, enlisting in the Marines early in life. He was a veteran of the Vietnam War, touring from 1965-68, mainly performing with covert and special operations. Quickly climbing the ladder and involved in black ops soldier training, he had finally had enough and opted out of the life, never looking back. His wife and new family had become his priority.

James and his wife, Bethany, had a son of their own named Sean, but Bethany died of complications during childbirth. Sean, who was twenty-one years old, was very close to his father, and in turn, James was incredibly proud of his son. Sean had never known his mother, but his father had more than compensated for the two of them.

A highly decorated Navy SEAL sniper and accomplished in his own right, Sean Woodford was already making an impressive name for himself in the Navy, finishing top in his class in SEAL training in San Diego, California, an elite soldier by any measure. This distinction more than elated his father.

James was immensely proud of Sean, and the resemblance between Sean and Sebastian deepened that pride when he met Sebastian nearly two years ago.

Sebastian had entered the ranger station with his mother, eager to present his invention—a uniquely designed, safe bear trap. His enthusiasm and intelligence were evident as he explained the trap's intricate design, which balanced practicality with humane considerations.

James was captivated by Sebastian's ingenuity and passion, seeing in him the qualities he cherished in his own son—intelligence, creativity, and a drive to make a difference. This connection grew into a valued mentorship forged through shared interests and mutual respect.

Sebastian's invention was more than just a bear trap; it symbolized potential and promise, reminding James of the enduring impact one person could have on another's life.

Sebastian lost both of his parents within a day of each other in a bizarre twist of fate, and James couldn't avoid the sense of sadness for the young boy as he did for Sean for never knowing his own mother. It was a tremendous amount for the boys, or any child, to endure at such a young age.

Sebastian had developed significantly in those few months; he had grown taller and broader with that boyish grin that could light up a room. Sebastian was a handsome, charismatic young man, and everyone he encountered gravitated toward him. James was certain Sebastian would not suffer from any social limitations by either of the sexes as he matured. Though still thirteen, Sebastian was becoming a man literally before James's eyes.

There was much speculation surrounding both of Sebastian's parents' deaths, which made many people wonder about Sebastian.

Over time the rumors had died down, almost forgotten by most at this point, giving way to other more important and pressing gossip circulating throughout the small town.

Sebastian had been in this orphanage for over nine months, and James enjoyed checking in on him from time to time during the week. In addition, they had a business arrangement which required frequent discussions and essential decisions to be made. They both sat down in the reception area, and he smiled at Sebastian, "How are things, Sebastian?" James would ask.

This time, Sebastian responded, "I hate it here, James. I'm one of the oldest, and I've realized that no families really want me. They want babies, James, not me. I honestly feel like I could do better on my own. I'm not like these kids; you know what I mean? I feel like I think more like an adult than a child. I mean, I am a mature thirteen-year-old, you know?"

James smiled and sat back in his chair, valuing Sebastian for a moment, and said, "Well, thirteen, but yes, Sebastian, you are more like an adult than a child—mature, intelligent, and resourceful. More mature, in fact, than most adults I encounter." Sebastian smiled at the compliment.

Sebastian's life experiences forced him to mature early and very quickly. Most would be overwhelmed by this measure, but Sebastian almost seemed to flourish within the responsibility and embraced life's challenges. He didn't dwell in his somber actuality as most would; he embraced the moment and decided to thrive in the opportunity and reality he was given.

This was a solid truth, thought James, but Sebastian was part of the system now, and he was also correct in he was too old as most young parents wanted babies or smaller toddlers, not potentially problematic teenagers when adopting.

"I realize it isn't easy, Sebastian, but things have a way of working themselves out, and you, young man, are going to be phenomenal in everything you do. In just a few years, the world will be at your feet. Stay focused and positive, and you will see that everything will make sense, and your own journey will become clearer."

"On that note, Sebastian," he continued, "I have some excellent news. After what seems like forever, the patent for the Bear Hugger looks like it is going to go through, and I have a few manufacturers interested in the prototype. This could be exciting. Your dream is finally coming together perfectly."

Sebastian flashed a grateful smile, his eyes gleaming with genuine appreciation. "James, that's incredible. I can't thank you enough for helping with the trap. I couldn't have done it without you. I really value having you as my partner in this."

He paused, his expression growing more serious and thoughtful. "Were you able to look into setting up that trust for the patent and any future changes, as we discussed? I want to make sure everything is legal and properly set up to protect our vision."

James laughed and nodded yes, grinning fervently at Sebastian's maturity, and understanding of legal matters and real-world adult situations. He continued, "There's the 'acting like an adult' thing we discussed. What thirteen-year-old understands *legal trusts* and lawful matters?"

"That reminds me, here are the legal papers that go along with the trust option. The judge had to sign as your custodian because you are a minor, without your parents being around, but he also appreciates your interests being protected. Now, on that note, I have taken care of all of those specifics, Sebastian, but I have to disagree on a portion of our partnership and agreement, young man."

"I reluctantly agreed to the 10 percent ownership of, which you were very insistent upon me receiving, which was more than generous to me because I am happy to help you with this project as a courtesy to you. I don't need to make anything on the proceeds coming from this venture, Sebastian. Thankfully, I have a retirement of my own. I simply want to encourage you, and I love that this gadget doesn't hurt bears."

"After all you have been through, you need someone in your corner, and I want to do this for you, Sebastian. I don't need to own any of it, son. But when the judge said when you two spoke, you insisted I receive a 30 percent stake and also be named custodian of your trust, I was truly taken aback. All I can ask myself is why?"

Sebastian smiled, sat back in his chair, like a man three times his age would do, and said, "James, you are the only person in the world I trust. Well, maybe Sean, too, but you two are the only ones. You have never wanted anything for yourself, never asked, ever. You have helped me because you are decent and good to me and have looked out for me, always. You are the closest thing I have ever had to a father, which means a lot to me. Please accept this from me and aid me further when I don't know what to do. At least until I don't need your help any longer, which will probably never happen. For your help and guidance, I want you to have this part of the ownership. Assist me for now and for my future. Please do this for me, James. Please."

James thought about it for a moment, sat back into his chair, impressed with the boy's logic, and finally said, "Okay, Sebastian, I will also trust in what you think is right, and I will accept this arrangement because you wish it to be so, and I can tell you have put a lot of thought into it, but we can always change it in the future if you decide. And I thank you, too, as this is going to change a lot of things in game and fish and all attributed to a boy that's only thirteen years old. It truly amazes me someone so young can achieve so much so quickly."

Sebastian smiled, extended his hand, and said, "Perfect. So, James, we have a deal. We are officially partners." He and James shook hands, sealing their agreement, as Sebastian reviewed the documents before him. Sebastian had no legal background but read the Agreements carefully, trusting James and the Judge had his best interest at heart.

As Sebastian reviewed all the documents, James relaxed into his chair and took a moment to appreciate this exuberant young individual. He observed him for a time as he settled within his chair, knowing the review of the documents would take a while, simply adoring the young man sitting before him. Sebastian constantly reminded him of his son, Sean; they were the same in many ways.

They were both exceptional young men, poised for success and talented in anything they set their focus on.

Sean and Sebastian had met roughly four months prior when Sean was on leave, and the head of the orphanage, Mrs. Salazar, allowed James to take Sebastian for the week and remain within his care.

Sebastian was hesitant about meeting Sean, understandably, as he was foreign to him, and Sebastian was not terribly trusting of adults at that time in his life. They had all failed him in some way. He and Sean had a lot in common, and they became fast friends despite their age difference of eight years. Sean was an only child and enjoyed having Sebastian as a "little brother."

That week was a revelation for Sebastian, both therapeutically as well as enlightening. It proved to be a healing experience for all three of them. By the end of it, Sebastian found himself profoundly connected to James and Sean, who had become his two favorite people in the world. Their bond, forged through shared experiences and mutual respect, transformed his outlook and brought a newfound sense of purpose and camaraderie into his life.

Sean spent time teaching Sebastian skills he had learned in SEAL team training and was astounded at how quickly Sebastian developed these talents and techniques. Sebastian was eager to learn and was not afraid to push the limits as Sean would increase the force and impact in their exchanges within their close-quarter combat training.

James studied them through the kitchen window of the rear porch. He was fascinated as Sean and Sebastian wrangled and scraped on the backyard lawn. Their concentration and intensity often building to a point where James would walk outside with intent on impeding these amateur bouts for fear of Sebastian getting hurt during these skirmishes. James would hold back, not interfering, but it usually ended up with Sebastian flat on his rear on the lawn. But then, he would hop back up, look at Sean intently, and smile, often taunting Sean. "Again, Sean, and stop holding back. A SEAL? Bleh . . . *more like a WHALE*, if you ask me." Sebastian enjoyed teasing Sean when given the opportunity.

Sean would look at Sebastian, often laugh, and then glance at his father and shake his head. Sebastian would then plant his stance for yet another round, and they would continue these bouts. These exchanges would go on for hours in a day, stopping sometimes only to eat or help James with a chore around the house.

As the week progressed, Sebastian's abilities and understanding grew exponentially. Each day brought new challenges and opportunities for growth. He absorbed combat strategies from Sean and James like a sponge, but he didn't stop there. Sebastian would take their teachings and integrate his own unique style, often enhancing the exercises or techniques during their training sessions.

Sean and James observed in amazement as Sebastian swiftly adapted and innovated. His natural aptitude and creativity pushed them to elevate their own teachings. They began introducing more advanced concepts, delving into a broader array of combat styles. The trio explored the intricacies of assault weapons and ammunition, experimenting with different types to understand their strengths and limitations.

Covert tactical training sessions became a highlight of their days. Sebastian's quick thinking and adaptability made him a natural in scenarios requiring stealth and strategy. He mastered antidetection techniques, learning how to move unseen and unheard, turning the forest and urban landscapes into his personal playground.

The dynamic between the three became electric, each pushing the others to new heights. Sean and James weren't just teaching anymore; they were collaborating, expanding their collective knowledge. They delved into the psychology of combat, understanding the mind games that could be as crucial as physical prowess.

By the end of the week, Sebastian was no longer just a student; he had become an equal, a prodigious talent whose insights and improvements elevated their training to an art form. Sean and James recognized the rare brilliance in him, and together, they formed a formidable team, each member contributing to a collective expertise that was greater than the sum of its parts. Their bond was forged in the crucible of intense learning and mutual respect, a testament to the power of collaboration and the relentless pursuit of excellence.

Within his SEAL outfit, Sean's concentration was on weaponry and munitions, being a SEAL sniper, and they were able to test Sebastian's marksmanship on the 100-acre farm behind James's house. Sebastian was able to bull's-eye a Coke can and consistently hit it from five hundred yards out, which was beyond the talents of most snipers. In addition to Sean and James, Sebastian seemed impressed with himself until he witnessed Sean annihilate 4/5 bull's-eyes from 1,500 yards out. "Damn, Sean, that's exceptional. I want to be able to do that someday. You really kicked my ass," said Sebastian.

James would pipe in, "Ease up on the language, boy. What, were you born in a barn?" "Sorry, sir," replied Sebastian.

Sean smiled. "You said hold nothing back, remember, Sebastian? Besides, this is my calling. I was born to be a sniper. You will get better; you are way ahead of where I was, Sebastian, at your age."

Sebastian replied, "Well, know this, Sean, I'm going to keep working on this; I'll catch up to you. Just you watch and see."

Sean laughed. "Oh, I have no doubt, none at all."

As they walked to retrieve the cans, Sean was ten yards ahead of them, and James used the opportunity to speak with Sebastian and said, "Son, you amaze me every day. You make me proud, Sebastian; both of you do." Then he whispered what he thought was out of earshot of Sean, "And just between you and me, I think you just about have Sean beat in close-quarter combat."

"I heard that!" shouted Sean. Despite having eight years on the boy, he realized what his father said may well ring true.

Sean enjoyed watching and teaching Sebastian, as did his father, and Sebastian was a worthy pupil. Sean never had a sibling, and Sebastian was as close to a little brother as he would ever get. They both appreciated his value in knowing himself, opening up his range, and being unafraid of pain or failure but embracing it and learning from it.

Sebastian and Sean possessed no sense of fear; they shared a subtle confidence that radiated around them. Intuitive of each other, balanced, and graceful in their execution of everything they did. It was a sight to witness and enjoyable to experience. They both exuded enormous physical and mental strengths while in their presence. One could sense the power they projected. Sebastian couldn't get enough of the training and knowledge Sean and James were eager to bestow upon him.

On the second to last day of Sean's leave, the boys were again brawling in the backyard one morning as James came out to enjoy the two of them sparring and sat down with a cup of coffee. At this point, no punches were being held, no hesitation, and no lack of passion in the least. There were a lot of bumps and bruises to exemplify the tolls of their training thus far. Sebastian wore those wounds with pride, badges of honor, all of them.

Sebastian swung, missed, and followed through the turn with the momentum of the failed blow. Capitalizing on Sebastian's mistake, Sean countered with a hard punch to the side of his abdomen, and Sebastian went down to one knee. "Damn, Sebastian, are you okay?" apologized Sean, sometimes forgetting Sebastian was a young teenager. Sebastian put up his hand to stop Sean for a moment. The gesture made him aware he was fine but needed a beat to gather his thoughts.

Sebastian closed his eyes, not from pain but from a deep, introspective analysis of his own failure. He meticulously recounted the specifics of the melee—where his mistake had occurred, why it had happened, and how it had unfolded. In that moment, he replayed the scene in his mind countless times, dissecting each movement and decision.

He absorbed the lessons, adapting his strategy and pinpointing the adjustments needed for the future. James and Sean evaluated in respectful silence, recognizing the intensity of his mental process. They understood that this was not mere reflection but a profound recalibration, a methodical approach to mastery that turned failure into a powerful tool for growth.

Sebastian impressed them with his ability to internalize and learn from his mistakes. His eyes remained closed as he visualized new techniques, integrating his insights into a refined combat strategy.

The quiet determination etched on his face spoke volumes about his resilience and intellectual prowess.

When he finally opened his eyes, there was a steely resolve and clarity that hadn't been there before. James and Sean exchanged a knowing glance, both aware that they were witnessing the evolution of a formidable mind. Sebastian's process of learning, adapting, and applying was not just impressive; it was a testament to his unyielding pursuit of excellence.

James and Sean recognized the turmoil in Sebastian, his relentless quest for perfection, and the struggle within. James set his coffee down and straightened in his chair, watching as Sebastian, crouched on one knee on the lawn, navigated through his mental battle.

Sebastian's focus was true, his expression intense as he dissected his mistakes. Each second was a testament to his commitment to self-improvement. Sean admired the boy's ability to confront and learn from his errors, transforming flaws into steppingstones toward mastery.

James could sense the turbulence swirling within Sebastian's head, like reading words on the pages of a book. Sean narrowed his focus, concentrating on Sebastian's face as he was well aware of what the young man was experiencing, and stood up slowly to avoid disrupting his concentration.

Sebastian focused intensely, eyes closed, dissecting his moves, anticipating Sean's countermoves, mapping out the physical exchanges, all while extrapolating his own missteps in his mind. He remained motionless on the grass, analyzing it all until he had achieved the clarity of what he must do and how he would achieve it. They simply remained silent and studied the young man.

When Sebastian rose, a sense of understanding replaced his earlier turmoil. James and Sean exchanged a glance, understanding they were witnessing the crafting of a awe-inspiring individual and his self realization. Sebastian's journey was far from over, but each introspective moment brought him closer to greatness.

He felt stronger, engrossed, and resolute, achieving an almost invincible state of mind. He saw the lucidity in his execution and the mission before him.

His torment was resolved. All barriers were gone now, and he had become a machine, honed, and aligned in its purest form. There were no impurities any longer, nothing to stop or alter his execution. He determined what he must do.

James intently watched his young protégé and knew in the moment, Sebastian had changed. He theorized what was to follow, but he couldn't interrupt the inevitable. He was part of it now, caught within the mechanism of Sebastian's transformation, his metamorphosis, once Sebastian gently stood up, eyes intense, narrowed, and determined.

He switched his focus to Sean and studied him in the moment, and for the first time since Sean could remember, he felt within his core, deep down, something foreign, in a place he had never felt before that day. What was he experiencing?

Then it hit him . . . . *It was fear.*

Very serious now, all the playfulness aside, the taunting long past, Sebastian said in a soft voice, "Again, Sean. I want everything you have and the best you've got. Don't disappoint me, and don't hold back. Promise me, Sean." Sebastian gestured with his fingers, outstretched, for Sean to come at him with everything he had.

Sean cautiously nodded in agreement as he assumed his combat stance.

This twenty-one-year-old young man, in the prime of his life, a decorated Navy SEAL, squared up with a thirteen-year old human anomaly. On the surface was a seemingly grossly mismatched pair to the casual observer, but on the inside, all advantages, assumptions, and disadvantages were cast aside. Standing before each other, two warriors focused on the prize, appreciating the integrity of the moment.

They were equals. All past exchanges or victories were irrelevant at this point. This was the space in time defining it all. It was the moment that mattered most. The pinnacle of all of the training leading up to Sebastian's metamorphosis. James unhurriedly stood up, watching the two as Sean shifted his weight, centering his balance and almost leaping to his assault, expecting to catch Sebastian unprepared.

Sebastian was in his unadulterated zone, complete in form, ready as Sean leaped at him with a strong right, grazing Sebastian's left cheek. But his reflexes were honed, and Sebastian anticipated Sean's intent, avoiding the full impact of the blow.

Sean collected himself quickly as his full weight came down on his legs following his jump; reflexively, he began to turn as Sebastian lay a right hook into Sean's cheek, slightly lacerating his jaw, then a calculated roundhouse kick into his abdomen, knocking him backward. Sean shook it off, then came at Sebastian. Anticipating this in the same instant, crouched down, sweeping Sean's leg, sending him on his back, dazed.

Before he could recover, Sebastian was atop Sean, left hand at this throat and his right fist up, clenched and cocked for the final blow. Sean, unable to react, was stunned and, in realizing his predicament, defeated. It all transpired in a moment, perfect and flawless in execution.

His performance was immaculate, indefensible, and advanced in all facets; Sebastian was centered in the moment. He knew he had won. There was no contest and no question he was the victor. He held his position, primed and ready to strike but didn't, and relaxed his hold as he quickly got up.

James was about to intervene when Sebastian pounced on Sean but then hesitated when he witnessed the restraint in Sebastian's attack. Sean looked intently into Sebastian's eyes, "I knew you would surpass me, little brother. Just didn't think it would be this fast."

"Nah, I just got lucky, Sean," Sebastian replied and smiled at him. They all were well aware luck had nothing to do with it.

As James appreciated the exchange from the porch, he thought to himself, what focus and humility, "What was it with this boy?" Sebastian helped Sean up to his feet, noticing a small cut on Sean's face from Sebastian's attack as they walked back inside the house, arms wrapped over the other's shoulders. No anger, hate, or animosity, only adoration and appreciation of each other and their respective talents.

James heard Sebastian yell out, "Jumping in the shower, out in a few." The triumph was already forgotten. James's focus was still fixated on the spot where the boy's skirmish occurred a few moments before, replaying the brief battle in his mind.

Sean approached his dad on the porch, appreciating the view beyond the yard as dusk settled in. Pausing for a moment, he touched the small scrape on his face. Respecting his father was deep in thought. Sean then said, "That one's an exceptional breed, Dad, gifted beyond all others I have ever come across. And so young, it's amazing." Sean shook his head in disbelief.

James said, "I know, Sean, you both are."

Sean replied, "I'm good, Dad, but you don't need to sugarcoat it with me. We both know. Sebastian is something else. He almost . . . isn't human. And at his age, unbelievable. His intuition . . . I've never experienced it or witnessed anything even close to it. He adapted, adjusted, moved, and overcame in seconds, whereas for most soldiers, it takes years of experience to develop that acute awareness, and most never do, and Sebastian's already has sharpened the skill."

"He learned my shortcomings, exploited them, and manipulated how best to counterbalance them and leverage my weaknesses against me. It's both exquisite and bizarre, all at the same time. I've never known anyone to be able to learn an opponent's flaws and counter them so quickly. He has taken all of our military training and modified the techniques, making his attacks difficult to oppose or defend. It's extraordinary."

James quickly suggested, "At some point, I think we need to have someone take a look at him, don't you think?" Sean agreed, "Yeah, I do, Dad, when he's ready. Are we both thinking of the same person?" "Yes, we are, Sean. In due time, she will need to see him," replied James. Sean continued, "You know, Dad, I think he could take half of the guys in my SEAL unit. How is that possible?"

Shaking his head, James didn't know how to answer his son's question and said, "We need to help him, Sean, guide him, nurture him. He has a gift, and we must help him understand and develop it."

James turned to his son and smiled, ". . . and he kicked your ass, handily today." He pinched Sean's shoulder, nudging him slightly. Teasing of Sean and Sebastian was commonplace within their household.

Sean said, "That he did, Dad. I won't be mentioning this to anyone in my unit, and I'd appreciate it if you didn't as well, Pops." He grabbed his dad by the back of the neck and squeezed affectionately.

James replied, "Agreed. This will be our little secret." Sean headed back inside, "See you inside, Dad."

As the sun began to dip over the treeline miles away, James retraced his steps to consider the significance of the day. Almost as astonishing, Sebastian's miraculous feat of besting his son was the first time in twenty-one years that he had noticed this new trait in Sean. He had never seen his son experience that type of fear.

But he witnessed it in his son when Sebastian stood up, focused, and determined in the moment. He noticed fear in Sean's eyes that evening, and it was the first and last time he would ever see it.

In the same moment, he also had the eerie notion the trepidation he witnessed in his own son's eyes was a fear that Sebastian would instill in many others in his lifetime. There was indeed something unique in him, and James and Sean would help him develop and refine his gifts.

James went back inside, entered his office after closing the door, sat down at his desk, and thought for a moment. He then turned to his Rolodex, still old-school, and found a number he hadn't dialed in many years.

He slowly picked up the receiver, hesitated for a moment, and then dialed. After a few seconds, the call was picked up. "Hello, this is Bastini," a woman's voice responded.

"Hello, Hillary, it's James Woodford. It's been a long time . . . Yeah, all is great. Anyway, I'm sure you are busy, but the reason for my call is that I have someone you should take a look at, at least at some point. He is young, but the rawest of talent I have ever witnessed . . ." They spoke for a time before hanging up.

Thinking back, James Woodford was in awe of this young man from the moment he met him years before. "You ok, James?" Said Sebastian for the second time, shaking James from his trance.

The orphanage was about to serve lunch, and Sebastian didn't want to miss the mashed potatoes; they were always the first to go. "Of course, son," he looked at Sebastian, knowing the young man would become someone powerful someday.

Having finished with the documents, Sebastian handed them back to James. Smiling, James said, "Before you go to lunch, Sebastian, I talked to Sean last night. He says hello, and he is coming out next month. Not to get your hopes up, but I may have another surprise for you at the same time. We will see," said James.

Sebastian smiled at hearing this news. They stood up, and Sebastian hugged his dear friend and said, "James, thank you for everything. I'm so fortunate to have you and Sean in my life." James squeezed him harder than usual, appreciating the young man's loneliness within. Life's challenges were aging this young man far too quickly.

Sebastian turned and headed through the hallway, but not before he turned. "See you in a few days, James?" asked Sebastian. James quickly responded, "You certainly will, young man. Give 'em hell in there." Sebastian smiled, gave a thumbs-up, turned, and waved again as he disappeared down the hall.

James stood for a moment, watching him leave. How he respected this young man and was excited to be a part of Sebastian's journey. He had such high hopes for him and was curious about his aspirations as he matured.

He also worried for him like a father would for the life that lay ahead for young Sebastian. James stood, and in thought, he wondered what the next few years would mean to the both of them and hoped Sebastian was ready for the next chapter he was to enter as it would be a defining moment for him—for all of them.

James had heard through the administrators at the Orphanage that Sebastian was widely admired by the other children as well as the Orphanage staff.

They were all excited to see how his life would develop, but none more than James and Sean Woodford. Little did they know then, but this young man would later help shape countries and become a strategic weapon to several presidents and their administrative prowess. Sebastian Storm would be instrumental in shaping a political movement and presidential candidate that would reshape America in the years to come. He would become an instrument and force the United States had never before possessed.

Vienna, Austria
Present Day

Sebastian smiled, looking over the ad in Outdoor Life, thinking about one of the few happy memories it brought him during his adolescent life. The bear trap patent, directed through James Woodford's lead, secured a contract with a major manufacturer that later fabricated the mass production of the Bear Hugger line of traps, originating with Sebastian's bear trap and eventually to many of his other designs as well.

In the seven years following signing those documents with James in 1997, their venture became successful well beyond their expectations. At the end of the sixth year, the company's products had saturated the entire globe. It became the front-runner for all animal traps worldwide and performed an impressive $12.4 million in revenue the prior year.

The company had grown to thirty-four employees and was relocated to Big Sky, Montana. Sebastian chose the spot as the headquarters because he fell in love with the area, and it was the optimal location to test many of his traps. Their plant was situated outside of Gallatin National Forest.

James ran the show, retiring from the park service, but Sebastian cleared all major decisions despite remaining primarily "silent" as a partner despite being the majority stockholder.

In their seventh year, James approached Sebastian following his twenty-second birthday with an opportunity that had come before the lucrative company.

"Sebastian, you know I have cherished and loved this company since we started all those years ago, and even though my pension with the park service yielded an unimpressive $97,000 in thirty-four years of service." He rolled his eyes at the facetious statement. "Because of Bear Hugger, I now have over $7.3 million in savings, which makes my pension look like pocket change. This nest egg I have is entirely because of your generosity, Sebastian. I will never want for anything thanks to you, but I also need an exit strategy. I want to live the rest of my days enjoying the world and spoiling the grandkids you and Sean will eventually bless me with." He laughed at the remark.

Sebastian beamed. "James, I completely agree. As you must be aware, I'm not as passionate about this company as I once was. It's a business to me, and although I have adored it, I am more than happy to entertain an exit for both of us. It's no secret, my interests now lean in far different arenas. Tell me about our options," curious about what James had to say.

James laid out the framework, "There are two options, as I see it. First, we leave the company status quo, replace me with another individual or board to take my place and potentially take it public, and let the machine run as it has done beautifully for the last seven years. The second option, a group out of the Midwest in Indiana, approached me this week. After disclosing basic numbers with expenditures, our zero debt, and profitability, they generated an enormously gracious figure to you, Sebastian."

Sebastian frowns. "Well, first, James, it's ours, not only mine, and second, spill it, old man. What did they offer?"

Laughing, James continued. "Yes, right. 'Ours,' and the figure was an astounding $22.8 million to acquire the company. I think we could do a little bet—"

Sebastian interrupted, "Done! Take it. Sold, James. And this is how it will go. You and I will each take 50 percent of the sale. I won't negotiate this. Make it all happen . . . *yesterday*."

James laughed, then quickly replied, "Sebastian, I can't accept that option. I don't need that much money. You have graciously given me fifty-five times my retirement, and that was far too generous as it was. Remember, I live very simply."

Sebastian countered, "Fine, James, you drive a hard bargain. This is my final offer. Of your 50 percent, 25 percent will go to you, and the remaining 25 percent will go to Sean, or I won't sell. Period. If you wish, you could donate your half to whomever you desire, but that is how this will transpire. Think about how this will benefit Sean, too. I will no longer bargain with you on this, James," Sebastian joked halfheartedly.

James was always amazed by the vigor Sebastian displayed. Even at only twenty-two years old, Sebastian always held all the cards, and this game proved to be no different from any of the others they had faced together.

He realized arguing with Sebastian was pointless, and the money didn't matter to either of them nor would it be for anything Sebastian would ever do in the future. Sebastian had made nearly $21 million from the company in salary and dividend disbursements in the past seven years. He had not spent one dollar of the proceeds in those seven years, so it had grown to over $47 million for Sebastian in that time period with the proper investing and his other business investments.

The Bear Hugger was just one of Sebastian's many successful business ventures; James was aware he had several others. For Sebastian, money was never the primary focus. This was about something far deeper: family, trust, loyalty, and doing right by those who mattered most to him.

Each venture he undertook was infused with these principles, reflecting his unwavering commitment to the people he cared about.

The Bear Hugger, though profitable, was a testament to his ingenuity and a symbol of his dedication to a cause greater than himself. It was about safeguarding the wilderness and ensuring safety for all, driven by a sense of responsibility and integrity.

James admired this about Sebastian. He saw in him not just a savvy entrepreneur but a man of profound values and unwavering loyalty. The bonds Sebastian forged were rooted in trust and mutual respect, qualities that set him apart in a world often driven by self-interest.

For Sebastian, every business decision was a reflection of his character, a pledge to uphold the ideals of family and loyalty. It was this blend of intelligence, passion, and ethical commitment that made him not just a successful businessman but a truly exceptional individual.

James knew it, and he was also certain Sebastian was aware of it as well. His life had become enriched because of this young man. They had both taught so much to each other, equally and amorously, over the years, so without hesitation, James responded, "That's more than fair, Sebastian, and thank you for including Sean. That amount will set him up for life and give me peace that both of you would never want for anything. Plus, the two of you get everything I have anyway."

Sebastian replied, "Of course, James. Sean is like a big brother to me. I would never desire for any of us to suffer financially, and now, there is no chance it will happen. Pretty wild, all of this coming from a couple of hillbillies from Roanoke, huh?"

James replied, "Ain't that the truth, Sebastian, ain't that just the damn truth." They both laughed together.

They closed on the business acquisition three months following without so much as a hitch. Upon selling their business, Sebastian called James many months later to say, "Hey, James, I'll come out in a few weeks when I'm done with my work here. How does that sound? I coordinated it with Sean, and he thinks he can make it just a couple of days after me."

With a smile, James replied, "I would love that. It's been too long since I had you both together. It's no secret. I would love to know what you are up to, but also aware there is no way you will tell me."

Sebastian responded, "You know me all too well, James . . . Talk to you in a few."

Sebastian sat in the café, remembering those simpler times and how he longed to have them back, but he felt deep down the reality was not his to have or enjoy. The exhaustive training days with Sean and James were his most memorable as a teenager. He missed those days, but above all, he missed James. The only father he knew in those years.

Sebastian reminisced of that time, roughly eighteen years prior. So much had happened before and since that time. He couldn't help but feel honored to have James in his corner at that critical time in his life.

The trip they planned later that year was the last time he would see James alive again, a tragic end to a tremendous familial bond. Later, after James's passing, his advisory role would be replaced by his son, Sean, who would later prove to be Sebastian's greatest guardian angel in many ways.

Vienna, Austria
Present Day

Sebastian trusted his intuition more than most, a guiding force that had consistently served him well throughout his life. Deep within, he felt a nagging suspicion that something was amiss, and he trusted from experience that such a notion usually preceded a significant event.

This heightened awareness was one of his clearest assets, a commanding weapon in his arsenal. The inkling gnawed at his essence, disrupting his focus, and compelling him to scrutinize every person and situation with an intensity far beyond his usual vigilance. It was as if his subconscious was sounding an alarm, urging him to prepare for whatever lay ahead.

The more he sensed this unseen disturbance, the more his mind sharpened, becoming hyper-aware of subtle cues and hidden motives. This intuitive edge had always set him apart, allowing him to navigate complexities with a deftness that others often lacked. Yet, it also weighed heavily on him, a constant reminder that his instincts, while powerful, demanded his undivided attention and relentless scrutiny.

As he moved through his thoughts, the sense of impending change kept him on high alert, driving him to anticipate and adapt. It was both a gift and a burden, a dynamic force that shaped his actions and defined his approach to the unknown challenges that inevitably lay in wait.

Sebastian hesitated for a moment, then pulled out the encrypted phone from his breast pocket he always carried with him. He stared at the screen for a few seconds before retrieving an all-too-familiar number up in his mind and punching the numbers he retained only from memory into the miniature QWERTY keyboard.

He again wavered for an instant, indecisive, brooding over the screen before typing a single string of two letters, *SS*, and after a moment, pressing the SEND button and immediately erasing the text once sent.

He was well aware the single text would begin a chain reaction that he only utilized when he felt it was utterly necessary, and he was getting a feeling that this was one of those instances.

Chapter 13

A Father's Fate

Roanoke, Virginia
1995

Jonathan muttered a string of curses under his breath, his disdain for the forest evident in every word. He despised the incessant hum of insects, the rustle of unseen creatures, and the pervasive grime that clung to everything. The sun was sinking below the horizon, casting long, sinister shadows through the trees. As the twilight deepened, Jonathan's sense of urgency grew. The encroaching darkness promised to shroud the dense foliage, making his search for Sebastian increasingly futile. He was certain that once the last vestiges of sunlight vanished, the forest would become an impenetrable labyrinth of shadows.

He cursed his fortune in that moment for forgetting to bring a flashlight, making his situation all the more challenging. With a sense of desperation in his voice, he called out again, "Come here, boy, I know you can see me. Come on out, let's discuss this. You have nothing to be afraid of," yelled Jonathan in an attempt to appeal to Sebastian's sense of fear of the repercussions he would face once he was caught. Hearing the words echo through the forest, Sebastian lay on the ground, unfazed and silent. . . listening to his father's words, sensing the desperation in his voice. He couldn't see him, only hear him at that point, giving him an unnerving sense.

Sebastian had everything to fear if his father caught him. Everything.

Jonathan continued through the natural channel of the ravine, shaped by the forest landscape and terrain. It was at that point that Sebastian's father came into view, clad in a brightly checkered shirt that stood out noticeably against the natural landscape.

As the shadows thickened with the fading light, Sebastian's eyes adjusted, allowing him to discern his father's figure more clearly. It was then that the glint of the shotgun barrel in his father's right hand caught his eye. Curiously, his father hadn't brought a flashlight. This was unexpected, yet Sebastian had no need for one himself, confident in his intimate knowledge of the terrain. He moved with practiced ease through the darkening landscape, his familiarity with every twist and turn guiding him as surely as any beam of light.

Sebastian found it peculiar that his father had opted for a gun above any other supplies. If his sole intention was to search for him, what purpose did the weapon serve? Concealed in the shadows, Sebastian remained undetected even as his father moved closer, his movements cautious and deliberate. The distant howl of wolves reached his ears, a rare and unsettling sound this close, yet he dismissed it without concern. His focus remained on his father, questioning the true motive behind the armed search.

As his father trudged through the underbrush, Sebastian noted the tension in his posture, the way his eyes darted nervously through the gathering gloom. Why would he bring a shotgun if he was merely looking for his son? The incongruity gnawed at Sebastian's mind. He knew his father to be a pragmatic man, not given to unnecessary displays of force. There had to be a reason, something lurking beneath the surface of this search that Sebastian had yet to uncover.

The wolves' howls grew louder and more insistent, a chilling reminder of the wild and unpredictable nature of the forest. Sebastian's heart pounded in his chest, but he forced himself to remain still, his breathing shallow and controlled. He needed to understand his father's intentions before revealing himself. Every instinct screamed at him to stay hidden, to quietly wait.

As he tracked his father's path, it appeared almost aimless, driven more by anxiety than purpose. The shotgun, clutched tightly in his hand, was a symbol of fear rather than aggression. Sebastian's thoughts raced. Was his father afraid of the wolves, or was there something else out there, something more dangerous?

The minutes ticked by, each one stretching into an eternity. Sebastian's mind whirled with possibilities, each more unsettling than the last. The forest around him, usually a place of familiarity and comfort, is now oddly alien and threatening. He knew he had to make a decision soon: to stay hidden and gather more information or to step into the open and confront his father, demanding answers to the questions that gnawed at his soul.

The howls in the distance grew fainter for the moment, and the oppressive silence of the forest returned. Sebastian took a deep breath, steeling himself for whatever was to come. He needed to know the truth, no matter how dark it might be.

At that point, Jonathan was angling slowly southeast of Sebastian's position and approaching his second of four preferred trapping sites.

Sebastian studied his father's position inquisitively, curious, and even impressed that his father had made it well over a mile to this location within the forest. Jonathan was now within two hundred yards of Sebastian's lookout spot, and Sebastian became concerned if his father didn't deviate from his current path in the next one hundred yards, Sebastian would have to relocate to a new position and risk being detected.

As Sebastian tracked his father's movements, anger simmered within him. He loathed his father, despising everything he stood for and the way he had treated Sebastian and his mother. The loss of his mother intensified his hatred. He was convinced his father contributed to her death, stealing her from him forever.

Sebastian's fists clenched as memories of his mother's suffering replayed in his mind. He forced back tears, refusing to show any weakness. His father, now searching the forest with a shotgun, emulating more like a predator than a parent.

In the darkening forest, Sebastian's resolve hardened. He was no longer a frightened boy; he was determined to confront the truth. The shadows became his ally, concealing his presence as he followed his father's trek. The truth would come to light, and when it did, his father would face the consequences.

Unbeknownst to him, Jonathan began approaching the proximity to one of Sebastian's rabbit traps. Sebastian's eyes narrowed as his father quietly stepped within a few feet of his small animal trap. Jonathan hesitated for a moment, looking at the trap, examining the apparatus then continued slowly and purposefully forward, looking for his son.

Suspecting Sebastian was observing him, Jonathan again yelled out, "Please, Sebastian, let's talk this through. I promise you; I just want to talk." Then in a fit of frustration and anger, true to Jonathan's nature, he followed with, "Get over here, Sebastian, I demand you come out!" Sebastian quietly examined his father's body language; he concluded it would be a mistake to expose his position. He imagined what his father would do if he were to catch him, especially after having to trek this far into the forest.

The howling of the wolves was drawing closer now but blending with the natural sounds of the forest. As Jonathan stepped forward softly, a click and slide were detected as the pressure of his foot, along with the weight of his right leg, triggered the concealed *Bear Hugger* trap, making a "whooshing" sound as the apparatus initiated and clamped down on his right foot and leg firmly, yet painlessly, securing him tightly to the 100-plus-pound trap. Although there was no discomfort, Jonathan yelled out reactively, instinctively dropped his shotgun, and began attempting to pull the weight away and release the locking mechanism, confused, and startled by the trap itself.

Frustrated and frantic, Jonathan thrashed about, attempting to shake the bulky device from his foot and leg. His flailing inadvertently caused him to meander back in the direction of where he had come from initially and leaned over to inspect the boot but couldn't find any obvious way to unlock it, which was precisely its design.

"Sebastian, get your goddamned trap off me!" he cried out, becoming frantic now. Sebastian patiently waited from a safe distance, immediately satisfied with the performance of his invention.

Although it wasn't designed to trap a human, it was proving equally effective, more so in fact, because a bear was two to three times the size and strength of a human and able to manipulate the weighted boot far better. In his father's case, surprisingly, it held him nearly immobile, especially after he had hiked in the opposite direction for thirty feet, exhausting himself in the process.

At that point, Jonathan sat upon a fallen tree to catch his breath and continued tampering and desperately pulling at the boot to no avail, his temper rising in the process. Sebastian patiently and quietly evaluated with anticipation and intrigue. Considering his father intently, Sebastian experienced no empathy or concern, examining his helplessness as he imagined his mother must have suffered every day of her sorrowful life with this man.

The disgust for his father was at its pinnacle as he viewed him struggling, enraged at the contraption encircling his leg and knowing his own son was the architect behind its design. Sebastian had his father in a direct line of sight all the while, but Jonathan was still unable to locate Sebastian's position as he hid well within the forest landscape, camouflaged by the shadows of the darkness. Only the moonlight was present but bright that evening, illuminating the terrain far better than Sebastian would have desired.

Savoring this shift of power, Sebastian reveled in his father's anguish over his predicament. The remote control that operated the Bear Hugger trap was firmly grasped within Sebastian's hand. Being well within range, a simple activation of the button would disarm the trap, but Sebastian simply clutched the device, maintaining his control, and held his father's fate within his grasp.

Just as he considered aiding his father, Sebastian saw the first wolf enter the area a mere fifteen feet from where his father sat, unaware. Jonathan's focus was concentrated elsewhere, tinkering intently with the mechanism, swearing and oblivious to the skulking creature in his midst.

Sebastian tensed slightly when he saw the wolf but then eased and relaxed, watching as the second and third wolves began to approach, now circling his father. They studied, circled, and waited, weighing the risk versus reward of the victim before them.

He need only stand up, run to his father, or even shout to warn him, but neither option was utilized nor coveted. Sebastian need only turn the mechanism with his specialized hex tool or the remote control, and his father would be freed. But Sebastian chose fate to decide his father's outcome. He nuzzled back into his position and simply watched the story unfold before him.

At that moment, Jonathan heard a sound behind him and turned abruptly to see the wolves poised in their position, circling their prey.

Sebastian was fixated and appreciated his father's karma as it unfolded. Jonathan was seemingly frightened at this point, knowing his options were thinning by the second.

He had an enormous weight bound to him, tired from hauling it over the past few minutes, not to mention he had foolishly dropped his shotgun too far to retrieve at that point. He had all of this to contend with, as only the moonlight was available to him, inhibiting his visual senses.

There were now thirteen wolves within this pack, focused entirely on their prey, surrounding Jonathan, helpless as he sat in anticipation. Unlucky, the number thirteen, thought Jonathan, but fitting somehow. He cried, "Sebastian, I know you are out there. Help me; help your father!"

Sebastian started to shift his weight again, considering coming to his father's aid, but thought better of it, his moral compass in a tailspin as he pondered the complexities of this moment in time.

The remote held firmly within his hand, sweaty within his grasp. He needs only to press the button to disarm the trap and free his father. He stared at his finger, shaking over the disarm button, but he simply could not press it. He was unable to achieve that simple task.

Would his father consider him a hero for aiding him in his time of need? His father would think nothing of heroism. He would be angry and disheveled over Sebastian's trap. Sebastian would only suffer if he intervened. He calmed his nerves and settled back into position once again. No, he preferred to just simply . . . watch and see how this story would play out. He slowly slid the remote back into his jacket pocket.

His father was on his own now. The more valiant of the wolves, the apparent leader, a large black with a gray razorback, ventured closer to Jonathan, unwavering from the shouting and flailing of Jonathan's arms.

The wolves gritted their teeth, sharp canines dripping with anticipation, growling, and imposing their intimidation upon their weakened prey. Jonathan realized he was in trouble, his options quickly diminishing.

After what seemed like minutes, the lead wolf inched forward further and, without warning, jumped at Jonathan, catching his left hand between his jaws, and violently shaking his large head in an instinctive tearing and jerking motion.

Jonathan howled, tugging for a moment before ripping his hand back to safety, but not before seeing the mauled extremity shredded and mutilated in front of him. His hand was half severed off, now a mangled heap of flesh with two metacarpal bones protruding through his skin, twisted, and contorted, no longer usable, saturated from his own blood, his hand useless and broken. Jonathan cried out again, but this time in excruciating pain.

Sebastian's focus sharpened, the scene unfolding before him in a detailed slow motion. The first wolf's assault ignited a frenzy within the pack, its feral instincts awakened by the scent of blood. In a blur of fur and fangs, the second and third wolves lunged at Jonathan, their eyes gleaming with a predatory hunger. They attacked with precision, each one targeting a different limb with savage efficiency.

In that moment, the remaining wolves sprang upon their hapless victim, realizing their risk was depleted, seizing the opportunity now befalling them, each desiring their own take and claiming their prize.

Sebastian stalked in horrified fascination as the wolves tore into his father. Each wolf latched onto him, their powerful jaws clamping down with relentless force. The air was filled with the sounds of growls and the sickening crunch of bones, a brutal symphony of nature's raw power. Jonathan's screams echoed through the forest, a stark contrast to the eerie silence that had preceded the attack.

Amid the chaos, Sebastian remained frozen, his mind racing. The spectacle before him was both horrifying and mesmerizing, a primal dance of life and death. As the wolves ravaged Jonathan, Sebastian's emotions surged, a complex mix of fear, anger, and a dark, vindictive satisfaction. This was a reckoning, a savage justice meted out by the wild itself.

The forest, once a backdrop of shadows and whispers, now pulses with a life of its own, bearing witness to the violent retribution unfolding within its depths.

Jonathan's hollers turned to shrieks as the wolves tore flesh from bone and heartedly dismembered his father in front of him until the screams were reduced to mere murmurs and breaths and eventually replaced by the sound of the wolves chewing through the disemboweled carcass that was once human.

Despite the gruesome attack before him, Sebastian's view never diverted. He remained fixated and focused on the ferocious spectacle fate had brought him to witness.

Sebastian became an isolated spectator of his father's mortality.

His subconscious urged his yearning not to miss any of the horrific display of nature that was occurring. He wanted to witness every instant and appreciate any and all the suffering his father must have endured during the ghastly exchange between man and the unforgiving environment that befell him.

The creatures all claimed the spoils of his father and scattered in various directions within the forest, enjoying the specific portion of their kill and savoring their claim.

Sebastian closed his eyes. It was done. His father's judge and jury were determined by nature and the beasts that claimed him. Sebastian no longer suffered any guilt or sadness. His father deserved this fate through chance, and Sebastian was satisfied, deep in his heart, that his father was let off easy.

He started to dream of a happier life now, a better place, and his peace, finally, at long last. All was calm now within the forest, the sounds returning to normal.

He was all alone now, abandoned by both his mother and father. The weight of solitude pressed heavily on him, yet there was an eerie calm that settled over Sebastian as he lay beneath the canopy of trees. His heart rate gradually stabilized, each beat echoing the acceptance of his new reality. Exhaustion, a relentless force, began to claim him, and he felt his consciousness slipping away, pulling him into the embrace of sleep.

As his eyes fluttered shut, the events of the night replayed in fragmented images behind his eyelids—the violent attack, the piercing screams, the primal chaos. Yet, amidst the turmoil, a strange sense of peace washed over him. The forest, with its ancient wisdom, appeared to cradle him in its depths, offering a sanctuary from the horrors he had witnessed.

Sebastian's breathing slowed, his body sinking into the soft earth beneath him. The sounds of the forest, the rustling leaves, and distant animal calls, became a soothing lullaby. His mind, weary and overburdened, began to surrender to the need for rest. The tension in his muscles released, and he drifted into a deep, dreamless sleep.

The dawn would bring with it a new day filled with the uncertainties and challenges of survival. But for now, under the watchful gaze of the stars and the whispering trees, Sebastian found a brief respite. The forest, with its mysteries and dangers, had also become his refuge. As he slept, the line between man and nature blurred, and in that delicate balance, Sebastian began to find his place in the world anew.

The sunrise approached. The distinctive resonance of various feathered animals chirping, singing their harmonized morning ritual, and the constant buzz of cicadas crept into his subconscious, wresting him from a deep sleep where he lay on darkened forest earth.

Sebastian awakened early the next morning at first light, took stock of his surroundings, and replayed the gruesome details of the night before several times in his head before getting up. Was it possibly just a vivid dream? A hope, a blessing maybe, or was it his actual reality that he was simply returning to and not just a fantasy he created within his mind?

He swallowed hard; he realized it wasn't a dream at all. Fresh in his mind, vivid and clear, he was more than aware of what he witnessed, and he was content in nature deciding his father's destiny. Sebastian got to his feet and looked around. All eerily appeared normal and calm, almost tranquil, as a new day began. The fragrance of nature filled his lungs as he stretched his arms, feeling lighter and less burdened on this crisp summer morning.

He slowly walked down to the trap, noticing a rabbit contained within. He loosened the hatch and let him out, closing the door and resetting it. The rabbit scurried away happily and disappeared under a nearby bush. Sebastian unhurriedly ambled toward where his father had last been, 25–30 yards from his position, until he came up to his bear trap.

Blood saturated the landscape, crimson splattered on the large leaves of bushes everywhere, and also on the trees, shrubs, and ground around him. He instinctively avoided stepping on the areas to avoid disrupting the vicinity. He noticed the trap upon its side. Crouching down, Sebastian gently turned over the trap and fell backwards. His father's foot and lower half of his leg were bulging from the boot, the shredded bone of the tibia and fibula mangled and protruding, illustrating a hideous visualization of the aftermath of his father's death.

The veracity of life was all very surreal and vivid to Sebastian now. Warranted and justified, he thought of his father's plight. He was confident his father deserved every ounce of agony and torment he endured the evening before. Yet, Sebastian was still very aware of human frailty and its unrelenting imbalance.

Sebastian sat and thought for a moment as the sunrise emerged, shedding more light on the surrounding landscape. After several seconds, he got up, removed the specialized tool from his pocket, and meticulously opened the bear trap. Although disgusted by its sight, he carefully removed his father's leg from the apparatus, taking care not to disrupt the limb, and laid it upon the ground. Sebastian then dragged the trap back to its original position adjacent to the smaller rabbit trap.

He carefully and meticulously wiped the bear trap down with a wet cloth he had retrieved from the maintenance box he kept at the site. He then reloaded the trap and set leaves and dirt over it, making it appear like it had never been activated.

Using a branch, Sebastian swept the leaves and dirt over the tract that the trap had made in the ground from both his father dragging it the night before and Sebastian returning it to its original position, careful to avoid the blood-spattered areas as best as he could. He could feel intermittent sprinkles of rain were beginning to fall upon his shoulders.

He found the shotgun his father had dropped, picked it up, cracked the barrel, and found the two shells within, careful only to handle it with a towel and avoid touching it with his fingers or hands. Removing the shells from the chamber, he placed the two of them in his pocket.

He swept the area below where the gun had fallen, returned it to the location where he had left the limb, and threw the shotgun into the bushes a few feet away, then retraced his steps, ensuring the environment was in its most natural, unaltered state.

Sebastian was attempting to make the area appear as if his father had come into the forest, was attacked by wolves, and forgot to load his gun with shotgun shells, thus unable to protect himself from their attack. A gentle rain increased in intensity as he finished.

His work had taken only thirty minutes as he sprinted back to his house, throwing the two shotgun shells into the forest along the way. He sluggishly went up the stairs, carefully listening for the woman who had been with his father the evening before, but she was long gone. Sebastian was confident she didn't want any part of all the drama.

He went to his parent's bathroom and carefully flushed the two small, bloodied towels separately that he had used in the forest. Sebastian was intuitively careful and wrapped the soiled towels with additional clean towels while in the forest, ensuring that he didn't transfer any of his father's blood to himself.

He was vigilant in ensuring there was no blood on his clothing or hands. He was certain he was clean, but he didn't want to make any mistakes that would connect him to the incident.

He then went back downstairs to his room, removed his clothing, and inspected all the garments for anything that could tie him to his father's accident, placed the items in the washing machine, and started the cleaning cycle before getting into his pajamas, and settled into bed, and slept for a few hours before he heard a knock at the door he knew would eventually come.

Chapter 14

A Blaze of Fury

Vienna, Austria
Present Day

Fury, Hammer, and Nail stepped off the private jet in their tailored KAM suits and were transported covertly to their private villa within the city in less than an hour.

Tobias spared no expense in maintaining complete obscurity with all of his missions. This one was especially sensitive and warranted a pristine clandestine operation to support its furtive importance. Therefore, the flight was not recorded, making their excursion to Vienna appear as if it never existed. If Sebastian or Hillary ever got wind of their arrival, the operation would likely be severely compromised and aborted.

A black SUV was waiting for them, along with two escort SUVs at the base of the plane's steps. Hammer and Nail proceeded down the stairs first, as Tobias's protocol dictated. All senior officers on site were last to depart, respecting their individual stations within the organization.

As the senior ranking officer on site, Fury stepped off the jet and paused for a moment, taking in the bitter evening air, crisp and cool. It reminded him of his early mornings in San Diego, where his military training had begun almost sixteen years prior.

Fury was Tobias's best, his longest active military weapon. Born Derek Thomas Allen, he had always wanted to be an elite soldier. It was Fury's dream as far back as he could remember. He finished high school in Henderson, Nevada, as an all-state football receiver but chose, at seventeen years old to enter the military to become a Navy SEAL (acronym for Sea, Air, and Land; a member of special naval warfare, trained for unconventional multifaceted warfare) and take his rightful place within the navy's best.

Once accepted into the SEAL program, he achieved their highest distinction and became one of their most highly decorated, holding several records in SEAL training school that would have held today if not for the temper young Derek was unable to contain nor control.

Following his SEAL training, he graduated top of his class but later proved a liability determined by the higher-ranking chain of command. Anger management and insubordination issues limited his promotions, but he was known for executing his missions and getting the job done.

He logged four successful tours in Afghanistan and hundreds of effective special operations but was moved from team to team because of discipline and/or team compatibility issues.

He proved such a talent but was never given his own team, unable to conform to the systems set by the Navy and SEAL protocol, dubbing his nickname "Fury" stuck with him indefinitely. He got the job done but habitually with muddled consequences that often left him having to answer to his superiors. Fury detested the label but was gifted in close-quarter combat and small arms, matched by few. The name Fury fit him aptly so.

He used his abilities to his advantage in many a barroom brawl and often with his own team members in the soldier's barracks, landing him in lockup more times than he could count. Regretfully, his superiors found Fury before them for disciplinary action time and time again.

He was an introvert, recluse, and eccentric, and although he ultimately succeeded in his missions and operations, they were regularly untidy and aggressive in his methods of execution and often ended up with his lieutenant tearing him a new one following the operation.

Fury had been serving his country with relentless dedication for six long years, a soldier marked by his destructive efficiency and fiery passion. His missions were executed with a precision bordering on ruthlessness, his every move calculated to inflict maximum damage on the enemy. But it was on his last mission that Fury's unbridled aggression truly came to light. In the heat of battle, he became overzealous, his actions crossing the line from strategic to savage as he eliminated local combatants with a disturbing zeal. There was a disquieting glint in his eye, a sinister enjoyment in the act of killing that did not go unnoticed.

The aftermath of the mission left his comrades uneasy, their silent glances filled with unspoken questions. His lieutenant, a seasoned officer with a keen sense of duty, couldn't ignore what he had seen. Concerned for the safety of the unit and the mental state of his soldier, the lieutenant submitted a request for a psychological evaluation. The decision was not made lightly, but it was necessary. Fury's behavior had become a liability, a ticking time bomb needing to be defused.

When Fury learned of the evaluation request, his reaction was explosive. The very idea his mental fitness was being questioned ignited a fire within him that was almost palpable. He felt betrayed, his years of service and sacrifices reduced to a single, scrutinized moment of overreach. His reputation, built on the battlefield with blood and sweat, now hung in the balance. The prospect of an evaluation was a direct affront to his identity, a challenge to the core of who he was as a soldier.

He stormed into the command post looking for his lieutenant, his fists clenched, and his jaw set in defiance. The tension in the room was thick as Fury confronted his superior, his voice a low growl of indignation. The lieutenant stood his ground, his resolve unshaken by Fury's intimidation. He met Fury's blazing eyes with a calm, steady gaze, reiterating the necessity of the evaluation for the safety and cohesion of the unit. It was not a matter of punishment but of ensuring Fury continued to serve effectively without becoming a danger to himself or others.

Fury's internal struggle was fierce. He was a man of action, not introspection, and the idea of delving into his psyche was anathema to him. Yet, deep down, a part of him recognized the truth in his lieutenant's words. The battlefield had changed him, hardened him in ways that were both his strength and his curse. The psychological scars hidden beneath his tough exterior were real and undeniable.

As he left the office, his mind churned with conflicting emotions. The path ahead was uncertain, but one thing was clear: the journey through the shadows of his own mind would be his greatest battle yet. The evaluation would be a crucible, testing not just his sanity but his very essence as a warrior. And in the heart of the struggle, Fury would have to confront the darkest parts of himself, to emerge either reforged or broken. At the very least he could continue missions until the psych eval . . . . *but then, that was taken away from him and Fury had enough.*

Once he received word of his suspension until further notice, he was grounded until a more detailed analysis was completed. Upon hearing the news, Fury promptly marched over to his lieutenant's private quarters and loudly banged on the door.

The lieutenant abruptly opened the door and screamed, "What the fuck is your problem, Allen?" To which Fury aggressively replied, "You are, LT, you are my problem! Fucking asshole grounding me on a psych eval? That's a career killer, and I'm not going to let you fuck up my future over this."

His lieutenant retorted, "Well, you already did, Allen. You may be one of the best and brightest at what you do, but you are a head case and a butcher, and I won't tolerate it within my company despite your talents. I saw what you did to those enemy soldiers on this morning's mission. You are out of control on every level, Sergeant. All the other LTs have been afraid of you, but I sure the fuck am not! I thought I could tame you and keep you under control, but you are hopeless and an utter headcase."

The Lieutenant continued, "You're done, and I'm gonna end you, once and for all. No one else around has the balls, but I do, and here they are . . ." As the lieutenant gestured toward his groin for effect, Fury became so enraged and couldn't control himself any longer. He kicked the lieutenant in the testicles, then right hooked him, shattering his jaw as he went down hard in agony.

The lieutenant dropped to the floor, screaming in pain, wriggled on the ground, trying to say something, but the words were scrambled from his jaw being fractured in multiple places. Only drool, blood, and slobber managed to emerge from the lieutenant's mouth as Fury turned on his heels and promptly walked out of the officer's barracks and returned to his own. Only gurgling noises were heard from the Lieutenant writhing in pain behind him but Fury didn't care any longer.

Several minutes later, entering his own barracks, Fury sat on his bed and closed his eyes in an attempt to calm himself in silence for a brief moment or two before six military police officers quickly filed into the room with assault rifles, all trained squarely on Derek. The red dots of the scopes are centered on his head like dancing beads.

His colonel walked up behind them and formally stated, "Sergeant Derek Thomas Allen, you are hereby under arrest for the assault of a senior officer. Come quietly with us, or I will have these men pepper your ass all over the south wall. Get your sorry ass up, soldier!"

Derek slowly stood up, grasping the full force of what he had done and also realizing regardless of what any psych analysis concluded, his career as a SEAL was over.

The SEALS don't tolerate such blatant insubordination. He realized he had been a liability for the navy for far too long now, and despite his military effectiveness, the brass couldn't look the other way any longer. The MPs cuffed his wrists and shackled his ankles, escorting him out of the barracks in front of all the other soldiers to the military police lockup.

The MPs escorted Fury, and the colonel said on the walk to his cell, "You were one of the best, Derek." Shaking his head, he continued, "But that temper of yours . . . I always figured it would be your downfall. Never thought it would be a bullet, EID, or a soldier's knife that would take you down, Sergeant. No, I was sure it would be yourself, notably your own worst enemy, son. What you did to the Lieutenant will end his career as well as your own. Of that, there is no question." He shook his head again at the waste of such a tremendous soldier as the MPs escorted Fury into his individual cell and closed the bar-encased door. The door slammed behind him.

The colonel walked up to the cell door, thick steel bars separating them and looking into Fury's eyes, said, "A true spoil of a talent . . . It's a fateful waste. I wish you the best of luck, Derek. The U.S. Navy has finally had enough of you."

The colonel then turned in and about and walked out of the cell block.

Sergeant Derek Thomas Allen, one of the most highly decorated Navy SEALS to come out of the academy, was stripped of his rank, his training records rescinded as well as any mission commendations at the academy or in combat, and lastly, given a dishonorable discharge from the United States Navy. He was spared prison time for his immeasurable service to his country, but that was the best he would receive. He was let off easy.

Several days later, after processing him as a military criminal and granted leniency from the colonel, he was escorted to the front of the base, leaving him with only a military-issued knapsack, $56 in his wallet from his final paycheck with nowhere to go.

Abandoned and outcast from his unit, he was now considered a failure among them. No one was present to see him leave or wish him luck. He was left a man without a home and worst of all a dishonored name.

He found a small dive bar a mile from the base to help ease his pain, went in, sat down, ordered a bourbon on the rocks, and held it, numb to what transpired in the last week.

A sense of sadness and failure over his inability to control himself when it mattered most began to settle in. Fury possessed unhealthy anger and temper issues, spawned since adolescence but never addressed or controlled.

In his despair, he hadn't noticed the tall blond man who slipped in beside him as the bartender approached and asked the man what he would like to drink. The man hesitated, looked over at what Derek was drinking, and said, "I'll have what he is having . . . and put this soldier's drink on my tab as well."

Without looking initially, Fury raised his glass in thanks and sluggishly turned his head and said, "Mister, thanks for the drink, but I don't much feel like talking. But I have to ask . . . how did you know I was a soldier?"

"Ahhh, I know a lot about you, Sergeant Derek Allen. To me, you are nothing short of a hero, a little misunderstood maybe, and your talents poorly recognized or utilized for that matter, but a hero, nonetheless. I know your stats like sports fans know their favorite football players."

The stranger smiled and continued, "I'm quite certain by the end of this conversation, we are going to be fast friends, and things are going to be changing for you, Sergeant Allen. Changing for the better, I might add. Your luck is about to take an upturn today."

The man stuck out his hand and smiled again as Fury reluctantly shook it. "It's a pleasure to meet you, Derek. My name is . . . Tobias, just Tobias for now. Hear me out. Listen to what I have to say. I can make you a wealthy man, Derek, of that I'm certain if you consider the value and tremendous opportunity I will explain to you. I promise you, you won't be disappointed," continued Tobias.

For the next several hours, Fury listened to Tobias intently. He came to view Tobias as the savior he needed. Fury rose from the remnants of his life and ascended to a place where he was appreciated and respected.

Tobias was correct; his life did change. He no longer served God and country. It was time to redirect his motivation and concentration on himself, on a more significant cause, and to those who prized and valued his faculties.

There at the bar at the end of the three-hour discussion, Tobias looked at Fury and finally said, "And for the record, Derek, you ever take a swing at me like you did your LT, I'll put you right down myself, no questions asked. That scenario won't end the same way with me on the end of it, I can assure you."

Derek looked at the intensity in this man's eyes for a long minute. Despite his confidence and personal abilities, Fury believed Tobias was telling the simple and absolute truth. There was no question about the sincerity of his statement and the underlined threat that came with it.

Fury had never feared anyone in his illustrious career, but this man, Tobias, was on a different level entirely. Fury was confident the man would provide the environment and culture to learn the most from, and his new focus would have no limits.

Fury had a focus now, a purpose, and Tobias provided an arena for him to truly exercise his talents. No limitations were put on him save for any failures. They were not allowable nor tolerated.

He didn't consider Tobias a friend so much, but rather a mentor. Fury anticipated Tobias appreciated his abilities, having sought him out. Tobias valued his talents, however raw and visceral they may have appeared to be, with no constraints or limits ever put upon him. "Get the mission completed. How you do is not a concern," was their only mantra.

He couldn't complain about the income he made under Tobias's organization. Fury's income level working for the United States government was paltry at best. He made more in a year with Tobias than he would for an entire career for the government. Tobias was his liberator, and Fury would be loyal to him to the very end.

Atop the plane's stairs, the moist air made him think of that time all those years ago as he began descending the jetway to the entourage waiting before him and the twins.

Their contact on the ground, Mueller, was waiting in their black SUV to brief them on the activity to date. He had maintained a distant observation of Sebastian and HB over the last several days, losing them often due to his distance and obscurity, but still able to provide some scattered intel on their whereabouts. Mueller was also maintaining contact with their source within the heart of HB's Division. The combination of all intel was also proving invaluable.

Sebastian was rather elusive. However, Mueller was confident Sebastian hadn't detected him as yet but could at any time. Sebastian's steadfast use of antidetection protocols made him difficult to track for long periods. Mueller had been able to isolate Sebastian to within a four-block grid and was closing in on his safe house, he was certain.

These laborious efforts were appreciated by the team. It was enough for Fury and his team to begin to form a locational perimeter and begin the process of closing in on Sebastian for the last time.

They had Sebastian Storm in their sights.

Vienna, Austria
Present Day

Sebastian awakened earlier than expected in his Vienna loft. Something stirred in him as the darkness still loomed outside his window. His mind drifted into a myriad of various thoughts.

Tobias was undoubtedly plotting something substantial; they were certain. His meticulous nature and cunning had always been a cause for concern, but this time, the stakes were far higher. His greatest concern was HB had not yet uncovered any significant intelligence to confirm their suspicions. The silence was deafening, and the lack of concrete evidence was unsettling. Yet, HB was acutely aware of Tobias's potential for orchestrating a momentous operation. Their instincts, honed over years of fieldwork and analysis, demanded respect, having been proven reliable time and again.

Tobias had mastered the art of secrecy for a decade, weaving a web of misinformation and compartmentalization within his organization. Each thread was meticulously placed, ensuring no single operative had the full picture. This labyrinthine structure was both his strength and HB's greatest challenge. Information was tightly controlled, leaks historically swiftly dealt with, and loyalty secured through a mix of fear and reward. Tobias's ability to keep the specifics of his plans under wraps was unparalleled, making it nearly impossible for HB to infiltrate his inner circle.

HB's Division was on high alert, every operative working tirelessly to piece together the fragments of intelligence they managed to gather. The urgency was palpable; they sensed something monumental was on the horizon and was an ever-present shadow over their operations. Analysts meticulously scrutinized intercepted communications, satellite images, and financial transactions, seeking any clue that provided valuable insight into Tobias's machinations. Field agents were risking their lives to penetrate deeper into Tobias's network, hoping to uncover the elusive details that would reveal his endgame.

The tension within HB's Division was mounting. The clock was ticking, and the pressure to prevent whatever Tobias was planning was immense. They knew that his operations were always meticulously planned and executed with precision, leaving little room for error. The fear of the unknown gnawed at them, the potential consequences of inaction driving their relentless pursuit of answers.

HB's intuition, her sixth sense for danger and deception, was their guiding light in this dark and convoluted mission. It had saved them countless times before, and they clung to it now more than ever. Every lead, no matter how small, was pursued with dogged determination. The pieces of the puzzle were scattered and obscure, but HB's Division had faith in their ability to assemble them before it was too late.

Tobias's ability to stay one step ahead was a testament to his formidable intellect and strategic prowess. But HB was aware that no one was infallible. They had cracked impossible cases before, and they would do it again. The battle of wits was on, a high-stakes game where the cost of failure was unimaginable.

In the shadows of this clandestine war, both sides moved with calculated intent, every action laden with significance. Tobias, shrouded in secrecy, and HB, driven by an unyielding resolve, were on a collision course. The outcome was uncertain, but one thing was clear: when the dust settled, the world would be irrevocably changed by the events set in motion by Tobias's machine and HB's relentless pursuit.

His mind also often trailed off to thoughts of Adriana, her touch, her sensuality, and even the softness of her skin. The way she seductively connected with him, even while sleeping, was constantly weighing on Sebastian's mind.

Sebastian had not spoken with her over the last day, but she was curiously contained within his thoughts. He needed to see her again, though he knew it would be a mistake. She was a weakness for Sebastian, a substantial one, and he was acutely aware of any kind of relationship with her would entail and the risk he was subjecting her to. He had not let anyone inside his circle in years, and he feared if he did, their lives would be forfeited, which was a consequence he could not bear.

He wasn't sure he would ever see her again, but he had his ways of finding her. With an hour remaining until sunrise, Sebastian drifted back into the memories of his childhood, always wondering and fascinated by the aftermath of his parents' untimely passing.

It was when his life took on a new journey, a path ultimately leading him to who he is today and crafting him into the killing machine he had become.

Roanoke, Virginia
1995

The sharp knock at the door jolted Sebastian, even though he had been expecting it. He sat up abruptly, his heart racing. He hadn't been sleeping, just lying awake, lost in anxious thoughts. The moment he had dreaded had finally arrived, and much sooner than he anticipated. A second hard rap followed at the door with more intention.

Sebastian swung his legs over the bed, took a deep breath, and walked to the front door. The morning light cast long shadows through the obscured glass panes of the door, mirroring his uncertainty. He saw the figures pacing in front of the door, yet they could not see him.

The figures outside appeared stern and imposing, their movements erratic and ominous. The air was thick with tension. Sebastian squared his shoulders, attempting to induce some semblance of confidence. He determined from that moment on, nothing would be the same in his life.

Vivid and poignant in the moment, the reality of his situation had not faded from his thoughts. He realized they would eventually come and thought he was ready when they did, yet the pounding fists on the door still surprised him even after the second time.

He glanced at the clock on the wall: 9:14 a.m. The pounding at the door came yet again, louder, and more insistent. The forceful banging reverberated through the house now, each thud echoing his growing apprehension. This was the third time, and he knew he couldn't ignore it any longer. There was no one else to answer, no one else to face whatever awaited on the other side.

His mother's loss was still ever present, as was his father's grisly death. It was just a matter of time before they came with questions. He needed to let them in before they forced their entry into his parent's home, as that was sure to follow.

Taking a deep breath, he steeled himself. The urgency of the knocking left no room for hesitation. The noise intensified, a relentless demand for attention. With a final, bracing breath, he reached for the door, his hand trembling.

Sebastian unlocked the deadbolt and slowly opened it. Standing on the porch deck before him were two deputies, Detective Todd and, finally, Ranger James Woodford, all staring at him blankly.

Detective Todd was the first to speak. "Good morning. Took your sweet time answering the door, son. Could we come in? We need to talk with you for a bit." Ranger Woodford nodded as if to let Sebastian know it was okay, yet all wore a somber look upon their faces. "I don't know if my dad is here, I thought he would answer the door. . . . *sorry*. He leaves sometimes," lied Sebastian, attempting to substantiate his innocence and deflect any assumptions they may have harbored. He knew why they were there, and he would play the part as well as he was able.

Awkwardly, Ranger Woodford replied, "That's okay, son, he isn't here. That's why we are here to talk to you. We have come to talk about your father, actually." Sebastian nodded at this news and opened the door further, welcoming them in, rubbing his eyes as if he was still tired.

He was glad James was among the men in the small party. He didn't particularly care for Detective Todd and how filthy he seemed. James was the only man he trusted at this point.

Sebastian gestured them into the hallway and led them to the kitchen. Taking a seat at the kitchen table, Sebastian guided the men to a small dinette set with four chairs around the table. The burnt food Sebastian's mother had prepared was still sitting where she had left it only two days prior. Sebastian pulled out one of the chairs and sat on one knee and looked at the two men.

Following Sebastian's lead, Detective Todd and Ranger Woodford also took a seat on either side of Sebastian. The two other officers looked around the house while the three of them spoke in the kitchen.

"Son, our deputies are going to take a look around if you don't mind, and I'll explain why in a bit. We wanted to come by and talk to you about your father. But before we get into that, we need to ask you some questions first. Is that okay?" asked Detective Todd, and Sebastian deliberately shrugged and nodded his reluctant consent to both the questions and deputies in the home.

Detective Todd looked over at Ranger Woodford, then back at Sebastian, and said, "Son, did you see your daddy last night before dark?" Sebastian looked blankly and shook his head at Detective Todd as he continued. "Did he hunt much in those mountains? Or go out after dark to hunt that you can remember? And when did you see your father last?"

Sebastian briefly considered the series of questions and softly responded, "Why did you say 'did'? Has something happened to my father? I don't know where he is. And I usually don't know where he goes when he leaves. He would never tell my mom or me where he would go. He would just leave, sometimes for days at a time." His elusive answers were deliberate, avoiding the questions asked of him.

Both men looked at each other, then refocused on Sebastian as Ranger Woodford took the initiative this time and spoke, "Sebastian, did your father ever hunt? Maybe sometimes take you with him, or did he ever go look at your traps with you in the forest?"

Sebastian always liked James Woodford, trusted him, and smiled slightly to say, "He did hunt sometimes; he never asked me to go, but he didn't hunt a lot. I don't think he ever went with me to look at my traps, but my mom always did. You met her, Ranger, you remember? She liked to learn about them and see what I was doing in the mountains, I think. She died yesterday."

Saying those words saddened Sebastian, but then he smiled, remembering the positive light she always shrouded him with; she was the best thing he had in his life. "I know, Sebastian, and I'm very sorry for that. She was a fine woman and a good mom," replied James.

His face lit up when he spoke of his mother. Detective Todd asked, "How did you get that scratch on your cheek, son?"

Touching the right side of his cheek, Sebastian thought about it for a moment and remembered his father grazing him in the face with the swing of the bat the night before. He looked blankly at the two men and replied, "I don't remember. I just scratched myself, is all. Sometimes it happens when I'm in the forest, I'm there a lot. It happened yesterday late morning." Hoping neither of the men detected it was a day fresher than he claimed. They didn't challenge his explanation and accepted him at his word.

James Woodward nodded, then used the opportunity to ponder his response before replying, "Sebastian, your daddy was in an accident, we think, while hunting last night. And well, I don't want to beat around the bush with you, son . . . . He won't be coming home. He passed away while in the forest; we think last night sometime. Do you understand what I'm trying to say?" James Woodward asked.

Sebastian tilted his head down, feigning remorse, then looked up at James and asked, "You mean he is dead? Like my mom is dead?"

Ranger Woodford replied, "Yes, son, I'm so very sorry." He didn't want to include the gruesome details of the wolf attack in his explanation.

Sebastian looked at the two men for what seemed like several awkward seconds, troubled not by what happened to his father but more so when he was finally all alone. There was no one left for him, no one at all. That reality hit him far more than the loss of his father.

He was saddened by fate, by his lot in life. Why couldn't this have happened to his father two days before, he thought? Then, he and his mother could live blissfully, free of his father's tyranny and cruelty. But as fortune would have it, he was left all alone now, just a day late. That is what consumed his thoughts.

It had only been forty-eight hours, and in that time, he had lost both of his parents tragically. Sebastian's entire life had been turned upside down. He would grieve for years over the loss of his cherished mother, yet no regret or penitence for what happened to his father, none in the least.

Sebastian had already come to accept his father's death. He got what he deserved, and in a way that was truly symbolic of the way he lived his life and treated others.

At that moment, a single tear emerged from his eye for the memory of his mom and also for himself, for on that day, he became a man. Whether by choice or not, prepared or otherwise, it was now the existence that lay before him. The ranger and detective interpret Sebastian's tears for the loss of his father, not knowing where Sebastian's true desolation lay.

Sebastian muttered, "What will happen to me now, Ranger?" Detective Todd took the question and explained the state's protocols for parentless children to Sebastian over the next thirty minutes. Because there were no immediate relatives of either parent, he explained there would be a progression, and he needed to be patient with the process. The state would also provide a counselor if he needed someone to aid him in dealing with his grief.

When completed, Detective Todd and James stood up along with Sebastian, gathered some clothes from his room, and packed a small suitcase. The officers accompanying went through the home looking for any evidence that might prove useful. They walked outside together as one of the deputies led Sebastian into the back of a police car.

Sebastian quietly slid into the backseat, looked at James, and said, "Ranger Woodford, will you still help me with my traps?"

James Woodford responded, "Of course I will, Sebastian. You and I will get that all squared away once things settle down a little, okay?"

Sebastian smiled and mouthed quietly, "Thank you." James replied, "I'll be checking in on you from time to time, son." The deputy closed the door and tapped the top of the car twice, indicating to the driver he could go.

Detective Todd and James stood on the porch in silence, both staring out over the front of the Storm driveway in front of the home until the police car was safely out of distance. Then the detective turned to James and said, "Unusual this whole thing, James. I thought he would be more upset. He never asked what happened to his father. That is a peculiar detail to me. He is a strong kid, though, I have to give him that."

James replied, "Yes, he is, Detective. He probably needs time to process all of this. It's a lot for anyone, let alone a kid. He did just lose his mom yesterday, and now his father within a day. That would be a lot for anyone, let alone a young boy. I may be off, but I'm not sure there was much love lost over the death of his father, honestly."

Detective Todd replied, "You know, forensics had a field day at the scene on this one, James. Storm's body was torn apart and strewn over one hundred square yards of terrain. Although it seems obvious the wolves apparently got the best of him, I find it interesting he never got a round off with his shotgun, not a one, but a couple of unused shells were found in the area. Not to mention, his shotgun was found quite far from him, 'bout twenty yards from where most of the torso was in a bush. Doesn't that seem odd?"

James responded, "Yessir, it does, Detective, much like everything else about this case and his mom, too."

At that moment, a young officer came up to the men still standing on the porch holding a bat in a gloved hand and said, "Sir, we found this bat in the corner of the parent's room with a part of the door trim broken on the inside of the upper portion of the door frame. Some blood though, strange, on the bat, you see here," as he pointed to the small blood smear but was unsure if it was related.

Detective Todd looked at James and confirmed, "Another peculiar item." He took the bat from the officer. "Like everything else around this place and that young boy, something about him I can't quite put my finger on, James."

Detective Todd continued, "They even mentioned unusual tracks in scattered areas but attributed it to the wolves dragging and fighting over the body parts. Something isn't adding up, but I'm unsure just what it is. It's all bugging me . . . But there is something we are missing, I'm certain," he said as he tipped his hat off and itched the top of his head with the same hand.

"Run the blood through the lab," said Detective Todd to the officer, and then he turned and left.

James replied, "Hmmm, interesting, all of it. Give the kid a break, Detective, he has been through hell and back. Do you think the boy knows more than he was letting on? You know, there was a bleep on Sebastian's bear trap at that location last night just before dark, but the rangers had gone home for the evening and didn't detect the reading until this morning, and the trap was reset to, *not activated.* It sometimes occurs when the trap is activated, discharged, bumped, or rearmed. Also, the remote can reset or disarm it as well, but I'm not sure if that matters. They asked me about it but figured it was an 'wire short' or some anomaly, which happens. The boy doesn't have all the kinks worked out yet. We didn't know about the accident out there at the time. When do you suppose Storm bought it? Did you look at the trap up there, Detective?"

Detective Todd responded, "As a matter of fact, we did, and it looked like it hadn't been touched, or I should say, *activated,* but the ground around the area had been tossed and turned . . . but that may be from the struggle too or activity in the last few days around the site. It was all hard to speculate by the team up there."

Detective Todd continued, "It's a crime scene nightmare with all the dirt, trees, and bushes, not to mention there was a light rain this morning as well. Nothing is really for certain. It appears it occurred around nightfall, but it is difficult to be exact. There are just too many loose ends and variables as to Storm's presence up there at that time of day, the day after his wife's death . . . just odd. Who really knows? Maybe he was clearing his head, thought he'd hunt to get his mind off things. We didn't even find all of Storm's body. Thirty percent of him is still missing. It's a mess."

Sympathetically, James said, "Imagine losing your parents within a day of each other. What are the chances?" shaking his head, then asked, "What's going to happen to the boy, you think, Detective?"

Detective Todd slowly replied, "Honestly, James, I think he will fall victim to the system. Young parents won't want him because he is too old. They want crying babies who shit, eat, and repeat when adopting. The state won't know what to do with him, and he will go to a foster home, most likely, or several, I would imagine. You know how those places can be on a teenager. The state will hold him for a while and then most likely turn him over to the downtown orphanage. It's a sad situation, James, but it is what it is, you know?"

Sorrowfully, James said, "Yeah, I do, that poor kid. My son Sean grew up without his mom, and no child deserves that, let alone losing both parents. Keep me posted, would you, Detective?"

Todd said, "I sure will."

Sebastian rode in the backseat of the police car in silence, thinking of his future. Today would be his life's new beginning. Today would mark the point where he would never let anyone hurt him ever again or those important to him. He would protect those foremost in his life by any means necessary.

Sebastian knew his calling was to protect those who couldn't defend themselves. Despite his youth, he had already witnessed profound suffering. The pain he had seen left deep scars, driving him to build an emotional fortress to shield himself from such anguish. Each encounter with adversity strengthened his resolve. He realized that true strength lay not only in physical power but in remaining compassionate and resilient. With every life he touched, his purpose was reaffirmed. In a world of darkness, Sebastian stood as a beacon of hope, committed to defending the vulnerable and ensuring they never faced the pain he knew so well.

Sebastian Storm would now emerge from the chaos, reborn like a phoenix from the ashes.

Vienna, Austria
Present Day

Dreaming of that time, a bittersweet relief washed over Sebastian, mingling with guilt and sorrow. As he lay in his bed, memories of the morning after his father's death resurfaced with haunting clarity. He could still hear the knock at the front door, heralding the uneasy arrival of the police. They had come to deliver the grim news of the accident.

The anxiety and fear he had felt then were palpable, each heartbeat echoing his dread of the uncertain future. The realization that both his parents were gone had seemed insurmountable, an overwhelming burden for his young heart and mind. The world had felt vast and empty, a daunting expanse without the anchors of his family.

In his dream, the echoes of that fateful morning played out with agonizing precision. The officer's solemn face, the weight of their words, and the crushing reality of his orphaned state all returned with vivid intensity. Yet, amidst the sorrow, there was a flicker of relief—relief that the nightmare was in the past, even as its shadows lingered in his present.

Seeing James Woodford was an unexpected, yet pleasant surprise that morning despite the circumstances surrounding their visit. It was then that Sebastian's relationship with James would evolve further. At first, Sebastian worried James Woodford's involvement stemmed from pity, but later, he realized that they had a commonality.

Sebastian constantly struggled with the loss of his mother and whether he could have done something to alter her fate. He would have saved his mother had he fought against his father, defended her, or never left home that morning to run into the woods to escape it all. He failed her that day, and he would always blame himself on some level. She needed him, and he disappointed her as well as himself.

Unwilling to save his father, Sebastian had chosen not to aid him in his time of need. It would have been relatively simple to create a commotion, retrieve the shotgun, or simply yell at the wolves, which could have caused their disorientation, making them run off to regroup. But he chose not to and left his father to his own fate, his own chance, and ultimately answer for all his wrongdoings. Sebastian was content with the decision he had made that evening. The abandonment of both of his parents dying tragically weighed on him tremendously.

Life was leading Sebastian on this journey, paved by the decisions he made during those two days, and it forever set his course.

He waited and watched as his father was overcome and dismembered, and there was a small part of him that enjoyed watching the man suffer. In that moment, he did experience a vague perception of guilt, but a larger, more substantial sense of satisfaction and justice achieved.

Sebastian valued his appreciation for nature in its purest form, claiming what it was due, and that debt was repaid with his father's life, his existence extinguished.

His father was sacrificed for his depravities and died alone, essentially by Sebastian's will. He could have stopped it, but he chose not to, and he was satisfied, though initially conflicted with the decision he made that day. It gave him a sense of peace knowing he controlled, to a degree, his father's eventual fate that evening so many years ago. He questioned his moral high ground at the time in doing so. That day spawned a change in him to protect those oppressed, his father being the originator of that drive and ambition.

Sebastian mused on the cyclical nature of life, reflecting on the inevitable return to the earth, the eternal transition of ashes to ashes, dust to dust. His father had paid the ultimate price for his transgressions, a poignant reminder of life's inescapable justice. Who was Sebastian to alter his father's predestined fate, if such a thing as destiny truly existed? Perhaps it was the will of a higher power, should one have faith in such notions. That summer night, under the somber cloak of twilight, Sebastian stood as a silent witness to the irrevocable judgment that had befallen his father. The air was thick with a sense of finality, and in that moment, Sebastian felt the profound weight of fate's unerring hand.

Deep within his young heart, despite his father's cries of torment that night, his thrashing, and resistance to his inevitable end, he finally gave in to what he deserved, and Sebastian was finally placated and absolved. Sebastian's conscience was clear, his existence vibrant again, and his mother avenged at least to some degree.

There were no funerals for either of them, only a detached closure for him, and he would have to accept that end for both of his parents. Sebastian was finally at peace and made free of the filth, cleansed of the darkness that clouded his childhood.

He thought about those days as they began to fade in his memory. The years passed, and a portion of the memory dwindled as the years went by.

As he lay watching the ceiling fan spin in the same mundane fashion, he was content with who he was and what he had achieved in his lifetime.

His mother would always be missed, but he shed little remorse for the loss of his father.

His eyes began to drift as Sebastian succumbed to sleep that had evaded him most of that night. Little did he surmise that he would be tested again soon enough.

Sebastian's eyes snapped open, his heart racing in the predawn silence of his Vienna loft. The first rays of sunlight began to creep through the curtains, casting faint, golden patterns on the wooden floor. He was certain he had heard something—an elusive noise that had yanked him from the depths of sleep. His senses tingled with an inexplicable awareness, a creeping sense that he was not alone. Every shadow seemed to pulse with hidden life, every whisper of the early morning air laden with unseen intent. Something was definitely off, and Sebastian could feel it in the marrow of his bones.

These recent distractions, his occasional lack of focus, lapses in judgment as he contemplated his past, his childhood, James, Adriana, Tobias, Sean, the older man on the street, the hooligans, and Hillary. What did it all mean, he wondered? He had to find out.

He had pushed and suppressed many of these memories deep into his subconscious, but something had brought them all back to the surface. These were the moments when his guard was weakest, unprotected, and he was the most exposed.

Something jolted Sebastian's subliminal triggers as he delved into his psyche's deep crevasses. He looked at his clock, 5:05 a.m.

The hair on his neck stood on end when he heard a creak from the fourth step coming from the rear stairwell.

Lying on his back, in simply a black tee shirt and matching boxers, he reached for his 9mm under his pillow, always close, always ready. He slowly and quietly eased the slide back, arming the weapon as he sat up and gently shifted his legs off the bed and onto the floor, careful not to make a sound that could expose him, and listened intently.

Anyone else in the building might have hurried up or down the stairs, their footsteps a quick patter of urgency. But this was different. Sebastian knew the value of stillness, the art of listening with intent. It was a skill that had saved his life countless times before. He strained his ears, evaluating every creak and whisper of the old building. Patience was his greatest ally in these moments, often the thin line between survival and demise. The ability to discern the subtle shifts in his environment was quintessential, a finely honed instinct that could spell the difference between life and death.

He had lived his life on both sides of this paradox, thus remaining deathly quiet.

His heart jolted at the sound of the second stair creaking, this time from the twelfth step, several seconds after the first. The extended interval between the creaks set his nerves on edge. Anyone merely returning to their loft early that morning would have ascended with a brisk, rhythmic pace, no more than two to three seconds between steps. But this gap was nine to ten seconds—a deliberate, cautious ascent. This wasn't someone stumbling home; this was someone creeping with intention, each footfall a measured act. The realization sent a chill down his spine. Someone was there, methodically making their way up, and their purpose was anything but innocent.

Someone was ascending those stairs with purpose and with one focus.

They had found him.

Chapter 15

Mortality Recognized

Roanoke, Virginia
1995

Sebastian awakened, immediately filled with dread and unhappiness. He had been living at the orphanage in town for nearly thirteen months following his parents' deaths.

The staff and employees seemed cordial enough but left him alone mostly, tending more to the younger children inhabiting the facility. His favorite memories revolved around James's visits and when Sean was on leave.

Sebastian relished the intense training sessions whenever Sean was in town, yearning for those electrifying moments. His most profound learning experiences occurred when both Sean and James were present, immersing him in a wealth of combative strategies and captivating stories. James's vivid recollections from his days in

Black Operations were filled with adrenaline and intrigue, painting a picture of a shadowy world of high-stakes missions. Meanwhile, Sean's tales as a SEAL sniper, with their precision and peril, were equally thrilling and inspiring. These sessions were more than training; they were a gateway into a realm of elite expertise and adventure, igniting a fire within Sebastian to master his own skills and rise to their legendary prowess.

At the orphanage, many children had come and gone to the facility often. Sebastian thought it wasteful to get to know any of them on any significant level, as most would only stay at the orphanage for a few days. Eventually, a doting young couple, eager to fulfill some void in their lives, would come by and procure one of the children for a modest fee and relieving the state of its obligations.

Young parents were arriving at the orphanage almost daily, shopping for that particular child they would happen upon, making them joyful and content and satisfy them in some way. The supportive husband and eager wife would walk by the line of children the staff would arrange shoulder to shoulder in the main living space of the facility. The daily ritual was a mandatory obligation of its inhabitants and avoiding the ritual was met with harsh disciplinary action if avoided or missed.

It was a circadian ritual, sometimes several times in a day, more so on a given Saturday or Sunday. These zealous "parents to be" would continually browse by Sebastian without so much as a glance, perusing the children like pages in a catalog. It was daunting and fruitless for Sebastian's sake, but James had reminded him several times to be respectful of their rules and obey the elders that ran the orphanage. He did as he was told and always performed at these ceremonies so as to placate his place within the hostel.

He was far too old, by several years, to be selected compared to the other younger children and infants available to these optimistic young couples. These prospective parents wanted youth, not a potentially difficult and burdened teenager. As a result, he mainly kept to himself for that year.

The younger children looked up to and respected the older Sebastian. He would play with the adolescent kids on occasion or teach them, when outside, methods of protecting themselves from bullies and oppressors that may terrorize them when they got older. He tolerated no bullies within the confines of the orphanage, and the administrators appreciated Sebastian's militant order of things, and all the children followed his example.

Sebastian took a particular appreciation in showing the kids who were willing the art of self-defense just as James and Sean had shown him. It was the highlight of his tenure there at the orphanage, and it kept him busy and occupied and gave him purpose on some level.

James Woodford stopped in a few times a week to check on Sebastian after he had spent the week with him and his own son Sean months earlier. The orphanage would allow James to take Sebastian one to two weekends per month, and those visits became the high point for both James and Sebastian, as well as Sean when he was visiting.

James felt a kindred connection to Sebastian after that initial week and the several weekends that followed, witnessing the uniqueness that Sebastian held within, unrefined and not fully appreciated or fathomed by either of them at that point.

Sebastian possessed a strength and power that neither the young man nor James had yet fully realized. James was compelled, on some level, responsible even, to encourage Sebastian to nurture the talents the young man acquired. Sebastian appeared more than eager to learn anything he could from both James and Sean. He enjoyed his training and eager to learn as much as possible.

One Tuesday evening in the winter of 1996, Sebastian was nearing his fifteenth birthday and was summoned to the front office. Assuming it was James visiting, though not his usual arrival time, he hurriedly came to the front of the orphanage and turned the corner to see not just James but also Sean as well.

The excitement and adoration on Sebastian's face were apparent and all the appreciation James and Sean needed. He was astounded to see Sean because he usually was warned when Sean was on leave from his SEAL operations and, of course, was always welcome, but this time, he was completely surprised to see Sean accompany his father.

They talked for a few moments in the front foyer, then James said, "Sebastian, I'm not sure you are open to this, and you probably won't be, but what would you think about coming to live at the farm for a bit?"

Sebastian asked, somewhat confused, "What? Like come live with you, James . . . and Sean?"

Sean nodded, and James replied, "Yep, that's about the extent of it. What do you think? I mean, you probably don't want to, but . . . ."

Now picking up on the teasing tone, Sebastian added his own and said, "Nah, I'm good here, you know, I'm kind of a senior consultant to the other kids and all." Sean and James looked at each other with some amazement. Then Sebastian added, "Of course, I would! Just teasing!" They all laughed, Sebastian hugging them again before looking up at them again, making sure they weren't still teasing him.

Sean said, "Go pack your stuff, killer! Let's get out of here."

Sean softly added, "I just had to be here to see your expression when Dad asked you, Sebastian."

As Sebastian ran to his room and threw the meager amount of clothing and personal items into a military pack Sean had given him a few months back, they were off.

Sebastian would never set foot in that orphanage again, and he grinned as he walked down the front steps, his new life off to a tremendous start with, above all, a family that cared for him and the two people that meant the most in his life. Sebastian would later become one of the Orphanage's strongest financial supporters having a special place in his heart for those that lost their parents at a young age.

James had begun the adoption process soon after, and although it would take months, the state agreed to let James take Sebastian until the necessary paperwork could be processed.

He decided to hold off on telling Sebastian that part of the news until it was confirmed, but he thought the idea of coming for the next few months would help both test the waters. It was time to expand on Sebastian's training and to comprehend better what it took to become a soldier. It was time that Sebastian began to understand his place at the table.

Vienna, Austria
Present Day

As the knots in his stomach tightened, Sebastian realized with a chilling clarity that he had been compromised three times in as many days. The source of the breach remained elusive, leaving him haunted by uncertainty. Was it back in London? Or perhaps the bathroom at the Hotel Sans Souci? And now, disturbingly, right here in his own loft. The proximity of the threat sent a jolt of adrenaline through his veins—this was far too close to home. He needed to act swiftly and decisively to uncover the source of his vulnerability and reclaim control before it was too late.

The uneasiness of his exposure was apparent, confirming there was a security breach. He wouldn't be able to fight whoever was after him forever. They would eventually succeed. It was just a matter of time.

He needed to end this, cut it off at the root, and permanently purge this force from his life. He was quickly and quietly to his feet now, pulling up his workout pants and APL sneakers. He swiftly accessed the panel to his adjacent loft to ensure an additional layer of protection from the impending threat he was certain was closing in on him. Once inside the adjoining loft, he had access to a myriad of arsenal and technology arranged and organized for any occasion.

Sebastian always used a unique holster apparatus positioned just under his left pectoral muscle, with the muzzle resting in the space just below his armpit, which worked with a magnetic system. Being right-handed, Sebastian could place his 9mm gun to his left chest, activating the magnet that held the gun to his body and only his hand/palm print could deactivate the system to release the firearm. The holster proved effective, maneuvering back and forth between hand-to-hand melee and gunfire on the fly, and improved his effectiveness tremendously.

In addition, he placed a specialized encrypted tech piece into his left ear. Although rarely used, this inimitable earpiece had proved to be his immeasurable savior a few times and was reserved for only very particular situations. It was specialized in that it only detected Sebastian's specific speech patterns, recognizing his timbre, cadence, and vocal fluctuations, much like a fingerprint, unique only to him.

Within a few seconds, once Sebastian had the earpiece and holster placed and activated, he softly uttered, "SS activate. Confirm. Fallen Angel in jeopardy." Within a few seconds, the response followed, as always, "SS activated Guardian Angel on watch south visual. Confirm and advise Fallen Angel." Thankful for the response, Sebastian waited patiently, unsure what he was about to face but also aware that the first two attempts did not go well for his adversaries, and anyone worth their weight would not let a failure occur for the third time. They would bring a full force down upon him this time; he was certain of it.

It was then that he saw the first assailant cautiously enter the adjoining living room, assault rifle drawn and in the ready position, unknowing that Sebastian was behind the mirror glass to the man's right. His hands were gloved, his assault rifle poised, and his finger on the trigger, controlled and assured with every intent to kill.

A trained professional to the core, Sebastian surmised that this man was here to exterminate and eradicate. The assailant wore a unique black suit with a tie, which seemed oddly inappropriate to Sebastian. A second man, larger in size, entered through the front door, which Sebastian could monitor on his camera screens—the pair using lockpicking instruments to enter the premises from both entrances without knowing Sebastian's adjacent room. The soldiers were taking every precaution, covering all exits.

Sebastian noted that both men moved methodically, were very well trained, and similar with their gait and movements, though vastly different in stature. They almost appeared like . . . *Twins*, but then dismissed the thought.

Pulling his 9mm from his magnetic shoulder holster, Sebastian focused the weapon on the first subject he had a direct visual on, tracking him through the glass mirror as he activated his tailored earpiece to report real-time intel.

Sebastian held back from firing at the first assailant, knowing that the gunshot would alert any other soldiers within their company. He understood the critical advantage of maintaining the element of surprise for as long as possible. Patience was key; he needed more information before making his move. By eliminating the targets one by one, he could significantly reduce the risk. The situation demanded precision and cunning, and he was acutely aware that nothing would come easy. Every decision had to be meticulously calculated, every action perfectly timed. In this high-stakes game, he had to stay one step ahead, turning the shadows to his advantage.

Sebastian whispered in a low voice, "Guardian Angel, two perps, possible body armor."

The same man's voice from earlier replied in a low and deep tone in Sebastian's earpiece, "Confirm, Fallen Angel, a third bogey identified at the base of the building."

Sebastian started to respond, "Confirm—" But he never finished the sentence. At that moment, the first man turned abruptly to his right and pumped six silenced rounds through the mirror/window, surprising Sebastian as he lunged awkwardly behind the left wall, avoiding the spray of bullets.

The window shattered, glass crashing to the floor and erasing any advantage Sebastian might have had. He cursed under his breath—he should have eliminated the target when he had the chance. Instead, he had opted to wait, trusting that patience and more data would serve him better. Now, that calculated decision felt like a costly mistake. He couldn't dwell on the misstep; he needed to adapt swiftly and find a new way to regain the upper hand before the situation spiraled further out of control.

Crouching to the floor behind a wall, Sebastian returned fire in kind with three rapid response rounds, center mass, into the man's chest, knocking him back hard but failing to put him down as Sebastian's shoulder holstered his gun while simultaneously rushing toward the assailant capitalizing on the man's confusion. Other than the strong force of impact, the shots proved ineffective and literally bounced off the protective gear the soldier was wearing, thus not having their desired effect. Sebastian quickly ascertained that Nail's suit was equipped with a type of weapon's fire protection technology. He would have to improvise.

But adaptation—*that was his specialty.*

Sebastian immediately closed the gap between them, taking advantage of the effects and impact of his earlier shots to Nail's chest. He engaged him in close-quarters combat, effectively insulating himself from the other intruder two rooms away. Sebastian hit the man upward and hard into the support pillar that braced the ceiling, his strike minimized due to the body armor, but Nail anticipated this, clasping both his fists, and coming down hard on Sebastian's back, pain ripping through Sebastian's spine from the blow.

The second larger man was twenty-five steps away and unsure of which room Sebastian was located in. He immediately stepped up his pace as Sebastian put his fist into Nail's unprotected throat, partly crushing it and causing him to swing wildly in defense. Sebastian whip-reversed his torso and put the full strength of his elbow into Nail's face, knocking him to the ground semiconscious and dazed, nose broken. That would buy him a few precious seconds.

Sebastian quickly turned and whip kicked Hammer in the face as he emerged through the doorway blindsided, his rifle falling to the floor. Assuming he was clad in the same protective gear as the other assailant, Sebastian realized that exposed skin was the only vulnerable spot these soldiers possessed. Hammer was much larger and barely fazed by the blow, dismissing the strike, and responded with a double fist punch to Sebastian's sternum, sending him hurling backward into the wall and then falling to the floor hard.

Sebastian realized he was dealing with opponents of a different caliber.

Sebastian's earpiece squawked, "Fallen Angel, third perp on the move, one min ETA. Guardian Angel ON window safe." Sebastian knew what that meant.

"Working on it," mumbled Sebastian as he jumped to his feet quickly and met the bigger soldier head-on. As Hammer swings and misses, Sebastian takes advantage of the bigger man's slowness and puts an iron-like fist directly into the man's left knee, causing Hammer to yell out, grabbing a chair to stabilize himself. The KAM proved effective against small-arms fire but not as protective against blunt objects or concentrated high-impact melee attacks. His opponents underestimated Sebastian's close-quarter effectiveness.

Hammer stood with all his weight on his right leg as Sebastian kicked and swept Hammer's supporting leg. The man went crashing to the floor. Sebastian was atop Hammer instantly, barraging him with quick punches to the face and then began choking him. Still, physically, Hammer was able to fend off Sebastian's attacks and eventually threw him off toward the mirror glass wall that had emerged from earlier.

Never having witnessed such innovative and responsive attacks before, Hammer was somewhat mystified by Sebastian's agile prowess and edginess. These made close-quarter combat very difficult when engaged with Storm. Fury had warned them about Sebastian, but he still underestimated the man and his adaptive nature.

As Hammer attempted to recover, Sebastian was already sprinting toward him. In a fluid motion, he launched into a scissor kick, but Hammer deflected the attack with ease. Sebastian hit the ground hard but swiftly drew his 9mm and fired two rounds at Hammer's head. Hammer, anticipating the move, raised his right forearm, the specially designed KAM suit fabric absorbing the impact. The bullets struck his arm, only to bounce off harmlessly and fall to the ground with a pitter-patter. Hammer's defenses were formidable, but Sebastian thrived on overcoming the impossible.

Hammer slowly stood, but Sebastian couldn't get a clear headshot. Knowing this, Hammer began to charge him deliberately but limped with his left leg badly damaged. Sebastian re-engaged his firearm into his holster, knowing he needed both arms for what he had in mind.

Vision somewhat obscured, Hammer led with his forearm obscuring his view, which allowed Sebastian to come in low, assaulting with a combination of right and left uppercut to Hammer's jaw and stomping hard laterally against Hammer's left knee again. A cracking sound was emitted, squarely breaking it this time, which was Sebastian's intent, knowing the big man would go down after that blow.

"Arggghhh!" screamed Hammer as his leg gave out, and he went down hard to one knee. Sebastian seized the opportunity, grabbed Hammer's left arm, twisted it, and hyperextended it at the elbow. A crack was again heard, breaking his arm in the process this time. Hammer was amazed at Sebastian's combative improvising. All of it happening so fast.

Nail was gathering himself, knowing his brother needed him, and began to get up, blood in his eyes from his fractured nose. Without hesitation, Sebastian then rotated and maneuvered toward Hammer's back, pulling his gun in mid-movement from his magnetic holster, and without looking, emptied three bullets, rapid-fire directly into the base of Hammer's neck and severing his spinal cord, killing him instantly. Hammer went down hard with a thump as he hit the floor, becoming a heap of a massive bloody mess.

Sebastian then repositioned to a semi-crouched position. He looked down at Hammer's body for a moment, satisfied he was no longer a threat. He caught his breath as he was tackled from the side by Nail, crashing both of them into the nearby wall and through it to the adjoining room. His gun fell from his grasp from the impact, out of reach.

Nail pulled his KA-BAR knife, slashing at Sebastian. Finding its mark, Nail's blade sliced deep and penetrated Sebastian's left forearm as he attempted to defend against the barrage of cuts and thrusts. A second and third quick slash followed and connected with Sebastian's abdomen.

Countering Nail's attack, Sebastian responded with an exacting jab from his right fist and combination of his left then right fist again to Nail's face while grabbing the assailant's right hand, wielding the knife. Sebastian decisively twisted Nail's index and middle fingers, breaking them instantly and causing him to drop the knife in agony.

Nail was nimble, though, recovered quickly, and responded with rapid-fire jabs and connected with Sebastian's abdomen and face. Ribs cracking, trying to defend against the pounding, Sebastian accepted the onslaught, beginning to lose the contest. He needed to get closer to the window.

This was Nail's craft, his forte, and Sebastian took the full brunt of Nail's rage, retribution for the execution of his twin brother only moments before. Sebastian attempted to go on the offensive, but Nail abruptly and effectively dismissed every effort Sebastian made. Sebastian expended his energy fighting Hammer before and little was left to contend with Nail.

Sebastian turned to see the large bay window in his peripheral vision, 15 feet away. He evaded Nail's flurry of punches as he squarely connected with Nail's knee, making him stagger and wobble backward two steps, which was all that Sebastian needed.

Sebastian had his own bag of tricks, and this was what he needed to buy some time. Sebastian seized the opportunity and scrambled, fending off the severe pain riddling his body, inching toward the sizeable exterior window exposing the outside. The sun was just peeking through the window now.

Nail regained his composure, in no hurry, and felt confident he had Sebastian now, grabbed his KA-BAR knife from the floor, and began confidently walking along the wall toward Sebastian. Slowly making his way to the window, Sebastian need only reach it, but Nail had Sebastian squarely within his sights.

Nail lunged forward, knife outstretched, and connected with Sebastian's hip, the cut deep and with intent as Sebastian winced from the pain. His intention wasn't to kill at the moment; Nail wanted Sebastian to suffer. Sebastian swung but missed, and Nail jabbed into Sebastian's stomach, missing vital organs, but its effect was still devastating. Sebastian fell to his knees, his back squarely to the large window now, holding his stomach and side, the blood trickling profusely as Nail stood above him, facing the window, knife in hand, knowing he had his query where he wanted him, his victory was imminent and guaranteed.

Sebastian, weaponless, looked up into Nail's eyes as Andrei said in broken English, "You killed my brother, and for that, you will suffer slowly until you beg me to end you. It's nothing personal, Mr. Storm, strictly professional. I hope you understand."

As he raised his KA-BAR knife, ready to strike, Sebastian quietly said while looking into Andrei's eyes, "I do understand . . . . *Drop him.*"

Nail squinted, eyes diverted, confused. "Wha—" managed Andrei before his head exploded, liquefied brain and skull spraying the wall behind them as the 50mm bullet tore through Nail's skull as if was a mere balloon. His body fell limp, inert, with only the shell of a man left, defeated and motionless. The threat was eliminated and obliterated.

Sebastian was still on his knees when Fury rushed into the room. He took stock of the situation and surroundings and quickly noticed his fallen SET comrades. He lifted his assault rifle slowly and leveled it on Sebastian squarely as a second slug from the 50mm caliber hit Fury straight in the center of his chest. Simultaneously, Fury squeezed off a single round. The round was off mark but struck Sebastian's left shoulder.

Both men were knocked back from the impact, but Fury was nearly fifteen feet from the large-caliber thump, dropping his assault rifle from the force of the blow. The KAM suit saved him, but the technology was not designed to stop such a substantial caliber and certainly not a direct hit.

Guardian Angel attempted to line up a second round at Fury, a headshot, if possible, but Fury managed to crawl beyond the shooter's line of sight as a third round penetrated the wall and the floor below, through several inches from Fury's thigh. Had it hit him, the impact would have severed his leg in two. "Fuck, 50 Cal's, who the fuck is that guy," said Fury under his breath as he moved down the hallway, insulating himself from the cannon.

Fury quickly slid himself along the hallway to the stairwell, knowing he was now exposed to a sniper if he remained in the loft and that Storm's backup would be arriving within seconds. Fury needed to get out of the building as soon as possible.

Storm's expert sniper was not a contingency they had foreseen, and it proved fatal and costly to their mission. Fury's pain was immense; he suspected a collapsed lung and broken ribs along with internal bleeding from the impact. He could feel the blood pooling beneath his suit and realized this fight was not to be won that day.

Sebastian was lying on his back, hit hard by the last bullet that ripped through his shoulder. "Fallen Angel, immediate Exfil," Sebastian heard over his earpiece as he began to lose consciousness.

He managed a subtle smile and said, "Thank you, Guardian Angel, thank you . . ." Sebastian trailed off, succumbing to his unconsciousness as the darkness began to consume him.

Sean Woodford eased up slightly on his trigger, yet still fixed on the loft from eight hundred yards away, his scope expertly trained on Sebastian and the adjacent rooms. "Copy Guardian Angel, exfil Fallen Angel, thirty seconds, Cover." came a third voice over the earpiece.

"Confirm, area clear, two perps down, third perp still present but hit. Fallen Angel will need medical. Area clear," Sean responded a few moments later. The exfiltration team pulled up by the back entry in matching SUVs and immediately entered the building.

Six heavily armed soldiers quickly ascended the two flights of stairs, entered the loft, and promptly removed Sebastian, the twins, and all weapons from the premises. The exfil teams were very disciplined and diligent in their performance.

Sean Woodford contacted the ex-fil team just after receiving Sebastian's initiating text several minutes prior. The entire loft was semi-cleared within 30 seconds, and they immediately vacated the premises, exiting back down the rear stairs and into a pair of black Mercedes vans waiting on the street in the alleyway. People came out of their respective lofts asking questions but were met with silence from the masked men in black.

The initial exfil team sped off with Sebastian in tow as well as the two assailant's bodies. Sebastian was in dire need of medical attention and was fading fast.

A Special Division 'cleaning crew' passed the exfil group and filed into the loft to remove any evidence of Sebastian's safe house as it was now blown—blood, tech, laptops, or any vital information that could expose Sebastian or Hillary Bastini's Special Division.

The cleaning crew did not officially exist and were spared no expense to keep it that way. The location was now burned and had to be thoroughly cleaned. Minor repairs were made, and damaged items were promptly removed from the loft. Other tenants milled around, but the crew worked diligently and with no distractions. Sebastian's secret compartments were all cleared in just under two minutes. The incendiary device was intentionally activated destroying the laptop within. Their sole assignment was to make the loft generally appear unaltered as much as possible. Eventually, the landlord would enter the premises and see its occupant had vacated with some damage, and that was the intention. The gunfire would have made this scene less than inconspicuous, but little evidence was left.

Sean watched this impressive operation through his scope until it was completed before moving to a secondary location within his building to avoid being tracked himself. There was risk to him in holding a static position, he needed to be on the move.

After the two prior shots on Nail and Fury, he would have been compromised. Sean was frustrated with himself for not eliminating Fury, but he didn't have a headshot; only the body was exposed. That specialized suit saved Fury's life that day.

The atmosphere was thick with uncertainty. Would Sebastian defy insurmountable odds and survive? His life was hanging in the balance.

Chapter 16

A Trigger Emerges Within

Vienna, Austria
Present Day

Fury's head was spinning. He was having difficulty breathing and coughing up blood. Hemorrhaging badly from the bullet that was partially lodged in his left chest, Fury relied on the KAM suit to mitigate the bullet substantially. However, there was still significant damage to Fury's upper abdomen.

Finally, the black Mercedes G-Wagon SUV was in sight several blocks from Sebastian's loft, and Mueller noticed him coming, hurried out of the driver's side door, and opened the back passenger door for Fury as he stumbled in. Mueller looked at him in silence as if to ask, "What of the twins?" Fury simply shook his head, and Mueller assumed they had not survived their mission. His first thought was of the men, but the second was Tobias's disappointment in their failure.

Once the SUV was moving, Fury spoke, "Fuck, fuck, fuck. That was a shitshow, and the twins were bested, Goddammit! Storm was ready for us, and he had an overwatch sniper, a good one, covering his six."

Mueller continued his probe cautiously, afraid to aggravate Fury further, but he had to ask, "Was Storm terminated?"

Fury replied, "I don't think so. He was roughed up by the boys badly, but I don't think they fatally injured him. I got off one shot on Storm before I was taken out, but it wasn't a kill shot. Damn, this was bad, and the boss will be livid. Fuck! That fucking sniper was throwing .50 calls, and I caught one of them. Nail caught the other, and Storm killed Hammer. Get me to the jet, Mueller. I need to return ASAP and report this to the boss. Scrub everything here and make it squeaky clean, got it?"

Mueller promptly replied, "Yessir, will do." He opened his phone and dialed a number. "It's Mueller, fire up the jet. We are coming in hot, one returning with a gunshot injury, so have it ready yesterday." He hung up the phone and sped off toward the Vienna airport. Fury also leans up to Mueller's ear and softly says, "And, Mueller, find out who the fucking shooter was. I'm adding him to my hate list!"

Sebastian, startled, woke with a jump; seeing numerous faces hovering above him caused a brief panic. Blood was everywhere as one of the soldiers was compressing his gunshot wound while another, with paramedic training, attempted to place an IV in his right arm. HB was trying to settle Sebastian, "Stay with me, okay, you are a fighter, Sebastian. Talk to me, stay with me. . . . Sebastian!" Faces were coming in and out of focus.

"He has lost a lot of blood," exclaimed one of the paramedics. Sebastian's vision was dimming as the paramedic yelled, "We're losing him, he's coding, get me the defib . . ."

"Charge!" yelled the paramedic, looking at the LED display on the defibrillator. The intense cold came over Sebastian, his life slipping away into darkness. The cold, it was so cold.

"Clear . . ." said the second paramedic as his voice trailed off. One could hear the steady tone of the blood pressure machine emitting the sound of a stopped heart.

Roanoke, Virginia
1999

"Damn, Sebastian," yelled Sean, looking through his distance locator binoculars. "That was 1,351 yards, dead bull's-eye, nice job. I thought the 8 mph crosswind might throw ya." Sebastian smiled. He was proud of his shot. It was his longest to date, and he looked to Sean for affirmation. Sean's adoring look was enough.

From the ranch home over a mile away, James monitored them on his Super Mag binoculars. James pinpointed where Sean and Sebastian lay in the thickets and tracked their target, which was over one thousand yards away. His vantage point was ideal from this perch as Hillary Bastini stood admiringly beside James, appreciating Sean and Sebastian's triumphs quietly from afar, a silent observer.

James smiled and squawked over the walkie, "I knew you would nail it, Sebastian, quite a shot! Keep 'em coming."

"Thanks, James, I'm getting better," he said into the walkie, then clicked off. He turned to Sean and asked, "What's your greatest distance, Sean?"

Sean smiled as he answered, "1,808 yards. A nasty dude in Afghanistan, so it meant a lot more to me. But don't sweat it, kid. That last shot of yours will beat out almost any other Navy SEAL sniper. You are the man, bro." Their banter was always teasing and gregarious as if they were ten-year-old schoolboys.

Always complimentary, Sebastian said, "Your record, Sean, was over a mile. That's tremendous. I will get there someday."

Sean said, "No question. Practice. Study and understand wind variables. And . . . more practice. Master velocity drop and keep those nerves under control, which probably won't be an issue for you, Sebastian. And lastly, practice and then more practice." Both laughed, and Sebastian smiled as that advice was precisely what he would follow, and all three of them were certain of it.

"Lock and load let's do another one," yelled Sebastian as he chambers another round.

HB was present in a covert capacity, watching their young protégé taking form in his maturity. "That last shot would put him second in my outfit, James," whispered HB. They heard another crack from the rifle a mile away.

James chuckled softly, "Second? . . . . That would be one spot lower than he would expect. Demand even, Hillary."

HB smiled and then responded, "Love overachievers. When do I have the privilege of meeting him? I've dissected all the close-quarter combat, recon, mission sequencing, and mock covert ops videos you have sent me on this kid, but I still need to meet this young man. His skills are exceptional. Off the charts even. All of those stats are impressive, but I need to look him in the eye, James. I need to see the killer instinct and if he can maintain control and execute when needed. I need to see and feel it; there is no other way around it."

James put his binoculars down, leaned against the porch railing, and looked at Hillary Bastini for a moment, "You will be even more impressed with him when you do meet him; of that, I can assure you, HB. But soon, I think. Honestly, there is not much more I can teach him, and the same goes for Sean. We are both beginning to learn from him, in fact. His perspective and intuition are a marvel to behold—a fresh and different approach he has to the modern combat mentality. He has the battle analyzed, fought, and executed before it even begins, Hillary. He makes it almost . . . artistic in its execution."

James continued, "Sebastian has definitely made Sean a far better soldier in many ways. Sean's bar had been raised considerably since he began training with Sebastian. On these trips back here from San Diego, Sean longs to make himself better, to make him an even better soldier. Sebastian tested him far beyond what they do on base at this point. He has said he made him a stronger SEAL, which astounds me a decorated soldier like Sean could learn from a seventeen-year-old kid." James adjusts his position and shakes his head at the mere reality of his statement.

HB said excitedly, "Well, James, let's make it sooner than later. I'm very curious about this one. I'm anxious to get started. I have a 5:30 p.m. flight, but I'll be in touch."

James laughed. "Oh, I know you are, Hillary, I know you are." As James heard over the walkie-talkie, "Jesus Fuck, Sebastian, 1404 yards and with 11 mph crosswind? I'm not playing with you anymore," scoffed Sean. James smiled as his two boys laughed at the comment.

"You see that one, James? I'm catching up, Sean," yelled Sebastian over the walkie. James picked up his binoculars and, after a few seconds, replied, "Impressive, Sebastian. Shoot for 1500 next." The delay in James's response caused Sebastian to look over at James's position on the porch.

"Who's the blond with you, James? You on a date?" asked Sebastian, laughing through the walkie-talkie. Both boys laughed at the comment especially knowing James hadn't been out on a date in years.

James glanced at Hillary and dropped his head in a melodramatic slump mouthing the word "Shit." "She's just here delivering a pizza," he replied as Sebastian said softly through the walkie, "Must be a meat lovers then. I have my eye on you, old man. I have to look out for you and always with one eye open." They all laughed together.

James turned to Hillary and said, "Well, we have been made, Hillary. You had better roll out of here." She took the hint, walking down the stairs to her waiting SUV. "Boys will be boys. We will talk soon. Sooner than later, James," said Hillary, waving as she stepped into her SUV and drove off in her typical fashion.

In the four years since Sebastian had lost his parents and left the orphanage to come to live with James, he flourished beyond belief. Halfway through his last year in high school, Sebastian took advantage of what James would teach him about soldiering, nature, people, and life.

He was always eager to learn from those he respected, and James and Sean were at the top of his list. Sebastian especially enjoyed Sean's visits, which occurred several times a year, where his training would escalate to new and exciting levels, testing him, and pushing his limits well beyond their expectations.

Sebastian's abilities expanded as he focused on his close-quarter combat, marksmanship, covert maneuvers, and sniper skills, all becoming exceptional in precision and execution. He would practice with James several hours per week, and when Sean would come home on leave, he would hone his skills further with more advanced combat training followed by rigorous tests and trials crafted by Sean and James, all the while pushing his limits daily.

When alone, Sebastian often would develop his skills privately, spending hours in the morning before school or in the evening meditating, focusing, yoga, Pilates, or martial arts as his daily routine necessitated his discipline. Balance was a key element and constantly in practice for Sebastian, and he maintained the development of those skills every waking moment.

Sebastian continued through high school but was uninterested in normal adolescent social group activities his age typically surrounded themselves with. His interests were less juvenile than teenagers his age, and he strived to make a difference in his future.

Young people his age didn't understand his personal training regimen or his dedication to it and had trouble relating to him physically and mentally on many levels. Many misunderstood Sebastian and thought his demeanor was mysterious and stoic. He maintained a perfect 4.0 GPA as school and studies were austere and tedious at best for him. School was a necessary path, James always said; therefore, he persevered through the monotony of that part of his life and simply used it to bridge the more essential life lessons he gained during that time frame.

By no means was he like the other adolescents his age. His goals had far more significance. He strived to make his life worthwhile and substantial. Sebastian learned this lesson early, and his focus on that point made him somewhat of an enigma to other teenagers in his school. Sebastian didn't mind; he was perfectly accepting of the label.

Sebastian and James's business was performing extraordinarily, but it required much of James's time these days. Sebastian remained involved when his schedule permitted and often, after school, was at the shop developing new and innovative designs for their traps. James always thought it interesting Sebastian was already a millionaire and yet none of his classmates had any notion of the fact. His humility remained intact, and Sebastian navigated through his adolescence beautifully.

James had retired from the park service two years before and was dedicated full-time to their endeavor. James kept the machine running smoothly, handling most of the financial aspects and business operations, whereas Sebastian worked with the design team and engineers on product development. It would be another year or two until James fully disclosed how lucrative and remarkable the young business was actually doing.

Several months later, Sebastian and James had stopped to refuel the truck after returning from work one afternoon. Sebastian ran into the convenience store while James filled the tank and noticed several of his classmates had congregated within the store, looking at him curiously when he came through the front entrance. He immediately sensed something was amiss, tensing slightly as a result.

Two masked men had three students, and the convenience store clerk held at gunpoint; the third, largest one had crept up behind Sebastian when he came through the door and put the cold muzzle of his handgun to the base of Sebastian's neck. "Don't be a statistic, kid," the man whispered to Sebastian and then yelled to the others. "Everyone. . . hand my associates your phones, now!"

Seemingly frantic, the man with his gun to Sebastian's neck yelled at the attendant. "Clean out the drawer and do it now!" Pushing the urgency of his order.

The second accomplice said, "Jeez, Josh, settle down, man." Sharply, the leader turned and said, "Don't use names, dumbass." He ushered the employee to move and do as he was told.

Sebastian closed his eyes and considered the situation carefully. Having swiftly assessed the three assailants, he determined the leader standing directly behind him was the most confident of the trio, and the other two were clearly as afraid as the hostages. The leader was a larger man and seemed very confident, which posed more of a challenge for Sebastian because of his variability and sheer size.

The leader's handgun was still pointed, pushing on the back of Sebastian's neck. In that moment, Sebastian determined the leader was right-handed, over 230 pounds, as the leader's bark resonated more profoundly in Sebastian's left ear. Sebastian had all the necessary information stored within his head; he simply needed to execute it.

Sebastian closed his eyes, then . . . . *unleashed.*

Without warning and in a blur of motion, Sebastian quickly turned to his right and grabbed the man's gun with both of his hands, simultaneously thrusting backward and upward, bashing into the man's face squarely, breaking his nose as he fell to the floor.

Sebastian abruptly turned toward the other two after flipping the man's gun in their direction and firing two bullets at one assailant. The first bullet struck his right shoulder before he could react, making the man drop his gun, and the second slug ripped into his right leg, missing the femoral artery by a few inches. His objective was not to kill the men but to leave them incapacitated, which he did with a fastidious manner and execution.

Sebastian angled toward the last assailant and immediately put a round into the man's hand and the second into his opposite hand as he went down in agony. "Move over by the freezers and call 911, please," Sebastian said calmly to the hostages.

Josh, their leader, recovered slightly from behind, stood up, and launched himself at Sebastian. Sidestepping the attempt, Sebastian left-hooked the man, making him stumble, but he was crazed now and heading right at Sebastian. Putting a slug into each shoulder, Sebastian had carefully aimed as the man went down hard. Relentless in his perseverance, trying to stand up, Sebastian finally had enough and kicked the man hard in the face, knocking him to the ground. He spit out two teeth, dazed and confused, his face bloodied.

James, after hearing the initial gunshots, burst through the door. As the leader was shaking his head and attempting to rise up yet again, James put a square right fist into the man's jaw and dropped him once again as Sebastian kicked the guns away and pulled the three assaulters to a pile in the middle of the store, all writhing in pain and confused over what had transpired.

Sebastian still had the handgun directed at the three squirming on the floor as James stepped over them and motioned to take the gun from Sebastian. Satisfied with the status of the situation, Sebastian willingly handed the weapon to James.

One of the high school kids said, "That was the coolest thing I've ever seen. He took the first guy out and shot the other two in like a second." Sebastian feared the publicity surrounding the incident would surely surface as the first officer arrived a few minutes later, and the attendant and high school kids fought over one another to tell their side of the story.

When they finally came to Sebastian, James stood behind him in support as the gurneys wheeled the shackled offenders out through the front door. The leader, his name Josh Strickland, grabbed at Sebastian's sleeve while passing, face bloodied, front two teeth missing and nose broken, and said with a strange lisp, "This ain't done, kid, I have friends. I'll make you suffer for this!"

Sebastian yanked his arm back and glared at the leader as he turned back toward the officer and proceeded to lay out the account, in every detail, the way it transpired, to which the officer replied, "That's quite a story, young man, and all four of the people, within the store, basically told it the same way. They think you are a hero over there. Me? I would have let them have what they wanted and let 'em leave," he said, surprising Sebastian, who quipped, "And let them get away with it, do it again, or worse, kill someone? No disrespect to you, sir, but those people couldn't help themselves, officer. They needed someone who was willing to take a risk. I'd do the same thing again without hesitation," he said as James nodded in agreement.

The officer looked weary and said, "Fair enough, son. Take him home, Ranger. You will see quite a circus outside." As they left the store, the media had begun its frenzy over the event. A worthy news story in this quiet little town, it was undoubtedly their highlight of the month. James quickly escorted Sebastian to the truck. A reporter got in front of them to ask, "How did you take out those three assailants all by yourself, young man?"

A second reporter butted in to ask, "Do you have military training?" Yet another cut the second one off to say, "Those people, the hostages, think you are a hero. What is your response to their statements? How old are you, Sebastian?"

James puts his hand up, the other on Sebastian's shoulder, and steps in to say, "No comment. The boy simply did the right thing; no two ways about it. Now leave him alone, please."

He opened the door, ushered Sebastian into the passenger seat, then walked around to the driver's side. "No comment, no comment," he repeated as he loaded himself in, easing through the numerous cameramen, reporters, and media mobsters as they drove away in silence for the next few moments.

James watched the mob in the rearview mirror. After several seconds, Sebastian said softly, "I disappointed you in there, didn't I, James?"

James replied, "Nah, you didn't, son, but had something gone wrong and you took a bullet, or worse yet, were killed? I just don't know. I never would have been the same, Sebastian. You are like a son to me. The truth is, had Sean been in that situation, he would have done the same damn thing. Who knows? I may have, as well. Your instincts kicked in, Sebastian. I can't entirely blame you for what you did. Not sure you had much of a choice."

"The scary thing was that by chance, a stray bullet or your actions could have caused one of those hostages to take the hit or, worse, killed. If that had occurred, all of this would have had a far different outcome. There are always consequences, Sebastian. The media wouldn't have thought you a hero, but something far worse. They would have eaten you alive."

Sebastian quickly responded, "I wouldn't have let that happen, but I know it all set into motion so quickly. It was like my mind went blank, and my body went into overdrive. I remember thinking, I have only one goal, eliminate the threat. It was so strange. I couldn't stop myself, James. I just had to . . . initiate and execute. Those three guys were mere obstacles in my path. Speed bumps. I played out how it was going to happen before it even did, and then, it's like I simply instigated the sequence of events, letting it all unfold but already knowing the outcome before it even began."

James hesitated a moment before responding, "It's because you are a soldier, Sebastian, a warrior elite. This is your way and all you know. Sometimes, I'm so excited for you and what you are learning, how quickly you have progressed, and what you are becoming. Sean thinks this, too, but then I'm also saddened at the same time. It's such a lonely and solitary life, and I don't want that for you, either. But I know deep down, it's your calling . . . like breathing, for you, and I know it's what you dream of and yearn for to complete you. You have a set of talents beyond anything Sean or I have ever seen before. . . in anyone, Sebastian. How could one stifle those faculties when it's truly a wonder to experience?"

James continued, laughing out loud, "I'm just imagining how you made quick work of those three idiots in the store. They probably never understood what hit them. I'm certain, Sebastian. Underestimating you all the way. Above all, you had a choice in there."

James became serious, "You could have killed every last one of them, but you didn't. That in itself . . . was the most remarkable thing you did today, son. You chose correctly. You spared them, and that . . . was the most impressive to me. Your decision made me the proudest I have ever been of you."

James nodded his head in appreciation of Sebastian's decisions made in the store.

Sebastian listened to James's words knowingly and said, "This is what I want, know, and believe in, James. I don't think I would be happy doing anything else. I'm ready to enlist. I would love to serve with Sean as a Navy SEAL if they would consider me."

James thought about what Sebastian said and replied, after a moment, "It's a possibility, Sebastian, but Sean and I think you may have an interest in something bigger . . . but let me sleep on it, then we will discuss it, is that okay with you?"

Something bigger, thought Sebastian, but he reluctantly smiled and said, "Okay, sounds good."

They sat in silence for a time, following the emotional moment that had transpired, and it caused the image of his father to creep into Sebastian's mind until he felt he needed to tell someone, and he trusted James above all. The incident at the gas station gave him a sense of power, the same elation he experienced when, in some form, he controlled the fate of his father all those years ago in the forest.

Sebastian broke the silence, "There is something I need to tell you, have wanted to tell you, but I'm afraid you may be disappointed when I do, James." He turned to look at his reaction.

James quickly said, "Aw, Sebastian, you won't ever disappoint me. You can always tell me anything and know I'll never judge you . . . ever."

Sebastian started slowly. "It's about my dad and the day he died." James was curious as to what was to follow as he drove, concentrating on Sebastian's words.

Sebastian continued, "The evening he was attacked by the wolves. He had been looking for me in the forest that night. It was dark, and my trap caught his leg by mistake, and he dropped his gun while he tried to remove the trap from his foot and ankle, and the wolves . . . got him . . . as I watched, James . . . I could have helped him, but I froze and let them. I let the wolves attack him that night." Sebastian's head slumped after he told his story to James.

James abruptly pulled over to the side of the road off on the shoulder and stopped, putting the truck in park, and turned to Sebastian and said, "You can't blame yourself for that, Sebastian. Your father . . . was not a moral man. I understand why you hesitated that day. Some people just . . . aren't worth saving. You can't blame yourself," James said, watching Sebastian closely.

Sebastian felt a sense of ease and lifted his head as he said, "I don't think I do, James, but I had to tell someone. It was my trap that kept him from defending himself, and I do carry some guilt over that, but less as I get older. I've accepted my father deserved what he got. I only wish my mom could have held out a little longer."

James looked at Sebastian and asked, "If your father had found you, what do you think he would have done to you?" Sebastian looked into his eyes and thought for a moment, "He would have killed me, James. I saw it in his eyes back at our home, and the same while he looked for me, there is no question. I would be dead if he had found me before the wolves got him."

James responded, "Then there is your answer. I would have done the same thing you did, Sebastian. I would have let it happen the same way. That man deserved exactly what he got. Don't feel guilty for him, son." James looked in his rearview mirror, then his left mirror as he pulled back out onto the road.

They never spoke of the incident again.

Sebastian was always the unassuming champion. They sat in silence before coming up to the house. "Well, this delayed us a few hours; you saving the world, Sebastian. Take care of those chores before it gets dark, would you?" asked James, but both laughed at the comment.

Sebastian replied, "Sure. Sorry about the . . . interruption. And also, thanks for talking. It really helped." He hopped out of the truck and walked into the house.

"I'll be inside, in a few," said James, and Sebastian waved as he entered the front door. Once the door closed behind Sebastian, James pulled out his phone and reluctantly dialed a number he knew he would be calling at some point soon. He just didn't think it would be this soon.

After a few rings, the word "Bastini" came from the other end.

"Hey, Hillary, it's James," he said with hesitation, followed by, "I think it's time." HB replied, "Excellent! I'll arrive in the morning if that works, James. I saw the news story at the gas station."

James said softly, "Yep, big day for him. That'll be fine on time, HB; see ya then." He pressed the 'End' button on his phone.

As James slipped the phone back into his back pocket, his gaze again settled upon his land in appreciation of its simplicity and uncomplicated innate beauty just as the sun was beginning its descent. It would be dark soon.

James was experiencing an inner struggle as his conflict was battling within. Was he finally giving Sebastian the keys to the kingdom and furnishing him with the opportunity to reach his full potential with Hillary Bastini, yet sealing this extraordinary young man's fate, stripping away his youth, in reducing his life to the confines of the elite supersoldier?

James was confident Sebastian would ultimately become that very force. He couldn't visualize Sebastian being anything other than a soldier.

The image of a college life, hounding coeds, and a domestic domicile environment was the farthest from what Sebastian wanted. He always strived to be the best at what he did, and James did not doubt he would achieve that very feat.

Bastini's organization would show Sebastian things he had never seen before and unlock the true magnificence of his aptitude. The newest and most profound chapter of Sebastian's young life was about to begin.

The question was . . . . *was the world ready for him?*

Chapter 17

A Shining Light Lost

Roanoke, Virginia
1999

The morning following the incident at the gas station, Sebastian abruptly woke and turned to the clock on his nightstand. It read 5:23 am. It was early, with the sun beginning to rise from his eastern window.

He overheard indistinguishable voices emerging from beyond the kitchen. Curious, thinking only he and James were in the house, Sebastian threw on his SEAL hat and jacket and warily exited his bedroom, sauntering into the kitchen, cautiously listening. He vaguely noticed through the porch window James speaking with someone. Sebastian determined from their dialogue it was a female voice responding to James.

Sebastian quietly opened one of the French doors leading to the outdoor porch where James and a female guest were sitting and enjoying a coffee. James said, "Ahhhh, Sebastian, good morning, buddy." He began to stand up.

Sebastian replied, "Good morning." He smiled at James, "Ma'am," tipping his hat to the female guest, intrigued about the woman as she stood up. He had seen the woman before, watching from the shadows.

James explained, "This is The Director of the Anti-Terrorist Division (ATSD), Hillary Bastini, Sebastian. An old friend."

Sebastian shook her hand firmly and respectfully nodded. Sebastian said, "Very nice to meet you, ma'am." James ushered all of them to take a seat.

Hillary said, "Oh, Sebastian, please don't call me that. Bastini, Hillary, or preferably HB, but nothing too formal. I don't need the label to feed my ego or remind me of my advancing age." She lightly laughed.

James smiled and said, "Sebastian, in light of yesterday's events, I thought it might be a good time for HB and you to meet. I explained a little about the debacle at the gas station."

HB inserted, "And quite the news story I saw as well. An impressive display, Sebastian. I'm sure it may be a little confusing on what I do or why I am here this morning?"

Sebastian hesitated, then replied, "I recognize you from afar, Ms. Bastini, either when practicing maneuvers, sniper training, or during close-quarter training here or at our gym over the past year. I didn't think much of it and assumed James here would let me know when it was time to put a name with the face. So curious, yes, I suppose I am," Sebastian said with a slight smile.

"I didn't remain inconspicuous enough, I see, or little gets past you. I would venture to guess a combination of both, maybe?" HB responded with a soft, subtle smile.

Sebastian humbly said, "James and Sean have trained me well, Ms. Bastini. I have them to thank. Observation and awareness . . . fortunately come easier to me than for most. I'm fortunate, I suppose. I was kinda lucky yesterday. As James and I discussed, it may have gone an entirely different way, too." He tested HB a bit.

HB responded, "That you were, Sebastian, and yes, along with some subtle humility as well, I see. Do you have any idea what I do or why I am here this morning?"

Sebastian ventured a guess, "I suppose you and James see something in me most people wouldn't notice, and I'm assuming James's reference to 'Director' when he introduced you would lead me to believe you work with the government, specifically the Department of Defense or Navy SEAL division, possibly? And fairly high up the totem pole, I'm guessing. Am I close?"

James simply smiled at the exchanges between these two people with whom he had enormous respect. HB smiled, too. "Partially correct, Sebastian. The branches of the military you mention are certainly among our elite, promoted in a way as an instrument to largely facilitate the media, and have kept this country safe for many generations, much like what your friend James did before I came on the scene. He was partially responsible for my own training, but that was a long time ago, wasn't it, James?" She turned to James, acknowledging his nod in agreement.

"But my group, Sebastian, is . . . well, it's tremendously different from those military sects, though enormously respectable in their own right. Mine is unique . . . *special even*," HB said with a soft and genuine smile.

She preferred not to dramatize or publicize her division's existence, yet what she said was undeniably true, though deliberately vague. Her division was shrouded in secrecy, its purpose, and operations obscure even to her superiors. Much of its work was off the books, cloaked in layers of confidentiality that made it nearly impossible to explain. When she did speak of it, only a select few deemed worthy enough to listen were given a glimpse into its enigmatic nature. Balancing transparency and discretion were a constant challenge, but essential to maintaining the division's covert integrity. This made explaining her division a daunting task to anyone unfamiliar.

Attempting to find the correct words, HB went on to say, "My group is small, and elite . . . Sebastian, specialized, and a well-oiled machine that executes without fail. This division is as close to a 'sure thing' as there is from an elite covert military standpoint."

HB and James studied Sebastian as he took this information in and processed what he was hearing. Though intelligent, he was still struggling to fully comprehend what HB attempted to explain. She couldn't blame him. It was difficult to explain and understand for anyone not directly affiliated with her division.

Finally, Sebastian asked, "So a specialized unit but not part of the Navy SEAL program or associated in any way with the special forces within the army or any other military branch? Yes, Ms. Bastini, I guess I am still confused. I'm sorry. I have thought a lot about this and my plan for the future."

"I want to be a Navy SEAL like my brother Sean. I'm aware of their training protocols because of him, and James. I wish to serve my country in that capacity. I'm not sure how another outfit could be any better, honestly. Those are considered the best of the best, aren't they? Sean is a part of it, and I want to be a part of it someday, too." HB and James looked at one another, unsure of how to proceed.

Sebastian was passionate and getting slightly agitated not understanding where this conversation was heading. James stepped in. "I think we are speaking of the same thing, Sebastian. I beg of you, listen to what HB has to say."

But a spark of rebellion was igniting within Sebastian, compelling him to stand his ground. "James," he pressed on, his voice steady yet intense, "We have discussed me joining the Navy, then entering the SEAL program. Isn't that the path I should take? Isn't that what you and Sean would want for me?" His eyes bore into James's, seeking affirmation, yearning for validation of his burgeoning resolve.

James was now starting to become impatient and said, "Sebastian! Sean supports this, but we don't think the Navy SEALS are the best fit for you."

Sebastian's voice cracked with frustration as he cried out, "What? I've spent a third of my life training for this, James, and now you don't think I'm good enough? Why have you wasted my time if you think I can't make the grade?" The intensity of his emotions betrayed a raw immaturity, a desperate need for validation that he had rarely allowed to surface. His mind raced, trying to decipher their true intentions.

Without waiting for a response, Sebastian abruptly stood up, the legs of his chair scraping harshly against the floor. He stormed towards the exterior door, each step fueled by a mix of anger and confusion. Reaching the doorway, he leaned his forehead against the cool glass, his fists clenched tightly on either side of the door frame, eyes squeezed shut as if trying to block out the world.

The environment buzzed with a charged tension, the silence heavy and oppressive. James and HB exchanged a quick, concerned glance before rising from their seats. They moved towards Sebastian with urgency, their footsteps echoing in the suddenly too-quiet confines of the porch.

James reached out first, placing a firm yet gentle hand on Sebastian's shoulder. "Sebastian," he began, his voice low and steady, "It's not about thinking you're not good enough. It's about making sure you're ready for what's ahead."

HB stepped closer, her voice softer but no less earnest. "We've invested in you because we believe in your potential, not simply your current abilities. They are but a steppingstone of your true potential. This isn't about doubting you; it's about preparing you for something greater."

Sebastian remained motionless, his breath fogging the glass in front of him. The words of James and HB began to pierce through the haze of his frustration, slowly calming the tempest within. He took a deep breath, the tension in his shoulders easing slightly.

Finally, he opened his eyes, staring out at the world in the reflection beyond the glass. "I simply need to ensure that all this has a purpose," he said quietly, his voice barely above a whisper.

James squeezed his shoulder reassuringly. "It does, Sebastian. Every step you take, every challenge you face, it all leads to something greater. Trust us and trust yourself."

HB nodded in agreement. "You've come so far, and you have so much further to go. We're with you every step of the way."

Sebastian nodded slowly, feeling the weight of their words. He straightened up, turning to face them. The fire in his eyes was tempered, but it still burned bright. "Alright," he said, his voice firmer. "Explain to me the full meaning behind your words."

James and HB exchanged a look of relief and determination. They were aware that this was only the beginning of Sebastian's journey, and they were ready to guide him through whatever lay ahead.

HB said, "Sebastian, you would make a tremendous SEAL; there is no question of that idea from any of us, and if that is what you truly want to do, then we will all support you fully in that decision, but Sean and James want me to train you, and I don't train those 'types' of soldiers, Sebastian. They don't want you to be a SEAL because they fear it would be too . . . *limiting* for you and your talents if that makes any sense. Let me continue."

Sebastian turned and said, "Limiting? What does that even mean when they are considered to be the best? What do you have that they don't, Ms. Bastini? What possibly could your organization offer that the SEAL program cannot offer me?"

HB met James's gaze as he gave her a subtle nod, a silent "tell him" conveyed through the exchange. Taking a deep breath, she turned to Sebastian, her eyes filled with a blend of determination and empathy.

"Sebastian," she began, her voice steady and compelling, "The reason Sean, James, and I hesitate to endorse your path to becoming a Navy SEAL isn't because we doubt your abilities. Quite the opposite, in fact. We have no question; you'd be a valuable asset to their ranks; they would be fortunate to have someone of your caliber. But here's the thing—the SEALs, while elite and highly specialized, represent only a fraction of what you're capable of achieving."

She paused, allowing her words to sink in before continuing, "The SEAL training regimen is grueling, and it forges incredible soldiers. But there's another echelon, a level beyond the most prestigious special forces. This isn't about diminishing the SEALs; it's about recognizing your potential to transcend those limits."

James stepped closer, adding, "You've already shown us glimpses of what you can do, Sebastian. But to unlock your full potential, to reach that next level, you need a different kind of training, one that goes beyond traditional military frameworks."

HB nodded in agreement. "Think of it as an evolution of your skills, an opportunity to become something more than you might imagine. We're talking about capabilities that surpass conventional warfare, strategies that blend intellect with combat prowess in ways the world has never witnessed."

Sebastian's eyes widened slightly, intrigue replacing his earlier frustration. "What are you talking about?" he asked, his curiosity piqued.

HB's lips curved into a knowing smile. "Let me explain," she said, stepping forward. "There's a program, one that's as secretive as it is transformative. It combines the best elements of special forces training with cutting-edge technology and advanced psychological conditioning. It's designed to create operatives who can operate independently, think several steps ahead, and adapt to any situation with unparalleled precision."

James continued, "It's about more than simply physical strength or endurance. It's about mastering the art of strategy, understanding the nuances of human behavior, and utilizing technology in ways that appear almost futuristic. This program doesn't only train soldiers; it cultivates leaders and innovators on the battlefield."

Sebastian asked sarcastically, "What do you train then, Ms. Bastini? What is so special about your soldiers?" James softly chimes in, "Let her explain, Sebastian. It will all make sense once she does. Give her a minute." Sebastian gave her the minute out of respect for James.

HB's voice was earnest, her eyes locked onto Sebastian's with a plea. "Please, Sebastian, think this through. I don't train soldiers or even specialized, commercialized soldiers like the SEALs or Special Forces. No, I train a different breed entirely—the best of the best."

She paused, letting the weight of her words settle. "James is aware of it, Sean feels it, and now, seeing you, I recognize it too. Deep down, in your core, you know it as well. I'm certain of it. You sense it, you live and understand it, Sebastian. The SEAL training, as rigorous as it is, won't be enough to harness your true potential."

Sebastian's eyes widened, a mix of realization and curiosity flickering across his face. HB continued, her voice gaining intensity. "Your talents deserve more than simply elite training. They require a program that goes beyond the conventional, beyond what the SEALs can offer. You have the potential to transcend the limits of traditional soldiering."

James stepped in, his tone reinforcing HB's words. "What we're offering is a path that will push you to the very edge of human capability. It's about mastering not only physical prowess, but the art of strategy, psychological insight, and technological innovation."

HB nodded, her eyes never leaving Sebastian's. "This is about becoming more than a soldier, Sebastian. It's about becoming a force of nature, a leader, and a game-changer. You have what it takes, and we see it. Now, it's time for you to embrace it."

"In essence, Sebastian," HB said, her voice intense and unwavering, "I train soldiers who would, quite frankly, eliminate an entire SEAL team singlehandedly. Yes, that's the kind of soldier I develop—one type, one focus. I train elite supersoldiers, and that's you, Sebastian. A lethal, unstoppable human weapon."

Sebastian's heart pounded as HB's words sank in. This was more than he had ever imagined, a path fraught with danger and unimaginable potential. The moment seemed to pulse with the weight of her declaration, and he sensed his destiny crystallizing before him.

"You're not simply joining a team," she continued, her eyes boring into his, "you're becoming a force unto yourself. The training will be grueling, the challenges unparalleled. But you, Sebastian, have the raw talent and the iron will to rise above them all. The SEALs are elite, but what I'm offering you is beyond that. It's about becoming the epitome of human combat prowess."

James nodded in agreement, adding, "This isn't just about physical strength or combat skills. It's about mastering every aspect of warfare—psychological, technological, strategic. You'll be pushed to your limits and then beyond, forging a new level of soldier that the world has never seen."

HB's voice dropped to a fierce whisper, "You have the potential to be a game-changer, Sebastian. A lethal, fucking human weapon. The question is, are you ready to embrace that?"

Sebastian's breath caught in his throat. The magnitude of what was being offered was both thrilling and terrifying. But deep down, he realized this was his path. "I think, ma'am, I think I have always known I was ready," he said, his voice resolute. HB and James exchanged a look of satisfaction. They knew they had recruited a future legend.

James continued, "We all want what's best for you. Your country needs you, Sebastian, and HB needs you." James added, "You have the potential to be the best, Sebastian, and HB's outfit is the only one that will provide the tools to get you there. The only one."

Sebastian asked, "And Sean feels the same way? You will train me to eliminate an entire SEAL team. Is that even possible?"

James quickly replied, "Sean is the one that suggested it, Sebastian, and yes, it is. He believes in this without question. Have I ever steered you wrong or lied to you about anything, Sebastian?"

Sebastian stood a little straighter, almost at attention. "No, sir, you have not."

James said, "Well, I ain't about to start today, son. Trust in this and the people that love you the most."

Sebastian, now feeling more assured, said, "Yessir. I apologize for my outburst, Ms. Bastini." HB nodded, understanding.

James continued, addressing HB, "We would continue the training with some help from you, HB, but he needs to finish school. And when he does that and is ready, we will ship him off to you for training and to receive his degree at the same time. An educated and intelligent soldier is a better soldier. Agreed?"

Sebastian turned to her and said, "HB, I want to be the best. If you can get me there, then I am all in. I want no ceiling to my training." HB smiled at his response. His reply pleased both HB and James. Proud of him and satisfied the United States had Sebastian Storm fighting on their team. She would make him into a force never to be reckoned with.

HB replied, "Spoken like a true champion. We will train you, Sebastian, and we have every confidence 'the best' is exactly what you will be, and you will train with the most talented out there. I have a particular soldier I think you will admire. I think the two of you will respect one another greatly. His name is Tobias."

Sebastian said with a smile, "I look forward to it."

HB finalized this conversation with, "Fair enough, gentlemen, good talk." She put her sunglasses on and headed down the porch stairs to her black sedan, the driver waiting quietly for her return. She waved slightly as the driver opened the rear passenger door, and they were off.

James turned to Sebastian and said, "You possess talents we haven't yet begun to uncover, Sebastian, and I'm proud to be by your side and watch as it develops and help in any way I can. I'm always here for you. Sean and I have little else we can teach you at this point. You have evolved beyond our scope, and this is why this is the best decision for you."

"HB told me of this supersoldier, Tobias. He is every bit your equal. She said he is extraordinary."

Sebastian then said, "I'm excited about meeting this man. Thank you for always having my six." Sebastian smiled as James squeezed his shoulder and said, "As HB said, when the government had an issue that's sensitive, covert, and quasi-secretive, they would send in a seven-man SEAL team to attain the national and international media exposure like what they did with Bin Laden. This is because that is what people expect from those publicized groups, but when they need a high-value target eliminated, secrecy an absolute, or their SEAL team fails. Well, then . . . that's when they send you in, Sebastian. There aren't two ways about it. That's why the SEAL team is too limiting. I want what's best for you, too. Remember, you and Sean are my boys, my family, and my future."

Sebastian smiled at the thought of what he may achieve over what a SEAL team failed to accomplish. He wanted to be a super soldier.

Roanoke, Virginia
2004

The grass was damp, slick with dew from a rainy night, the sun long set, leaving the world in shadow. As he lay on his stomach, dazed, and disoriented, fragmented memories from seventeen years ago began to crystallize in his mind. The images were vague at first, distant echoes of a fateful day, but they grew sharper with each passing second.

He lifted his head, blinking away the haze. The sight before him was harrowing flames consuming the home, his home. *James's home*. The fire fiercely roared; its heat palpable even from his prone position. The crackling of burning wood a dreadful soundtrack to his resurfacing memories.

Seventeen years ago, it had all gone up in flames. He could almost hear the panicked shouts, the cracking embers and supports filling his ears. The bitter scent of smoke filled his nostrils, mingling with the cold, wet earth beneath him. He remembered the terror, the desperation, the heart-wrenching loss. The greatest loss he had ever experienced dwarfing the death of his own mother though her memory had long since faded.

The present and past collided in his mind, the intensity of the moment nearly overwhelming. It wasn't the fire destroying a building; it was the obliteration of a piece of his history, a part of his soul. He had lost so much that day, and the resurgence of those memories brought with it a surge of determination.

Pushing himself up, he recognized a burning resolve solidify within him. This time, he wouldn't be a helpless witness to the destruction. This time, he was ready to fight back, to confront the ghosts of his past and carve out a new future from the ashes.

His head was aching from the explosion, unable to remember why he was on the back lawn. He stood up on one knee, gathering himself, noticing strange details such as not wearing shoes. His skin tinged by the heat of the blaze upon his face, looking at the flames immersing the dwelling, recalling now, being awakened by a faint odor—the aroma of propane gas. The image played out of that fateful day, filling his mind with painful memories.

He had been visiting James to celebrate the sale of their company and only arrived from Munich that evening, only hours before. He had been with HB's outfit for nearly four years now and, sadly, had not been able to see James as much as he would have liked.

But he had taken this time to honor his mentor with a visit; he owed him tremendously. James deserved far more than Sebastian gave him, but James never asked for anything in return. James fostered and appreciated the importance of what Sebastian did for his country. To keep the American people safe.

Sebastian had told James he'd arrive at 11:00 pm, but in reality, he'd taken an earlier flight, landing at 7:00 pm. His intention was to surprise James, adding an element of spontaneity to his visit. After grabbing an Uber from the airport, he arrived at the house under the dusky twilight, the sky a canvas of deep purples and blues.

Sebastian's heart raced with anticipation as he approached the front door. He rang the doorbell, opting not to alert James beforehand, wanting to witness the genuine surprise on his friend's face. The moments stretched out, each second amplifying his excitement.

The door swung open, and the look of astonishment on James's face was worth every bit of Sebastian's subterfuge. "Sebastian? What are you doing here so early?" James stammered; his eyes wide with disbelief.

Sebastian grinned, his eyes twinkling with mischief. "Couldn't wait to see you, James. I've missed ya. Thought I'd give you a little surprise." James laughed, shaking his head in amazement. "Well, you certainly succeeded. Come in, was just beginning to prepare dinner for you." He hugged Sebastian tightly and said, "Damn, son, I've missed you." He pushed him to arm's length to look at him again as he beckoned him through the front door. "This is your home, Sebastian. You can always simply walk in, you know. What's this knocking bullshit?"

As they stepped inside, the warmth of their friendship enveloped them, setting the stage for an evening filled with shared stories and rekindled camaraderie. The unexpected reunion marked the beginning of an unforgettable night, where past memories and future plans intertwined seamlessly, igniting a renewed sense of adventure in both their hearts.

Not expecting anyone to his home at that hour, James was so happy to see Sebastian's smiling face standing there as they opened a bottle of wine, all grown up and appearing quite the man, distinguished, and dignified.

Admitting to James, "Well, wasn't sure if you may have a lady friend around, old man," says Sebastian. James simply says "ha" at the comment as he winks at him as if to say, "One never knows." The old familiar aromas of his youth entangle his senses as James says enthusiastically, "Can you tell what I'm making?" "Steak. My favorite, the familiar aromas of my adolescence, James, very much missed of late," replies Sebastian.

"Welcome home, son. I was making this for you and going to cover it until you got here, but your early arrival nailed it perfectly on timing," says James as they both sit down to enjoy their dinner and talk about the old times and the new ones.

"There's a lot of unrest, James," explains Sebastian as he shakes his head. Quietly pondering the stories and issues facing the world, James considers the information Sebastian shares with him, fully aware he is keeping a lot to himself for security reasons but also knowing Sebastian is keeping the world safe at the same time.

They spoke of Tobias and their conflicts since meeting and some of the basic missions, at least what he could discuss openly without putting James at any risk.

They talk for a few more hours before James says he needs to call it a night but will continue it the following day. They walk down the hall, coming to Sebastian's room, first stopping in front of the door.

"It's good to have you home, Sebastian. I worry for you and Sean but also realize you are on the front line, and I thank you for that, and knowing you two are there makes me sleep better at night."

Sebastian hugged him and replied, "You have been more of a father to me than I could have ever imagined, James. You made me the man I am today, and I am certain if you were aware of the full level of what I do every day, you would be proud beyond belief. Or at least, I hope you would be. We are doing good things out there while the world spins along."

"I know you are, Sebastian, in my heart, and I am proud of you more than you will ever fully know. Enjoy some sleep. I'll see you in the morning. Let's go hunting if you are up for it," said James, and Sebastian nodded, always enjoying those moments with James.

He so adored the man, and despite the missions, he fought for God and country; all he wanted was to make James proud of him. He looked at James admiringly, knowing that for all practical purposes, James had become the father he never had and appreciated him more than he would ever comprehend.

Sebastian opened his mouth to tell him those simple words but then thought better of it. He would tell him when the time was right.

He watched in admiration as James continued down the hall to his own room at the end, and he appreciated all the man had provided him over the past eight years. As the door closed to his room behind him, his heart was heavy in adoration for him more than usual that evening. There was no way to know that it would be the last time Sebastian would ever speak with James again.

He briefly remembered smelling the propane gas and walking to the kitchen from his room hours later that night, detecting the faint odor but also noticing through the window that the valve on the large exterior propane tank had been removed. Thinking that the large tank was more the issue, he quickly walked outside and down the back porch steps when the explosion occurred from within the house, hurling him thirty feet onto the back lawn.

The explosion knocked him unconscious for over a minute, and it was at that moment he stood up and realized that James was still inside and rushed up to the porch, but the flames and heat were far too great to enter the home.

He yelled, "James, James!" He immediately went around to the side and front of the home, but all the exits were overcome with flames pouring out of the broken windows, billowing upward into the sky with a thick black-and-gray smoke.

Sebastian heard the sound of a revving engine in the distance behind him, far to his right, causing him to turn to see the battered truck take off two hundred feet away. He made out a partial plate ending with the license number --P3547. He thought it significant because the truck was driving away from the fire versus towards it, which would have been more of a common reaction of someone in the area following an explosion in the dead of the night.

Turning back, Sebastian helplessly observed as the fire and the dwelling devoured fully consumed his home. No one could have survived that explosion, and he certainly would not have either had he not been several feet outside when the explosion occurred. Several minutes had gone by, and he heard the sirens in the distance as the north and west walls collapsed and the roof fell inward. He felt so helpless, and his heart saddened that he had lost the only person who had adored him as much as his mother so many years ago.

Two police cars were the first to arrive on the scene, with the two fire trucks following in their wake. The police officers and two paramedics approached Sebastian to ask him if he was okay, and he quickly dismissed them. "Yes, I'm fine. I'm certain James Woodford was in there, though. There are no exit options . . . Please just get that fire out. I couldn't save him. I just couldn't," shaking his head, Sebastian responded but was saddened at his helplessness. The fire trucks put all available hoses on the home, shut down the gas valve, and began containing the blaze.

The police officers approached Sebastian as he studies the blaze, still burning strong in front of them. He had that all too-familiar sense of despair similar to the day he had remembered being at his home years ago when his mother had died, discovering her at the bottom of the stairs.

"Sebastian, I'm Officer Jenkins with the Roanoke Police Department. We met a few years ago when you were a little younger. Were you and James the only ones in the home that you know of?" Sebastian didn't respond immediately, distant and dazed by the dancing of the flames engulfing the house.

Without turning his head, he slowly responded, "Yes, Officer, only us. I was here visiting James. I arrived a few hours ago, about 7:30 pm, from out of the country." Sebastian was in a monotone state, uninterested in the specifics of the questions he knew Officer Jenkins had to ask and knowing nothing would bring James back. All of it seemed irrelevant. "We barely had a chance to talk, to even say goodbye." He said out loud to no one in particular.

Jenkins responded, "I'm terribly sorry, Mr. Storm. Of course, as you probably are aware, we will need to confirm if anyone was inside before the report can reflect that and, if so, the cause of death, but we don't need to deal with that right now. Do you mind if I ask you some questions?"

Coming back to the present and to the moment at hand, Sebastian said, "Not at all, Officer. I realize you just need to do your job."

Jenkins responded, "Thank you for understanding. It appears as if the gas lines were possibly tampered with both inside and outside of the home, which we are checking and verifying. Also, it appears the valve was intentionally removed on the outside propane tank, making the area a flammable hotbed. Obviously, we have a lot to sort out. Why were you outside if you don't mind me asking?"

Sebastian spends the next few minutes explaining the detailed accounting of what he recalled before the explosion. He realized that they had to consider him a suspect, although they didn't disclose that to him, and it was subject that he was able to avoid the blast, or at least the brunt of it, and he was the only known witness to the events surrounding the explosion.

Sebastian purposely did not mention the truck and partial plate he had recovered. He had nothing against the Roanoke Police Department, but he wasn't overly impressed with their efforts surrounding his mother's death years before. He was going to pursue that angle on his own.

At that moment, the firefighters had reduced the flames to a manageable size when the lead fireman came up to Jenkins and Sebastian and said, "Officer, there appears to have been only one person inside, male, but we would need to confirm dental records through his dentist and CSI for his identity, but most likely he died of smoke inhalation." He looked at Sebastian and said, "I'm sorry, sir." Sebastian nodded then said, "Trent . . . Wood, that's his dentist, Dr. Trent W. Wood in Roanoke, if that helps." The firefighter nodded and headed back toward the containment area.

Officer Jenkins took the doctor's name down and asked Sebastian a few more questions, and when there seemed to be an extended pause between the questions, Sebastian said, "You think we are good for now, Officer? I need to call James's son, Sean, about this. I'll be around the area for a bit if you should need me." The sun was just beginning to rise, giving an entirely different perspective to the destroyed home.

Officer Jenkins replied, "Thank you. I'll call once we receive the forensics completed on the victim, and again, I'm sorry, Mr. Storm." Sebastian nodded, giving him his and Sean's contact information, as he noticed the paramedics push the gurney with James's body, encased in the plastic body bag, lifeless and still through the broken wood, debris, and bricks, to the awaiting ambulance. So much life to the man was extinguished in an instant.

He endured a sense of sadness and anger at the thought of not ever being able to talk to him again, those moments forever locked now in his memory. Sebastian knew this was not an accident. The truck he saw drive away was the key to the homicide, and he certainly didn't want to involve the police. He would handle this personally.

He grabbed his phone and dialed HB's number. "HB, I need a favor . . . Would you find out everything you can on a partial Virginia License number --P3547, say, late eighties Ford flatbed, navy blue? James was killed tonight. The propane tank exploded. HB, I need to know who and why."

HB went quiet and then said, "Jeezuz, Sebastian, I'm . . . I'm at a loss. Of course, anything you need. I will research everything on this that's out there and be back with you soon. I'm so sorry, Sebastian, to you and Sean."

He muttered, "Thanks, HB." then hung up to think about the situation. Sebastian's phone began to ring. He flipped it over in his hand and saw that the letter S was emitting from the display as he shut his eyes hard, hesitated, then pressed the *Accept* key and said, "Hey, Sean . . ."

The dream Sebastian was experiencing from afar began rising from behind his head, lifting higher above him, initially the focal point. The picture expanded to include him standing on the lawn, his burned home, fire trucks, and people milling about the scene and the land around James's home, all in view. Rising further into the sky, the image now, into the clouds, the house a distant dot in his thought, as he abruptly awakens.

The recurring dream, vivid and genuine, was as real as the day it all happened. Sebastian, foggy-eyed, strived to focus and looked around at his surroundings. He was lying in a hospital bed; the room encased in glass, an IV connected to his left arm paired with the "beeping" of medical equipment monitoring his various vitals. HB was asleep in a chair next to the bed.

Sebastian was experiencing incredible pain throughout his body, but mainly from the gunshot and multiple knife wounds that occurred in Vienna. His whole body ached; every inch reminded him of that moment within his loft.

The doctor came into view, walking along the exterior of the glass walls, concentrating on Sebastian's chart before entering the room, unmindful that Sebastian was fully aware and coherent. As he walked through the door, he was startled to see Sebastian awake and so quickly convalesced, saying, "You are awake, Mr. Storm. Welcome back from the dead."

HB began to awaken after hearing the voices and smiled, seeing Sebastian was back among them. The doctor continued, "Impressive recuperation, Mr. Storm. Quite the statistics you racked up. Six knife wounds, fourteen contusions, four broken ribs, internal bleeding, two broken fingers, and a gunshot wound to the upper left shoulder, to name a few. A normal human would not have lived. I believe you will recover fully after a little R and R."

Mouth dry and hoarse, Sebastian seriously said, "Thanks, Doc. How long will I be stuck in here?" Sebastian was already thinking of his next move.

The doctor replied, "HB is demanding a rigorous rehab regimen for you, Mr. Storm, upon your awakening, which now you have fulfilled. She must want you out there saving the world again, I'm guessing. I'd like a month, but she is only allowing a week in addition to the time you have spent here, sorry." The doctor glanced at HB and turned with a shrug.

Sebastian looked at HB and asked, "A week, huh, HB? Hmmm. . . You are all heart." The doctor noted the light tension and sarcasm in the statement, knowing he wasn't entirely desired in their conversation, so he took the hint, turned, and headed out of the recovery room door, saying in an authoritative tone, "I'll be back to check on you in a few hours and will initiate rehab up here to set a schedule together."

After the good doctor left and the door closed, Sebastian turned to HB and asked, "What happened, HB?"

She replied, "It appears Tobias's elite force had plans to eliminate you, Sebastian, and they came damn close this time. Too close. He appears to have escalated his talent. And we have a mole I need to exterminate. Your Guardian Angel saved you, Sebastian. Sean saved your life on this one."

Sebastian closed his eyes, trying to remember what transpired that morning in his loft, and was so thankful he had Sean to back him up. They made an amazing team, he, and Sean. The day before the attack, he texted the "SS" in the café, which was his and Sean's code for "need immediate assistance," following the beacon the satellite phone emitted for the bearer's location. Sean dropped everything going on leave and was on a private charter within the hour to Vienna to aid his brother in his time of need.

Sebastian said, "Those guys were highly trained and almost had me. I'm fortunate Sean was there. I've had an eerie notion since I left London."

HB responded, "You two took out two of them and almost a third. Coincidentally, they were brothers, twins actually. Their leader, codenamed 'Fury,' excommunicated Navy SEAL we discussed in the barn in Vienna, escaped but not before Sean put a 50mm caliber round in him that slowed him up considerably, to live to fight another day, I'm certain. Sean is aware of the guy from reputation, and, I guess, has quite a list of accolades in the SEAL unit as a bruiser, this Fury. That suit of his saved him. When we evacuated the brothers, we found they were equipped with the latest armor tech suits. It's amazing technology."

Sebastian figured, "That explains why I barely made a dent. Only exposed areas, head or joints seemed vulnerable as well as blunt attacks. I had to really work at it. Those guys were fucking robots."

HB responded, "Lucky for us, these machines didn't stop the illustrious Sebastian Storm. Yes, impressive enough that my guys will reverse-engineer that tech. It was remarkable, not to mention in cocktail attire, too. Bastards were even wearing ties. GQ assassins are so in vogue these days, it seems." Sebastian laughed, then winced from the pain. HB continued, "I realize a week is a short time, especially with broken ribs and a gunshot wound, but Tobias is making a move, and all we have been able to determine is that it's happening somewhere in Europe and fairly soon. We are narrowing in on him. We need to get out in front of this."

"Okay, okay then, I hear you," said Sebastian. "Get me out of this bed then."

HB instructs, "I've taken the liberty to set you up down the street, Sebastian. I believe you are familiar with the area." HB fashioned a crooked smile for his amusement.

"I know what, well?" asked Sebastian, wondering what she could mean and realizing he didn't realize where he was.

He asked, "Where are we, HB?"

HB hesitated for effect, then answered, "Why, we are at Lake Como, Sebastian. It's in Italy, in case you didn't know." As if he was unaware of where Lake Como was, she continued, "Don't you have a little place close by? Get well soon, Sebastian. We have work to do," explained HB as she stood up and walked toward the door.

"There is very little that Mother Hen doesn't know about her ducklings, my dear. I might add that it is all being set up covertly as we speak. And I chose a real charmer to be your rehab specialist. I think you will like him. He is so your type. You two should get along well. Good luck."

"Great, can't wait. How many days have I been here, HB?" asked Sebastian.

"Four days, so let's get a move on, chop chop," responded HB, and with a wink, she was gone.

Sebastian lay in his bed for a moment and thought, "How does HB know about the villa here in Italy?" He shook his head. Of course, she was aware. She's aware of everything. She made it a point to be for everything and everyone.

He was naïve to think that she wouldn't know about his little private oasis, but he was also pleased with the thought that there would be no better domain for him to recover than his. . . *game room.* He smiled at the thought.

He was excited about his rehabilitation. A little pain and suffering only sharpened the senses, and he was confident he would have his fair share of both in the following days.

Tobias had gotten too close, and now it had become personal. His focus realized, he knew what he needed to do.

Dublin, Ireland
Present Day

Crashing through the clinic's double doors, Fury refused to be placed on a gurney or in a wheelchair, pushing them away upon entering Tobias's private medical facility within the complex. The exclusive private medical infirmary was more than aptly prepared for Fury before he arrived, and all personnel were well versed concerning his stubbornness. "I don't need that shit," he said, referring to protocol and pointing to the wheelchair. "I can walk on my own. I'm not an invalid!"

He had lost a lot of blood in transit, and the entire front of the KAM suit was saturated, crimson in color. Once they were able to calm him down and placed on an examining table, the attending chief surgeon came into the bay and evaluated the extent of the wound after removing his clothing and ordering a few chest X-rays of the injured area.

The doctor knew he couldn't mince words with Fury, saying, "Derek, you are one lucky soldier. The KAM suit stopped 50 percent of the bullet's impact, but a few small fragments are still lodged in your chest, close to your heart, and you probably have a partially collapsed lung, I suspect. You have lost a lot of blood getting here, and numerous ribs are fractured. I need to remove those fragments and put some blood back in."

"Okay, Doc," Fury said, "Get it done, but I need to report to Tobias ASAP, so make me battle ready, you got me?" demanded Fury.

The doctor nodded and then ordered his team to commence with surgery, "Okay, prep him." They immediately prepared him, getting Fury ready for the operating room. The surgeon wanted Fury sedated before he changed his mind or his temperament, more importantly.

The surgery went well, but Fury suffered tremendous blood loss and needed several transfusions. The bullet fragment was also relatively easy to retrieve but had broken up when it came into contact with the KAM suit but still penetrated Fury's chest. Fury recovered well after the surgery and was heavily sedated in the recovery unit for several hours.

An hour later, Tobias, sitting at his desk, had hung up with the chief surgeon two floors below. Despite hemorrhaging tremendously, Fury would recover fully. He had the KAM suit to thank for saving his life. The surgeon was dumbfounded that Fury was still standing, not unconscious from the blood loss, but attributed it to his vigor and obstinacy.

Though relieved that Fury was not slain, the utmost pain that surged through Tobias's veins was the loss of the twins, Andrei and Shura. Admirable and loyal soldiers to the core, the two of them would leave a substantial void within his ranks. And worse still, Sebastian Storm was still at large and was once again at the root of it all.

He had underestimated Sebastian at every turn and sacrificed several of his best men in the process. Sebastian Storm quickly became his principal focus, along with the delicate operation that was to occur in two weeks' time in Berlin, Germany.

He thought of the importance of his mission in Berlin but then considered the possibility of killing two birds with one stone. If he could only lure Sebastian to Berlin at the same moment, he might be able to both ensure his operation a success and eliminate Sebastian, all within the same stroke. He sat in thought and contemplated his next move, knowing exactly how he would do it.

There was a knock at his door. "Enter," came Tobias's words. Due to Fury's injuries, the second in command of his SET guards, Boomer, entered the room to give Tobias updates.

"Sir, as you are aware, Fury will recover fully and give you a full report concerning Vienna shortly, but in the meantime, with the loss of Hammer and Nail, I'm certain you have considered their replacements, sir?" he asked. Boomer, a master of explosives, both on a large and small scale, had served Tobias loyally for over five years and would play an integral part in his plan for Berlin. With the exception of Fury, Boomer had eliminated the most targets for Tobias while under his employ.

"Yes, Boomer, I have, as a matter of fact. Bring up Turner and Elias into the queue. Their names will be Axe and Trigger, respectfully, and fitting I believe to their talents," said Tobias.

"Aptly named, sir. I will bring them up and initiate their preliminary training protocol and inform Fury when they are ready," replied Boomer. Never one to overstay his welcome, he abruptly turned and headed out the door, leaving Tobias in silence.

Tobias had another soldier that was nearly ready but he wasn't yet determined that Inferno was prepared enough. Inferno was the experiment he was going to unveil soon.

Lake Como, Italy
Present Day

For seven strenuous and arduous days, Sebastian worked tirelessly to overcome his injuries within the confines of his villa, no venturing out, HB's orders.

Hours were devoted every day to regain his strength, such as intravenous nutrients, steroids, anti-inflammatories, and healing enhancers. Although exhausted after the relentless rehabilitation, he felt his determination and strength growing every day, inspired by his recovery, medication, and self-discipline. It was rigorous but effective.

His expansive and beautiful villa was situated on a small peninsula directly upon the north bank of Lake Como, Italy. The location gives him one of the more splendid views of the lake from three of the four sides of the expansive property.

The villa fashioned an Old World design, with most of the structure built in the early 1800s and completely modified and updated the year before by Sebastian after he acquired the property.

It was meeting and exceeding Sebastian's every expectation in its design. The elaborate stone was strewn throughout the small castle, though it towered over fifty feet in height, with four floors, boasting an eight-car garage on the east and north end and a boat dock on the south side. On the east portion of the property, a helicopter pad sat where his Eurocopter X3 sat covered on his retractable landing pad.

Touring the shores in his helicopter proved one of the most therapeutic skills he had ever attained. Learning to fly nearly 15 years before, the skill proved useful many times, both professionally and personally, and always enjoyed any moment where he spent more time piloting the powerful aircraft.

The castle project was designed through an intermediary directing a designer so that Sebastian orchestrated the entire renovation without meeting any of the third parties directly, strictly to maintain his security and protect his anonymity. The project had taken two years, and he spent that time at his ranch in Montana while it was completed.

HB arranged, along with the trusted doctor, to have Sebastian's basement fully modified into a complete rehabilitation center, which wasn't that difficult a feat because Sebastian's elaborate gymnasium was set up already on the basement floor as well, making the transition relatively simple in design.

Sebastian's ornate bedroom was on the top floor and proved to be one of the most laborious tasks set forth daily for Sebastian. Simply navigating the four floors up and down several times daily was more than daunting but a welcomed daily challenge. He was not allowed to use the elevator, which he wouldn't have utilized anyway.

Sebastian embraced the pain and welcomed it on some level as his body was undergoing its own transition and rebuilding in some peculiar way. It fed him and pushed him in some lewd and twisted fashion; he thrived on the discomfort. Sebastian always welcomed the pain; he embraced it as it represented his progression based on the bodily changes occurring.

He needed it and thrived on that pain to push him through. Sebastian was at his weakest and most vulnerable while in this condition and surmised Tobias would not rest until he was eliminated.

The three soldiers in Vienna were exceptional in performance, and Sebastian recognized that Tobias suffered an immense setback in the loss of the twin soldiers, causing his hunt for Sebastian to intensify all the more, he surmised.

His focus was on the mission and his recovery, but Adriana's image and the memories they shared relentlessly infiltrated his thoughts. He thought of her often, her presence a powerful motivator driving him to heal faster and return to the life he imagined he might have, if he was deserving enough. A life he deserved. Adriana embodied everything he desired in a normal, balanced life, a tantalizing glimpse of stability and passion that made him feel more alive than ever before.

Despite knowing the risks, he couldn't resist the pull. Adriana consumed his thoughts, her smile, her touch, the way she made his heart race. The intensity of his need to see her again was overwhelming, pushing against the boundaries of his better judgment. He craved the way she made him feel, the electricity between them, and the promise of something more profound. Something he had to pursue at least to fully understand.

He had a mission to complete, responsibilities that couldn't be ignored. But the thought of Adriana, the possibility of holding her once more, was a siren call he couldn't resist. He needed to see her again, to experience that alluring spark, before returning to the task that awaited him. He had to let her know she had not been forgotten, not forsaken. He needed to explain, through honesty, who he truly was and what he represented.

Determined and driven by a mix of longing and duty, he made his decision. He would find her, even if only for a fleeting moment, and then he would dive back into the mission with renewed vigor, fueled by the memory of her and the promise of more understanding of who he was and his mysterious past. The path ahead was perilous, but the thought of Adriana made every risk worth taking.

But, above all . . . . *Sebastian needed to stop Tobias Teague.*

Chapter 18

A Fallen Hero Avenged

Roanoke, Virginia
2004

Sebastian hung up the phone with Sean, explaining every detail surrounding the incident to him. It was a very difficult call to make as Sean and Sebastian adored James beyond words.

A heavy silence hung in the air after Sebastian finished speaking, each second stretching into an eternity. Finally, Sean broke the stillness, his voice unexpectedly composed. "I'm sorry, Sebastian. I think I'm simply in shock. I'll catch the first flight back from San Diego. Thank you for calling. I'll send you my travel details as soon as I have them."

Sebastian could sense the underlying tension in Sean's voice, a controlled calm that belied the turmoil he must be feeling. He imagined Sean, thousands of miles away, grappling with the weight of the news he'd sadly delivered. The distance between them seemed to amplify the gravity of the situation, the urgency of Sean's return palpable even through the phone.

"Take care, Sean. We'll get through this," Sebastian said, trying to infuse his own voice with strength and reassurance.

Sean sighed, a sound laden with unspoken emotions. "Yeah, we will. I will miss him."

"Me too, Sean," Sebastian said after hesitating a moment. "Sean, I'm so sorry I couldn't save him. I feel like I let both of you down," he said softly.

Sean interrupted, "No, Sebastian, you didn't let us down. It would have been worse had you been inside as well. It looks like that was also the intention. Just promise me this: when we find out what happened and who did this, then that will be the day of reckoning, and I will need you more than ever before, Sebastian. You hear me?" responded Sean, sadness and hate in his tone.

Sebastian agreed. "Without question, Sean. I will be here for you in any way you need me to be." Sean continued, "Someone fucked with our family, Sebastian, and there will be vengeance for that error. And now you are my only family. Dad deserves this of his boys."

Sebastian felt enormous pride and hoots, "Hoorah, Sean, hoorah! Someone will pay for this; I promise you that."

"Thank you for that. Thank you. I'll call back with my arrival details." Sean said before he hung up the phone. Sebastian sits down at their backyard park bench table, the only structure still standing and undamaged on the property.

After the call ended, Sebastian couldn't shake the sense of unease. Sean's outward calm was a thin veneer, barely concealing the storm brewing beneath. He knew his friend well enough to understand that the real impact of the news would hit Sean once he was alone with his thoughts on that flight back from San Diego.

Sebastian took a deep breath, bracing himself for what lay ahead. The coming hours would be a test of their resilience and strength, a harrowing journey that would push them both to their limits. But with Sean by his side, he clutched for a flicker of hope.

They had faced the impossible before, and together, they would face it again but . . . . *together*.

The sun was just beginning to rise above the tree line. It was always so beautiful looking out over the lush greenery as was every morning at their home. This home would never be the same, and the thought pained Sebastian tremendously.

Watching the scorched wood and infrastructure dripping in moisture, the fire now entirely out, Sebastian recalls the images of Sean and James, all laughing together upon the very bench he was sitting on. Teasing one another, paired with the training over the years, brought out in him a controlled calmness, almost a peace, to his damaged heart.

James and Sean made Sebastian the soldier he had become. The man he had become. They made him the killing machine he had been bred for, a fierce weapon and a force with no equal. When HB learned more about this puzzle surrounding James's death, she knew the effect it would have on Sean and Sebastian. James's loss would forever shake them to their core. They, as a weapon, would be unleashed without pause or hesitation on those foolish enough to cross their paths.

The people responsible for James's death would suffer a punishment that would be swift and just, and they would feel the full weight of Sean and Sebastian's anger and retribution.

Later that morning, HB called Sebastian back with vital and relevant information. "Sebastian, it took me a little longer than I thought, but I have some news you and Sean will want to hear." Sebastian replied, "Good, HB. Talk to me. Sean will be here early this evening, and we won't want to waste any time on this. The police called a few minutes ago, confirming through dental that it was James, and are deeming it a homicide but don't have much to go on, so tell me what you have, please."

HB reported, "The license plate came back registered to a Clint Pedersen. You know the name by chance?"

Sebastian replied, "No, I don't, should I?" seemingly puzzled by the question. HB continued. "Well, he had a couple of priors along with his buddies, one being 'Bobby Johnson' and the other being . . . Joshua Strickland. Anything ring a bell?"

Sebastian replied, "I feel like I know the name, but from where, I'm drawing a blank. HB, forgive me, but I'm a little fuzzy and tired today, having been up most of the night. And for a woman priding herself on candor and directness you aren't on your game today. Sadly, I don't have it in me for guessing games this morning. Please, HB, just get it out." Sebastian was running on about two hours of sleep and couldn't be held accountable for his lack of social etiquette and poise under the circumstances.

HB apologizes, forgetting for a moment what Sean and Sebastian were going through, "Sorry, Sebastian. Johnson and Pedersen were let out of jail about a year ago for good behavior, but the third was let out of the Virginia State Penitentiary the day before yesterday for robbery and grand theft. Sebastian, these three—"

Sebastian interrupts, "Wait. . . . . Were they the bastards at the gas station several years ago?"

HB said, "Yes, Sebastian, they were, and reading the police report from that day, it mentioned Strickland, their leader, threatening you primarily when he was being wheeled out of the gas station that afternoon after you shot him up. I'm guessing the two little ones didn't have the balls or inkling to put this arson together, but once their buddy Strickland got out, he had been planning this for the last several years, I'm sure, and his first thought was to make you pay for that day. I'm sending you pictures of the three of them right now."

At that moment, a ping occurred on Sebastian's phone, and the three most current images of the men popped up on the screen while still on the phone call with HB.

Sebastian studied the pictures closely, and something seemed vaguely familiar when Clint Pedersen's face came up. He thought long and hard for a few seconds before saying, "Shit, HB, this Pedersen. I saw him at the airport last night as I got off the plane before meeting James. They were watching me, knowing I had arrived back in town. Something was vaguely odd about him, but

I didn't think much of it. He looks very different than he did a few years ago, Prison hardened and aged him. Damn, I wish I had caught it last night. This could have ended a lot differently."

Sebastian questioned, "All this over a foolish $100 robbery? James actually told me the most impressive thing about the day at the gas station was I didn't kill them when I had the opportunity all those years ago. I would so much rather have that day to do once again. The outcome would have been far different." He fantasized about making them suffer in agony before extinguishing their lives if he had the chance again.

Sebastian was all business, his demeanor steely and focused, as if he were preparing for an intricate and perilous mission. HB listened to him closely, recognizing that he was in his element. She knew him to be at his best during these moments of intense planning. His mind was a whirlwind of strategies and contingencies, each detail meticulously evaluated and prepared for. She didn't dare interrupt his flow, knowing that his "mission mode" was sacred territory.

This mission, however, was unlike any he had undertaken before. It was deeply personal, striking at the core of his very being. Its importance transcended any professional objective he had ever faced. The stakes were higher, the risks more profound. Every decision carried the weight of his past, present, and future.

His thoughts were a symphony of tactical precision, each element harmonizing into a coherent strategy. The air around him buzzed with the electric energy of his concentration. He was thinking of a strategy and the best way to handle the situation.

HB could sense the intensity in his thinking as he expressed his thoughts; the unwavering determination that drove him was evident. This was more than a mission; it was a reckoning. As he meticulously crafted his plan, she was overwhelmed with a surge of admiration and concern. She understood that this operation, more than any other, demanded the full measure of his abilities and resolve.

Sebastian paused for a moment, his gaze turning inward as he visualized the execution of his plan. Every possible outcome played out in his mind. Each scenario tested against his rigorous standards.

The weight of the mission bore down on him, but he embraced it, fueled by a fierce resolve.

He glanced up. His focus spoke volumes, "This is it," he said quietly, yet with a resolve that echoed over the call. "This is the one that matters most for Sean and me . . . . *and for James.*"

HB nodded, her support unspoken but palpable. She knew he was ready, and in that moment, she believed there was nothing he couldn't achieve. The mission was set, and Sebastian was prepared to face whatever lay ahead, his mind and spirit honed to perfection.

HB stirred, "Sebastian?" His focus was vacillating.

Sebastian responded, "Yes, HB. Sorry. I only wish I had that day to do over."

Sympathetically, HB said, "I completely understand, Sebastian. Once you implement your plan, you should get with Sean and consider, hmmm, having a little chat with those boys in a covert kind of way, keeping it friendly, of course. I happen to have an address—1239 East Fairmont Lane. Please keep it on the down low, keep it smart, and do what you need to do for you and Sean to have some . . . *closure.* I'll send over any additional information on them and all pictures I have as well on the secure server."

Sebastian thought for a moment and then replied, "Closure, yes. I think it would be good for Sean and me. . . . and James, of course, would appreciate it as well. Thank you, HB." He hung up the phone.

Lake Como, Italy
Present Day

Sebastian was up at 4:30 am, just before sunrise, beginning the morning ritual of getting out of bed. His pain was less today but still excruciating, given the circumstances. It had been seven days since the incident, including the three days of rehabilitation.

Despite his agony, he often reminded himself how the other three had fared in the skirmish, so he considered himself quite fortunate all the way around.

With only a few days into rehabilitation, he was progressing reasonably well, especially with all the enhancers the doctor was pumping into his body. He eased down the long flight of stairs to the gym below and stretched, easing his sore muscles, which had grown stiff overnight from the previous strenuous workout. At 5:00 am, Hyzen arrived at the estate after passing Sebastian's overly cautious security protocols.

Hyzen was a tall, muscular Austrian man who HB had retained to put Sebastian through his daily physical sacraments, knowing they both would push each other to the limits, and that's precisely what they accomplished.

"*Hallo, Sobaston, let's get on the rise and the shine,*" he said. Hyzen would begin every morning in his thick Austrian accent, and each morning, Sebastian would correct him, "No, Hyzen, it's *Sebastian*, not 'Sobaston,' and 'let's rise and shine.' There is no 'get on the' or 'the' in there whatsoever." Hyzen always responded the same way, "Ja, das what I say, 'get on the rise and the shine, let's go, chop chop!" Sebastian simply shook his head as he commenced with the required torture for the next eight to ten hours.

On the eighth day, HB stopped in toward the end of their workout at 5:00 pm, watching the two spar on the mat. Hyzen was respectful of Sebastian's injuries but pushed him further every day. With over thirty pounds and four inches on Sebastian, Hyzen was a physical menace.

Boxing maneuvers were good for Sebastian's core, ribs, and shoulder, and he kept pace with Hyzen until he ended the session each day. "Sobaston, you strong herr, you keep up good, ja, good jobs," said Hyzen.

"'*Good job*,' not 'jobs,' ahhhhh, never mind. See you tomorrow, Hyzen, and thank you," Sebastian said. Hyzen waved him off, grabbed his towel, and made his departure, barely breaking a sweat.

"Looks like you are regaining your form, Sebastian," HB said. "Hyzen is a brute on every level, but probably what I need," replied Sebastian. HB smiled, "That's good, excellent progress. We need to get you out of here. I've got a little more intel on Tobias's operation, but not much. As you know, he had been quiet for well over the last decade or more, developing his profile, covertly building his clientele list, and gaining capital to finance his 'unveiling,' if you will, and now he seems almost cavalier in his confidence."

Why would he be this reckless now, thought Sebastian? Something wasn't adding up, but in the moment, it hit him. Tobias wanted him there, in his arena, and he was taunting Sebastian in his own twisted way.

His goal was to show the world his might and eliminate his nemesis all in the same stroke. If that was the intent, thought Sebastian, then he was going to oblige Tobias in any way he could.

Roanoke, Virginia
2004

United Airlines Flight 436 landed on time at 4:36 pm, sixteen hours after James had been killed. Sean walked through the terminal exit and saw Sebastian waiting in an Adidas workout outfit, somber and saddened. Locking eyes and nodding to one another as they approached each other, no words were exchanged, nor had to be, only a strong embrace acknowledging their adoration for each other. They were brothers, not by blood, but by circumstance, by life, and by fate.

Both lost their parents far too early and now were inextricably connected. Both were seasoned men, yet soldiers now, not only in years but more so in life experiences. They had seen it all on so many levels, more death than life between them.

Sebastian and Sean silently walked toward the truck until Sean was the first to speak. He said, "Sebastian, we need to find these guys, and they need to pay for what they did. Promise me they will pay." Sebastian nodded and replied, "Without question or hesitation, Sean. I have a plan, and I have worked it up. They will be dealt with accordingly, swiftly, and justly. I know where they are, Sean."

With the news, Sean was content knowing what a strategist Sebastian Storm was and revered for his planning acumen. He nodded, then looked sharply at Sebastian and nodded. "Let's go to the house. I need to see it. I need to see dad's final resting place." replied Sean as they hopped into the truck and headed for their home.

On the ride over, Sebastian had spelled out the broad strokes in his conversation with HB earlier, letting him know the details of who was accountable. Sebastian harbored responsibility for what had happened. Sebastian explained, "If I hadn't interfered at the gas station that day, James would still be alive. James thought I was a little reckless in doing what I did." Sebastian was now shaking his head.

Sean raised his hand to stop him, his expression a mix of intensity and understanding. "Don't, Sebastian. Don't even start. It was the right call, and more importantly, you didn't kill them. You could have as I probably would have had I been there instead of you that day. But taking their lives at such a young age would have haunted you and tormented you to this day. You did the right thing; please don't blame yourself. It's fate, man, simple fate. It was Dad's time, and nothing could have changed that, nothing. You know he would say the same."

Sean's voice softened, his eyes reflecting the depth of their shared loss. "He had a remarkable life, Sebastian. He loved working with you on the Bear Hugger venture. Those were some of his happiest times. We need to honor him, to remember him for the man he was, and to avenge him in a way that upholds his legacy."

Sebastian's guilt began to shift, transforming into a sense of acceptance and fate. Sean's words resonated deeply, igniting a fierce determination within him. They would honor their father's memory, not through revenge, but through justice and continuing the work he loved. They would channel their pain into something meaningful, something their father would be proud of.

As the weight of Sean's words settled, Sebastian felt a renewed sense of purpose. Together, they would face whatever challenges lay ahead, driven by the memory of their father and the unbreakable bond between them.

Sebastian and Sean both stepped out of the truck in what was once the front yard of his father's home. Sean shook his head at the devastation before him. It was difficult for him to see his home demolished and decimated. Once his happy domicile, full of childhood memories, experiences, training, and laughter, now simply reduced to despair and sadness for the loss of his father.

The home was now destroyed and ruined completely. They walked through the remains of the dwelling and came to what used to be James's room. He could see where his father had finally rested for the last time. Sebastian gave him a moment alone as Sean needed to make his peace and say goodbye in his own way to his dad, his mentor, and his friend.

After a few minutes, he turned, walked back to Sebastian, and put his hand on his shoulder, saying, "Now, let's go bury Dad, then take care of business." Sebastian's only response was, "Copy that, brother."

James Woodford was laid to rest at Blue Ridge Memorial Gardens in Roanoke, Virginia, on June 23, 2004, three days after his death. Over eight hundred people were in attendance, with ten individuals speaking on behalf of James's character, including friends, people he worked with from the ranger station, and the governor of Virginia. Sean gave the eulogy, bringing tears to those in attendance.

After bidding farewell to the last of the guests paying their respects, Sean and Sebastian politely excused themselves as the stream of well-wishers dwindled. The solemn atmosphere lingered, but their minds were already shifting to the task ahead. As night cloaked the landscape, they regrouped at the firearms shed in the northeast corner of James's property.

They now stood amidst the arsenal, the weight of their purpose pressing heavily upon them. The sun had long since dipped below the horizon, leaving the world in a shroud of darkness. This was the hour they had been waiting for, the moment when their true mission would begin.

The shed's interior was dimly lit, the glow of a single overhead bulb casting long shadows over the racks of weapons and equipment. Sean moved with practiced ease, checking their gear with methodical precision. Sebastian, equally focused, loaded magazines and double-checked their plans. The air was thick with unspoken determination.

This night was more than a beginning; it was a convergence of their grief, their anger, and their unyielding drive for justice. Every piece of equipment they handled, every strategy they reviewed, was a step towards avenging their father's legacy. They painted black slashes upon the skin and clad in black with gray baseball caps to match their ominous spirit.

Outside, the world was silent, unaware of the storm brewing within the shed. As they finished their preparations, the brothers exchanged a look that spoke volumes. This was their moment, the start of a harrowing journey that would test their limits and forge their paths forward.

With their gear secured and their minds steeled, they stepped out into the night. The darkness embraced them, but within that void, they carried a light of purpose that would guide them through whatever trials lay ahead. Their night was only beginning, and with it, the first steps towards a reckoning that had been a long time coming.

They suited up quietly, silently, packed lightly in black military gear, each with a silenced sidearm of their choice with multiple loaded clips within their belt, though unsure they would even need them. It was not the first mission for either of them, but it was the most important one to date for both boys.

"Ready?" Sean asked, his voice low but charged with intensity.

Sebastian nodded, his eyes reflecting the fierce resolve within him. "Ready."

They reviewed their plan once more, with no deviations or alterations made. Having done the reconnaissance well before, Sebastian drove the twelve miles and parked well off the path on an old dirt road two miles from the predetermined location. Without pause, they exited the vehicle and headed north in a synchronized, moderate jog, closing the distance within about fifteen minutes.

They came up on the house with the old, faded navy truck in the driveway, license plate number XMP3547. They had the correct location. The dark of night was used to their advantage and more than adequate camouflage for their covert infiltration.

"That's it," whispered Sebastian, referencing the old truck as he indicated for Sean to go to the right and behind the house while Sebastian was to head to the side of the home per their plan. Sebastian taps his ear as they separate, indicating to go to ear comms, and Sean nods his acknowledgment.

Guns drawn, both headed to their various selected waypoints. Sebastian hugged closely against the house as he made his way to the side door.

He peeked through the windows and made out two men sitting on a soiled sofa, drinking beer and watching television in the living room. "Confirm visual on Pedersen and Johnson, negative on Strickland," softly spoke Sebastian into neck voice piece.

"Visual confirmation of Pedersen and Johnson, copy," replied Sean. The home was old, dilapidated, and poorly maintained. Entry inside would not be a problem. Sebastian reached the side door first, followed by Sean, reaching the rear door a few seconds later. Both indicate they had reached their breach points via comms.

Sebastian whispered, "Breach in. . . . 3 . . . 2 . . . 1 . . ." They both rushed their respective doors, easily shattering the locking mechanisms on both entrances. Pedersen and Johnson were sitting on the sofa, stunned and confused, as Sean immediately had his gun trained on Johnson, and Sebastian had his sights honed in on Pedersen.

"Easy boys, where's Strickland?" demanded Sean.

"He isn't here. What the fuck are you doing in my house, and who the fuck are you?" asked Johnson, dumbfounded, looking at Sean and then glancing over at Sebastian. After a moment, suddenly recognizing him, he said, "And you, motherfucker. You fucked all of us. You shoulda burned as well . . ." Sebastian put a single silenced bullet right between his eyes, shutting him down cold. Sebastian carried no remorse or regret for ending the man's life right then and there. They weren't there to talk.

Sean and Sebastian were not going to be putting up with any lip from either of them. They had no intention of discussing or negotiating. This evening all three of the men responsible would be terminated with extreme prejudice.

Sean and Sebastian were judge and jury that day, and banter was not part of the evening's program. Pedersen looked at his friend and saw the single trail of blood dripping down his nose, eyes still open, motionless. Pedersen turns and gasps, "Okay, okay, man, don't shoot. Put your gun down, I'll tell you. He is hooking up with some girl tonight." He was now holding his hands up as if to protect himself.

"Where?" asked Sean.

"If I tell you, will you let me go?" pleaded Pedersen. "Maybe," said Sean. Pedersen whimpered, "He's at his house. It's off Braffle Lane, a few miles from here."

Sean, seeking some closure, asked, "Why did you kill my father? What did he ever do to you?"

Pedersen said, "It wasn't about him, man, it was about you."—pointing at Sebastian—"It was Josh, man . . . all him. He had been pissed since he shot all of us at the gas station. Josh has been obsessed with ruining him and wanted to blow up the house. It was all his idea. He wanted it to look like an accident, but your dad was in the wrong place at the wrong time. He made us go, or he would have killed us if we didn't. He planned to return and finish the job in the next day or two. You should have let us take the money that day, man. Strickland hates you. . . ."

Without warning, Sean put two slugs into his forehead. Sean and Sebastian weren't interested in excuses or rhetoric from these men. They were in their professional mode—no emotion or hesitation. They were now machines set into motion on a path that would not end until their mission was completed.

When these men chose to take out James and attempt on Sebastian, their lives became forfeit. Their privilege to live and breathe was revoked, and that decision was not negotiable.

Sean stared for a moment at the two lifeless bodies before him on the sofa, the beer still in Pedersen's hand balanced on his leg, perfectly still. Sebastian grabbed the three shell casings and finally had to shake Sean's focus, saying, "We need to go, Sean."

They had both witnessed death many times before, but this time, it was personal and hit far differently. Being a professional, death all around you was inevitable, but a death based on a personal level came at a much higher price. There was to be no alternative for Sean and Sebastian. They simply did what they had to do.

Sebastian and Sean quickly departed the home from the back door and crept slowly along the side to ensure they were not spotted. No one seemed to be around at the late hour. The closest home was over two hundred yards away, and the lights were off in the neighboring house. They quickly jogged to the truck and headed off toward Braffle Lane.

Lake Como, Italy
Present Day

Sebastian pressed the accelerator further to the floor as he let out the clutch, taunting his Ferrari 488GTB up over 150 mph, relishing the straightaway, welcoming the unrestricted freedom of the road before him. Adrenaline peaking, the lush landscape and stone walls whirred by in his peripheral vision as Sebastian navigated the Italian mountainside.

He savored the enjoyment of a performance vehicle on the open road almost as much as he relished following the ambling shoreline in his X3 helicopter; both had their place and provided sheer excitement for Sebastian.

This time, it was the road game. Other vehicles on the highway, noted but insignificant, became mere obstacles in Sebastian's path, opportunities to demonstrate the Ferrari's prowess and handling. He expertly piloted the precision machine around them, weaving through traffic as if the other cars were standing still. The frustrated honks and startled faces of fellow motorists barely registered as Sebastian whizzed by in a blur of sleek, black speed.

The Ferrari's engine roared with a fierce, intoxicating power, the acceleration a rush that sent adrenaline surging through his veins. The RPMs spiked into the red, the car's high-pitched whine signaling it was nearing its limits. But Sebastian possessed no fear, no hesitation. He was in complete control, every movement precise, every decision instinctive.

The eloquent castles and stretch of Lake Como whizzed by, a kaleidoscope of color that only heightened his sense of invincibility. Each turn, each swerve, was a testament to his skill, the Ferrari responding to his every command with flawless grace. He was pushing the boundaries, not only of the car but of himself, reveling in the sheer, unadulterated freedom that came with such a force.

As he navigated the labyrinth of asphalt, Sebastian's mind was a razor-sharp focus, his senses heightened to a near-superhuman level. The world outside was a blur, but inside the cockpit, everything was crystal clear. This was his domain, his sanctuary, where the mundane rules of life were suspended, replaced by a pure, exhilarating dance of man and machine.

The thrill of the chase, the roar of the engine, the wind whipping through the open windows—it all combined into a symphony of sensation that fueled him, driving him onward. In those moments, Sebastian wasn't just a driver; he was a master of his destiny, a force of nature hurtling through the night with unstoppable momentum.

Popping in the clutch, he downshifted the car to third gear, revving up the RPM as he approached the all-too-familiar S curve before the mile-long tunnel. The engine roared and quieted as his speed dropped to 70 mph to maneuver the turn expertly. He made a quick soft right, followed by an immediate left as he entered the tunnel, accelerating out of the turn, hitting the fourth, then fifth gear within a second or two.

He could see the light at the end of the tunnel as he punched it further to 160 mph, then 170mph, coming out of the tunnel, slowing and bringing her down to 60 mph as he approached his villa.

Reaching under his visor, he hit the boosted RF signal remote as he swerved into his drive bay and quickly into position four of his eight-car garage, the door closing immediately behind him. He stopped hard and shut the beautiful automobile down. All eight bays were filled with toys, not a spot open for anything new.

He vigorously hopped out of the car, more confident and feeling healthier with each passing day, appreciating his long row of vehicles within the garage bay as he walked by them into his home.

It had been eleven days since the ordeal in Vienna, and he was eager to get back into the game, but he cherished these moments of elation tremendously with vigor and excitement. They validated his resolve and made him feel alive once again.

The doctor cleared him for active duty, and he planned on leaving first thing in the morning. Sebastian was far from 100 percent, but his yearning to be "back in the fight" was beckoning him, tugging on him to return to his next project. He had unfinished business that needed resolution.

Sebastian was never one to sit on the sidelines; he thrived in the heart of the action. For the past week, he had been pouring over the data HB had provided The information was scattered and fragmented, making it challenging to piece together Tobias's exact plans. Yet, one thing was clear: Tobias was gearing up to make a bold statement.

Sebastian's mind raced as he connected the dots, each fragment of intelligence sparking new hypotheses. The urgency of the situation fueled his determination. Tobias's organization was a formidable force, and whatever they were planning promised to be catastrophic. The ambiguity of their intentions only heightened the stakes.

He couldn't afford to wait for more clarity. Action was necessary, and time was running out. The weight of responsibility pressed heavily on him. He knew that uncovering Tobias's scheme and thwarting it was imperative. The lives of countless innocents depended on it.

Sebastian's resolve hardened as he considered his next steps. He would have to dissect Tobias's motives further and get closer to the source. Every instinct, every ounce of his training, screamed for him to dive into the thick of it, to be the spearhead of their counter-operation. This was his arena, and he was ready to dominate it.

As he finalized his plan, a fierce determination blazed in his eyes. Sebastian wasn't planning to deter Tobias's threat—he was going to dismantle it altogether and eliminate him as a threat once and for all. With steadfast determination, he prepared to launch himself into the fray, knowing that his actions would be critical in safeguarding everything he held dear in the coming days.

He had one more delicate piece of business to handle before he gave Tobias his complete attention.

Roanoke, Virginia
2004

Braffle Lane was an old country road on the east side of town. Josh Strickland's family had owned a once successful dairy farm that was originally over 1,000 acres in size. The parcel had reduced in size to a trivial 50 acres after the last three generations sold off the land over the years to satisfy their bar tabs and legal troubles, preserving less for each generation that followed. The small estate wasn't worth much at all anymore.

The original farmhouse still remained modest and failing, as the property had not been kept up over the years. Most likely condemnable by this point, but the authorities rarely made it out that far and left the Strickland home alone.

Joshua was the eldest of two brothers, but his younger brother "Stitch" Strickland was serving an eight-year sentence upstate for rape, having two additional years to serve before he would be released.

"Stop it, Josh, stop. I said no!" said the girl, tearing her arm from his grasp but not before he slapped the girl hard across the face.

"Git on out of here then, go on. Git," said Josh Strickland, kicking her in the rear as she ran down the broken stairs jumping the last two and hopping into her rusty El Camino, but not before she yelled, "You're a dick, Josh, same ole asshole, should have died in prison." She started the engine. Irritated, Josh threw his half-drained beer bottle the thirty feet or so at her windshield, shattering the bottle and breaking her windshield in the process.

She flipped him off. "Ha, I still got it," he muttered, impressed with his throw as she tore off in her car, a cloud of dust in her wake. Josh simply laughed as she recklessly drove down the dirt road standing there on the dilapidated porch until he couldn't see her taillights anymore, then said, "Fuck, that was my last beer, that bitch." He strolled back into the house, scratching his rear, and slammed the door.

Sean and Sebastian watch from afar as the debacle occurs between the two. The girl left the house quickly, giving Sean and Sebastian little time to take cover. They were reasonably confident she wouldn't be returning, and from the look of Josh, he didn't seem interested in pursuing her. From about a hundred yards just inside the tree line along the road, they studied him standing on the porch looking their way, but they were out of view and remained quiet, watching him until he went back inside.

"That's our boy. He appears to be alone," whispered Sebastian, looking at Sean. Not responding immediately, Sean simply focused, eyes narrowed at the space where Josh had been standing only moments before, thinking of what he would do to the man once he got ahold of him. Sean slowly turned to Sebastian and said, "He's mine, Sebastian, no two ways. He needs to suffer for what he did to Dad. Just have my back. Fair enough?"

Sebastian understood and said, "Of course, Sean. You do whatever you need to do. You know I will always have your six." Sean nodded, verifying their brotherhood. Sebastian knew he didn't even have to ask, but it was his way of saying that no matter the circumstance, Sean would be the one to put this man down in any way he saw fit.

He didn't want intervention. He didn't want judgment. He simply wanted full autonomy to proceed in any way that satisfied him, whatever that may be or entail. They slowly stood up, and with guns drawn, they proceeded over the driveway and made their way to the front of the home.

Sebastian approached the porch first, slowly, and quietly taking two steps at a time, and took his place at the side of the front door. Sean followed and began to ascend carefully up the four stairs individually, but upon stepping on the third, a crack emitted as his foot went partially through. "Fuck," Sean whispered.

They hear rustling from within, followed by a yell from inside the house, "You back, bitch?" from Josh as he made his way towards the front door, Sean and Sebastian hearing the heavy footsteps approaching the door from within.

Sean was loosening his foot free when Josh pushed the door open and said, "What the—" He started to rush toward Sean. Anticipating, Sebastian, being in position on the side of the door, fired a fist at the side of Josh's head, stunning him slightly.

As he staggered back and to his right, it only infuriated the crazed man as he tackled Sean onto the grass in front of the stairs. Josh swung hard at Sean but missed wide. Josh Strickland was enraged and wild, mixed with alcohol and drugs. This made for an overwrought assailant. Sean, on his back, gave two quick jabs, but Josh was 230 pounds and a barroom brawler and suffered little from the blows.

Sebastian needed to buy Sean time and quickly flipped upside down from the top stair, connected his boot to Josh's face with a flip kick, taking the blow hard. He fell off Sean and to the side and quickly stumbled to one knee. Immediately recognizing Sebastian, he said, "You, you should be dead," he rushed Sebastian, but it was no contest. Sebastian sidestepped the bigger man and did his left-right combination to Josh's face, taking the hits squarely and dropping to his knees.

Sebastian, taking advantage of Josh's confusion, roundhouse kicked him squarely in the face, knocking him back and onto his rear as Josh shook his head to clear it, unsure of what just hit him.

At this point, Sean was back on his feet, waved Sebastian back, and stood before Josh, looking at his face, bloodied and swollen from the myriad of blows he had ungraciously accepted from Sebastian.

Numb from alcohol and drug use, Josh rolled to all fours, still hunched over, then brought up one knee again, hands resting on his thigh as he looked up at Sean standing in front of him several feet away. He turned his head and glared at Sebastian in the background, but off to the right, he looked back to Sean.

"My fight isn't with you," said Josh to Sean, attempting to catch his breath and trying to equal the playing field. Sean strikes back with, "Oh, but it is, Joshua. When you messed with Sebastian here and killed our dad, it became every bit my business and sealed your fate," Sean spoke softly and deliberately.

Josh shook his head, attempting to shake himself sober. He wasn't sure how he would maneuver out of this and sat there for a minute, weighing his options, but there was little he could do. In a blur, Josh rose to his feet, set his balance, and began to rush the ten feet to Sean.

Anticipating Josh's desperate attempt, Sean pulled out his silenced 9mm and put two slugs into Josh's right knee, then immediately one into his left. Both knees shatter instantly, with Josh crashing to the dirt hard, face first, his right leg almost completely severed in two, contorted and twisted unnaturally.

Josh let out a shriek as he held both knees, unable to curb his pain, intently glaring at Sebastian and Sean. "You fuck, Storm, you fucked my life!" Josh spits out as Sean fires a round into each of Josh's elbows, making them useless and increasing his pain further.

There was no remorse on Sean's face, only anger and hatred for the man who killed his father.

Sean had to be mindful of the pain level he was inflicting so as not to induce shock, which could lead to unconsciousness, and he needed to keep Josh lucid for the time being. He replied, "No, Josh, you fucked up your own life. Simply being born was your mistake." Sean was now walking around Josh in slow, methodical circles. Josh was writhing on the ground, but he was eyeing Sean as he circled and paced, blood saturating the earth around him.

Josh was in intense pain at this point and still was intently watching Sean as he circled him, unsure what would transpire next. Surely these boys wouldn't kill him, thought Josh. They were war heroes in those parts and Josh assumed they must uphold the law, at least to some degree. Yet their actions told a different story. He was sure they wanted him to suffer.

Sebastian stood, arms folded, and simply guarded over the spectacle. He knew he had to leave Sean to his misery and justice. Sean needed this, his pound of flesh, to deal with it in a way that satisfied his hurt and hate for this man. There was no interrupting the process, and he would never interfere with what a soldier must do to achieve his own closure and, least of all, Sean. Sebastian had Sean's back ultimately and would follow him into any depth of what this scenario would bring.

Josh was now begging, "Just kill me, man, you fuckers, just do it!" Sean looked at him and shot him in the right hand, and Josh winced. Sean explained, "No, I need for you to agonize, Josh, just like my dad suffered from being burned alive."

Josh called out, "You fuc—" Sean shot him in the lower jaw, splintering and fragmenting it, not wanting to suffer the heathen's words any further; he no longer possessed the right.

Sebastian continued to watch as Josh began to cough and gag on his own blood and bone, trying to move a jaw that no longer functions. Josh mumbled, "Fuuuccking . . ." Sean put another round into his groin as Josh's eyes started to roll to the back of his head.

Sebastian asked, "Time to end it?" He looked at Sean as they both watched the man twisting in pain. Moments flashed back of Sebastian's father being dismembered by the wolves. Josh was now a wretched victim facing his own fate for what he had done.

Sean waited a moment before replying, then said, "Nah, Sebastian, I think we will leave him to it. Let him think about what he's done before he bleeds out." He looked over at Josh, "That okay with you, Josh? Yep, I thought so. Say a prayer. You'll need it." Sean looked to the sky and softly said, "This is for you, Dad. We miss you," as he began to walk away.

Sebastian looked at Josh as he picked up the eight 9mm casings. His father's image filled his thoughts. The reflection was the evening so many years ago when his father was caught in his own trap, torn apart by the wolves encircling him.

Josh deserved the same destiny his father endured the day after Sebastian's thirteenth birthday, to die in pain, helpless, and . . . alone. Jonathan and Josh, no one would miss them. . . . *No one.*

Sean walked down the driveway as Sebastian caught pace with him. They began to leave together, side by side, along the long dirt road in silence. Josh lay quietly upon his back in front of his steps, broken and beaten.

The pain had taken over completely, and shock had begun to set in. His body became numb as he appreciated the stars in the sky above. He deserved all this, he thought. If there was a God, Sean and Sebastian have been sent to answer for his sins, and he would no longer be running from it. He delved into the depths of his soul, grappling with the gnawing question: Had Sean and Sebastian been as lost, as corrupted by darkness as he had been? Why was it them that was chosen to seal his fate? Were their spirits tainted with the same shadows, their hearts hardened against the light? Would they, too, one day stand before the divine, summoned to answer for the burdens they carried? Yet, in this sacred moment, such thoughts seemed distant, almost insignificant. In the moment it was not about them; it was about him.

Today, the spiritual reckoning he had long feared and anticipated had arrived. He felt the weight of his sins, not just as a burden of guilt, but as a profound spiritual dissonance that had distanced him from his own soul. The universe, with all its mysterious and unfathomable wisdom, had aligned to call him to account. The day of atonement was here, and the echoes of his past reverberated through his spirit, demanding reconciliation.

He sensed the presence of something greater—a force beyond human comprehension—guiding this moment of truth. It was as if the very fabric of his being was unraveling, revealing the full extent of his moral and spiritual failings. There was no escaping this divine judgment, no running from the truth that had finally caught up with him. Sean and Sebastian had become his Grim Reaper, in a sense, selected for him and only him. Today, he would face not just the consequences of his actions, but the profound spiritual reckoning that would define the essence of his soul.

For the first time in his life, he gazed into the heavens and prayed. He prayed not for himself initially but for the people he had hurt along the way. He hoped in doing so, maybe God would forgive him just enough to save his soul, but then thought better of it. He wasn't worth saving.

For the first time since Sebastian intervened in the gas station all those years ago, Josh realized he was to blame. He created the mess he now found himself fully immersed within. Josh was so driven by hate and rage for what Sebastian had done he needed to take responsibility for his own actions that day.

Rolling the dice the afternoon was his fatal mistake in the gas station and went up against someone better, outmatched, and now he had to face his fate. He had absolutely no one to blame but himself. He concentrated on the stars and placed his right hand over his heart as if it meant something significant. His last breath slipped from his lungs, his eyes open, fixed in time, to the final image of the brilliant stars above.

He left with one final thought, hoping and praying there was a heaven. His last breath was long and drawn out as his lungs emptied completely. Justice had been served, and Josh Strickland would never again hurt another person.

Sebastian and Sean rode in silence when returning to James's farm, stripped their clothes off, burned them, retrieved the guns, and broke them down into separate parts along with the eleven bullet casings from the evening and scattered them in ponds and wells that had been there for years, several miles away and apart from one another.

They both knew how to eliminate any artifact or evidence connecting them. Their work took an hour, not a word uttered, until they were both back in the truck headed back into town.

Sean was the first to break the silence. "Sebastian, what you did for me back there will never be forgotten, and I love you like a brother more now than ever. Dad would be proud of us, and I thank you for bringing justice to his name and honoring his life with me." Sebastian simply nodded.

After a moment, he replied, "I would do it every day of my life if I could only have him back, Sean."

Sean replied, "I know you would, brother, but you have repaid the debt in full, and if you ever need me, well, you know." Sebastian replied, "We did what needed to be done, and we did it for our dad." Sean nodded in agreement as he continued. "Four things, Sebastian. One, let's never speak of this again. It's done and finished, and we must move on. Dad would want us to live and not dwell."

"Second, there will invariably be fallout and questions once those boys are found, and their identities connected to the gas station incident. I ask that you field those issues and handle them for me, Sebastian?" Sebastian nodded again.

"That brings me to the third item. I want us to keep the farm. Its memory is too strong, and I don't want it ever to be sold. The fourth and final 'ask,' Can you drop me at the airport? I need some time to process and refocus, but I will . . . and then I'll find you. Agreed?"

Sebastian nodded, yet had many questions, but he respected Sean's wishes. "Of course, Sean, to . . . *all of it*," replied Sebastian.

They arrived at the airport a few minutes later. Sean said, "Remember, if you ever need me for . . . anything . . . anything at all . . . you simply text '*SS*' on a secure line to me at this number," handing Sebastian the number—"and I will be there to cover your rear, no questions asked. You will always be my brother, Sebastian, and I'll never forget what you have done for me. You taught as much to me and Dad as we ever taught you. Always remember that." Sebastian held back his tears knowing Sean and James were the best thing that ever could have happened to him.

The cipher Sean offered became the unbreakable bond that tethered the two men together. If one ever needed the other, it was an unspoken pact: no questions, no judgments, just unwavering action to achieve the necessary outcome. This principle was their lifeline, an unspoken promise that transcended words and circumstances.

They lived by this creed, a testament to their loyalty and shared experiences. Fittingly, they referred to themselves as "*SS*," a moniker derived from their shared initials and a symbol of their unyielding alliance. This code, this honor, was their guiding principle, etched into their very souls.

In the darkest moments, when the world seemed to close in around them, the cipher served as a beacon. It reminded them of their unwavering commitment to each other, a silent vow that echoed through every mission and challenge they faced. Their bond was more than just a partnership; it was a brotherhood forged in the crucible of shared trials and triumphs.

The code was their shield and their sword, a reminder that no matter the odds, they would always have each other's backs. It was this bond that gave them strength, fueling their resolve and sharpening their focus. Together, they were a formidable force, a dynamic duo driven by a creed that demanded excellence and loyalty above all else.

In the end, the cipher was not just a tool—it was a testament to their enduring friendship, a symbol of the trust and honor that defined their relationship. And as long as they lived by this code, nothing could stand in their way.

It was their Lethal Decree.

Sean got out of the truck, grabbed his bag, saluted Sebastian, and walked into the airport. Not another word was ever uttered about that night again between them.

"Hoorah, Sean, hoorah," Sebastian quietly said as Sean disappeared into the airport and then pulled away from the curb and drove away.

He memorized the number Sean had given him, leaned over while driving, and opened the glove box to retrieve a lighter James had always left there.

The lighter is silver, old, weathered, and a figure of a bull etched on both sides. He had remembered the lighter being there since he was a kid. How appropriate, Sebastian thought, there being a bull embossed upon the handle, which is precisely what James emulated, and he honored and appreciated him for that.

He pulled the lighter out, remembering the occasional cigars James would light with it, and used it to burn the piece of paper Sean had given him.

Holding it within his fingertips, he let it burn until nearly nothing was left. He dropped it from the window, watching it smolder out on the asphalt through his rearview mirror.

He looked at the lighter once again, still in his hand, before returning it to the glove box and softly said, "I'll miss you, James, more than you will ever know."

Chapter 19

To Close for Comfort

Vienna, Austria
Present Day

Adriana Mercer left her room, took the elevator to the main floor, walked up to her hotel's front desk, and smiled at the reception clerk who had helped her numerous times. "Hello, I'm Adriana Mercer, and I'm in 1802. Are there any messages for me?" asked Adriana, smiling at the attendant. She could sense he enjoyed speaking with her on any chance he would get and was always more than eager to serve her in any way possible.

"Pleasant day, Ms. Mercer. Of course, I know what room you are in. Let me check for you. One moment." The attendant perused his computer before looking up and said, "No, ma'am, it appears not. Oh, here is a note." Adriana's expression brightens, "It appears your flight this evening is delayed forty minutes, but it's all I have at the moment." He smiled as if his news would bring her some comfort. But it did not.

"Excuse me, what is the temperature outside today?" the attentive clerk looked at his computer screen and replied, "It is a beautiful 25 degrees Celsius, and the sun is out with not a cloud in the sky, Ms. Mercer." She smiles and thanks him again and is content that her outfit is the perfect selection for her morning walk to the office.

Her stay in Vienna had taken far longer than expected, nearly four weeks to close a large and most lucrative contract with her company. She wasn't complaining; she enjoyed the time of year in Vienna.

To complete the deal, several patents had to be executed, and if they weren't finessed correctly, her firm could have lost the entire account. But in the end, she prevailed and secured a contract worth over $500 million for her firm over the next five years. She also smiled as it was the largest commission she had ever received, totaling over seven million (USD) personally.

Although she had thought of him on many occasions, she hadn't spoken with Sebastian in over ten days, and although she was secure and focused on her work at hand, she couldn't help but miss his banter and, as much, his touch. He was unique and equally mysterious and elusive, and those attributes were both exciting and frustrating to her. She supposed he looked at their tryst far differently than she and it disappointed her.

Sadly, she had no way of contacting him, and he, like her, was supposedly there in Vienna on business, but she couldn't imagine him still being in Austria after all of this time, especially if she had not heard a word from him in over a week. She would never know of the arduous rehabilitation regimen he endured in Italy during that time.

She had to admit that she was slightly surprised that he hadn't reached out in some fashion after their last night together. She was certain they had connected on a deeper level, far more even than their first night together. Maybe it was because of her questions and probing about the scars on his body. Was it what pushed him away? She would never know.

Although her business had taken quite a bit longer than anticipated, so she feared it had simply been a fling for him, but she refused to let herself believe or consider she had been so gullible and foolish to think it could be anything more than the torrid affair it appeared to have been for him.

Adriana had an entire day before her flight and was going to go into the office to tidy up a few loose ends before returning home in the evening, back to the United States.

She decided to go into the lounge where she and Sebastian had first met and took a seat at the same table where he had initially greeted her. The lounge presented far differently during the day versus when they had met that first evening. Reminisced about that magical night, Adriana recalled the passion, the intrigue, and the intoxication, and even with an additional dose the night following, she couldn't get enough of Sebastian Storm. But he vanished without so much as a note.

Adriana decided she needed to concentrate on other things and filed the memories of him deep into her thoughts. She sat for 30 additional minutes and returned emails on her computer before looking at her Breitling, noticing it was just after 8 am. It was getting late; she needed to get to the office. She had a few hours of work left to do before her departure. Adriana placed her computer in her bag and made her way to the hotel exit.

Well concealed, he studied her from a distance as she exited the Sans Souci Hotel. It was 8:05 am, and Adriana Mercer looked every bit the consummate professional as she descended the hotel stairs to street level. Her crisp attire and purposeful stride exuded confidence, masking any turmoil or disappointment she may be harboring.

She turned east, her intended direction clear, and he mirrored her movements, descending the stairs across the street with practiced ease. His gaze never wavered from her; each step calculated to maintain a discreet yet vigilant distance. The city around them hummed with the morning rush of people and traffic, a perfect backdrop for his covert observation.

———

As Adriana navigated the bustling sidewalk, she seemed unaware of his presence, her focus on the day ahead. He, however, was acutely aware of every detail—the sway of her coat, the way she glanced at her phone, the rhythm of her steps. Each moment was a piece of a larger puzzle he was determined to solve.

His mind raced with possibilities and scenarios; the stakes of his surveillance high. There was an air of mystery surrounding her, an enigma he was both drawn to and wary of. His mission was clear, but the lines between duty and curiosity blurred with each passing second.

The city's bustle masked his footsteps, but his heart pounded with a mix of adrenaline and anticipation. He knew the importance of this shadowy dance, the significance of staying hidden while remaining close. The streets of Vienna offered countless places to hide, yet none could conceal the intensity of his purpose.

As Adriana turned a corner, he quickened his pace, ensuring he remained just out of her line of sight. The game was afoot, and he was ready to pursue it through to the end, whatever that might entail. His eyes, sharp and unyielding, tracking her every move, a silent promise that he would uncover the truth she so carefully concealed.

Computer bag in hand, she intended to walk the eight blocks to her office as she had done for nearly a month, often varying the path slightly to maintain a sense of variety and experience new things along her journey. The city of Vienna offered so much, and she appreciated its visual and historical diversity.

He knew her schedule intimately, researched her route, and was more than aware of the general path, taking into account her occasional trip variations to maintain her daily excitement. He had studied her cell phone tracking signature through the software he utilized to monitor her various movements over the last few weeks. He had the time and patience, so he used it to track her closely.

It was a warmer morning, allowing her to wear a perfectly contoured mini dress with a flowy button-down blouse complete with wedge espadrilles.

Her brunette hair shone beautifully in the morning sun, capturing an early glow, making many a passerby turn to appreciate her as she walked elegantly past them along the sidewalk. If there was such an image that could emulate the concept of stopping traffic, it was exhibited in Adriana Mercer. She expertly strolled down the busy boulevard.

Adriana always looked the part and attracted the attention of both men and women alike. That would be his challenge, to grab her without anyone noticing. She received no shortage of attention.

He would have several opportunities along her route; he simply needed to choose the optimal location and timing, and when he did, he would strike.

She continued along the busy avenue for a few blocks. He persistently follows her from across the street in a nonchalant manner. She wouldn't notice him with all the people walking about as he blended well within the Vienna cityscape.

She knew the route well, having taken it so many times in the past, yet she did find herself lost on occasion if she felt the urge ever to modify her path. Today was just such a day. She felt good and was excited about what the day would bring. She couldn't put her finger on it, but she had a good sense that today would be special for her.

Succumbing to her whimsical nature, she turned onto a smaller street, assuming she may save a few minutes, hopeful of the new shortcut she had chosen. Not quite an alley, but there were no storefronts, only brick walls overshadowing her on either side of the narrow street.

Adriana became aware the busy street noise had diminished as she was no longer walking on the main road but now a couple of blocks inward, further insulated from the bustling street. It was far quieter, and fewer people were present, and she was beginning to think taking this particular shortcut may have been a mistake. He watched her very closely now, patiently waiting for his chance.

He used the opportunity to cross the road and close the gap between them, gaining on her position and seizing the chance if he found her isolated for even a few seconds.

She seemed slightly lost now and was experiencing an uneasy feeling as a result of her impulsive decision to trek off the reservation. She questioned why she even strayed off her ordinary course at all, a route that had proven effective countless times for her in the past. She cursed her foolishness and impatience for wanting to find a faster way.

He tracked her closer now, careful to remain hidden and discreet, watching from only several yards away. She wasn't aware of him yet, but it was only a matter of time. He was aware she was very intuitive, and if she identified him, all would be compromised.

She stopped for a moment and fumbled with the GPS on her phone, attempting to pinpoint an accurate bearing on her current position, but the tall buildings, concrete, and the myriad of metal objects and structural supports created cellular interferences that inhibited her precise location, essential to ultimately locate the corrected path to her office. She sighed. She was lost.

He saw her on the corner and decided to go around the other side of the building to obtain a better position and vantage point, though she would be out of sight for the better part of 45-60 seconds. The risk proved fruitful as he was fortunate as she was still engrossed with her phone to catch him entering an exterior stairwell door, assuming her path would lead her in his direction once her GPS became calibrated.

The gamble paid off as she now realized where she was and had a mere four blocks left until she came to her building. She crossed the small street, a woman in a workout outfit and earphones was 50 feet in front of her, but she was essentially alone.

He became hopeful as she approached his position, the door only slightly ajar so as not to be discovered. As she approached, she appeared to be walking directly toward him. He couldn't have asked for a more ideal position in which to take her.

As she stepped up to the curb and sidewalk, she began to pass directly in front of the exterior stairwell doorway the man had entered only seconds before her arrival.

As Adriana passed the door, it flew open. The man came up behind her with his left arm holding her around her chest and his right hand cupping her mouth. He quickly pulled her into the stairwell, slammed the door, and then quickly shoved a knife into the door jamb to prevent anyone from entering.

Adriana had been taken, and a single, chilling thought consumed her: this might be the end. Bound tightly from behind, she sensed he was a sizable man. The darkness around her was suffocating, amplifying every sound. The heavy breathing of her captor, indistinct and menacing, only deepened her terror.

Her mind raced, each heartbeat louder than the last. Shadows clung to the corners, where indistinct figures loomed, watching her every move.

Her blood ran cold. Despite the overwhelming fear, a spark of defiance ignited within her. She knew that whatever lay ahead would be a battle not just for survival but for her very soul. The true nightmare was only beginning, and she was determined to face it head-on.

She abruptly turned and met his gaze with unyielding resolve, ready to fight for her life. The room seemed to close in on her, the air thick with tension.

Roanoke, Virginia
2004

After Sebastian dropped off Sean at the airport and burned the note he was given, he drove back toward his hotel, deep in thought, wondering where his life had taken him and how a turn of events beginning with his parents' deaths and now James's had set his life toward a particular path.

He respected many events happened for a reason and appreciated the journey he had chosen or, rather, had been chosen for him. He blinked, looked up into his rearview mirror, and saw the flashing lights from the unmarked police car ushering him to pull over to the side of the road. He slowly and cautiously pulled off to the shoulder, unsure why he was being detained.

Sebastian had his 9mm between the seat and center console, out of sight but nearby if needed. The glare of the police cruiser's headlights made it difficult to determine clearly as a heavyset man in plain clothes slowly approached the driver's side of Sebastian's truck.

Something was familiar to Sebastian about the officer's gait, but he couldn't pinpoint it. When the officer came to the window, he immediately recognized him as Detective Todd, who had investigated his parents' deaths several years prior. "Good evening, Sebastian. It's been a long time," said the man.

Sebastian said, "Yes, sir, it has, Detective Todd. Over eight years, I think."

The detective responded, "Yep, that's about right. You were just a little boy at the time. It is a sad business with your parents and such all those years ago. And now, with James's passing, he was a good man." "Yessir, he was the best, actually," replied Sebastian.

"Anyway, I stopped ya because we need to speak with you and Sean Woodford down at the precinct. We have some questions. We couldn't seem to locate him. Do you have any idea where he may be?"

Fearing that Sean's flight had not yet departed, Sebastian replied, "No, Detective, I sensed after James's funeral, it was especially hard on him, and he needed some time to clear his head. Maybe he went target shooting. Honestly, I'm not certain. I didn't want to pry. He seemed like he needed space."

Knowingly, the detective replied, "Oh yeah, target shooting, interesting choice of words, Sebastian. That's kind of what I need to talk to you boys about. Do you mind following me down to the station to answer some questions?"

"I'd be happy to," Sebastian lied, remembering his promise to Sean to "field" any inquiries that came from their actions that night. Then he asked, "This have anything to do with finding James's killer, Detective?" He attempted to deflect the focus on the bigger issue at hand.

The detective didn't give away much as he replied, "You could say that, yes. See you in a few minutes. Follow me." The detective slapped the top of the door twice before walking back to his car.

Detective Todd got into his car and pulled onto the road, and Sebastian followed him for ten minutes to the police station. They parked next to each other outside the station and walked into the precinct together in silence.

Sebastian had not stepped foot into the station since the day his mother died, and the old familiar chill returned to him as Detective Todd sat him down in the same room he had been put in all those years ago. The room had not changed or been updated in those eight years. The holding room was still filthy, cold, stark, and frigid.

A deputy came through the door and remained standing within the room. He handed Detective Todd the manilla envelope as he entered the holding room and sat down opposite Sebastian. The detective thanked the deputy as he stood at attention next to the door. Sebastian didn't understand why a deputy needed to be in the room but gathered his reputation most likely preceded him. Sebastian was a national hero. Stories of his valor saving Presidents outshined his more clandestine missions that had saved countries. He was considered a hero in Virginia.

He took a long, hard look at Sebastian and said, "You look a lot like your dad, Sebastian." Sebastian simply glared at him, unsure if he meant it or whether Detective Todd was trying to ruffle his feathers. He didn't comment either way on the statement and reacted even less to the jab.

Detective Todd continued, "I know what you have been through. Losing James is tough. Hell, he is a good buddy of mine, Sebastian—well, *he was*, but I need to ask you and Sean some important questions."

Sebastian responded, "That's why I'm here, Detective. I only want to help and apprehend those bastards that killed James. Ask away."

Detective Todd looked at Sebastian quizzically after his statement and asked, "Those? Another interesting choice of words.

What makes you think more than one person is involved in James's death?"

Fuck . . . . thought Sebastian. He needed to be smarter in his responses but replied, "I think we both know, Detective. One person couldn't have done this. Well, at least it seems so. I'm no detective, but it doesn't take much to ascertain all of this took more than one individual." His attempt was to save the situation but was unsure if he adequately dodged the bullet.

Todd thought for a moment, then said, "Hmmm, well, maybe. As it were, you may be correct. Do you recall a Clint Pedersen, Bobby Johnson, or Joshua Strickland?" Sebastian appears to consider those names for a few seconds before responding.

Finally, Sebastian said, "I recall, Detective, those are the boys I had a little altercation with at that gas station a few years back. What do they have to do with James's death? Aren't they still in the state prison for that crime? Well, I hope they still are incarcerated, at least."

Detective Todd replied, "Well, as luck would have it, Pedersen and Johnson got out some time ago, and Josh Strickland got out only a few days ago. He was in there longer being the ringleader of that little debacle as well as not the best track record while in prison. Guess he knifed another inmate about 3 years ago, which added to his sentence. We have a possible connection between these three and the explosion at James's home. But herein lies the rub—the three of them were all found dead earlier this evening." Sebastian appeared shocked at the news but was afraid it was less than sincere.

Detective Todd opens up the manila envelope and lays out dramatically three 8 × 10 inch glossy photos in front of Sebastian for optimum effect. Detective Todd continues, "This is the current status of these three men, Sebastian. As you can see, someone put their lights out professionally and extremely personally. Strickland seemed to take it the worst. Kinda interesting, right?"

The photos were grisly and gory and depicted the deceased well. Sebastian didn't feign any reaction and didn't need to. He noted that pictures always looked worse than the real-life snapshot he had in his mind of the incident. He remembered well as he was present at each of the men's executions.

Sebastian slowly replied, "Terrible what happened to these boys, but unsure what the relevance is to me, or Sean for that matter, or why am I here? This has nothing to do with me, Detective."

Detective Todd replied, "Well, son, I guess what I'm asking is, did you have anything, or did Sean Woodford have anything to do with the deaths of these three boys? I mean, you both had a motive, and you both are certainly capable. It's no secret that Sean is a decorated Navy SEAL, and you are some hotshot with Homeland or the CIA or whatever. We are both aware, Sebastian, that you have some special gifts and talents after what happened at the gas station all those years ago. Didn't you save passengers over some foreign country and a president or two as well? Not to mention your Bear Hugger outfit. You are both kinda thought of as local heroes around these parts, and for good reason, I might add, but I still have a job to do. I hope you can appreciate that. But, regardless, I am curious: where have you been for the last few hours?"

Disregarding the backhanded compliments, Sebastian confirmed, "Sean was with me at my hotel following the ceremony. We sat and talked about James's estate in my room for a few hours following the funeral. Then about an hour ago, Sean said he needed to clear his head and left on his own. I'm not sure where he went; he didn't say. I gave him the space he asked for, Detective, not much else I can tell you."

"When were they killed?" Sebastian asked, attempting to deflect the detective's inquiries.

Detective Todd answered, "Well, Strickland was found first by some estranged girlfriend that said she and he had a fight with him earlier in the evening, and she left in a huff, I guess, but had forgotten her purse, went back and found him all shot up and left to bleed out, it appears. She found him dead in front of his home. His arms crossed over his chest like he had a moment with God. It was definitely a personal hit based on the pattern of the gunshot wounds. Someone wanted him to suffer. The other two boys were together and found by Pedersen's mom, and she immediately called 911. We are guessing it's been a few hours. These killings are pretty brutal execution style. Without question, someone very angry, and honestly, you two are about the only ones with any motive from what we have determined. No one else much cared for these boys, so the two of you are kinda at the top of our list, no offense." Sebastian put up his hand accepting the statement.

Studying Sebastian for any kind of inflection or reactionary nuance. Detective Todd noted no adverse reaction. Sebastian gave him nothing. Sebastian replied, "Honestly, Detective, I can't help you on this, and you mentioned this only just occurring in the past few hours. Sean only left me an hour ago. Who knows, maybe it was a drug deal that went badly or something else illegal. These boys were shady and criminals at best. Any number of things may have occurred, and we both know it. And why would Sean be considered a suspect? He didn't have anything to do with them; only I did. And you only *now* mentioned that they had anything to do with James's death. Do you have any proof that connects Sean or me with these boys and what happened to them? I sincerely doubt it. I will not lose any sleep, Detective, knowing these guys got their due. I'm sure they deserved it."

Todd wondered and said, "Well, that there is the trick, Sebastian. We found traces of explosives at Josh's home that matched those found at James's home, which caused the house to go up like a match. We have a working theory, and the evidence corroborates that these boys may have had something to do with James's death. Do you two have any idea about that? I mean, I can't imagine how unless you have a crystal ball or something, as we only just obtained the connection an hour ago. I can't really imagine how you would have known that before we did." Sebastian simply shrugged, agreeing with the detective and his logic.

Of course, they had something to do with it, thought Sebastian. That's why they were terminated. But instead, Sebastian said, "Wow, no, we had no idea. I mean, you only just mentioned it to me but said they were killed hours ago. So again, Detective, maybe they got what they deserved, karma and all?" He shrugged as if to strengthen his point and exemplify his lack of interest in the subject of the brutality of these boys' demise. Sebastian simply, did not care, and Detective Todd could easily sense that was the case.

Detective Todd asked again, "Sebastian, did you or Sean have anything to do with the deaths of any of those boys?"

Sebastian sat back in his chair to think about the question. He replied, "Detective Todd, we didn't care anything about those boys. I applaud whoever took them out, however. If they had anything to do with James's death, then they fucking deserved exactly what they got. And you only just obtained the information about the explosives and mentioned it to me only moments ago. Doesn't that basically exonerate the two of us? Is Sean, or am I being charged with a crime, Detective?"

Detective Todd shook his head, to which Sebastian replied, "Is there a law against wishing someone was dead? So, if not, drop it. If you have no evidence supporting your accusations or insinuations, I'd let it go and concentrate your efforts on finding their true killers or those responsible. Who's to say they didn't do it to one another? Respectfully, Detective, I think we are done here."

As Sebastian stood up, he looked at Detective Todd blankly and walked to the door. Before opening it, he turned back toward Detective Todd and said, "Those guys were bad news; they just were, Detective. You know it, and I lived it. I put them in their place several years ago at the gas station, and this time, someone else put them into the ground. I wish I had myself years ago because James would still be alive today if I had. They deserved what they got then, Detective, and they deserve what they got today. If you are correct in that they were responsible for James's death, then they definitely got what they deserved, and the person or people that eliminated them should be praised and rewarded for what they did, not hunted down."

Sebastian turned back towards the door, hesitated for a moment before opening it, and started down the hallway. Detective Todd looked at Sebastian, who was walking down the same hall he had been in with his father all those years ago.

A sense of Déjà vu came over Detective Todd as he called after him. "Sebastian . . . Sebastian." He turned to look at Detective Todd one last time. "Tell Sean to contact me. He has become our prime suspect."

Sebastian replied, "Copy that, Detective," He waved and turned back toward the hall. Sebastian left the building, got into his truck, started it up, and pulled out of the police station and onto the main road, leaving the precinct in his rearview mirror before he pulled out his phone and dialed HB.

Sebastian said, "Hello, HB; hopeful you may be able to help with something. Sean and I are getting a lot of heat from local law enforcement here in Roanoke over a few local boys . . . Ahhh, getting shot up around here that more than likely deserved what they had coming. A detective, Barry Todd, is pushing hard to get ahold of Sean and questioning him up and down like he just did me. Trying to save Sean the headache, not to mention he ex-filled about an hour ago to clear his head. I feel we all need to respect the time that he needs, most of which is from the Roanoke Police Department. Sean is heading back to San Diego soon, and I don't want those plans tripped up for him. Any chance you might smooth the way on this and maybe have the police look elsewhere?"

HB understood Sebastian loud and clear and went immediately into business mode and said, "Let me make some calls and poke some bears and see what I can do."

Sebastian said, "Thanks, H; I really appreciate your help on this. You always know what to do," and hung up.

HB had a special and unique ability to make messy situations disappear. She didn't throw her weight around often, but it was effective and final when she did.

She made a few calls and had Sean and Sebastian were completely cleared and removed from any focus surrounding the murders of the three men in Roanoke, Virginia.

Chapter 20

The Master Plan Develops

Vienna, Austria
Present Day

Adriana's heart raced as he pinned her against the door, her life flashing before her eyes in vivid fragments. The grip was firm, unyielding, yet he hesitated. As seconds stretched into an eternity, her initial terror gave way to a turbulent mix of fear and curiosity. What was he planning? She remained on edge, a cocktail of adrenaline and dread coursing through her veins, her mind whirling with the possibilities of his next move. He held her fast like a vice grip, his strength unyielding.

Still holding his right hand over her mouth, he slowly leaned in and whispered, "Did you miss me?" Her eyes widened as he loosened his grip, and she turned immediately towards him. . . .

"Sebastian! Oh my God, it is you," as she kissed him deeply for several seconds, realizing in the moment her fear, pulling slightly away only to slap him hard across the face without warning.

"I suppose I deserved that," caressing the side of his face, certain it was flushed but smiling, knowing he would have a lot more explaining to do beyond that simple gesture.

"Two of the most magical days in my entire life, then you utterly disappear. I don't know whether to kiss you or slap you again!" exclaimed Adriana.

"Well, I think you effectively did both, but I enjoyed the prior far more than the latter," responded Sebastian as her hand came up to strike again at his comment, but this time, he caught her wrist in mid-flight, surprising her with his agility but melted away as he kissed her again.

He grabbed each of her wrists with his hand above her head and held them against the door as his kisses emerged deeper into her soul. His weight against her body made her realize what she had missed for so long as his lips drifted to her neck. She presses her breasts to him as her leg glides between his legs, wanting to feel and know she is exciting him.

She smiles, confirming her effect on him, so she continues to rub him with the inner part of her leg, slowly up and down. The impact of his kisses upon her neck spins her wildly with anticipation as his left hand releases her right wrist first and drifts to her throat initially as her hand instinctively moves to the back of his head, his hair cascading between her fingertips, urging further as he works diligently on her neck both with his lips and his hand mildly squeezing her throat causing her to gush as she assumed she would with his sensual and attentive touch.

His right hand now releases her opposite wrist as he begins to squeeze her breasts, already heaving, her heartbeat quickening as her free hand moves to his chest, enjoying the carved muscle below his tan shirt.

She grips under his left pectoral muscle, and he winces from the recovering fractures, ribs, and bullet wound, still on the mend.

Sensing his discomfort, hesitating for a moment as he meets her lips with his own. Her right hand finds its mark below his belt as she strokes him, remembering how good he felt the last time they were together.

His own hand now eases to her stomach and slides down her skirt as she begins to undo his belt. She repositions her leg now to give him full access as he begins to hike up her skirt to her hips, only to slowly slide his hand over her mound again, appreciating her omission of panties yet again. The notion of instant access stimulates him more as he notices her heat emanating, eager to anticipate her moisture and excitement; he knows she has for him every time he has touched her.

She moves to his shirt and begins to unbutton each from the bottom to the top as he enjoys her creaminess, lubricating his fingers. Their lips are still entwined as her hand pushes away his shirt over his shoulders so she can see and appreciate his carved chest and abdomen.

Adriana first noticed the stitches, causing her hand to pull away from him slightly, but her human nature was piqued as she needed to visually confirm what she already felt. It was then that she saw the extensive bruising and multiple sutured areas on his stomach, shoulder, and arm that bothered her the most.

"You're hurt, Sebastian . . . *badly*." Her look of concern was genuine, but she equally questioned the reasons behind the injuries. Everything about this man was a mystery.

He took her head in his hands, looked down at her, and said, "I have so much to my story, and I will tell you it all, Adriana. I want to tell you everything, but you must trust me; the reasons are bigger than only us."

She looked into his eyes, and she wanted to believe him, wanted to trust what he said were not lies, but it was difficult with the scars she observed in the bathroom to these recent injuries. It was all a lot to take in. It would be a lot for anyone.

The words were one thing, but when she looked into his hazel green eyes, they told her the truth in what he said, and although it may appear strange and bizarre, she trusted an explanation to all of this and validation of everything he promised her.

She could not resist him as she put both hands behind his head and pulled him to her, firmly and seductively. She needed to savor him, to feel him connect with her again.

His belt had loosened already; she unbuttoned his pants while she caressed him, easing down his zipper, anticipating her reward beneath, excited as if it was their first time once again. She looked back up at him as she stroked slowly and deliberately his fingers, finding her wetness inviting, ready for him.

He teased her skirt up further and cradled her rear cheeks firmly in his hands, easing her up several inches as she straddled him where he stood. Her arms now around his neck, he gently positioned her onto him as he slowly found his spot and began to enter her. Only a tease at first, but as she kissed him, he began to ease himself all the way inside her until there was nothing left for her to take.

Sebastian's stature and strength were enough to support Adriana as he began to rhythmically thrust against the door softly at first, then quickened the tempo as her moan increased with each plunge. Slow and methodical, his cadence strong and dominant as she felt every stride penetrate, not disappointed in any way.

His hands supported her rear as he pushed and pulled with every glide, quickly bringing her to euphoria after only a couple of minutes. As she approached her orgasm, she lost muscle control. He fully supported her weight as she surged, contracting her muscles, squeezing him tighter in her spasm.

She pulled him close, slowing his rhythm as it incited too much for her to bear, overstimulating her to the point of losing control. She held him deep inside for a few moments before easing down his legs, letting her feet touch the ground as he slowly slid from the moistened folds below her skirt.

She kissed him, biting his lip slightly as she cupped his moistened member with her hand and stroked firmly. She crouched down, kissing his tip, slowly tasting his ridges as her tongue encircled his entire circumference. She would occasionally look up at him as she began to take him in further.

Gently stroking his entire length while she savored what he fed her, cherishing him with each pass. Her pace begins to quicken, further enlightening him, knowing what she wants from him beyond anything at that moment.

Sebastian relishes her efforts and appreciates her talents and dedication to her endeavor. She feels him grow considerably more, a product of her efforts, which only seem to entice her exertions further.

She senses he is close, and she wants to taste his sweetness upon her lips and swallow his warmth and all of his essence. Adriana wants it all and won't stop until she collects all of it; none wasted or lost is her goal.

Sebastian's left hand rests against the door, his other holding the side of Adriana's face as he feels the mild perspiration on her face and caresses the bulge of her cheeks when she takes him completely within her mouth.

The simple action and pulse of her stroke and pressure begin to drive him over the top. To the point of no return as he bursts inside of her all that he has as she is his vessel, her tongue lapping every drop of him until she has recovered all of him.

Slowing her stroke, Adriana accepts all of him, leaving nothing behind, and continues for a time until she is certain she didn't miss a drop. She puts her hands upon his chest from below and gently raises back up to see his eyes know he is content with what she provided and he to her.

Yearning for this moment as her head rests against his chest for a moment. She licks her lips, still tasting him and enjoying his flavor. She smiled to herself, gratified in how he stimulated her but more so that he had found her. Her value must be significant to him on some level.

She pulls his pants up, zips them, and begins to button his shirt as he puts his thumb and forefinger to her chin, tilting it up to look at him and softly says. "I will explain it all, Adriana, I promise you. I will be gone a few days in Berlin, but when I'm finished with my.

. .Uh, project, I will find you and answer every question you have of me. *I promise you this.* I just needed to see you again it has been what has driven me over the last week and half."

He smiles at her, searching her eyes for some kind of affirmation, but she simply nods and softly replies, in almost a whisper, "I know you will, Sebastian. I don't know whether to trust your words, but I trust your eyes more than what you speak, and that is all I can do at this point. That is simply all I can allow." She licks her lips one last time, ensuring she has his every drop, with none wasted.

Smiling back, Adriana pulls her skirt down, runs her hand through her hair, and puts her hand against his chest, once again feeling the stitches beneath, knowing and wondering about the story behind those scars. The new scars, as well as the old, they all had a story. A tale she yearned to hear.

Grabbing her computer bag and purse, Adriana turns for the door but hesitates for a moment before turning towards Sebastian once again.

Her hand reaches for his cheek, and she simply says, "Find me after. Do what you need to do then . . .*find me,*" as she pulls the knife from the jamb and hands it to Sebastian and slips through the doorway and closes the door behind her. She is gone, like a subtle breeze passing through a window.

Sebastian rests with his back against the door, collecting his thoughts for a moment. He is amazed by this woman on so many levels, not only by her substance as a person but as much by the aptitude and understanding she can bear, not fully comprehending exactly what he is. That is what mystifies him most about Adriana Mercer.

All Sebastian thought now, and his only ambition was the desire and needed to explain who he was to her. He felt she was the only one who could truly understand his burden and pain.

Mueller noted as she left the stairwell door, writing notes surrounding the specifics of his observations. A second man had picked up the tail for Adriana Mercer.

He had been following the woman, but as he noted his observations, he witnessed Sebastian Storm emerge from the same stairwell door nearly 90 seconds later. This was a surprise to Mueller, but Tobias would be happy to hear the intel within his report. The woman's value increased tenfold.

Tobias will be very pleased.

Berlin, Germany
Present Day

Sebastian was thirty minutes from arriving in Berlin, Germany. HB booked him on the company's Citation Excel private jet to get him back into the game quickly, as they were running out of time. She had allowed him to stop in Vienna on the way, but time was slipping away.

In the final moments before landing, he took a mental inventory of his recovery. At 85%, his healing was substantial but not complete—a concern given the urgency of their mission. Yet, there was no time to wait for full recuperation. Tobias had to be stopped, and the clock was ticking. His mind raced, balancing the risks of his current condition against the critical need for swift action. The stakes were high, and the margin for error, razor thin.

The Citation landed safely in Berlin and proceeded to the private jetway designated for American government officials. He stood in front, waiting for the copilot to pass through the exit and clear the cabin, signaling to the flight attendant to open the door, and as she did so, the bright sun burst into the compartment, blinding Sebastian slightly. He could make out the two black SUV silhouettes as he carefully descended the jetway stairs with the morning sun on their faces.

As his eyes adjusted, he first spotted HB standing by the car, her familiar face a welcome sight. But then, a jolt of exhilaration shot through him as he noticed Sean Woodford leaning nonchalantly against the SUV. Sean's casual demeanor, almost feigning boredom, belied the deep bond and sense of home that surged in his heart at the sight of his long-lost brother. The reunion was both unexpected and profoundly stirring, setting the stage for the mission ahead with renewed vigor and unspoken camaraderie.

As Sebastian took his last step onto the tarmac, Sean met him, embracing him, holding Sebastian tighter and longer than normal. Sean stepped back a half step, still gripping Sebastian's upper arms to appreciate Sebastian being healthy let alone, alive and nearly whole again. He was simply happy Sebastian appeared unscathed.

"Thought I may have lost you on that last one, Sebastian. I just couldn't allow that, and HB here grounding all communication with you in the last two weeks for security reasons about killed me," said Sean quietly.

Sebastian replied, "You saved me, Sean. If you hadn't watched over me, I wouldn't have made it out of Vienna. No arguing that point, my brother," smiling again at Sean.

Sean joked, "Always saving your ass, it seems." Sebastian smiled, knowing the truth in his words. "Spoken like a true big brother," replied Sebastian.

HB had given them a moment but then jumped in. "Sorry to break this party up, boys, but we need to keep it moving. Sebastian, I thought you might like to have Sean in on this one despite you being a one-person wrecking ball." Sebastian was now excited. "Hoorah, HB, now we have the varsity team all here. It's time to fuck up Tobias's little party and put him to rest."

HB gave instructions. "You guys take the first SUV, catch up, and get settled into the hotel. I'll send a driver for you two a little later, then let's get to work. We have a lot on our plate for this one." Sebastian gave his usual reply, "Copy that."

As Sean and Sebastian make their way to the first SUV, Sebastian flips the back of Sean's head, tormenting him as if they were long-lost brothers finally reunited.

Dublin, Ireland
Present Day

Sitting at his desk, Tobias was growing impatient over his timeline and working with his lieutenants to iron out the final points of his plan for the mission in Berlin. Tobias's advance team was already in Germany, scouting the venue and monitoring the activity in the city.

A knock came at the door. Tobias uttered, "Enter." The door promptly opened as the recovering Fury entered the room and stood at attention. Tobias said, "Ahhh, Fury, you are mending. That's good to see." He ushered for him to take a seat.

"At ease, Fury," he said.

Fury started to sit as he said, "Thank you. I failed you, sir, in Vienna. Here is the full debrief report. Apologize for the delay, but the doctor had me all bunched up for a bit." Handing the report and looking directly at Tobias. He would not make any excuses for himself or his men's performance. Tobias appreciated that quality in Fury.

Tobias hesitated for a moment before speaking, "Yes, you did, son, and lost two of our best in the process." Tobias looked directly into Fury's eyes and said, "He's only a man, Derek, like you and me, but he bested you. But you will have a chance to redeem yourself . . . in Berlin. I want our operation to occur without incident, and I want Sebastian Storm eliminated with no excuses in the process. After receiving Storm's location from our source inside, sadly, we lost him after this cluster in Vienna and haven't been able to locate his whereabouts for the last eleven days, licking his wounds somewhere in safety, I'm surmising. Plus, we have a plan to lure him to Berlin. He will pop up at any time; I'm quite certain of it."

Fury stood up and said, "I will not fail you again, sir." He turned and walked to the door.

Tobias asked, "Derek?" Tobias was the only one who occasionally referred to Fury as Derek.

Fury stopped, turned on his heels and replied, "Sir?" Tobias asked, "Are you up for this physically?" Fury took a step toward Tobias's desk, hesitating, he breathed in slowly before replying, "Sir, . . . I'm a professional, your most dedicated, sir, and I get the job done. As far as I can recall, it is the only time I have failed you. Storm killing the twins has made it personal for me. I will be going to Berlin, and I will eliminate him . . . or I fear I won't be coming home. That is the commitment I am making to you, and I will not fail a second time. I will see this through or die trying. The only thing that will supersede this mission is my protection of you, sir."

Tobias looked solemn, saying, "Fair enough. Good, Fury, make him pay . . . and suffer." And with that, Fury turned to the door and walked out of the office as the door closed behind him. Boomer was standing at the ready in the anteroom, waiting for his chief to emerge. Boomer walked up to Fury and nodded.

Boomer said, "Hey Boss, Sebastian Storm just landed in Berlin." Fury was happy. "Good. Tobias's plan is working." Tobias's strategy to leak information about Berlin had worked and brought Storm into their circle of destruction, an arena he would not be leaving so easily this time, he thought.

Boomer continued, "We also have news from Mueller that a woman by the name of Adriana Mercer appears to have some significance to Sebastian Storm. He was seen with her in Vienna just before he arrived in Berlin. We have a tail on her at the moment and providing us hourly updates. She could be key at some point." Fury nodded, "Brief Tobias on the girl and Storm and see how he wants to proceed."

"Assemble the team. We leave at 12:00 pm. What's your final number?" Boomer tallied it up. "Including yourself and me, along with Blast and Kick, make up our Set Team along with Prim and his elite team of ten. Finally, Tobias will join us tomorrow before the event."

Fury responded, "Very well. I'll meet you at 11:00 am to finalize the preparations and personnel positions for the mission. Timing will be key for this one."

Boomer replied, "Copy that, sir. See you in a few."

Dublin, Ireland
Present Day

Stepping from their SUV, Sebastian and Sean walked into the Hotel Adlon Kempinski, located in Berlin's Mitte district adjacent to the Brandenburg Gate and a fifteen-minute walk from the Pergamon and Bode Museums.

He stopped short of the entrance and looked cautiously up and down Unter Den Linden Street. Satisfied, they stepped into the parlor of the hotel. Mueller focused from afar, leaning against a government building less than a quarter mile away, south of the Hotel on Unter Den Linden, as Sebastian entered the property. He was equipped with telephoto sunglasses that had fifteen times magnification but appeared normal to the astute observer.

In both Berlin and Vienna earlier that morning, it was the closest he had ever gotten to Sebastian's immediate location without exposure. However, he had to be extremely cautious as far too many people historically had underestimated Sebastian Storm and ended up less than breathing. He didn't want to become another one of the man's victims.

Mueller was proud of himself as he internally praised his skills and anti-detection measures. Tobias and Fury would be pleased. He called the information in and reported the progress and content of his surveillance.

As Sebastian entered the building, he pulled out his phone and dialed his superior. "Hey HB, we are at the hotel. I've got a tail south of the Adlon reading a magazine. Blue suit, dark hair, six feet tall. Find out who this guy is for me. I don't think this is the first time this guy has been watching me. I've seen his face somewhere before. I just can't place it."

HB replied, "Copy, Sebastian. Hold on for a moment." HB barked some instructions to one of her agents nearby and waited a moment. He heard the agent report a "Got him."

HB continued, "Okay, Sebastian, we have him, identified as Erhard Mueller with Interpol. He was with German intelligence before being criminally discharged five years ago. We suspect he is one of Tobias's. He doesn't do the dirty work, only recon. We will stay on him."

Sebastian replied, "Copy that. He may be our only lead on this, and I want Tobias to know I'm here without him knowing I'm onto his guy. Don't let your men lose him, HB." He hung up the phone. Sean looked at Sebastian, surprised before saying, "How did you see that guy, Sebastian?" Sebastian smiled at the question and replied, "Just that Spidey sense I have Sean, you know, my Superhero shit. I'm always on high alert. Plus, you know I have a nose for bad guys, I can smell them from a mile away, and this guy reeks of it through and through." Sean laughed at the comment but also believed it to be true. Sebastian did have an extremely sharp sense of those things.

Sebastian looked around and nodded to Sean. If Tobias had a man outside watching him, they might very well have one on the inside as well. Sean knew from experience that without Sebastian saying a word, the scene was in play, and they had already started their mission. "Stay sharp," said Sebastian.

Approaching the reception desk, Sebastian checked them into the suite that was booked for them, using an alias for security. Although an alias, whether necessary or of any efficacy, was debatable at this point. Sebastian assumed everyone knew his arrival in Berlin wasn't as covert as he hoped.

"Damien, don't lose Mueller," whispered HB to her agent in charge as their surveillance tracked from both the third floor of a business building across from the hotel and their unit on the street.

They retained a mobile unit, but those were much easier to spot, hidden within a delivery van a block away on a back street behind the Adlon Hotel. "Ma'am, Mueller is on the move . . . moving away from the hotel," said Damien.

"Stay on him, and for chrissakes, don't lose him and don't get spotted. We need to keep this guy in play," she said.

Prim, Fury, and Boomer landed at 3:00 pm and met with the advance team upon deplaning. The group assembled in a safe house a few miles from the Pergamon Museum. They spent the better part of an hour reviewing the specifics of the mission and team positioning. Blast, Kick, Prim, and Fury were all to take a group of two of Prim's elite soldiers, both men and women, dressed in plain clothes to blend within the environment. Boomer would then set charges while having two soldiers chaperoning, covering him as he placed the explosives throughout the museum.

More than one individual setting the charges could attract far too much attention. Therefore, Boomer was the only person tasked with that responsibility. Everyone else provided cover.

The explosives were to be set on strategic load-bearing walls, configured within a thin set of transparent adhesive sheets 8×8 inches, essentially the same thickness as a piece of paper containing a highly concentrated hydrolyzed C4 explosive. The specialized film would cause a wide-radius blast, cutting through six feet of reinforced concrete, and, when timed with others, had an exponentially powerful blast radius. Its intent was to inflict maximum damage.

Tobias's plan was intended to level the museum, and an anticipated three to four thousand fatalities would ensue. Based on the plans obtained by Von Sydow several weeks prior, it was determined twelve key support points existed throughout the museum that would secure the most damage when destroyed.

The twelve charges would be placed at strategic positions throughout the museum. A remote-activated chip embedded within each sheet would allow for a simultaneous synchronized explosion.

The transparent sheets, nearly invisible and virtually undetectable, were ingeniously designed to detonate remotely if necessary. To ensure redundancy, both Tobias and Boomer had their respective remotes, with Boomer's serving as the backup. Fury meticulously briefed the teams, outlining the precise scenario and sequence of placements they had rehearsed countless times. The tension was palpable as each member absorbed the critical details, ready to execute the plan with flawless precision.

Fury barked out the orders. "The four teams will be dispersed throughout the complex, solo or two-soldier groups, not congregated to avoid attracting attention." He pointed to the detailed layout of the complex on the table. One of Prim's soldiers piped up. "You don't have enough men to evenly canvas the area; it's not enough."

"Excuse me, Renaldi?" said Fury. Renaldi had been waiting for the opportunity to challenge Fury and display his competence in front of the other soldiers. Attending to his own agenda, Renaldi had his sights set on eventually becoming a SET soldier and thought this a way to receive the recognition he deserved.

Renaldi continued his challenge. "The museum's footprint is far too expansive for the number of soldiers in this operation."

Fury demanded, "Who put you in command, Renaldi? And we don't want an abundance of players in this arena to avoid attracting unwanted attention." He glared at Renaldi, seeing the door open in the far side of the room well behind Renaldi's field of view, and sensed Tobias walking through the doorway with two guards in tow, slightly diverting Fury's attention.

Logistics for the operation had been scrutinized numerous times, but Fury, Prim, and ultimately Tobias himself thought the number adequate. They even considered reducing the force by one or two men and improving efficiency.

Noticing Fury's shift of focus, Renaldi said under his breath, "Asshole." But Fury caught it; his eyes narrowed and hardened as he closed the gap between them and pushed Renaldi against a support beam in the middle of the room, his forearm forced up against Renaldi's neck, choking him.

A look of fear in Renaldi's eyes confirmed that he realized the level of his mistake. At that moment, Tobias was approaching alongside Fury, detaining Renaldi, and in a fluid motion, drew from the breast pocket of his long tan cashmere overcoat, his snub-nosed .380 with a silencer attached and without so much as a thought fired directly at the right temple of Renaldi as he walked by, killing him instantly all while keeping his stride, never missing a beat. Slightly shocked, a spray of blood splattered Fury's face but he remained unflinching. Fury then released the bloodied corpse as it slumped to the floor.

Tobias possessed an extreme side to his soldiers' discipline; Fury didn't always agree but kept to himself in these instances. Renaldi didn't need to die just taught a lesson.

This was the lesson Tobias thought apropos to the situation.

Tobias replaced the gun within his breast pocket before addressing the group as a whole, "Well, I guess we are a man short." Every man and woman in the room focused on Tobias intently, and rightfully so. Fury stood tall, face bloodied, dedicated to the message Tobias spilled forth. His crimson badge of dedication displaying his devotion to his superior.

He continued, "I don't have space or time for insubordination within my ranks. I don't fire people here; I eliminate them. Men don't walk out of here; they are carried out. No one crosses my leadership or me, is that understood?" he asked, looking at everyone in the room. All the soldiers in the room were now nodding in agreement.

The instructions continued. "Now, get this heap out of here." Several soldiers quickly moved Renaldi to the corner of the room, throwing a tarp over his body and quickly forgetting him. "Continue, Fury," said Tobias softly as he came to stand at Fury's side in support of the final steps and preparations being properly executed.

Fury at attention said, "Sir, we are primed and ready to display our full destructive force and aptitude to the world."

Tobias calmly replied, "Excellent, as I would expect, Fury." He looked at the rest of the men and women, hesitating for a moment. He looked at many of them closely, looking for any weakness or hesitation in any of their eyes, but he saw none.

When satisfied, he continued, "This is our moment to make our mark on the world stage, gentlemen. We have an opportunity to gain the power and respect that we deserve by instilling global fear and utilizing the Pergamon as our example and statement here in Berlin. Our objective is twofold. First, level the Pergamon Museum with precision-like accuracy; second, I want Sebastian Storm eliminated along with Sean Woodford and Hillary Bastini."

"A ten-million-dollar bonus to anyone that brings me Sebastian Storm's head and one million for either of the others. This mission must progress without incident; each of you was personally selected to ensure its success."

"Renaldi was a fool, questioned his superiors, and this organization and I will not entertain such lack of loyalty and disobedience on any level. Please don't make the same mistake he did; I will not tolerate it. Now, any questions?" In unison, the group was silent and yelled, "Sir, no sir!" Tobias nodded and knew they were ready.

The soldiers again go over the specifics of the mission and their individual roles with Boomer and Fury. They were now a man short; therefore, Prim opted to have only one soldier with him versus two.

There was a debate on whether to attempt to infiltrate the Pergamon at night to place the charges, but the issue was security patrols, night-vision cameras at the facility, and possible detection of the explosive sheets the following morning. Tobias quickly dismissed that option.

Prim served as the ground overseer and backup, ready to step in if any of the teams encountered issues or suffered casualties. His hunger for the ten-million-dollar prize for eliminating Sebastian surpassed that of anyone else involved. Determined to secure the bonus and improve his standing with Tobias, Prim positioned himself strategically, maintaining a slight distance from the main action to better his chances and to impress Tobias despite his previous lackluster performance.

At their base, Tobias monitored the mission with two technology experts by his side while Mueller personally assisted him. Known for their flawless execution, Tobias's team treated this operation as their most critical yet.

The mission was set to commence shortly after the 8:00 am opening the following morning. Tobias aimed to demonstrate his formidable destructive power to the world. His chilling estimate predicted over 5,000 casualties—double that of the World Trade Center attacks. This horrific figure would undoubtedly capture the attention of Hillary Bastini and the entire globe. Tobias was determined to make this day historic, not only by causing unprecedented devastation but also by finally eliminating Sebastian Storm.

Chapter 21

Tobias's Plan Takes Form

Berlin, Germany
Present Day

Damien Kerr was HB's chief assisting agent and followed her wherever she went. He was assigned to watch Mueller from a distance, along with two other agents who were assigned to his surveillance.

Kerr knew where all of HB's secrets and skeletons were buried and was a crucial instrument in her division. His vital role made him privy to important information that proved useful and lucrative to specific individuals if the price was right. With a daughter attending New York University and a second at Arizona State University, Kerr's paltry governmental income barely covered their respective tuitions. Mueller walked toward the Pergamon and Bode Museums, stopped before the front of the museum entrance, and made a call.

Mueller's mole within HB's group had gone dark after identifying the Hotel where Sebastian and Storm would reside. Each agent was flanking Mueller's position on each side and well outside of view, whereas Damien was directly behind him yet several hundred yards away and well out of sight.

Their configuration created a strategic funnel following Mueller's movements and adjusted as their query's position evolved.

HB communicated with all the operatives through their encrypted earpieces. It was the calm before the storm, and all of them sensed it; they simply needed to piece together the rest of the puzzle.

Looking out over the city of Berlin, Sebastian stood at the railing of the large terrace of his suite, appreciating the spacious views as dusk quickly approached.

For a moment, his thoughts drifted to Adriana, wondering where she might be in the world at that very instant. He was aware she had departed Vienna for the States that evening, but beyond that, her exact location was a mystery. The urge to track her movements was strong; knowing where she was would bring him some semblance of peace. However, he sternly forbade himself from giving in to that temptation, at least for now. With his extensive resources, Sebastian could pinpoint her location within minutes, but he resisted, refusing to succumb to his desire to know her immediate whereabouts.

He remained firm in this position to keep her life private. It was better he didn't know and attempted to put it out of his mind. At that moment, Sean came out onto the terrace and nudged Sebastian with a McCallum Bourbon 21-year with a large ice cube, his drink of choice. Sebastian happily accepted the cocktail as they both looked out over the city.

Sean understood Sebastian better than anyone, sensing something was deeply amiss. He could see the torment in Sebastian's eyes, but he knew better than to confront him directly. Sean was keenly aware not to push; Sebastian would reveal what troubled him when he was ready and not a moment sooner. Understanding the delicate balance and respect of their relationship, Sean chose to wait, knowing that the truth would emerge in its own time.

Sebastian enjoyed the drink and nodded his appreciation as they watched peacefully and quietly, looking out over the beautiful horizon. Toasting each other, Sebastian took a pull from his glass as Sean did the same. After a moment, Sean softly said, "That view somehow makes it all worth it." Without looking at Sean, Sebastian replied, "That it does," still mesmerized by the spectacular view that lay before him.

They stood in silence for a moment, and then Sebastian slightly turned to Sean and asked, "Do you ever feel like there's more out there for us, Sean? Do you ever wonder about the simplicities of a normal life and what it could offer?"

Sean was a little surprised about the question but then asked, "You mean like a family, children . . . a wife?"

Sebastian pondered, "Yeah, I suppose so. I don't know, something beyond the carnage and destruction of what we do. Or did we forfeit all of that long ago, I wonder?"

Sean replied, "That's a hard question, Sebastian, and with no simple answer given the complexities of life goals and the choices we have made. I've often thought of a simpler life, and personally, I don't think I could find anyone to put up with me. Plus, I would have a hard time subjecting a woman to my dangerous lifestyle. And you . . . We are cut from the same cloth, ole buddy; you would be quite the handful yourself." They both laughed at the truth of the statement.

Sebastian agreed, "I hear ya, Sean, but I met someone recently who made me think more about that life and less about . . . well, this one. The hunger has been growing within me for some time now, and when Tobias's group nearly took me out a few weeks ago, it made me question my place within the world. It made me doubt myself and my . . . *mortality*."

Sean was more than astounded to hear this testament coming from Sebastian Storm, as he always thought of him as the ultimate soldier, but he didn't let on the surprise Sean felt deep within from Sebastian's words. He was speaking from his heart, and Sean sensed it. He didn't want to discount the new perception Sebastian was contemplating, but he had also seen it before.

They both looked out over the city as Sean pondered this question and sensed more of the specific struggle Sebastian was experiencing.

Sean continued, "Hmmmm, met someone, I see. She must be something significant to push you out of balance. You never let anyone that close."

Sebastian replied, "She is. I met her in Vienna, and she's made me think about things differently. Alternatives and my options, I suppose. Anyway, that's not the crux of it. What matters is it's stirring something inside me, making me consider the option of reaching another level, something different. I'm not sure what it is yet, but there's a change happening within me, a longing for something more. It's almost like a rediscovering of myself in a sense."

Sean contemplated, having heard similar conflicts from other soldiers before. To him, it appeared Sebastian was questioning his place in the world, possibly in need of some reassurance. Despite the hesitation in responding, Sean understood the gravity of Sebastian's words. He was aware his friend trusted very few people, and he was honored to be among those few. This wasn't just idle talk—it was a call for help, a search for meaning.

"Sebastian," Sean began thoughtfully, "everyone hits a point where they question everything. It's not a sign of weakness but a sign of growth. Maybe you are on the brink of something significant, a transformation. But whatever it is, you don't have to face it alone."

Sebastian's eyes flickered with a mix of relief and contemplation. Sean's response wasn't simply a platitude; it was a lifeline. He felt the weight of his inner turmoil slightly lift, knowing he had someone to navigate this uncertain path with. The air between them thrummed with unspoken understanding, a bond forged in the crucible of shared battles and unyielding trust. Together, they would face whatever came next, their futures intertwined in a tapestry of loyalty and change.

Sean replied, his voice a blend of firmness and empathy, "Sebastian, you are a warrior, a soldier's soldier. You were born and bred for this life. You know you're the best, and even on your worst day, you could take me down—and I'm no slouch. You have no equal. This is what you were meant to do."

He paused, his gaze turning somber as he continued, "Soldiers like us, we don't get to have those 'normal' lives, at least not in any traditional sense. Look at Tobias. Losing Emily turned him into a monster. The pursuit of normalcy was his eventual undoing. She made him vulnerable, and she ultimately suffered for it, and he wears his guilt on his sleeve as a result of her death."

Sean waved a hand towards the city, the sprawling expanse glittering under the night sky. "It's our destiny, Sebastian. We protect all those people out there. Because of us, they sleep soundly at night. It's a heavy burden, but it's ours to bear. In many ways, I don't think we chose this life—it chose us."

Sebastian listened, his inner turmoil reflecting in his eyes. Sean's words resonated deeply, a mixture of truth and the harsh reality of their existence. He harbored the weight of his friend's understanding, the shared sense of duty that bound them together.

"But what if there's more?" Sebastian said, his voice barely above a whisper. "What if I'm meant for something beyond this, too?"

Sean nodded slowly, recognizing the conflict within Sebastian. "Maybe there is, and maybe you are. But whatever path you take, you don't have to walk it alone. We'll figure it out together. Just remember, being a warrior doesn't mean you can't evolve, or can't seek something more. It only means you'll bring that same warrior spirit to whatever you do."

The city lights shimmered in the distance, a silent testament to the lives they protected. In the moment, the two men stood united, their bond stronger than ever, ready to face whatever destiny had in store for them.

Sebastian said, "I know, Sean, but each life I take removes something from me, from my soul, and I don't want to eventually have nothing else left but the black hole remaining, the void, the abyss. That is why Tobias is devoid of understanding, mercy, or empathy. I never want to turn into what he is or stands for on any level."

As Sebastian shook his head in mild confusion and frustration, questioning the surreal conflict within his thoughts emerging. Sean said, "Think of the good . . ."

All of a sudden, breaking radio silence, HB announced through her earpiece, "Sebastian, we have a location on Mueller. He is currently outside the Pergamon Museum. We are well outside of the field of view, and he is on a phone call. We will continue tracking him. We are attempting to intercept the call."

Sebastian replied, "Copy that. Something's off about this, HB. It appears too easy in this situation; I just can't put my finger on what it is yet. I think we need a second layer backing up the three-man team you have in play. Tobias is far too cunning to leave Mueller this exposed."

HB responded quickly, "I've always trusted and relied upon your instincts, Sebastian. Team Delta, follow up Team Alpha, and I need your ETA, ASAP!" she barked into her earpiece.

Delta's team leader immediately replied, "Copy, Delta is three minutes out."

"Copy, make it two, double time!" replied HB, but all teams were copied on the conversation.

"Aye aye, Cap," replied the Delta leader as he shouted to his men to quicken the pace.

Sebastian nodded to Sean. "Let's continue this discussion later, Sean." They double-timed it to HB's safe house. Damien heard over the comms that they were bringing reinforcements to fortify their position. This was simply an observational mission on Mueller, so he was a little confused as to why Sebastian was concerned for Alpha Team, but he had come to respect and admire Sebastian's abilities to see things others often missed. Damien respected Sebastian's tremendous intuition and came to fear it as well.

If anyone saw through Damien's guise, it would be Sebastian Storm. It had saved all of them countless times, and he was rarely incorrect in his assumptions, but he admitted to himself that this call on the surface, appeared a little overly cautious. It could complicate things for him.

Sebastian's intuition could end up derailing Tobias's plan. Damien's exposure was imminent. Damien Kerr had now covertly supplied Tobias's operation with three distinct locations where Sebastian could be found: London, then Vienna, and finally there in Berlin. Their intercept teams had failed in the initial two locations, and this was his final time to provide them with this crucial and dangerous information.

Each of Tobias's failed attempts on Sebastian put Damien more at risk, but the three-million-dollar payout was initially worth the risk; it was only small pieces of information he disclosed. But, at this point, the gamble was becoming far too great. HB was getting close to finding who was leaking the information to Tobias, and because of their prior two failures, his own life was now in jeopardy. His job was only to provide the information; what Tobias's organization did with the information was not his concern.

Using his binoculars, he still had the visual confirmation of Mueller on the phone 380 meters to the northeast of his position, "Subject static, please advise," said Damien.

"Hold, wait for backup; do not become detected. Delta Team is three minutes out," came HB's voice over the earpiece. HB and her team were observing using drones and troops on the ground, but the area was heavily canvased by tree cover, making surveillance far more difficult for HB's team.

"Copy instructions, awaiting backup," replied Damien. He waited a moment longer and then sensed a presence behind him. As he started to turn, Fury fixed his K-Bar knife firmly to the right front of Damien's neck, just below his Jugular vein, drawing a small but effective trickle of blood, demanding Damien's respect for the situation.

Fury had his left hand gripping a silenced 9mm muzzle steadily against Damien's left lower back. Coming up close to Damien's right ear, Fury gently whispered, "Don't move. I imagine you have backup coming up to this and the other two positions, correct?" Fury's hot breath scorching his ear as he hesitated and didn't want to lie for fear that Fury most likely heard him only a moment earlier, confirming HB's call to bring reinforcements.

"That's affirmative," replied Damien.

"What's their ETA?" asked Fury. Damien was hoping to buy some time and potentially turn this altercation around, and knowing Fury possibly had not been privy to the discussion on when the reinforcements would arrive, hopeful Fury wouldn't call his bluff, he said, "Four minutes."

Fury replied, "Hmmm, I doubt it. You underestimate me, Damien, and oh, I wanted to let you know we are terminating your contract and won't require your services any longer. By the way, Tobias sends his regards."

Slowly, he breathed as he sliced Damien's neck with one stroke, carving through both jugular veins on each side and trachea in the process. Damien's hands immediately and reflexively rose to his throat to limit the damage, but any attempt proved futile.

Fury held Damien's weight while he bled out within a few seconds, then softly lowered him to the forestry floor.

"Primary down, eliminate the other two teams, reinforcements in less than three minutes. Take them out," Fury whispered into his earpiece, and both of HB's other troops were terminated tactfully by Fury's team.

Mueller was on the phone with Tobias at the time. He reported, "Tobias, I believe I may be being followed."

Tobias responded, "You are Mueller. Proceed quickly to the southwest exfil position. Fury will meet you there. He is handling the situation."

Mueller quickly responded, "Copy, exfil pickup point." He used the moment to escape while HB's team was in the dark about his whereabouts. He kept to the trees and maneuvered effortlessly.

The leader of the Delta team cautiously came up to the corpse of Damien Kerr, and as he clicked his earpiece, he was never given a chance to speak and warn the others. Fury, who had been positioned in a tree above, fired a single silenced round from his modified Barrett M82A1 Special Application Scoped Rifle into the left eye of the Delta team leader, killing him instantly, then turned ninety degrees to have a clear shot from 418 yards of the other Delta soldier and dropped him within seconds of the first. Boomer effectively and surgically took out the third team, and they quickly met at the rendezvous point without HB even being aware.

HB reached out to Damien with no response, and the Delta team leader also did not respond. "Get a Goddamn team down there and find out where everyone is . . . and where the fuck is Mueller? Get a call into Sebastian and get him and Sean over here ASAP," barked HB. The situation was unraveling before them.

Several minutes later, Charlie's team leader came on the headset. "Lone Star, this is Charlie Team, both Alpha and Delta teams were eliminated, no survivors, and the Bogey is MIA, Charlie out."

HB screamed out, "Fuck, they just surgically removed both our tracking teams, Goddammit!" HB then got back onto comms, "Charlie. . . and what of Damien?" "Also eliminated, ma'am," came the response. HB shook her head, amazed at Tobias's audacity. He was undoubtedly drawing a line in the sand.

The agent reported, "Storm and Woodford . . . ETA three minutes, ma'am." HB nodded.

Sebastian and Sean entered the situation room of their safe house and walked up to HB. They had been briefed on the situation as they were escorted in.

HB said, "You were correct in your assumption, Sebastian. Both Alpha and Delta were taken out. Entirely taken out." She continued. "This has Tobias written all over it, and I think he is making this personal. Eliminating our teams is his way of 'taunting' us, and it also makes me suspect we are getting closer to his true intention as to why he is here in Berlin."

Sebastian replied, "That brings me to a thought . . ." Looking at all the data before him, he focused in on Tobias's file which was strewn about on the large table. "Here's my take, HB. Something struck me as peculiar with this architect, Von Sydow, the one you flagged who died of 'natural causes' several weeks ago, but his death's MO follows more the style of Tobias's head of security, Prim, you mentioned to me back in Vienna."

HB responded, "I'm not following Von Sydow's relevance. He was only an architect, nothing more significant than that, and didn't he just come up because of recent news here in Berlin?"

Sebastian responded, "He did, but cross-referencing Prim's tactics and you placing him here in Berlin at the same time as Von Sydow's death made me put things together. I remember reading something connecting the architect to the Pergamon Museum here in Berlin. Then it struck me. Now, with Mueller ending up at the Pergamon and Bode Museums before escaping, where, ironically, Von Sydow orchestrated the remodel of the museum a few years back, makes this all a little too coincidental. My gut tells me he is going after the museums, and their one-hundredth-year anniversary happens to be tomorrow, which is also convenient. The museums will be full of people, wall to wall—a perfect opportunity for a mass terrorist attack. I question if Tobias has subtly left us a trail of breadcrumbs and in such a way has also led me here as well, which was always his intention."

Like a light went off in her head, HB replied, "That photographic memory of yours, Sebastian. How did you pull those together? We are here in a very veiled capacity, gentlemen, and the German government will not react without proof, and a hunch won't be enough for them. We are going to have to proceed in a covert manner, I'm afraid."

Sean asked, "HB, are you able to get us into the museums to have a look around?"

HB replied, "I'll see what I can do, but they will ask many questions. Also, we have just learned, there are some ties to Damien Kerr that can't be explained. He was among the deceased with Alpha and Delta teams, and we are beginning to suspect he may have been our mole. He's been with me for over eight years. We are vetting him personally at the moment, and it looks like some offshore accounts in his name have received some sizable deposits over the last few weeks. I never pegged Damien as a traitor."

HB shook her head in disbelief at the thought that her most trusted assistant was selling information and betraying her and her division.

Later the same evening, HB contacted Sebastian to let them know they had clearance to inspect the museum. After hours of inspection, they found nothing out of the ordinary after thoroughly covering the entire premises multiple times.

Museum security would allow HB's team entrance but allowed limited access within the museum. "Our teams can remain on-site as long as we provide real-time situational updates to German intelligence, museum security, and local law enforcement. They really don't want us around, especially on this, their anniversary."

"I'm not entirely sure this is the target, Sebastian," said HB as she, Sebastian, and Sean stood at the entrance of the Pergamon Museum.

"I have this feeling we are standing within the target, HB. And with the 100th Anniversary tomorrow, it is optimal for a horrific event. I think we should have a team here tomorrow, well before opening, and I'd like to head up the team with your permission," said Sebastian.

Sean chipped in, "I'm going to side with Sebastian on this, HB. His instincts are usually spot on, and our intel isn't suggesting anything else as an alternative from what we can see. I'm in as well."

HB replied, "Okay, boys, I'll let you have four agents on site, and we will run the mission from the base, follow up on some other leads we have, and cross-reference all of our data."

Becoming somewhat alarmed, HB's tension was running high because they had no clear line or understanding of what Tobias was up to or where he was in Berlin, but they all were certain he was in Berlin . . . . *Somewhere.*

The German police only agreed to increase security somewhat over HB's warning, but it would hardly make an impact based on the sheer size of the two large museums and the ground they need to cover. Not to mention, thousands in attendance.

An attack on one or both of the museums appeared logical but without any evidence pointing to either of the locations. Unfortunately, HB and Division would have to rely on real-time data as it would trickle in or develop the following day.

The Museum was a tactical and defensive nightmare, yet perfect for anyone wanting to make a statement.

The Pergamon Museums' 100th Anniversary was to be held the next morning, with over 10,000 people estimated in attendance.

Chapter 22

Plight at the Pergamon

Pergamon Museum
Present Day

Tobias's first team enters the museum immediately upon opening at 8:00 am that Thursday morning; each man enters staggered throughout the morning either separately or paired with a female to reduce suspicion.

The four teams arrived and entered the museum within the first hour of their doors opening. Blending well within the environment, they all were dressed to appear as if they were simply tourists with their objective crystal clear—cover Boomer as he placed the twelve explosive charges throughout the Pergamon and provided protection and intel if needed or obtained.

Fury and Boomer estimated the placement would take roughly 90 minutes. The timing was ideal as the museum would be at its full capacity of ten thousand in attendance by 9:00 a.m., with the one-hundredth anniversary festivities in full swing by then.

Sebastian and Sean were stationed at each museum entrance with two agents apiece, watching as the museum enthusiasts would enter. It was challenging to monitor and differentiate between any suspicious individuals within the crowd of nearly ten thousand people.

With the exception of Fury and Tobias, HB's team didn't know the identities of Tobias's outfit, which proved to be more of an issue in identifying the threat.

They communicated with their concealed tech earpieces. "All clear on the north entrance," said Sebastian.

"Copy that, negative on south entrance," replied Sean. They had been present for several hours, and the museum had been open for nearly an hour with no suspicious activity noted as of yet.

Sebastian shakes his head and mumbles, "Everything seems far too perfect and smooth." He began to question whether he had made the correct call on identifying the Pergamon Museum.

Boomer's team was last to enter the Pergamon. The two soldiers assigned to him entered the building several minutes before, one a female soldier, and walked just past Sean, holding hands and laughing with her counterpart. Sean didn't notice them at all.

Once past security, Boomer immediately entered the men's bathroom in the main hall as his escorts lingered in the souvenir store just across from his position. "Team One has a positive ID on Sean Woodford at the south entrance," said the woman soldier when in a safe and inconspicuous position.

"Copy that, Woodford ID, south entrance. Watch him, take him out if given the opportunity, but wait until all charges are placed," replied Mueller as Tobias acknowledged and nodded his approval.

Tobias's technicians had tapped into the museum security to study the movements of their own soldiers on the mounted cameras. They all wanted that ten-million-dollar prize but also knew better than to put their own interests above that of the mission. That agenda was the quickest way to receive a bullet through the brain from Tobias.

When the camera catches Sebastian at the north entrance, the tension on the back of Tobias's neck erupts. "To all, Sebastian Storm is at the north entrance. I don't have to remind you of the bounty on his head. Execute the mission and take him out once the explosives detonate!" exclaimed Tobias over his headset.

Boomer left the stall to wash his hands as the last gentleman left the lavatory before leaving him alone. He quickly retrieved the small ceramic handgun from underneath the sink that had been placed there prior by one of the other teams to circumvent the metal detectors and X-rays at the entrances.

He placed it in the small of his back, held fast by his waistband. He gently pulled a single thin transparent sheet of the concentrated explosive material from his backpack and placed it at knee level of the supporting beam in the middle of the bathroom. The thin sheet was coated with single-sided adhesive to fix it in place. He removed the backing and quickly placed it on the flat surface of the rounded pillar. Virtually invisible and taking only seconds to place.

Being transparent, it blended and conformed very well with the light blue of the paint upon the pillar. Once securely placed, it was then armed through his remote device.

One down, eleven remaining explosives to place. The chip needs only to be activated with his remote detonator after several seconds of synchronization when the adhesive backing is removed, and it is considered armed once the synching with his detonator is completed, which takes 15–25 seconds per charge. That was his most vulnerable moment as the charge and detonator must be synched to arm the charge, and Boomer needed to pay close attention to the sequencing.

After nineteen seconds, Tobias saw the blip occur on his screen on the virtual map of the museum, signifying that the synching was complete as Boomer said over the earpiece, "Initial charge armed."

Mueller replied, "Copy, all clear on no. 1 charge." The computer screen in front of Mueller blipped as a single circle emitted, showing the first charge active. The process took all of thirty seconds, but the challenge was not being observed by a passerby as the sheet was placed. Boomer left the lavatory and made his way down the hall to the secondary placement position.

Sebastian was getting restless, it already being 9:00 am; he felt his window was dwindling. It was then that he caught a museum tourist eyeing him a little too closely and intently. "I got a possible bogey, in his forties 30 meters south of me, lingering at the program station, olive shorts and a white shirt. Appearing suspect, have museum security pick him up. He appears to be solo," whispered Sebastian into the earpiece.

"We see him, Sebastian," replied HB as museum security began approaching the man. The man appears to speak into an earpiece similar to Sebastian's.

"This is Murphy; I've been made." As he instructs Mueller through the comm. Murphy carefully removed his earpiece, subtly dropped it to the floor, and crushed it with his heel before he was inevitably questioned by security as he feared. Museum security approaches Murphy and asks to speak with him privately as they take him away. Without the earpiece, there is nothing Murphy has on his person connecting him to the operation.

Sebastian walks up to where Murphy stood after the man is escorted away. Kneeling down, he picked up the crushed earpiece as it broke into pieces between his fingers. It's hard to identify, but it's definitely an earpiece from what Sebastian can see.

Into his own earpiece, he said, "Storm here. If they didn't know we were here, they do now. The guy picked up was on comms. Press him and get something out of that guy, HB. Whatever it takes, we need information. This. . . . *is happening here, I can feel it.*" Standing up, Sebastian looked around and thought, if he was here, there were definitely more, and obviously whatever they came to do, they hadn't completed it as yet. There was still time. Sebastian turned, scouring the area, looking and evaluating each individual within his line of sight.

Sebastian called his two agents, and they began separately canvasing the area in hopes of finding something more substantial. At the same time, HB and her team attempted to obtain any valuable information out of the soldier they had detained. The apprehension confirmed Sebastian's intuition of the venue for Tobias's event; she said to all her agents running leads in Berlin, "All available agents to the Pergamon immediately. We have a situation brewing."

Within thirty minutes, Boomer had completed his fourth location explosive placement, all with relative ease. He was moving to his fifth position when he saw Sebastian in the distance around the Ishtar Gate and the Market Gate of Miletus exhibits.

He needed to position himself close to the supporting pillar adjacent to the Ishtar Gate but decided to move to his alternative target locations to avoid being detected by Sebastian and his counterparts, which would delay his timeline by a few minutes.

Sebastian Storm's reputation was far too illustrious to attempt to place the explosive within his focal view. He was fortunate that Sebastian did not know his identity but ran the risk of being spotted, detained like Murphy, or killed before placing all charges. It could ruin the entire mission. He couldn't risk it.

To avoid this obstacle, Boomer nonchalantly moved to his sixth position behind the cafeteria. He mocked a fake phone call, crouching down to tie his shoe, and placed the explosive on the circular supporting column with ease. While viewing the public milling about around him, he then synched the device without incident. He stood up and imitated conversing for a time on the phone to strengthen his muse before moving to the seventh position.

"Team, this is HB. This soldier apprehended is a tough one to crack. We haven't been able to get him to forfeit what they are up to here at the Pergamon. Sebastian? You will be happy to know the price on your head is ten mil and one mil for Sean and me, but that's all we have been able to press from him so far. HB out."

Great, thought Sebastian. All he needed were some trigger-happy mercenaries on his heels for a contract on his head as he dealt with a terrorist threat. He was certain Tobias planned to keep him off balance. With Tobias's team incentivized to eliminate him, paired with this current threat, Sebastian was most assuredly compromised on many levels. Shaking himself back into reality, Sebastian regains his focus. He needed to turn the tables, and he had an idea on just how he would achieve it.

"Storm here," he said into his earpiece. "I need everyone to look for men or women in tourist attire, adjusting an earpieces or acting in any way suspicious . . . anything! Please alert me immediately. Even if it is a false alarm, we need to flush more of these terrorists out. We need to turn up the heat a bit."

Boomer completes the sixth and seventh positions in the next fifteen minutes. The eighth position was difficult as it was to be placed adjacent to a door frame inside the Pergamon Altar exhibit. The difficulty was that he was exposed and vulnerable more than most of the other positions, and his chaperones needed to be diligent in protecting his flank while he maneuvered.

The female soldier, Moriarty, stood out by becoming far too stationary while Boomer placed the explosive. One of Sebastian's agents took notice of the irregularity and studied her more intently. "Storm, Franklin here. I may have a possible bogey here at the Pergamon Altar, a woman with questionable body language. Also, I can see an earpiece fitting the tourist description you mentioned when she adjusted her hair." As Franklin watched his subject fixedly, he heard Sebastian quietly say, "Be there in less than a minute. Don't lose her and don't let her see you, above all. Great spotting, Franklin."

In forty seconds, he was close to the exhibit as Agent Franklin called in with an update. "Sir, I think she may be on to me. She has moved her position toward the north side exhibit lavatories and picked up her pace. I'm on her."

Damn, thought Sebastian as he responded, "I will intercept, cover my six; we need precision on this. I need locations of storage closets or facility rooms on her route immediately."

Moriarty looked over her right shoulder for Franklin several times, attempting to elude him. "Maintenance closet east wall twenty feet in front of you, Sebastian," replied HB. "Copy," responded Sebastian. Perfect, he thought.

At that moment, Moriarty felt she might be too far compromised as she began to report her status to command, but before she could do so, a presence immediately filled her left blind spot, her vision blurred, and her knees became instantly weak as she now felt light-headed, nearly collapsing where she stood. Her body jerked, and her right ear went numb.

Sebastian gripped the back of Moriarty's neck, heavy pressure on the jugular with his thumb and in her right ear with his index finger, crushing her eardrum with her own earpiece.

The pressure on her jugular reduced oxygen to her brain, and her crushed eardrum had limited discomfort, but an acutely induced vertigo sensation overwhelmed her, causing immediate light-headedness. Taking full advantage of his stimulated confusion, Sebastian quickly ushered her toward a storeroom as Franklin and the second agent, Daniels, engaged the people nearby, immediately distracting them with requests for pictures and/or directions.

With no time for traditional tactics or red tape concerning museum security, Sebastian pushed Moriarty into the storeroom together. Sebastian achieved the movement largely unnoticed and promptly closed the door behind them, locking it. "Wha, what are you doing? What did you do to my ear?" asked Moriarty, confused as she looked over her left shoulder directly at Sebastian in a dazed fashion.

He was taking a calculated risk as Moriarty may not be affiliated with Tobias's outfit, but he needed answers immediately. Her ear was already bleeding from being so severely damaged. Gripping the back of her neck more tightly, she let out a small scream, and Sebastian leaned up to her still operational left ear and gently whispered, "My name is Sebastian Storm. I surmise you have heard of me, and I also know you are more than aware of what my capabilities are in this instance."

Sebastian asked in this specific manner because he wanted her to know that he was sure she was part of this plot at the museum, and if she were aware of his reputation, he would not have to waste his time convincing her he was a force to be reckoned with. If she did not know who he was, she would simply be fearful of why a strange man had accosted her and shoved her into the storage closet.

Either way, he would have his answer.

How she reacted was essential to how he proceeded, and even the most seasoned professional could rarely react in a way that would deter how he progressed. The face and eyes rarely lied. He used it as if it was a human lie detector.

Sebastian had used this tactic many times in the past, usually with tremendous success. She looked at him, panic welling up, her eyes tearing from fear and pain. He said again, "Do you know me?" With hesitation, she nodded a few times in rapid succession, acknowledging her awareness of who he was.

There was his answer, simple but effective. He had her now and would stop at nothing to get what he needed. Sebastian replaced his right hand with his left in the more traditional choking hold as he lifted her 130-pound frame up and against the shelving, pulling her off the ground by a few inches to get her attention.

Moriarty seized the one moment to attempt an offensive movement against Sebastian with a knee to the groin, but he turned, sidestepping it easily, simultaneously repositioning his left hand over her mouth and grabbing her left hand. In doing so, he broke her middle and index finger immediately to regain her focus, which worked as she let out a suppressed scream over the pain he caused her. Her fear heightened as he anticipated.

"Make a sound, and I will end you right here. Your life is forfeit now. How you answer my questions will determine whether you live or die today. Do you understand?" Whispered Sebastian. She nodded, her comprehension of the situation she now found herself immersed in.

Sebastian's eyes narrowed. He was intent on terrifying her, and the tactic was proving successful. "Now, listen very carefully to my first question: If I detect you are lying to me, I will break your neck," said Sebastian. He released his left hand from her mouth but pulled her broken fingers up with his right hand to remind her to comply or face the consequences.

When Sebastian's hand was forced, there was no equal in the effectiveness and efficacy of his methods to extract information. Paired with the fact that the clock was ticking, in the back of his mind, he was certain he was losing valuable time with each passing moment; he needed some vital questions answered.

Sebastian softly and quietly asked Moriarty, "How many men have you got on site?"

She looked at him with such fear, her eyes darting right and left as panic gripped her, coursing through her body. Moriarty reluctantly replied, "Twelve."

Good thought, Sebastian, further confirming his dicey notion that he secured a valuable resource in Moriarty. Sebastian then responded, "Good. What is the mission Tobias had set forth here at the Pergamon? I remind you, do not lie to me. My retribution will be swift." His eyes glared at her, urging her to answer quickly.

She closed her eyes hard, shaking her head, fighting the pain and misery over her predicament. She said after a moment, "I cannot tell you. Tobias would—" Sebastian then broke her smallest finger without hesitation or warning as he began choking her with his left hand, stifling any scream she attempted. Tears were falling from her eyes at this point. Her pain increased with each passing moment. Intense pain paired with oxygen deprivation, Sebastian was fully aware, could be a very persuasive instrument.

He said menacingly, "You will tell me." His grip tightened, and she began to asphyxiate and reflexively thrash about. But Sebastian held her fast, controlled, and patient as she was about to lose consciousness. He released slightly, letting her regain the oxygen her lungs and brain so desperately needed.

She was terrified now. Moriarty had always feared Tobias, but Sebastian had no remorse or regret. He was like a machine in his execution. She assumed he would kill her without reluctance, but she was also aware he was a man of his word and that if she told him what he wanted to know, he said he would let her live. At that moment, she feared Sebastian more than she feared the wrath of Tobias, and she had to trust that Sebastian would protect her.

"You must protect me from . . . Them but most of all. . . *Him*." Referring to Tobias, he assumed.

———

Sebastian said, "Done. Tell me what I need to know." Intently looking into her eyes as HB sounded off in the earpiece, "Sebastian, Sit Rep." He replied, "Hold on, H. I need an extraction team to my current position." Sebastian turned to Moriarty. "See? I can be reasonable. I've made arrangements to get you out of here. The question is whether you will be breathing or not. I need it all from you. Now. But if this goes down and anyone is hurt, I will put a bullet in your head myself. You have until my team arrives to tell me everything, or you die," Sebastian lies.

Moriarty eagerly began by saying, "Explosives, set to go off in the next thirty minutes. Boomer is moving about the museum with organized teams. He is placing them all and activating and arming them as he goes."

Sebastian quickly asked, "What type and how many?" Moriarty replied, "Twelve . . . transparent sheets of a specialized concentrated C4."

Sebastian continued, "How will they be detonated?"

Moriarty replied, "Tobias has the primary switch; Boomer the secondary."

Sebastian asked, "How can they be disarmed? And describe this *'Boomer'* to me."

She aversely replied, "They can't be disarmed, I don't think . . . I don't know. Boomer is blond, and attractive, wearing white pants and a black short-sleeved shirt. He looks like a tourist."

Sebastian continued. "What else can you tell me?" She shook her head as if to say nothing.

Sebastian spoke into his earpiece while holding her gaze, frightening her even more. "HB, is the team ready?"

"Affirmative," replied HB.

"Initiate," said Sebastian as the door to the storeroom immediately opened within seconds. A woman entered, instantly injecting Moriarty in the neck with Diprivan, a sedative causing her abrupt unconsciousness as she slumped to the floor.

Sebastian then slowly and methodically exited the room in a casual manner as two other agents quickly entered the enclosed space, clad in maintenance clothing, and within thirty seconds, they all departed, appearing on the surface to be moving equipment from one location to another where Moriarty's sleeping body lay within, unsuspicious to the casual observer.

Sebastian was now speaking into his earpiece again. "Storm here. Team, we need to step it up. We have ten bogeys out there, twelve explosives, a thin transparent sheet type C4, and Tobias with the detonator. A guy by the name of Boomer—blond, attractive, with white pants and a black short-sleeve shirt—is placing the explosives. I'm unsure how many he has placed, but we need to take him out of play. They plan to detonate in the next thirty minutes, so they must be close to completion."

The plan was hinged on getting Boomer neutralized and luring Tobias into the fold; Sebastian needed access to both detonators. They had to operate covertly; an announced evacuation would cause a panic, and unknowing of how many explosives were set and active, it could be detonated at any moment if spooked. Their hands were tied.

"Storm, we have a possible match on the suspect described adjacent to the Pergamon Altar exhibit," announced an agent named Fitz over the earpiece.

"ETA sixty seconds," said Sebastian, and he began a jog toward the exhibit.

"HB, is there any chance of 'jamming' the radio frequency on these detonators?" asked Sebastian as he started to break into a light run.

"I'm on it," replied HB.

"Ma'am, should we evacuate the building?" asked one of her agents as a precautionary measure.

"Negative. That would cause a museum-wide panic, and until we get any transmission jammed in or out, they can set it off at any moment. We have to hope our team on site gets this done, or we will have a real mess on our hands," replied HB.

Boomer didn't like the exposed partition he needed to load with the sheet of C4 directly positioned by the Pergamon Altar. He could feel Sebastian's group closing in on him as Tobias said over his earpiece, "Two soldiers down, we need to wrap this up. All available soldiers to Boomer's position, located at the Pergamon Altar, to aid in his delivery of the package."

The pressure was mounting, and Boomer still had three charges remaining to place to complete the series of twelve. Tobias's engineers had calculated that they needed all twelve charges placed at their designated areas for the full effect of damage desired. Anything less than the twelve charges detonating would significantly mitigate the effective damage and radius of the desired blast.

Boomer located the supporting wall inside the exhibit area and stopped at the altar description platform, pretending to read the historical information in the museum program explaining the history of the Pergamon Altar. At the same time, he cautiously scoured the area for any of Sebastian's team. His cover team was in close proximity perusing the exhibit, but all seemed clear, so he slowly made his way to the supporting wall and leaned against it. With 10,000 people circulating through the museum, it was difficult to differentiate any relevant players within the museum grounds.

He took out his phone to appear like an ordinary tourist and blend in like so many others visiting the museum on this, their 100th anniversary, taking full advantage of the tourist chaos surrounding the altar. The area was bustling, being one of the more popular exhibits on this historic day, and Boomer was hoping to use this to his advantage.

Unknown to him, so too was Sebastian.

In the hall outside the exhibit, Sean and Sebastian arrived at the entrance of the Pergamon Altar exhibit at roughly the same moment. Agent Fitz, their team member who called in the initial sighting of Boomer, subtly nodded in the direction of the altar exhibit room and the subject in question. "South wall, I believe. I didn't enter for fear of alerting the suspect, but he is in there and with only one way in and out."

Their options improved considerably with only one entrance/ exit to the exhibit. Approaching the same wall, Sean meets Sebastian before the entrance, stops short so he won't be identified, and quietly says, "Sean, this guy in here has one of the detonators, but Tobias has the other. We need to take this guy out of play and flush Tobias out. We need both detonators and hopefully, HB will jam any incoming signal. I have a plan."

"You always do," came Sean's reply and smiled.

Sebastian laid out his strategy with Sean and then told the team via the earpiece comms before implementing his idea. Per Sebastian's instruction, Agent Fitz casually and cautiously walked into the exhibit parlor slowly and deliberately, reading the various historical metal placards mounted about the area.

Tobias monitored the surveillance and was the first to identify an American agent within the proximity of Boomer. He assumed they were closing in on his men and his mission. "We have an agent that has entered the Pergamon exhibit, Boomer. He is fifty yards northeast of you. Tan shorts and a white shirt, sandals." Boomer looked around and located the agent Tobias had identified.

"Boomer, set that charge and arm it," orders Tobias over the earpiece. Tobias's two agents in proximity, Solomon and Gaither, a male and female team, began positioning themselves closer to the identified agent while still providing necessary cover for Boomer if he should need any immediate assistance or protection.

Boomer needed to place the charge quickly, arm it, and vacate the area before he and the explosives were compromised, and the mission impeded.

Fitz was their decoy and proved a promising gamble as Tobias's soldiers had their focus reconcentrated towards Agent Fitz, identifying themselves in the process and allowing Sean and Sebastian to slip into the exhibit foyer unnoticed by Solomon and Gaither, all the while maintaining the blind spots the security cameras were missing.

Sebastian breaks radio silence. "We need to take these two agents out covering Fitz. Sean and I are on Boomer. HB, take care of those soldiers."

HB responded, "Copy that. We have them identified." Three more agents entered the arena. HB's teams were always well-trained, refined, and performed in unison like a well-oiled and efficient machine.

Gaither, the female soldier, was just out of camera surveillance view, taken from behind, intentionally at this point by one of HB's agents without so much as a struggle, as she was drugged by physical contact transmission a few moments earlier when an agent lightly grazed her hand with a powerful concentrated contact solution called Ricin, which impacts protein synthesis within a few seconds of contact. The effects of the concentrated Ricin were an immediate ill feeling, the onset of nausea, and then losing consciousness after several seconds following transmission. She appeared to have fainted by anyone observing.

With Gaither out of the picture, the agents moved on to neutralizing Solomon, who had not yet noticed Gaither's capture, as his focus was more on Fitz and protecting his primary, Boomer.

Once again, kneeling down to tie his shoe, Boomer looked through his backpack as he pulled out a sheet of the C4 explosive, which he concealed within the commemorative museum program brochure, to place at the base of the supporting wall. He needed only to activate this explosive in addition to the last three sheets, and he would have completed his portion of the mission, but the last few were proving to be difficult, especially this current one located within the altar surroundings.

He was the least protected in this position, but the location was critical to their plan and design. The sheet lays inconspicuously upon the floor as he fumbles with his shoelace, slowly looking about for his chaperones, but has lost sight of them with all the tourists walking about and impeding his depth of focus.

Boomer had to assume they were out there, watching over and protecting him. Placing the transparent sheet over the intended area was a relatively simple task. However, he still had to activate the sheet and add it to the explosive sequence upon his detonator. This proves to be more involved for this particular charge than he had anticipated, all the while being mindful that he does not alert suspicion in the process.

It was then that the hairs on his neck stood up as he heard, "Stand up slowly and turn toward me," instructed Sebastian quietly.

Standing together with Sean, they both stood a few feet behind him, out of view. Looking around before responding, Boomer weighs the options now facing him. He had to assume Gaither and Solomon had been neutralized without so much as a warning from Tobias and the surveillance team, making it most likely they were also unaware his escorts had been effectively compromised.

Boomer couldn't help but be impressed with Sebastian's team and their apparent resourcefulness. They played it smart, well executed, and on point. Boomer dropped his head, his options dwindling as he considered them. He hadn't been able to sync the current C4 charge, nor would he be able to place the remaining three if captured. If only he could arm the current C4 and Prim and Fury came to his rescue, he could get the remaining charges placed and armed, assuming Sebastian's crew was not aware of the intent and execution of their true mission.

He also had the gun placed under his shirt in the small of his back, wedged inside his belt if the situation turned sour. Touching his ear, he said, "I'm here with Storm at the altar—"

In a blur, Sebastian slapped his hand away, his earpiece flying out of his ear onto the ground as Boomer slowly stood up. He didn't like these odds. "Boomer, the bomb guy, I presume," asked Sebastian with Sean's silenced 9mm pointed squarely at Boomer's forehead. Once fully standing, Boomer slowly eased away from the wall, knowing the surveillance cameras would pick him up if he could simply position himself a few more steps toward them. "Don't move," warned Sean, now a second time.

People nearby noticed Sean's gun, and a tourist exclaimed, "He has a gun, he has a gun, help, run!" Panic began to overwhelm the immediate area, and people, unaware of the scream's source, began to run in various directions. The result was Boomer's intention.

Boomer seized his opportunity in the chaos as a woman and her small child ran between them. Seizing the easiest target, Boomer grabbed the young girl of roughly five years, held her as a shield in front of him, and grabbed his gun from the small of his back in the same motion.

The mother, suddenly dumbstruck and terrified as to why this man would take her daughter, fought with Boomer while clutching and pulling at her daughter to free her of the impending stranger. Putting a solid fist into her face, Boomer dropped the mother as she fell where she stood, unconscious.

Boomer was intelligent and calculating, manipulating the scenario to improve his odds. He held the young girl very close to his head with his gun held to her right temple, and he knew, as they all did, they didn't possess the high percentage shot.

People were still running aimlessly about as Boomer, Sebastian, and Sean stood nearly motionless, staring at one another. "Let her go, Boomer, it's over," quietly muttered Sebastian, referencing Sean, "and the best marksman in the world has his gun pointed squarely at your head. Let her go. If you don't, you won't make it out of here alive."

Sebastian looked at Boomer intently, trying to determine his devotion to this endeavor and loyalty to Tobias. Boomer wanted desperately to arm the explosive; Sebastian could ascertain his commitment to the mission, but he saw it in Boomer's eyes. He was a fanatic. Tobias did his work well and recruited soldiers loyal to his cause. Boomer smiled, "I don't think I was ever getting out of here alive, Mr. Storm."

Boomer's focus darted back and forth between Sebastian and Sean, keeping calm, trying to bide time. "Look here, as luck would have it, I have the number no. 1 and no. 2 most wanted right here in my sights. This must be my lucky day. Not sure if you are aware, but there is quite the hefty bounty on both your heads; I'll be a wealthy man," replied Boomer.

The moments were dwindling, and Sebastian knew he was running out of time. Sean pipes up, "Can't spend it if you are dead, mate." Sean once again says:

"Sebastian, I have the shot. . . . "

Chapter 23

Armageddon

Pergamon Museum
Present Day

When Tobias first detected Boomer moving into view on the surveillance camera with the young girl held in his arm, gun pointed at her head, he announced, "All teams to the Pergamon Altar, Boomer, Woodford, and Storm on site, triple time!"

Tobias sat in the shadows, his eyes glued to the unfolding scene with a mix of intensity and calculation. He was merely a spectator, yet the stakes were profoundly personal. His fingers drummed rhythmically on the armrest, betraying his underlying tension.

He was certain Boomer had failed to arm the charge in the altar room. The absence of the usual confirmation signal was a glaring omission, stark against the backdrop of otherwise seamless executions. Each placement had been confirmed meticulously, yet this one crucial task remained in limbo.

Tobias's mind raced, considering the implications. The success of their operation hinged on precision, and any deviation could spell disaster. The altar room was pivotal, its charge meant to be the linchpin of their entire plan.

His gaze hardened, and a sense of urgency gripped him. If Boomer had indeed faltered, the repercussions would be severe. Tobias knew he had to act swiftly, but the chaos of the moment demanded a careful approach.

As he continued to study the scenario, his mind whirred with possible contingencies. He was a master of strategy, and even now, he began formulating a backup plan. The room before him was alive with motion, each movement a piece of the puzzle he needed to solve.

In the dim light, Tobias's features remained inscrutable, but his mind was anything but calm. He was ready to intervene, to steer the situation back on course. The game was far from over, and Tobias intended to emerge victorious, no matter the cost.

Tobias had the yearning to detonate the existing armed device immediately, allowing him the opportunity to eliminate Sebastian and Sean at the same time but consequently losing Boomer in the process and compromising the full effect of the mission objective.

The loss of Boomer would be unfortunate collateral damage but well worth the award. Without that charge at the Alter activated, the overall damage would be significantly reduced; therefore, he had to rely on his teams to come through with their objective in the final moments as his mission was beginning to deteriorate.

"Hold your fire, Sean," said Sebastian quietly as his focus was intently fixed on Boomer's gaze, his 9mm Beretta squarely aimed at Boomer's forehead but remaining calm and collected.

He didn't want to kill Boomer because he needed to confirm he had the detonator on his person, as well as provide valuable information on his employer, Tobias, and their organization, and the magnitude of their terrorist display at the Pergamon. There were so many unanswered questions.

Boomer was roughly ten feet from Sebastian and Sean when Sebastian said again, "Let the girl go, Boomer." There was difficulty in getting a bead on Boomer because there were still hysterics from the crowd within the altar room, and people were running randomly throughout the area, affecting his line of sight.

Paired with the screaming and yelling, tracking the perpetrator was proving very difficult in the given setting. At that moment, Sean and Sebastian heard over their earpieces, "A bogey coming in fast from the northeast . . ." as Fury crashed in and tackled Sean, the one closest to him.

Boomer used the distraction to redirect his gun toward Sebastian and squeezed off a round. Anticipating this move, Sebastian diverted quickly to the right to draw the fire, then immediately left, avoiding the bullet, whizzing past his ear, missing him by only a few inches, yet the round struck a woman in the leg twenty yards behind.

Knowing immediately that he missed his mark, Boomer adjusted his aim, but not before Sebastian was atop him with a right square fist, directly into Boomer's face. Boomer dropped the young girl as she ran to her unconscious mother ten feet away.

Being the closer target of the two, Sean received the full impact of Fury's rage as the two of them slid twenty feet following the collision. Both men quickly got to their feet. Sean glanced at Sebastian and Boomer and determined that Sebastian seemed to have his situation under control.

Whatever happened, they could not allow Boomer to activate the device or risk detonating all the other explosives set throughout the museum. "SEAL to SEAL, Woodford, you won the first round in Vienna with that pussy sniper shit, but not today. Time to man up. You are on my most wanted list," said Fury as he came at him.

Sean was the smaller of the two and more agile than Fury, but he also was aware of the man's reputation back when he was at the SEAL training academy. Other SEALs often spoke of the notorious Derek Allen, one of the most gifted and talented soldiers to come out of the academy, yet also one of the most unstable, ultimately leading to his professional and occupational demise. Sean thought to himself, "Oh shit, he is a lot bigger than I thought."

Fury lunged and missed the more agile Sean Woodford, but hand-to-hand combat was more Sebastian's style. Sean was more comfortable navigating the large 50-caliber cannons that could blow a hole through a pickup truck. Sean realized he wouldn't last long toe-to-toe with Fury; he needed to bide time and think fast. An idea came to mind.

Studying Fury's profile, Sean remembered that the man's weakness was playing into his head. "Well, Derek, I think it's more like SEAL to dishonorably discharged ex-SEAL. Yes, I feel that is more apropos," he stated. This enrages Fury as anticipated.

Fury took a right swing at Sean, but Sean had eased back slightly, the miss grazing Sean's nose but allowing Sean to give Fury a hard right, then an immediate left combination to the kidney before stepping back. Fury winced from his bruised ribs, still healing, damaged from the altercation in Vienna, but held his wits. Sean was also aware of this and needed to exploit it further. He had learned much from Sebastian in close-quarter combat training and taken his teaching seriously. The practice was paying off. he was keeping up with Fury, but more importantly . . . *keeping him occupied.*

"You don't seem that tough, Derek," said Sean. The arena around them was clearing at this point. All the tourists within the exhibit had exited the large Pergamon Alter room as the four men were entangled in a flurry of combative maneuvers equally matched between the four soldiers.

There were over ten thousand tourists within the museum that day, which was far higher than usual because of the 100th anniversary of the Pergamon Museum and all the events' celebrations.

The timing was essential, and Tobias was losing precious seconds as he witnessed the portion of the museum that held the Pergamon Altar being evacuated because of the skirmish occurring within the main exhibit hall, and the young woman shot in the leg had alerted the full museum security detail to that location. Tobias had less than five minutes to detonate the explosives that Boomer had armed thus far to maximize damage, but his window was dwindling by the second.

Angry that the last four charges would not be detonated, Tobias surmised the damage would be tremendously limited, reducing the full potential of their intended mission; casualties would be substantially less than anticipated, which would be a considerable disappointment to Tobias and the goals he had set for this attack.

Boomer struck out with a myriad of thrusts and kicks aimed at Sebastian's head and abdomen, most deflected as Sebastian responded with combinations to the face and stomach, clearly dominating the melee. At that moment, Boomer determined he needed to end this or fail to complete the mission. He was twenty feet from the explosive he had set only moments before at the altar exhibit but had yet to arm it. He needed Sebastian neutralized or otherwise occupied.

He yelled, "Fury, help here!" Fury immediately looked at Boomer and Sebastian and realized what Boomer was thinking. He needed to help Boomer activate the explosive and salvage the mess that was occurring as their mission was unraveling. Disregarding Sean, Fury immediately turned and started after Sebastian, running at him with Sean directly behind him in pursuit.

Sebastian was forced to divert his attention from Boomer to Fury, who had become the more immediate physical threat. Leaning down, Fury then drove his uppercut, grazing Sebastian's left jaw, underestimating his defensive talent, thus failing to land a solid contact.

Sebastian retaliated with a roundhouse kick to the side of Fury's head, wincing at the impact, his injuries reminding him he was not at 100 percent. The impact to Fury's face did not slow him down significantly but seemingly infuriated Fury further.

Boomer took the opportunity to run to the explosive in an attempt to arm the specific and sensitive arming mechanism.

Fury, realizing that close-quarter combat was consuming far too much time, attempted to run hard at Sebastian with the intent to tackle him, giving Boomer the time he desperately needed. His goal was only to detain Sebastian for a few moments to allow Boomer the seconds he required to arm and sync the device.

Boomer reached the explosive and looked behind him, watching the development between Sebastian and Fury, elite soldiers engaged in battle. It was almost mesmerizing to watch, both versed in the art of warfare and closely matched.

He had the moment he needed to complete his task, but he didn't take into account. . . . *Sean Woodford*. Fury narrows his focus on Sebastian, once again charging him with all he had. Boomer assumed Sebastian would try to intercept the detonator again but had not considered Sean in his peripheral vision.

In a full run, only steps from Sebastian, Fury could feel himself firming his power as he was about to make full contact with his target. Sebastian's focus had been briefly diverted with Boomer and the explosive. Sebastian was just turning to look at Fury, coming at him with all the ferocity that Fury had mustered within himself. Suddenly, and without warning, his vision blurred as he felt his balance tipping to the left.

Fury accepted the full collision of Sean's impact into his side. Despite having a difference of thirty pounds on Sean, his impact hit him with everything Sean could gather. Achieving his intent, Sean knocks Fury off his intended path and stuns him in the process as Fury's momentum works against him.

The gamble was rewarded handsomely as Fury partially collapsed as he fell completely off balance. The motion and shift of the weight and his momentum made him hurtle to the floor, sliding across the tiled surface, deviating his trek substantially, buying precious seconds. Sean's sudden impact took him further from Sebastian and Boomer.

Boomer had just looked away, grabbed his detonator, and began the synching process he needed to arm the device. The process took fifteen seconds as he studied the display homing in and locating the transmitter within the explosive sheet—ten seconds remaining until the explosive was activated.

A fourth of a mile away, Tobias studied intently as Boomer's detonator display underwent the synching process, mirroring its progress on Tobias's computer within his command post. His finger gently hovering over the master detonator button, he fully planned to activate the explosives if there was any possibility of encompassing Sebastian and Sean in the explosion that would ensue. The loss of Boomer and Fury would be substantial, but he couldn't pass this opportunity to eliminate Sebastian once and for all.

Attentively watching the screen, his finger now resting lightly over the button as the estimated time of completion ticks on the view with less than six seconds projected until the process was completed.

Then five seconds left. . . . . four. . . .three and counting.

Boomer, stooped to one knee, fixated on his detonator screen as the seconds dwindled. This charge was crucial, the keystone to the mission's devastating effect. As he monitored the countdown, an unexpected twinge of pain seared through his left hand. Instinctively, he turned his head and was met with a horrifying sight.

His left hand, along with the detonator, had vaporized, replaced by a gruesome, bloody stump. Shards of bone protruded through the mangled flesh, and blood spurted rhythmically from the wound. The shock immobilized him for a moment, the agony and surrealism of the scene overwhelming his senses.

Time seemed to slow as he processed the grotesque reality before him. His mind raced, the mission's importance clashing with the immediate, visceral horror of his injury. Boomer's breath came in ragged gasps, the metallic scent of blood filling his nostrils, mixing with the acrid tang of the gunshot residue bellowing around him.

The dim light of the room flickered, casting macabre shadows on the walls. His vision blurred slightly, not just from the pain but from the adrenaline flooding his system. In the chaos, he could hear the distant sounds of exchanges between Fury and Sean, but his focus remained on the grotesque transformation of his hand.

Despite the excruciating pain, Boomer's mind remained poised. He needed to adapt, to salvage the mission somehow as it was slipping through his fingers. The blood dripping from his stump onto the floor was a stark reminder of his vulnerability, but also of his resolve. He clenched his jaw, forcing himself to think clearly, to find a way to turn this gruesome setback into a moment of triumph. But, it was too late.

He slowly looked right to see Sebastian with a gun in hand, saw the muzzle flash, and then everything went black.

Sebastian knew they were running out of time and suspected that Boomer had not yet activated the explosive's remote. When he found Fury had been delayed, he seized the opportunity to swing the momentum in his favor. Already drawing his gun from his specialized holster, he aimed directly at the detonator in Boomer's hand, having little concern for any collateral damage.

The desired effect achieved, his round obliterated both the detonator and Boomer's hand simultaneously, effectively terminating the synching process of the device, making the explosive sheet ineffective and inoperable. Disoriented, Boomer slowly turned toward Sebastian in awe as two shots exited Sebastian's barrel, center mass, directly into Boomer's forehead, his lifeless body slumping to the ground. His glazed pupils still pointed directly at Sebastian with an enigmatic stare of his eyes lifeless before him.

Tobias's screen froze at "Two seconds," and he closed his eyes and looked up, hands outstretched, yelling, "God damn it, Sebastian!" He had to assume Boomer had been eliminated.

HB was now on her earpiece again. "We've got exterior jamming of any incoming signals, Sebastian, but the explosives will take time to find and can still be detonated on site remotely. It looks as though Tobias has the only other detonator. We located only two RF remote signatures, and you eliminated one of them."

Sebastian responded, "I have an idea." But they still have Fury to deal with near the Altar. Sean was exchanging attacks with Fury and holding his own, but Fury, being the superior soldier in hand-to-hand combat against Sean, was gaining ground on him. It was only a matter of time before Fury would overcome Sean.

Sebastian needed to intervene immediately. Intentionally approaching from his blind spot, Sebastian rushed Fury, jumped forward, and hit him squarely with his fist in the back of the neck, stunning him as Sebastian followed with several rapid attacks and a solid kick from Sean into the chest, sending Fury hard against the wall behind him.

Getting up, Fury saw the dead corpse of his partner, Boomer, unmoving and realized they were losing this battle. Within seconds, Sebastian was on top of him with a flurry of fists, Fury attempting to throw him off but to no avail. Sebastian was repeatedly pounding him until his face was a bloody mess until, ultimately, Sean had to pull him off.

Sebastian shook it off and stood, saying in his earpiece, "I need a team in here to take this asshole out of here. I'll have some questions for him later." He considered the security cameras that had undoubtedly recorded the entire ordeal with Fury, now simply a gory heap behind him.

Certain of who was watching him, Sebastian slowly looked up, smiled, and said, "Sending boys to do a man's job, Tobias? Are you that cowardly? Why don't you come and get me yourself?" Sebastian pulled up his gun and shot both cameras.

"I think we will be seeing Tobias at any moment. Be alert," Sebastian said in his earpiece as Sean walked up alongside him with HB entering the room with several agents.

"That was a mess. Do you think Tobias will make an appearance?" asked Sean.

"That it is, and I think his ego will drive him more than anything. We need to neutralize these explosives, Sean," said Sebastian as HB got close.

"We are quietly evacuating the museum to avoid hysteria but still have a few thousand people in the various exhibits, and the exits are bottlenecked. We have not begun to look for the explosives, but they could be anywhere and everywhere. Tobias can detonate them at any time," explained HB as Sean and Sebastian nodded in agreement.

"Tobias wants me, and he has to be here to detonate the charges Boomer was able to place before we intervened." He showed them the thin sheet explosive, harmless unless activated.

HB and Sean handled the explosive in its benign and innocuous state. "The tech available these days is amazing. This is state-of-the-art," said Sean. Sebastian observed as the agents were secured, not far from them.

Shaking his head, Sebastian responded, "Yes, it is, and Boomer almost got this one activated. I have an idea that had he been able to, Tobias would have activated the whole series of explosives, taking us all out, in addition to several thousand tourists. We dodged a bullet this time. Well, so far, we have, but we are far from out of this mess yet."

Sebastian looked at HB, "You mind escorting the gorilla here back to his cage? Make sure he is handled, HB?" Referencing Fury as he was quietly escorted out of the area in cuffs and shackles, glaring at Sebastian as they walked towards him.

"Yeah, I'll have my best take care of him," replied HB as Fury yanked on his chains, stopping abruptly where they stood, looking at Sebastian in the eye, and said, "We will dance again, Storm, another day." He was pushed from behind in the forward direction by one of the guards. Fury glares at the guard and says, "I'll be killing you first," as the guard rolls his eyes.

Sebastian taunted, "Well, make sure you bring your A-game next time, Derek, because you sure as hell didn't today." Fury awkwardly laughs as he is ushered away by the two of HB's agents. "Oh, it ain't over, Mr. Storm, we are just beginning, just getting started . . ." He continues to laugh as he walks away.

Sean, Sebastian, and HB look at one another, all more than a little concerned at what the cryptic response could mean.

HB excused herself and followed Fury and her agents, then went out of the side exit to take a call as the agents continued down the hall with Fury. "I'm fortunate you hit him when you did, Sean, or this would be a far different outcome," said Sebastian, watching Fury nearing the terminal end of the hall towards the southwest exit.

"Again, saving your ass, it seems, Sebastian, kind of getting used to it," said Sean with a wink. "Always my guardian angel," replied Sebastian.

At that moment, the ground shook violently, and the glass atrium above the hallway exploded violently. Both Sean and Sebastian jumped to opposite sides of the hallway as a primary load-bearing steel beam supporting the atrium above dropped between them, and the walls started to crumble all around the museum, falling inward and crashing to the floor.

Sean hurled himself toward the exit side of the building, and Sebastian went back toward the Pergamon Altar, somewhat trapped, and saw Sean trying to find a way to him. "No, Sean, no! Stay back, get out of the building, I'll get out . . . somehow. Go!" screamed Sebastian as he watched Sean, not wanting to leave him but fully understanding why he must.

Sebastian figured Tobias had made his entrance. He must have been on-site to detonate the explosives. Maybe Fury's parting words were more fitting than they had initially thought.

Sebastian's position was far from optimal, but there was little he could do as the series of explosions shook the building and roof system, and large portions of the building were collapsing all around both of them. Sean tapped his ear as if to indicate he could reach him with his earpiece as he evaded falling debris, arriving at one of the exterior exits and getting safely out of the building.

Tobias . . .

He was becoming a menace, thought Sebastian as he avoided the falling pieces of roofing and wall supports. Looking back, Sean didn't see Sebastian as the remaining portion of the roof caved into the hallway. Shaking his head, Sean couldn't imagine anyone surviving that chaos. But then he thought again, Sebastian wasn't just anyone.

As the rumbling began, Fury immediately smiled, realizing what was transpiring and knew Tobias's final act had begun. Tobias was nearby, and he was making his appearance. The explosives had been detonated, most of them anyway.

Capitalizing on the distraction, Fury swiftly bumped the agent to his right with a stiff shoulder, knocking him to the ground. Turning quickly, Fury then double fist punches the agent to his left in the face with his shackled hands. The agent reacted slowly and reached for his now broken nose as Fury seized the opportunity and reached for the agent's gun, holstered on his hip while sidestepping behind him, effectively using him as a shield.

The agent on the ground aimed his gun, trying to hone a bead on Fury. His target moved swiftly, but the captive agent's body provided a partial shield. Seizing the moment, Fury maneuvered with precision, his eyes sharp and calculating.

Suddenly, the desperate agent on the ground fired, aiming for Fury's face. The shot went wide, obscured by the captive's head and the violent shaking of the structure around them. Debris rained down, and the air was thick with tension and dust.

Fury's instincts kicked in. He capitalized on the missed shot, advancing with fluid agility. The room seemed to pulse with danger, every second a potential turning point. His movements were a blend of strategy and survival, each step calculated to outmaneuver his adversaries.

As the chaos intensified, Fury's resolve only grew stronger. The agent's desperate act had inadvertently given him the upper hand. In the dim, flickering light, Fury's eyes glinted with determination. He was not just fighting for his life; he was fighting to bring order to the chaos and to ensure that his escape was guaranteed.

With the tumbling rocks and ceiling fragments falling and crashing all around them, the agent's aim was difficult to train, his target wavering and uncertain. Having to speculate at best, the agent discharges a second round, missing Fury by two inches but hitting the ensnared agent squarely in the right eye, killing him instantly and splattering Fury's face with blood and brain matter. Fury laughed at the missed shot and made his move.

Spitting out pieces of bone and flesh, Fury smiled and said, "I told you that you would die first." He was losing leverage with the dead agent, so Fury hurled the lifeless heap toward the agent still on the ground in an effort to shield himself. In an attempt to deflect the dead agent's mass coming straight towards him, the agent rolled to the left as the dead man hit the floor hard next to him facedown.

Two slugs struck the agent in the face as Fury utilized the disruption to finish the encounter. A large stone portion of the supporting column fell within a few feet of Fury, and he rushed over to one of the fallen agents, grabbed his handcuff keys and earpiece, unlocked his shackled ankles, and got up from the floor.

Gun still in hand, Fury started a light run for the exit as he unlocked his handcuffs, threw them aside, and placed in the Agent's earpiece. He wanted to see if he could pick up any information as it developed. "All agents, cover the exits. We need to sack Tobias; we cannot let him escape." That was the only piece of information that came through amidst the chaos.

The northern part of the Pergamon appeared to be hardest hit, and the agents escorting Fury were not responding.

"We have a clusterfuck on site, people. We need to pull this together. I need all agents to call in with respective validation codes to authenticate," yelled HB over the earpiece as the various agents began calling in. All but three agents called to verify, including Sebastian. She assumed he had a reason to keep his status private, but then she instantly became apprehensive and hoped he wasn't in trouble. HB had to assume the communications had been compromised and default changed the frequency channel to an alternate. Fury threw the earpiece away as he opened the door of the exit.

Little did HB know that Sebastian Storm would be put to the ultimate test in the moments that followed.

Chapter 24

Detonation

Pergamon Museum
Present Day

Sebastian was all too familiar with navigating through various perils. He couldn't recall the last time he had to pilot himself through disintegrating roof structures and collapsing wall segments while finding himself directly within the fulcrum of a terrorist attack by an all-too-familiar enemy.

In the past, his missions had often led him alone to be the consummate "architect" of such commotion and confusion, but here at the Pergamon Museum, he had become the quarry. But this time, Tobias was the true engineer of the Pergamon carnage and destruction, not Sebastian. There were undoubtedly going to be substantial casualties as a result of Tobias's premature detonation, but Sebastian and his team had significantly circumvented the potentially exponential human loss had the explosives detonated as planned.

Tobias's mission was still a momentous victory paired with the significant financial and historical damage that would surely follow. But that was not Sebastian's immediate concern.

Sebastian once again found himself in the Pergamon Altar exhibit, covered in soot and filth, desecrated, and largely destroyed. Yet, the Altar itself remained intact and stable for the moment, a shining beacon in what was otherwise a structural pandemonium.

Screams and shrieks from those injured or maimed filled the air from afar, but the Alter was uninhabited. The area had been evacuated earlier because of the altercation with Boomer just twenty minutes before the explosion, so no people were present.

Sebastian was alive, but was he alone?

The dust and debris left the area with low visibility, but the roar of stone cracking and metal twisting diminished as the moments passed, and the wreckage began to settle.

The Pergamon Altar, a symbol of veritable perseverance amid the insurmountable bedlam, was a true testament to history, thought Sebastian as a 9mm bullet whizzed by his left ear into the wall behind him. A wild attempt, wide and off, but more of a warning, it seemed.

He dropped to the exhibit floor in an instant, his movements fluid and precise. The limited visibility turned the room into a maze of shadows and indistinct shapes. Sebastian's mind raced, analyzing the situation with rapid-fire precision.

The bullet had lodged itself into the wall nearby, providing a vital clue. He quickly deduced the general direction of the shooter but lacked the exact position. His senses heightened, Sebastian's eyes darted around the room, seeking any flicker of movement or glint of a weapon.

He could feel the tension in the air, each heartbeat echoing like a drum in the silent exhibit hall. His training kicked in; instincts honed from years of experience. He calculated angles, distances, and possible cover positions, his mind a whirlwind of tactical assessments.

Without wasting a second, Sebastian began to move, using the exhibits as a makeshift cover. He needed to flush out the shooter and turn the tables. Every step was measured, every breath controlled. He listened intently, filtering out the ambient noises, focusing solely on detecting the slightest sound that would betray his opponent's location.

As he advanced, adrenaline rushed through his veins, a mix of fear and exhilaration. This was his element, the blend of danger and strategy that tested his limits. He tightened his grip on his weapon, ready to respond the moment the shooter revealed themselves. Sebastian knew that in this deadly game of cat and mouse, only one would emerge victorious, and he was determined it would be him.

The exhibit was now reduced to a quiet, dusty tomb, with destruction everywhere. Still, despite the reduction in visibility, the faint footsteps whispered ahead of him and to his right, he estimated. Sebastian pulled himself to a large collapsed wall segment as he drew his gun and listened.

"You are a fortunate individual, Sebastian. You just won't die, it appears," Tobias softly said as he moved positions for a better angle and to close the gap between them.

Sebastian closed his eyes. He had not thought of Tobias's voice in over a decade, and although he wouldn't admit it, the man's voice's resonance and timbre gave him chills. "You know, it's just the mission, nothing personal, so goes the cliché, Sebastian. Actually, fuck it, it is personal," said Tobias. Attempting to pinpoint Tobias's voice, Sebastian determined that he had moved closer and more central to his current location. Another round hit the wall behind him to the right. This time, Tobias hoped for that auspicious shot that may be fortunate enough to find its target.

Sebastian remained calm and fluid as he maneuvered several feet away to a location with better visibility. Staying in one location for too long often proved to be deadly; he needed to keep moving. A valuable lesson learned from James many years ago.

Running from one collapsed wall to another, Sebastian saw a glimmer of Tobias's black combat suit. He estimated him roughly fifty feet from his position, now drawing closer, closing the distance between them.

"I'm impressed, Sebastian, you managed to minimize the full impact of what was intended today. Bravo. I underestimated you, yet again," Tobias explained in an almost pleasant tone. Sebastian's current position touted both excellent protection and an idealistic view of the arena before him.

Two large pillars had fallen into one another, creating a superlative protective position and a potential tactical advantage if he was to climb one of the collapsed pillars quietly. However, this would leave him in a somewhat vulnerable position if Tobias approached the pillars from the southwest. From any other direction, the spot proved beneficial. Probability favored him. It was worth the risk.

Sebastian sensed Tobias was easing closer. The pillar climb was a gamble Sebastian was willing to venture. Grabbing two small rocks from the rubble, Sebastian placed them within his jacket pocket before meticulously ascending one of the pillars, giving him more of an overview of the arena below and attempting not to divulge his current position. He hadn't been blessed with Tobias's voice in a few seconds, which worried him.

The dust was settling further now, and the visibility was improving with each passing moment. Scaling the pillar, Sebastian was roughly fifteen feet above the ground. Turning his head to barely peek over the pillar, he obtained the advantage of seeing Tobias crouching and approaching, unsure of where Sebastian was located. Sebastian didn't have a clear shot, as it would expose him far too much if he missed.

Slowly reaching into his jacket pocket, Sebastian retrieved one of the small stones he had grabbed earlier. Positioning himself now behind the pillar, he was directly to Tobias's right and above. Fastening his firearm to his specialized holster, he leveraged his leg on the ridged support of the pillar. He would have to move quickly, noticing Tobias peering directly ahead of him, searching the rubble for any sign of Sebastian, unaware he was perched in a far different place than Tobias anticipated.

Tossing the stone to Tobias's left side and simultaneously pushing hard with his right leg to accelerate off and over the pillar, Sebastian's timing needed to be perfect.

Tobias heard the rock clatter, bouncing about over hard surfaces to his left, and began to turn in the direction of the reverberation before his instincts overrode his reflexes. He realized the sound was meant to be a distraction, intended to divert his focus. Cursing himself for this foolish and costly mistake, Tobias immediately turned back toward his right as Sebastian collided with him hard, knocking the gun from Tobias's hand, and it lodged between two medium-sized rocks.

Having fallen on his back, Tobias whipped up his legs and snapped them back quickly, leveraging his weight to land on his feet, and then stood up in a fighter's stance facing Sebastian. "Finally, at long last, I have you," muttered Tobias under his breath.

Realizing his handgun was thrown outside of reach, Tobias appealed to Sebastian's sense of sport and fairness. "Even better, Sebastian. Finally, we end this today," taunted Tobias.

"A man motivated only by hate, Tobias, is no man at all," replied Sebastian. Angered by the comment, Tobias jumped at Sebastian with an immediate right then left combination. As if Sebastian knew Tobias's movements in advance, he countered, deflecting, returning the blows with equal verve and effectiveness.

Tobias roundhouse kicked Sebastian hard in the chest, knocking him back a few steps. Sebastian flinched, reminded of the effects of the skirmish in Vienna. The healing ribs and abdomen, still fresh from the attack two weeks prior, plagued him as he winced from Tobias's impact.

Sebastian's eyes flicked to the gun in his shoulder holster, his hand hovering near the grip. He hesitated, his gaze shifting back to Tobias. In that fleeting moment, a whirlwind of possibilities raced through his mind. He could end this now, a single shot bringing closure to their dangerous game. The thought was tempting, resonating with a primal sense of justice.

But Sebastian was a soldier, bound by a code of honor and integrity. Every instinct screamed at him to act, yet his principles held him in check. The weight of his decision pressed down on him; the room thick with tension.

He took a deep breath, eyes narrowing as he measured Tobias. This was more than a moment of action; it was a test of his character. The appeal of a swift resolution clashed with his unwavering commitment to doing what was right, not just what was easy.

With a steely resolve, Sebastian made his choice. His hand moved away from the holster, signaling a decision to confront the situation head-on, guided by his unwavering principles. Tobias studied him closely, the touch of a smile hinting at his recognition of Sebastian's inner conflict. The stakes were high, but Sebastian's integrity would guide him through the storm.

Some profound sense of fairness tugged deep within Sebastian's core. There was an even bigger test facing him. All he needed to do was pull his gun and put a bullet into Tobias's head, which more than tempted him, but an arcane sense yearned and urged him to level the playing field against Tobias one final time.

He needed to prove this to himself. Who was the superior soldier? Who was the better man?

Chapter 25

Crafting of Champions

Quantico, Virginia
1998

A special division and training facility had been set up twenty floors below ground for HB and her operations. She liked it that way; it was hers, and it was secure—and hidden. Very well hidden.

She was grateful that the higher-ups in the Department of Defense left her to her own devices. Her operations were always effective, and as long as the results came through, they didn't care about the methods. Arriving slightly before 6:00 am on a Tuesday, she stepped into her "War Room," as she affectionately called it.

The room was a hive of activity, a stark contrast to the early morning stillness outside. Screens flickered with real-time data, maps covered the walls, and a low hum of focused conversation filled the air. She thrived in this environment, where strategy met execution and every decision could shift the balance of power.

Her team snapped to attention as she entered, their respect for her palpable. She acknowledged them with a curt nod, immediately immersing herself in the day's tasks. Here, she wielded her authority like a finely honed blade, cutting through bureaucracy and red tape with precision.

As she settled into her command post, she felt a surge of purpose. The War Room was her domain, a place where her expertise and instincts could operate unfettered. She relished the challenge, knowing that her unique approach and unorthodox methods were what kept their operations ahead of the curve. Here, in the heart of her carefully orchestrated chaos, she was in her element, ready to tackle whatever the day would bring.

She was rumored to have asked for such a headquarters numerous times before, yet she was always rejected. She was finally thanked privately by former President George W. Bush Jr. for her labors in circumventing a particularly sensitive situation in Kuwait.

She was awarded her War Room for the Division's efforts and for keeping the excellent results forthcoming. She used the victory as a platform to create the facility she desired to truly fulfill her station and clandestine operations.

That day, President Bush had said, "Hillary, if you ever need anything, anything at all, I will be at your disposal." Seizing the moment, she responded with unwavering conviction, "Well, Mr. President, there is one thing. If the President of the United States has a War Room, then I damn well deserve one too. Because I'm the one actually fighting your wars."

Her boldness caught him off guard, but he couldn't deny the truth in her words. From that moment, she secured the command center she needed, a place where she could orchestrate her operations with the same precision as the Commander-in-Chief.

The president responded, "Done!" No one ever questioned the notion nor the request, and the name stuck. HB got her War Room, and many unsavory people were eliminated as a result of the planning and execution that emanated from the room. Countless lives had been saved, and thousands of villainous individuals no longer came to be from what was decided within that sacred domain.

HB arrived with eager anticipation, keen to see the test scores results from Tobias and Sebastian from the previous day. Her longtime personal assistant, Thomas Simmons, was already waiting, ready to discuss the reports in detail. "How did they score, Simmons?" she asked, her eyes sparkling with curiosity. "I've been looking forward to this all morning."

Simmons enthusiastically replied, "I'm sure, ma'am. I have it all here for you, and believe me, you are going to want to see this." He fumbled with the two extensive reports; one fell upon her desk as he handed her the second report.

HB rolls her eyes at Simmons. Simmons was the best personal assistant she had ever had in her employ but acted more like a court jester on occasion. The thick reports included the comprehensive fitness tests performed on Tobias and Sebastian the day prior.

HB took the reports and laid them side by side upon her desk without opening them up. "Give me the summary, Simmons. You know I don't have time to read all this shit," referencing the thick reports lying on the table.

"Gladly, ma'am, as you would imagine, I have it all memorized," replied Simmons.

"Of course you do, Simmons, let's hear it," replied HB. Simmons disregarded her jab and continued, "Well, as you are aware, we have a stringent physical and quantitative baseline established from several respective military outfits including, but not limited to, testing regimens for the Navy SEALs and various covert and Black Operations Soldiers."

HB retorted, "Yes, yes, I am privy to all of this, Simmons. I aided in the development of half of it, for fuck's sake, Thomas. Let's get to it. How did the boys perform?"

"Yes, well, I'm getting to that, ma'am," replied Simmons somewhat rudely in his response. Simmons always abhorred HB's impatience.

HB smiled, "Well, Thomas, sometime today, will you?" She enjoyed teasing him. It gave her tremendous pleasure to push his buttons.

Once again, disregarding her taunts, he continued his analysis, "Well, ma'am, per your design, the parameters set forth to analyze most quantitative data are based on historical subjects' recorded ranges and ranking from their highest marks to the lowest scores. As a result, all subjects were ranked within the historical data range. Essentially, what I'm trying to say, ma'am, is when any new records or top marks are performed, though rare, the new mark would define the new cap for that given test. There are twenty-three individual physical tests and fifteen quantitative, or thirty-eight total qualitative tests, and as I mentioned, rarely is a new cap established. In fact, when we initially tested Tobias three years ago, his test average was 98.7 percent with several parameters right at the ideal range, giving him an adjusted 100 percent in several categories," explained Simmons.

HB hated when Simmons spoke overly technical; he could never just get to the point, but she knew his technical ramble was part of what she had to endure to finally arrive at the treasure eventually following.

"I'm still a little confused as to what this had to do with the tests given yesterday?" asked HB.

"It had everything to do with it, ma'am," he continued. "Tobias and Sebastian literally scored off the charts. Of the thirty-eight possible tests performed, they shared between them eleven new records. Eleven new records were broken yesterday!!! It's never been done before in the history of this type of testing, not even remotely close. Sometimes, we would witness 1–2 records broken, but not eleven. It's as if they pushed one another beyond normal limits. One hundred percent was considered perfect, but they redefined a new ideal in several categories."

"Because they broke several records, Tobias scored an adjusted 101.2 percent and Sebastian an impressive 101.4 percent. I've never certified or verified overall scores exceeding 100 percent in my sixteen years . . . and this test produced not just one but two candidates doing exactly that. I double-checked and triple-checked the findings. All verified," said Simmons.

HB sat back in her chair and considered this information for a moment. Both Sebastian and Tobias scored beyond their data ideals. She shook her head in amazement. "Specifically, ma'am, Tobias's records include tactical planning, explosives, close-quarter combat, reasoning, and logistics, to name a few, whereas Sebastian scored highest in firearms, close-quarter combat, sniper marksmanship, decision making, tactical execution, counter intuition, protocol, and tactical planning. Sebastian scored slightly higher because he outperformed Tobias in both close-quarter combat and tactical planning. It's almost like . . . a sibling rivalry. How do they get along, ma'am? When together? I've been curious," asked Simmons.

"As a matter of fact, they have . . . yet to meet one another, Simmons," replied HB, and continued, "That was to occur tomorrow morning, it should be an interesting meeting."

Simmons nodded, forgetting they had yet to meet, and then offered, "Their meeting should prove most enlightening, ma'am." HB smiled and responded, "Yes it should. . . . Either it will go very well, or it will be a total catastrophe."

"Tobias likes to be the top dog around here, but there is no one close to him on any level. Sebastian just changed that dynamic completely. I know where I'm putting my money," said Simmons.

"Yeah, me to, Thomas," replied HB.

Quantico, Virginia
1998

Arriving early, Tobias was waiting in HB's office, leaning against her credenza, reading his recent qualitative fitness report lying on her desk as HB and Sebastian walked into the room. Simmons wasn't far behind.

She smiled at Tobias and said, "Good morning, Tobias. This is Sebastian Storm. Sebastian, Tobias Teague. My two best." Sebastian went to shake Tobias's hand, and Tobias put a palm up as if to stop him in his tracks, uninterested in the introduction.

"Best, HB? This kid hasn't even completed a mission yet. How could he be the 'best' at anything?" Sebastian held his head high and reclaimed his spot next to HB, placing his hands behind his back at attention. I loyal lapdog, thought Tobias.

"Well, for one, Tobias, he outscored you in the qualitative and got six records in the process to your five. I'd say those figures speak for themselves, but I'm more impressed with the fact you both scored over the 100 percent mark. That feat has never been done before," HB explained, but Tobias didn't want to listen what she had to say. He was unimpressed.

"This is bullshit," said Tobias as he began to walk out. As he passed them, Sebastian gently grabbed his arm as if to calm Tobias, but it had quite the opposite effect. Seeing only red, Tobias was teetering on the precipice of unraveling. With his opposite hand, Tobias firmly grasped Sebastian's hand in an attempt to break his wrist and end the altercation immediately.

Sebastian, keen to the ploy, twisted his hand, releasing it from Tobias's grasp while simultaneously squaring a solid punch into Tobias's stomach to ensure some separation and causing him to step back two steps.

Tobias smiled, impressed with Sebastian's counter, "Oh, you want to play with the big boys, huh, kid? I have a few lessons for you." Tobias lunged, punching Sebastian in the sternum, then roundhouse kicked, which Sebastian deflected, grabbed his foot, and twisted, but Tobias rolled with the twist and released his foot in the process.

Tobias underestimated Sebastian and immediately reassessed the situation before him. They square up with each other once again as HB nonchalantly takes a seat in her chair behind her desk to study the spectacle as it unfolded. She simply observed and evaluated, a calm flower within the pandemonium occurring all around her.

The two exchange jabs and punches, equally matched, both giving and receiving damage with equal vigor and vitality. Tobias jumped and struck with a right fist to Sebastian's chest, sending him backward into the plate glass wall of HB's office, shattering the glass all over the entrance of her office and hallway. Taking the advantage, Tobias sprang toward him. As he approached, Sebastian swept kicked Tobias, sending him to the floor as well. Then responding with his own right hook connecting with Tobias's jaw.

"Enough! That will be quite enough, gentleman," yelled HB as three security guards came running up to the office, guns drawn. "Put the guns down, boys; everything is fine," said HB.

The head security officer asked, "What happened here, ma'am?" HB hesitated before answering, "The first day of training, Sergeant, nothing more." She walked out of the office but not before turning around and saying, "Get up, boys, that will be quite enough, and brush it off, and I'll see you in the War Room tomorrow at 7:00 am sharp."

She looked at the Sergeant and continued, "And, Sergeant, clean up this mess for me, please?" She nodded and walked out of the room with Simmons on her heels.

Chapter 26

Confrontation of Titans

Pergamon Museum
Present Day

Navigating the museum, rubble was strewn about, dirty and scuffed from the terrain and combat exchanges. Both men were tired standing before the Pergamon Altar. Sebastian and Tobias stood tall, glaring at each other from several yards apart. "I'm impressed, Sebastian. I thought you might take the easy way out, having the gun, thus the advantage," said Tobias as he focused on Sebastian, gaining valuable time to catch his breath.

They walked in a circle, like animals circling their prey, watching, learning, and sizing one another up. "Oh, Tobias, it wasn't even an option, though I have to wonder if you would have made the same decision had it been reversed," Sebastian replied, then continued, "I decided I needed to simply eliminate you myself. Like putting down an old rabid dog. You need to be retired, Tobias, today."

Tobias smiles at the taunt, attempting to keep his temper in check and his sanity balanced.

"I'm glad to see you finally gave up on sending your minions to do your wet work, Tobias. Since we all are aware of how they ended up," provoked Sebastian. Growing tired of the dialogue, Tobias leaped at Sebastian, but he was ready for him, knowing one of Tobias's weaknesses was his temper and hasty, reactive nature. Sebastian sidestepped Tobias's lunge, but Tobias relied on his own instincts as well, as he forearmed Sebastian directly on the jaw, stunning him slightly as he took a step back.

Sebastian ducked and connected with a right fist into Tobias's chest, knocking him backward. Tobias collected himself, then abruptly roundhouse kicked Sebastian's shoulder. The physical melee continued, two combatants locked in a battle built on hate and jealousy, fueled by the desire to be the best at their craft and claim victory over the other. If ever there was a historic battle of two evenly matched soldiers, a match worthy of study, every attack countered or deflected by the other as if they were teaching techniques to the casual observer.

Each assault was perfectly executed, a textbook in style and form. Both men exercised their technique and rhythm as if choreographed and practiced with precision and excellence. Neither man had the advantage over the other. Only the better-conditioned and disciplined would prevail, but there was no indication either possessed the true advantage in the conflict.

Tobias and Sebastian traded body blows and face punches with relentless intensity. Each hit echoes the sheer force of their determination. Neither man would allow himself to fall or yield to the other. The battle had transformed into a grueling test of endurance and willpower.

Strength and power were crucial, but the real contest was now a battle of minds. Each strike was a physical blow and a mental challenge, testing their resilience and focus. It was a clash of titans, and the victor would be the one who could outlast and outthink his opponent in this brutal dance of perseverance and resolve.

From the moment they met all those years ago in HB's office at Quantico, their hate and animosity are in full view now.

Both soldiers, legends within their profession slowly grew weary and fatigued over the physical exchanges close-quarter combat demanded. Tobias swung and missed, and Sebastian used the opportunity as he landed a solid right and then an immediate left to Tobias's jaw, throwing him off balance and staggering him backward. Tobias regained quickly and countered with a kick to Sebastian's abdomen but only accepted half the damage as Sebastian shifted his weight to soften the impact and protect his injuries; he was still recovering from weeks prior. Using this to his advantage, Sebastian vaulted toward Tobias with a second right/left combination to Tobias's face as he fell back and caught his heel on a stone, causing him to fall onto his back.

Knowing he might not receive this opportunity again, he jumped on top of Tobias, followed by a flurry of rapid-fire punches to Tobias's face and body. Sebastian's rage took over as he knew he was winning, driven by his hate for this man, hatred for his father, hate for Josh Strickland, and hate for all aggressors that came before him. Tobias's face was becoming bloodied as he attempted every effort to defend himself, but all were failing him now, knowing Sebastian Storm had bested him.

Tobias needed a miracle.

. . . He got one.

In the anteroom outside the altar exhibit, Fury came across the clash between Sebastian and Tobias but didn't have a clear shot as they were partially obscured behind fallen pillars and wall segments. Off to his right, several hundred yards away, HB and six agents navigated through the various debris to get to Sebastian's location.

Fury looked up and saw a dangling roof section teetering above Sebastian and Tobias's location. He fired three bullets into the roof segment above before it began to dislodge and plunge the forty feet below, his intended result. He emptied the remaining ten rounds methodically toward the numerous agents approaching, making them scatter about, taking cover after hearing the gunshots to slow their progression.

Hearing the rounds being fired, Sebastian hesitated and then focused on the source of the sound while attempting to look for the shooter. He took careful inventory of his surroundings. He could see a figure far away ducked behind a fallen pillar. Glancing back at Tobias, he saw his eyes widen as he looked beyond Sebastian, noticing a rumbling reverberation above him. He looked up, spotting the large piece of stone dislodging from the roof system.

Thinking ahead and optimizing the opportunity, Tobias pushes Sebastian off to his left. Tobias rolled to his right as the large stone and steel rebar crashed between them. A more significant roof segment began to sag and twist due to the structural disruption and crashed to the floor below, further separating the two men.

Sebastian and Tobias scampered in different directions as debris peppers both men. Getting up quickly, Tobias maneuvered around several large pieces of stone, limiting his view of Sebastian. The dust disruptive and blinding once again.

Upon getting up, Sebastian drew his 9mm, attempting to track Tobias in his sights as he expertly sidestepped the fallen walls and roof structure. However, with the recurring dust swirling about, Sebastian squeezed off several rounds but failed to find their intended target.

Unable to pursue Tobias due to the instability of the ground and destruction around him, he could not make out Tobias connecting with Fury over eighty feet away. He took a firing stance, aimed carefully, and took the low percentage shot, limited by any handgun at that distance.

Tobias reached Fury, cognizant of the agents south of their position, but the exit was several yards away while HB's agents were still more than a hundred feet from reaching them. "Sir let's get you out of—" Fury attempted to say over the gunfire and structural ruin falling all around them when Sebastian's bullet struck him in the right shoulder. He fell to one knee as he said, "I'm alright."

In that moment, Tobias was already moving. He grabbed the back of Fury's combat vest, thrusting him up and moving toward the side west exit.

Within seconds, they were through the door and lost among the thousands of people outside, immediately blending within the frightened and frantic mob on the lawn adjacent to the Pergamon Museum.

Haggard and beaten, both simply looked like all the other dusty and weathered tourists that had survived the Pergamon explosion. Invisible within the myriad of others who were fortunate enough to escape the disaster yet, unbeknownst to all, the actual architects of the horrific plot.

HB could see them exit and shouted into her earpiece, "Two bogeys just exited out of northwest doors, Fury and Tobias. All available agents in that area, do not let them escape." But it was too late. Fury and Tobias were able to blend themselves into the crowd immediately, mixing within the backdrop of the tourists, all amazed and confused as to what had transpired before them. HB didn't have enough agents to cover the entire area.

Sebastian was certain he had hit Fury but was unsure how severe his injury may be. He did not have a shot on Tobias, or that would have been his priority. He lost them both. Making his way out of the altar into the main hallway, he said into his earpiece, "Storm coming out of the altar. Please don't shoot! That would make this day extra shitty."

As he made the turn into the hallway, he saw the agents cautiously approaching with HB toward the rear. They walked toward one another until they met within the rubble.

"We have multiple—" said HB, "agents canvassing the northwest exit."

Sebastian held a hand as he interrupted, "He's gone, HB. I put a round into his bulldog, Fury, but how did he get away from you initially?"

"We found the two dead agents escorting him about a hundred yards down the hallway." HB pointed out down the hall. "But he took them out and came back up this way to likely help Tobias, I'm assuming."

Softly, Sebastian said, "He certainly did. I had Tobias . . . had him, HB! Then Fury fired at a weak area in the ceiling, and everything came tumbling down. I had him in my hands . . . Damn,"

"We will get him, Sebastian. We averted the worst of the damage here, though there are many casualties, and the museum was destroyed, but it could have been a lot worse," explained HB.

"Yeah, we will, HB, but after how many more lives are lost, how many lives are justified?" Sebastian needed the rant, and HB let him have his moment. Through the door came Sean walking up to them.

"I wish I could have been here for you, Sebastian," said Sean, shaking his head.

"There was no way, Sean. The building was falling apart. We are both lucky to have survived it," replied Sebastian.

"That's for sure. You look like shit," Sean teased. "It looked like Tobias used your face as a punching bag." Sean laughed.

"Yeah, well, you should see his face." Sebastian winked as they walked out of the northwest exit.

Tobias, bloodied and beaten, stepped into the exfil van, followed by Fury. Mueller handed both men silenced 9mm in case they encountered opposition on their exfiltration. Prim was already in the vehicle and waiting. Mueller closed the doors behind them and crawled in behind the wheel. They all drove in silence for a time until Tobias said, "We should have executed better, Derek. We failed."

Mueller spoke up. "Sir, the preliminary report has stated that there are over 500 dead or wounded at the Pergamon, so it isn't a total loss. You made a statement here today."

Tobias appreciated the sentiment but disagreed, "Not enough, Mueller, not enough," replied Tobias. "And Sebastian?" he continued, "We need to ruin him and everything important to him. That is my new mission."

Prim responded, "Sir, please, sir, we cannot let one man control what we do . . . . ."

Tobias glared, "I've had quite enough of you, Prim, and your mediocrity," as he pulled up his gun from the back seat and put a single round through the back of Prim's head shocking Fury and Mueller. Prim's head slumped to the passenger window, smearing blood. Tobias continued, "We will concentrate all efforts on Sebastian at this point. He has bested Prim three times and now me. He appears to be a step ahead of us at every turn, and we need Sebastian Storm completely out of the picture, or our outfit will never truly flourish." Looking at Fury, he instructed, "We must increase the timetable on Project Nerek, Fury. We need to concentrate on ending Sebastian's existence completely, and I know exactly what must be done. First, I want him to suffer and very aware what to take from him." The others within the SUV looked at Tobias, unsure of what Project Nerek was, but were far too afraid to ask. Fury was very aware of Nerek but was unsure if he was ready, it was still too early.

Fury simply replied, "Yes, sir," knowing not to question Tobias but thought Prim a fool for not respecting that simple point. There was a time to talk strategy and recourse, but that was not the moment.

Sebastian and Sean were riding in the rear seats of their black SUV in silence, making their way back to the hotel. Sebastian was staring out of the window, deep in thought. Normally, he would think of the mission, the lives saved, and the ones lost, but not today. Today, he reminisced about Adriana and wondered where she was at that moment and what she may have been wearing that very day. She reminded him of more pleasant thoughts. He needed something more, something positive to focus on, as there was a missing element to his being, to his reality: so much death and destruction in his life . . . in his existence.

Tobias had almost taken his life today. His organization was becoming much stronger and closer to its goal of eliminating him. Sebastian had been very fortunate that morning, but his luck would eventually run out. Sebastian slowly turned to Sean, hesitated, then spoke his mind to his longtime friend, "I'm not sure I can do this anymore, Sean. My perspective changed today."

Sean replied, "I can imagine. Maybe you simply need an extended vacation, Sebastian. I'm sure HB would understand and allow that for you. The credit you have built up with her is insurmountable. You are just burned out, Sebastian. Take some time, find your girl, relax in a remote place on the beach somewhere, and don't tell anyone where you are. Disappear for a while. Vanish."

Sebastian smiled and then replied, "We both know that HB won't let me disappear. It's not in her DNA. I don't think she would understand what I'm going through. She thinks of me as the forever soldier, Sean."

"Or maybe she just may surprise you, Sebastian. Try her." Sean said encouragingly.

Shrugging the thought off, Sebastian agrees, saying, "Maybe you are right. Thanks for always listening, Sean. I'll try to speak with her when the moment is right. I need to sort it out."

Tobias, Fury, and Mueller boarded their jet with Prim's body in the cargo bay, a substantial premium levied to get out of Germany. After what transpired earlier that day, a sizable price tag was placed on their heads. Enough camera footage was available to make them substantial targets when this was all sorted out.

The plane taxied down the runway to return to Dublin.

HB's team was on the seventeenth floor of the hotel. It was completely secure, per the strict protocol set up by HB and her Division. When traveling with her larger teams, she always occupied an entire floor of a hotel to ensure their safety precautions could be fully met and without exception.

Several hours had passed, and while walking down the hall toward Sebastian's suite, HB observed the medical team just leaving. As she approached them, she stopped and asked the treating doctor about the boy's status. "They are resilient, ma'am. They have a few cuts and contusions and are pretty bruised up, but they will recover completely. They took quite a beating, especially Sebastian," said the lead doctor. "That's our Sebastian, thank you," replied HB.

There was a knock at the door in the normal security-controlled method which changed daily. Today's protocol dictated it be two knocks, then one knock, and finally three knocks in rhythm. Satisfying the protocol, the two guards within opened the door and allowed HB inside the suite.

She left the two guards standing inside the room when she entered, and they quietly closed the door behind her. She found Sebastian and Sean sitting outside on the large terrace. She walked outside and said, "Looks as though you two will live to fight another day. I talked to the doctor as he was leaving. It appears you two will make a full recovery, he said. Excellent news."

Sebastian was now deep in his recurring dark thoughts. "We were fortunate this time, HB; It may not be the next time," he said, offering his cryptic response.

HB replied, "Ahhh . . . feeling somber this evening, I see."

Sebastian smiled. "No, not at all. I'm just realizing my own mortality these days, but we can talk about that later. What is the damage?"

HB responded, "Grim, regrettably. A total of 523 dead, though it could have been over 10,000 had you, boys, not been there. It was a good call, Sebastian, on the Pergamon, nice work as always. Sadly, over 500 casualties are still substantial, though." HB shook her head. "But I suppose it could have been far worse. They will be cleaning up that place for months."

"We also lost eleven agents: two covering Fury, six that were tracking Mueller yesterday, and three today in the museum. Overall, Tobias ended up winning this round, and with him and Fury escaping, it's just a matter of when they would strike next."

Sean piped up. "I have an idea that everyone sitting at this table will also be his priority and focus as well. Some new protocols will need to be set up, HB."

HB replied, "Without question, Sean and I have a team on that, but that's not all."

Sebastian interrupted, saying, "No, it isn't, HB. A task force needs to be formed to eliminate his organization completely. He is cancerous, and what's worse, he used to be one of us, making him tremendously more dangerous."

HB suspected Sebastian was right. She replied, "Agreed, Sebastian, and I've been thinking about this and how I would like to handle it. I think you should head up that task force. You can handpick your team, review all the material we have on him and his organization, and plan the best way to eradicate him and his group. Our recent intelligence has him at a fortified compound somewhere in Europe. I figured you would want 'point' on this, and I'm giving you the authority to move on this immediately." She assumed Sebastian would be pleased with this news.

Sebastian considered HB's proposal and contemplated the options carefully before responding as he sat back into his chair.

"I think an elite group is necessary, yes, without question, but I think it should be another team leader, HB. You have some very capable options in Steele, or Patteson and even Sean here," replied Sebastian, referencing his long-time partner. HB looked at Sebastian for an uncomfortable moment; both she and Sean were surprised that he wouldn't jump at the chance to head up the team to eliminate Tobias. Somewhat stupefied and perplexed at his response.

HB remarks, "Something has changed within you, Sebastian. I can sense the shift. Was it something on this mission?" Then she looked at Sean. "What's your take on this, Sean?" Sean throws up his hands as if to shrug and stands up, saying, "It's not my business. I'll leave you both to it. Good night, you two. For what it's worth, we did a good thing today," he turns and walks inside.

After Sean had stepped inside, HB turned to Sebastian and said, "Talk to me, Sebastian. You are far and above the best I have, but more importantly, you are my family. You know this, and I know this. We have been together for nearly 25 years. Everyone in the unit needs you. On every mission you are involved with, the team has more confidence with you being in the fold."

Sebastian thought about what HB had said. "I've lost my youth, HB. I'm well past it, in fact, and for what? What have I achieved? I know I have been a valuable part of the Division and have saved lives, but I am struggling for the first time in my life since I lost my parents as to what my identity really is. Who is Sebastian Storm? No one can answer these questions, but me, HB, and I don't know what those answers are right now."

HB looked at Sebastian for a long minute and understood this man's pain. She felt his struggle and that all great warriors fought with their identity at some point in their career; she somehow just assumed Sebastian dealt with it as he did with every other obstacle he faced, but this one was different, and she needed simply to support him as he navigated through it.

"Think about that while you take the next few weeks off and weigh your options, and I will support any decision you come up with and decide. I am here for you always."

Sebastian said, "Thank you, HB. I so appreciate you." He knew she was genuinely sincere and wanted the best for him.

HB stood up, put her hand on his shoulder, and said, "You are my family, Sebastian. Remember that always. We take care of our own." And she walked inside as well, leaving Sebastian outside with his thoughts.

Sebastian was a master within his role, his obligation, and the people that depended upon him. This life had been good to him, and he was at his peak, charmed even for such a long time.

Was he on borrowed time? He didn't know a life outside this one but also knew that he would have to make some of the most difficult decisions he'd ever faced in the coming weeks. He had a calling, an obligation to his country, HB, and himself.

He looked out over the city of Berlin in its beauty and elegance, and it made him think of Adriana. He now realized that he needed to find her. He promised her answers to her questions.

She played a part in his future; he wasn't exactly sure how, but she was a piece of the puzzle that he needed to pursue. He owed her an explanation and promised her to provide one.

He would hold true to that promise and now that the attack in Berlin was thwarted, his focus must shift to what he vowed to Adriana once his business was completed in Germany. He felt in telling her his truth, it would begin the process for a better understanding of himself. She would help him navigate through it; he was certain she would.

Sebastian Storm yearned to move forward and find the meaning within, deep in his core.

He sought to rediscover himself, delving into the depths and crevasses of his soul with a quiet, however, intense yearning.

Chapter 27

A New Beginning

Venice, Italy
Present Day

The memory of their time together played on a loop in her head, a tantalizing mix of excitement and longing. She couldn't shake the notion their story was far from over, even as reality chipped away at her optimism. The uncertainty gnawed at her, leaving her in a constant state of anticipation and doubt, wondering if and when Sebastian would reappear in her life.

Adriana sat quietly in the sun, savoring its warmth on her skin, as she relaxed at a remote trattoria in Venice, Italy. A last-minute decision had brought her there, a detour before heading back to the United States. With the major deal in Vienna wrapped up two weeks earlier, she finally had some time to relax. She had certainly earned it.

The morning air was cool, a crisp breeze weaving through the narrow streets, but the sun's rays bathed her face with gentle harmony. She closed her eyes for a moment, absorbing the serene beauty of Venice in the morning light, a stark contrast to the intense pace of her recent weeks. The tranquil setting was a perfect escape, a brief, blissful pause in her otherwise hectic life.

Several weeks had passed since Adriana had been in Vienna, yet thoughts of Sebastian lingered in her mind, growing more vivid with each passing day. Their encounter had been brief but undeniably exhilarating, sparking emotions she hadn't felt in years.

Adriana fashioned a simple white sundress with brown wedges. She was unassuming yet an elegant sight to behold. She read the newspaper, fascinated by the Pergamon tragedy and all the lives lost that day, then turned to more work-related, positive items. She had her laptop open, passively researching some patent legalities for work, a presentation she had later in the afternoon, and the subsequent contract she hoped to secure later in the month in New York.

Daydreaming of Sebastian's hands and lips upon her, Adriana reminisced about how he made her senses open up and the sensual effect he had on her body and mind. Adriana began to drift into a life she had fantasized about with Sebastian many times in those previous weeks.

Her thought trailed deeper into her colorful fantasy. Of all her vast travels, Adriana had adored traveling through Nice in Southern France or more so the Amalfi Coast in Positano, Italy. Enjoying the trattoria and solitude in Venice, she daydreamed of her and Sebastian lying in the sun on the beach in Amalfi for the entire day, holding hands and teasing and laughing with one another as they sipped the local favorite in exotic drinks and enjoying the warm sun upon their bodies.

She dreamt further about her favorite hotel there, the Le Sirenuse, where she and Sebastian would return from the beach and enter their room laughing as he tickled her from behind, teasing as he does in his special way. Running in front of him, holding his hand, they would enter the threshold, and Sebastian would close the door and pull her to him firmly.

She would look into his eyes as his hand would brush back her hair so he could simply see more of her face, and he would appreciate all her beauty and all she offered him in mind and body. He would smile, and her heart would melt when she touched his stubbly face and rested her head upon his chest. There was a tranquility in the thought, her mind serene and comforted in the moment—just adoring those few seconds and knowing he was drawn to her. Their connection pure in its happiness and calmness, was all she desired.

Adriana gazed up at him with a sultry smile, her eyes full of promise. He responded with a slow, passionate kiss, reigniting the fiery connection they had felt since their first encounter. Every touch from Sebastian sent electric shivers down her spine, their bodies merging into an irresistible dance of desire.

His absence only heightened her craving for him. She loved how he would pull her tightly against him, his embrace powerful and possessive. He would inhale her scent deeply, with a raw, almost primal intensity sending her pulse racing. Each moment with him was a thrilling blend of heat and anticipation, leaving her breathless and longing for more. The chemistry between them was undeniable, an intoxicating mix of passion and connection that set her ablaze every time they were together.

He then kissed her passionately, making her spontaneously jump up, straddling him. He catches her as her sandals fall to the ground. He supports her weight effortlessly as they slowly spin within the large room. The Amalfi Coastline is ever present from their room as they tangle within their adoration and chemistry in full bloom.

Sebastian lays her upon the bed only in her white lace crochet cover-up from earlier beach festivities. Her legs open for him to set his knees between them as he slowly kisses her toes, followed by her thighs as he pushes the coverup further apart revealing only her bikini below.

Adriana takes in his sensuality as she runs her hands through his hair, and he engulfs her body as he moves upward. She beckons him to loosen her bikini top and bottom and smiles as she imagines what is to follow.

He slowly sits up, enjoying her exquisite beauty and bareness as she lies there watching him as he unbuttons his shirt smiling at her all the while, seducing her with his eyes as she begins to rub her thighs and stomach enticing him further. Sebastian takes in his view and consumes the moment basking in her beauty as her hands slide over her skin, appreciating her contours and softness.

His shirt drops to the floor as she enjoyed him unbuttoning his swimsuit, and it too falls to the floor. She loves his tan skin, and her eyes light up in anticipation over the thought of what will occur next. She has never been more attracted to a man than she is of Sebastian. He positions himself atop her again, kissing her neck now as her hands hold his hips with anticipation.

She takes in his scent as both their sexual tension intensifies. Adriana eases her legs open, knowing he has already excited her to a point where she is more than ready for him. Sebastian was well aware and begins to softly kiss her supple lips as her hand drifts from his hip to his member, appreciating the effect she is having upon him as well, making her want him even more.

She looks into his eyes as she begins to guide him to her sacred place, they both want him to go and bask in the pleasure as he begins to enter her, slowly at first, but then, after a moment, she guides all of him in deep within her. She cherishes their lovemaking, and her oneness with him and connects deeply as she looks into his eyes, his soul, desiring every part of him as he is more than gifted at stimulating her spot and enjoy the moment.

He takes her to that euphoric place and oneness with him. Adriana pulls him closer as her muscles spasm, and she tightens around him, sending him immediately into his own paroxysm as he lets her have all of him until his mild convulsions and thrusts begin to cease.

With one sweep of his arm, he turns her over and sets her upon his chest. They talk for hours as the sun begins to set, and they simply are at peace in being together in the moment. He lightly scratches her arm as she gently falls asleep upon his chest, content in the moment, protected, and thankful.

She trembled at the thought and how the story would unfold as she pictured it in her mind's eye. Why was she having these intense feelings for him at this moment, she wondered?

The server came up to take her order as she politely asked for double expresso and a scone with fruit, per her morning ritual.

The server left to place the order, and she regained her composure, bringing her thoughts more to reality but knowing and smiling over the effect the thought was having upon her.

Inconspicuously sitting at a small outdoor restaurant well beyond her view, several hundred yards away, Sebastian intently studied Adriana and appreciated her beauty and strength along with everything surrounding her. The sun shone through the buildings, focused on her exact spot, as if she had been singled out by God himself, a spotlight of splendor . . . . *all that was Adriana Mercer*. He smiled, excited, yet nervous, to see her once again.

He had found her, using his resources and tracking her credit card use, leading him to Venice, Italy, a few days before. He had remained patient. Only observing and watching.

Wearing a white linen shirt, tan pants, and sandals, he was relaxed and calm in the moment. Sporting bronze aviator sunglasses, he simply studied her like he had done hundreds upon hundreds of times professionally in the past, but now for personal, selfish reasons. Sebastian had been patiently waiting in a nearly perfect position for some time, knowing the spot she had chosen for the last two days. She was predictable and consistent, and he enjoyed the quality about her.

He didn't wish to intervene, only enjoy and appreciate those moments life provided. He had waited in this time, attempting to formulate in his mind how he wanted to approach her. He wanted it all perfect, for her. . . . *for them.*

Thankfully, she was a creature of habit, and he predicted she would return to her favorite small ristorante at roughly the same time yet again that morning. Adriana didn't disappoint, as Sebastian speculated correctly. He didn't need any elaborate tracking hardware to determine she was predictable that way.

He wondered if she even thought of him, their brief interlude, their moment in time. Making a promise to find her again was what she left with the last time they were together in Vienna. He failed his promise. He wondered if she felt the strong sense as he did, or was it something different for her? It was unique and instant, the bond they created upon their first meeting only weeks before.

Would she be incensed with him for fading away from her the morning after returning from his recuperation in Italy? Sebastian couldn't be sure of her reaction.

Or if she was able to forgive him.

He hoped to tell her his story, all of it. She deserved as much, and he was confident she would understand if he could just explain . . *if he could make her understand.* His delay in confronting her rested on his uncertainty about how she would react. After he was able to foil Tobias in Berlin, he knew he needed and desired something different and time to process it before he found her.

The values and desires shifted within Sebastian, and he simply needed to embrace it, to understand and accept the metamorphosis tugging at him from within.

Munich, Germany
Days Before

In the days following the Berlin operation, after the debriefing, Sebastian met with HB at their European headquarters in Munich, Germany, just over a week later.

Sebastian knocked on her door, and she ushered him in and offered him a seat across from her desk. She had given him time to himself, as he had requested and didn't bother him during that time. She owed he and Sean as much.

HB started sensing she was losing him, "Sebastian, you know I don't thank you enough, but the U.S. government and every American, for that matter, not to mention the country of Germany, owe you a tremendous debt of gratitude. You never ask for anything, Sebastian . . . But thank you," she said, smiling at him.

He smiled at HB, always appreciating her and the endless sacrifices for her country. She was always on the job, a lifelong commitment. He envied her dedication but also appreciated the tremendous toll it had taken on her over the years.

Sebastian sat back in his chair, looked out of her window, and hesitated for a moment before responding. "Thank you for the time. I needed it. You know, HB," he said, "you don't have ever to thank me. It's just what I do, and after all these years, I'm always here for you, our country, or any government fighting tyranny or terrorism. It's just what I am. And hearing you say that I haven't ever asked you of anything . . . Well, I suppose there is always a first time."

"This past mission, and possibly me meeting someone has made me view things in a different light. I've broadened my perspective, I suppose. I realize I desire something more, HB. My focus has shifted. I've been a soldier my entire life since my training started trapping animals as a young kid in the hills of Virginia. Then living with James and all I learned from him and Sean, and finally, coming to work for you in my late teens. I was just a kid when you recruited me. It's all I have ever really understood. There was nothing more satisfying for me, HB, than putting bad guys into the ground and making the world a better place, but I can't do this forever. We both know this truth." He looked at her for some sort of approval.

HB said once again, "You are far and away the best there is, Sebastian, and we both are aware of it. Everyone knows it . . . Even Tobias realizes it and hates it. The United States, hell, the world needs you on its side, fighting the fight for what's good and just. You are still in your prime. You keep the balance set, the bar raised, Sebastian. Somehow your presence sets the order of things, keeps them at bay, and the chaos . . . *from winning and overtaking us all.*"

"The young agents look to you for guidance and as their beacon for what could be and what is right. You are their symbol of ideal, Sebastian, their champion. You emulate what is idyllic in this craft. Don't strip them of that. You have a lot of great years ahead of you, so much good you could, *and will*, do."

Sebastian softly responded, "Don't you think I've considered this, HB? My effectiveness, the catechism I would leave for you in my absence, the organization, and our country. I nearly lost my life four times on this last mission, and Tobias made me realize for the first time that I'm . . . *human.* Vulnerable and fallible, and it scares me. It really frightens me, HB, for the first time I have experienced. . . .*fear.* I have never had the sensation before, and frankly, it terrifies me. I've lost my edge as a result and with that . . . . . *I've lost my advantage.*"

Sebastian took a deep breath, then continued, "I've served my country with tremendous dedication for over twenty years, and I think I need to serve myself for a change. I need to feed this inner hunger I have . . . to be normal, simple, and content."

HB asked, "Do you think you would be happy or content in that type of simple life? A sedentary being with a wife or running after children? Do you see yourself in that scenario, Sebastian?"

He laughed at the picture she painted of his potential future and replied, "I don't know, HB, but a part of me must try and see if some fulfillment would come from a more austere life. I need to search for my truth . . . *my peace.* I need to find out. I honestly don't know about any of it anymore. I can always come back, right?"

HB calmly replied, "Of course, Sebastian. You know I will support you. If I understand one thing about you, I am certain you have analyzed and thought through everything, and why would this be any different? As I said last time we talked, we are your family. We will always be here for you, but remember, the idea of a simple life may sound alluring and attractive on some level, but it's not who you are. That is your curiosity, calling out for something unknown, but that small growl from within is no match for the lion you are, Sebastian. That lion summoned you, grew within you and you needed his fierceness to feed your thirst, don't forget that. Your roar is hearty and strong."

Sebastian stood up, smiled, and simply replied, "Thank you, HB, for always having my back. Who can say, maybe I'll be back before the end of the month with my tail stuck between my legs."

She laughed softly, a gentle sound that carried the warmth of their bond, yet beneath it, there was an undeniable trace of melancholy. "And I always will have your back, you know that. Above all, good luck, Sebastian, we won't be the same here without you," she said, her voice filled with a mixture of reassurance and the sorrow of inevitable parting. The words hung in the air, heavy with the finality that neither of them wanted to acknowledge but both knew was there. He nodded, appreciating the acknowledgement.

As Sebastian turned to leave, a profound sadness gripped him, tightening like a vice around his heart. Each step he took away from her office felt like walking through thick, suffocating fog, where every memory of their shared past replayed with a cruel clarity. HB was there for him in the beginning and now he possessed a sense of betrayal to her and the division. He descended the stairs, his footsteps echoing hollowly in the silence, each one a painful reminder of what he was leaving behind—of the connection that had meant more to him than he had ever dared to admit.

At the front door beyond the security desk, he hesitated, his hand lingering on the cold metal handle, a thousand thoughts racing through his mind. What if he turned back? What if he stayed? But the fear of what might happen, the fear of facing the emotions he had buried so deeply, kept him moving forward. He forced himself to step out into the world beyond, but with every inch of distance he put between them, the reality of what he was losing became more excruciatingly clear.

The door closed behind him with a finality that seemed to echo in the very depths of his soul, a sound that marked the end of something irreplaceable. He didn't look back, not because he didn't want to, but because he knew that if he did, he might never be able to leave. Yet, as he walked away, the sadness consumed him, filling the space where hope and meaning had once lived.

It was as if he had left a piece of himself behind—a piece he would never get back. The successes and adoration they had shared, the silent understanding that had passed between them so many times, now felt like ghosts of a past that would never be again. And with each step, the weight of what he had lost grew heavier, until it was almost unbearable, a melodramatic crescendo of sorrow and regret that threatened to overwhelm him completely.

But despite knowing they were his family he needed to press on….he *needed to endure*.

As he opened the doors, the sunlight hitting his face, his path endless as he embarked on the empty walkway, he immediately recognized his surrogate brother's all too familiar face at the end of the walk. Waving but not missing the opportunity to tease him, Sean said, "Thought you were going to get out of here without saying goodbye, didn't you?" He smiled at Sebastian and returned the gesture as he walked up to him.

Sebastian said, "Never, Sean, but I did opt out with HB. She gave me her blessing as I'm hoping you will as well."

Sean said, "I will always support you in any decision you make; always have your six and all, Sebastian. I would be remiss, though, if I didn't mention your departure will be a tremendous loss to this Division and the good people out there you protect."

He gestured with his hand to the building then said, "We do a lot of good here, but we will survive. They will have lost their greatest champion, but this you already know, and you have your reasons, and that is what I respect, and always will . . . . and I accept it, in addition to the man. I would never think to question you, Sebastian."

Sean sighed, then continued, "Go find what you are missing, Sebastian, but make damn sure you find it, okay? You will always have a home here." Sean hugged Sebastian and held him longer than usual, both shutting their eyes tight out of their pure adoration and appreciation they held for one another. As they released, Sebastian said quietly in parting, "Hoorah, Sean . . . Hoorah!" He pretends to punch him in the gut, smiles, and continues walking down the sidewalk, the sun to his back.

Sean simply appreciates the man as Sebastian's form begins to diminish in the distance and peacefully thinks, a true warrior, Sebastian Storm, your mother and James would be so proud of what you have become. And maybe even your dad too. You are indeed the best man I know. Godspeed, my brother. I hope you find what you seek.

Sebastian finally fell from Sean's view.

HB watched them both from her window several floors up, wondering what they had said to one another but knowing these two men had an unshakable bond forged from adoration, warfare, blood, tears, but most of all . . . *loss.*

It was the first time she was genuinely concerned for Sebastian. She realized he never had a chance to have a young man's life. HB had swooped in during his early adolescence, robbed him of his youth, and an enormous wave of guilt fell over her at the thought. Sebastian had always overcome his foes because he could see them, sense them but this new foe was one that he fought on a new battleground. One that he fought within and he was not certain how to overcome it. He was used to an enemy he could see but this was one that he could not. Sebastian was constantly debating whether he was a monster slayer or he himself was the monster. She then thought on a deeper level, maybe she was the true monster all this time, but none of them realized it.

After Sebastian was no longer visible, she thought about their conversation. HB returned to her desk, sat down, opened her laptop, and launched the encoded file she had just received.

Listed on the top of the profile was the name:

Carter Davis, CEO BlackThorn,
53 years old, father of one boy,
11 years old, divorced.

His profile didn't affect national security but came before her because several of the subcontractors BlackThorn used were sordid at best. He had come up on HB's *watch list* from his addiction to young underage girls and the sexual exploits he had kept somewhat enigmatic, but HB's organization had its ways of knowing these things.

What attracted her to his file was the CEO's sexual activities triggering her very secretive reflex and duty to Sebastian and his brand of justice. For years she had furtively, *and secretly* supplied him with these sensitive targets' dossiers, and he always came through when she determined these specific targets needed special attention.

Hillary Bastini was secretly Sebastian's anonymous source.

He may have surreptitiously guessed but never disclosed he was aware at all of her involvement with his personal clandestine missions, such as with South African Ambassador Zuma or Hiroshi Mikatani in Tokyo. These were terrible men, and she assumed Sebastian would do what needed to be done. He handled every one of their situations discretely.

She pondered the file for a moment, hesitating, especially considering the meeting she just had with Sebastian, but then initiated the file into her very reticent protocol, protecting her anonymity as she had always done for years. The file uploaded into the encrypted server was specifically designed to uphold the utmost in security and identity protection of not only her but also her organization as the file's source.

Once the process was completed, she needed only to specify her recipient. This entire system was set up years before solely for the benefit of only one person, one recipient, one liberator, and one hero that alone would cast judgment on the name she would provide.

His record spotless on every one received.

She wavered before finally pressing the button to send the file. The screen flashed, *"**Accepted: SStorm Confirmed**."* She had confirmation Sebastian would receive the encrypted file and handle it as he had done the hundreds of files before.

He had never rejected any of the profiles she sent to him in the past; it was what he needed, his passion, his obligation to defend those who couldn't protect themselves. HB appreciated all her agents, but above all, she understood Sebastian the most. Because of this, she contacted him fifteen years ago anonymously, heavily covert, encrypted, and cautious so as not to let him realize her secret identity as she had been his anonymous source for all this time.

She covertly fed his need and was initially worried she was putting him at risk in providing the information but also knowing she satisfied his basic need to do right by the victims of these stories and eradicate the atrocities of those people seemingly above the law or beyond apprehension.

She surmised the provided targets helped him cope with the guilt of what he was as a man and a soldier, so she provided the credible outlet for him time and time again.

She sat back in her chair and wondered, based on where Sebastian was emotionally as of late and if this secretive side to him would continue, evolve, or potentially cease altogether.

A few miles down the road, Sebastian received a text from his covert source. The ping indicated he had received a new encrypted file from his unnamed source.

File: Carter Davis CEO BlackThorn populated his inbox. In the past, Sebastian would immediately review the file . . . . *but not today.*

Today he would let the rest of the world run itself.

Sebastian Storm was officially off the clock for the first time since he could remember. Today, Carter Davis would be given a pass for all his past transgressions. Today, Sebastian didn't care. He put his phone in his pocket and smiled; he was completely content with that decision.

Sebastian faded back into his reality, quietly sitting in his chair at the local Osteria, obscure and unobtrusive and still watching Adriana enjoying her coffee from a distance and enjoying the sun in Venice, Italy.

Recalling his conversation with HB, he had made a decision that day, forever altering his life. He wanted to retire his past, bury it like the hundreds of people he had terminated throughout the years.

Deep within, he wanted to forget his past, his parents, Tobias, James, all of it. Starting anew was what Sebastian's focus was now, far different than his ordinary course. He was alive again; he wanted Adriana to be a part of it, despite her having no understanding of who or what he was. She would be swept up in his new direction.

A life of simplicity, a life of integrity, a life of normalcy.

He no longer wanted any more secrets. He wanted to create a life of honesty to himself and all surrounding him. Sebastian looked at her, still enjoying the sun, wrapped up in her tranquility. Her life was what he wanted, what he craved and visualized when he slept and when he woke.

Adriana did as she wished. Each and every day had no reason to look over her shoulder and lived her life to the fullest, and Sebastian wanted the very same for both of them. The world was hers, and he wanted to experience that with her intertwined within his own existence. A perfect merging of their worlds was what he hoped and yearned for as of late.

This was his wish, and he had the blessing of Sean and HB, although hesitant, and it was all that mattered to him. They wanted Sebastian blissful and content, giving him a sense of calm and elation. A sense he had not felt for a very long time.

He thought of his mother. Would she be happy for him? He was sure of it, making him smile at the thought. He missed her every day, but now he had something else to look forward to.

Adriana Mercer.

———

Sebastian couldn't wait any longer. He stood up and dropped a 100K lira bill on the table. He was smiling to himself. He had never been as excited as he was at this particular moment.

Walking through the front of the restaurant and into the sizeable cobblestoned patio many of the restaurants shared for their seating, he saw her sitting, unaware, from 100 yards away.

Adriana suddenly looked up as if she somehow sensed Sebastian's presence around her, his energy close somehow, slightly straining her eyes to confirm what she couldn't believe. Could it be him? Of course not, her mind was playing tricks on her. She hoped it was Sebastian in her heart, and she smiled at the thought that it could even be a possibility.

He was so handsome, casual, and relaxed and appeared somehow different to her than the other times she had met him. Lighter, unburdened . . . he was somehow transformed to her but not sure how exactly. Could it be he was fulfilling his promise, the promise he made to her in Vienna weeks ago?

As Sebastian walked toward her over the stone walkway, it was then he realized he had never spent any time with Adriana during daylight hours, save the moment in the stairwell, and smiled to himself at the simplicity of the thought. He had so much to explore with her. There was so much more about her he would discover, and he was elated at the possibility of knowing everything there was to experience with this woman.

She slowly stood up, straining her eyes and squinting as she watched him approach her direction. A large tourist group of sixty to seventy people walked between them, obscuring his view of her for a time, but he noticed her turning abruptly in the distance, almost unnaturally, until they all passed as he continued toward her. But she was no longer in the same location, which confused him, altering his perception of the moment.

But she was there, displaced, but the sunlight had shifted and made her look altered in her appearance for a moment to him. Something was different about her despite still being radiant and beautiful. He couldn't put his finger on it, but she appeared somehow different. Only glimpses and obstructed views as the tourists passed could be seen. Was it her hair, or her stance, it was odd to him? She was looking away from him now as if something had caught her attention behind her.

Sebastian didn't care; he smiled as he walked toward her, closing the gap between them when his phone chimed with a text alert upon the screen with a simple sentence reading,

"An eye for an eye, Sebastian. The time has finally come for you to truly feel my pain."

Upon reading the text, his heart sank, knowing something wasn't right. Instinctively, he glanced to his right, and several hundred feet away, he zeroed in on the familiar tall blond man watching him, dressed in a black suit, observing the arena he had created in the moment.

The spectacle had all been created for him, for Sebastian's benefit. Everything around Sebastian was a sole performance, all constructed for only his value and appreciation.

Fear crept into Sebastian's entire body in those seconds as he recognized the man quickly and realized, without question what was to follow. Standing next to the man, Fury smiled at the expression Sebastian held on his face and remembered his last words at the Pergamon, *". . . we are just beginning, just getting started. . ."*

Unconsciously, Sebastian turned back toward Adriana and instinctively began running toward her, but there were still people from the tourist group trailing between them. Sebastian frantically waved in her direction to get down and run from the area.

As expected, all the people hearing him were bewildered as the significance of the situation hadn't yet sunk in. He ran toward her, all in slow motion. Something was still off, strange about her, while standing in the distance, still partially concealed by the myriad of people in front of her. So many faces, blurred, distorted and distracting.

Still slightly turned away from him, he couldn't decipher what it was or what had changed, but it was in the moment the ground shook hard from the explosion detonated several feet behind Adriana. A billowing cloud of dust and rock erupted toward the patio, throwing Sebastian back twenty feet and against a table behind him, shattering it. Slightly dazed and mystified, he strained to focus on the source of the blast. Chaos ensued as the area swarmed with people and debris.

Sebastian slowly got to his feet as people emerged, running and staggering from the dust cloud engulfing the restaurant, but he began to walk and then run into the pinnacle of the destruction before him. Sebastian fought to get closer in as people were fighting to run from the blast. Bodies were strewn about, blood everywhere, tables overturned, and rubble scattered about the area.

He searched several bodies before he recognized a tan wedge dangling from a foot under a pile of rubble. Her white dress was soiled now, as her body lay in a heap below the numerous rocks piled atop her, smothering and crushing her. Her shoes, the wedges appeared darker brown before, far more soiled, but he was confused by it all. He was disoriented and confused from the blast, nothing made sense.

Sebastian approached where Adriana last stood, knelt, and frantically pulled at the rocks that had fallen on her until he was able to uncover most of her body. Her bloodied face was distorted and twisted; he couldn't even recognize her. His hands trembled as he reached out, desperately hoping against hope that he was wrong. He pressed his fingers against her wrist, searching frantically for the familiar, faint rhythm of life beneath her skin. But there was nothing—no pulse, no sign of the vitality that once flowed so strongly through her. A cold, paralyzing dread seized him as the awful truth began to sink in.

The silence around him grew deafening, each passing second hammering the reality into his heart with brutal clarity. He had lost her. The realization hit him like a tidal wave, washing over him with an unbearable sense of remorse and crushing sadness. How could this have happened? How could he have let this happen? His mind raced through the possibilities, grasping at any shred of denial, but it was futile. The finality of it all was inescapable.

He stared down at her, his vision blurring as tears welled up in his eyes. The world seemed to close in around him, suffocating in its stillness. The memories of their time together flooded his mind—every laugh, every touch, every word they had shared—now cruelly transformed into ghosts of what could never be again. The weight of his failure pressed down on him, a burden he knew he would carry for the rest of his life.

There were so many things left unsaid, so many moments they would never share. The overwhelming regret gnawed at him, and he felt as though a part of his own soul had been ripped away. He had lost her, and with that loss came the devastating realization that he could never go back, could never change what had led them to this moment.

The sadness was all-consuming, a dark, endless void that swallowed him whole. And as he knelt there, clutching her lifeless hand, he could only wish—desperately, hopelessly—that he had done more to protect her. Why hadn't he been there when she needed him most? But it was too late. All that was left was the emptiness, the crushing disappointment in himself, and the haunting sorrow of a life left unfinished.

He pulled her lifeless body onto his lap, cradling her head tenderly in his arms. His fingers gently caressed the side of her bloodied face, rocking her softly as if she were merely asleep. The aftermath of chaos surrounded them, the dust slowly settling like a cruel reminder of what had transpired.

Blood and lacerations marred her once beautiful features, each wound a testament to the violence she had endured. He held her tight, the weight of sorrow and remorse pressing heavily upon him. His heart ached with a pain that was almost unbearable, yet he remained dazed, trapped in the surreal horror of the moment.

As the world around him blurred into silence, he struggled to grasp the reality of his loss. Each second stretched into an eternity, his mind racing with what-ifs and regrets. The raw emotion of the scene hung thick in the air, a tragic testament to the love he had lost and the battle that had taken everything from him.

He could hear cries and screaming from the people in the area still as he looked around, taking in all the destruction. As the smoke and soot began to clear further, he looked again where he had witnessed the man in black standing, still there, the focus becoming clearer until the figure came into full view.

Tobias Teague stood smiling in his own warped and sinister way as he glared at Sebastian and reveled in his loss, enjoying Sebastian's suffering.

He wanted Sebastian to experience the same pain he had endured all those years before when he lost Emily.

The image still fresh of her decomposing head and her gaze even in death. He would never let go of that vision, forever seared into his mind, his compass, his focus ever-present, of what he must do and achieve. The image of his dead wife became the driving force for all he desired.

He simply wished to bestow the sense of sorrow upon Sebastian Storm to experience as he had years before.

At that moment, with Sebastian vulnerable before him, Tobias had the chance to end it all with a single bullet if he so chose. But a more sinister satisfaction filled him. Killing Sebastian would be too merciful. Instead, he had inflicted a far worse fate—he had stolen Sebastian's happiness, a wound that would fester and haunt him for the rest of his life.

The anticipation of Sebastian's enduring torment thrilled him and fueled his rage for a time. He wanted Sebastian to wake every morning and remember what had been taken from him, to feel the gnawing emptiness that would never heal. This was his true revenge, a punishment far more agonizing than death, ensuring every breath Sebastian took would be laced with sorrow and regret.

Tears welled up in Sebastian's eyes, a potent mix of grief, dust, fire, and smoke stinging his eyes. He could barely see through the haze, but his focus was unyielding as he locked eyes with Tobias Teague. The pain of her death was a raw, open wound, and every fiber of his being trembled with a mix of sorrow and unbridled rage.

Sebastian's breath came in ragged, furious gasps. His heart pounded in his chest as he stared down the man responsible for his agony. The flames flickered around them, casting ominous shadows that danced on the walls, the air thick with the acrid smell of destruction and death.

Tobias stood, a smirk playing on his lips, reveling in Sebastian's torment. He had orchestrated this moment with cruel precision. The agony in Sebastian's eyes was more satisfying than any death could ever be.

Sebastian's hands clenched into fists; his knuckles white with the intensity of his grip. His muscles tensed, ready to spring into action, driven by a fierce need for vengeance. The hatred in his eyes burned hotter than the flames around them, his mind already calculating the myriad ways he could make Tobias pay for this unimaginable pain.

But Tobias was prepared, his calm demeanor a stark contrast to Sebastian's visible turmoil. "Feel my pain, Sebastian," he taunted, his voice a venomous whisper. "That's the agony of everything you hold dear slipping through your fingers. And it's only just begun."

Sebastian's tears continued to fall, mingling with the grime on his face as he looked back down at Adriana's lifeless face. But as the sorrow coursed through him, it began to harden into a steely resolve. He would channel this pain, this searing loss, into a relentless pursuit of justice. Tobias Teague had made a fatal mistake, underestimating the strength arising from true, profound loss.

In that charged moment, amidst the ruins of his happiness, Sebastian made a silent vow. He would bring Tobias down, no matter the cost, and reclaim the honor of the life and the love so brutally stolen from him. The battle between them was far from over; it was only just beginning.

Knowing Sebastian could see him more clearly now, Tobias remained in the same position holding his smile, staring directly at Sebastian, unwavering and simply mouthed, "For Emily." Then slowly turned and walked away with Fury in tow.

Sebastian's voice echoed through the chaos, raw with loathing and desperation. "Tobias . . . Tobias!" he yelled, his shout piercing the roar of the flames and the crumbling ruins around him. His eyes burned with a mix of anguish and grief, fixed on the retreating figure of Tobias Teague.

But Tobias didn't turn around. He continued his stride into the distance, each step deliberate and unhurried. The destruction he had orchestrated shielded him, a barrier of fire and smoke magnifying the sense of hopelessness closing in on Sebastian.

Sebastian's heart pounded in his chest, the sadness surging through his veins urging him to pursue Tobias but another part of him no longer cared. The carnage Tobias had wrought held him back, every piece of debris a reminder of the suffering meticulously designed to break him. Tobias had won.

Their silhouettes grew smaller, shrouded in the haze of devastation. His calm, unwavering retreat was a stark contrast to the turmoil he left behind. The smirk on his face was almost palpable, a silent testament to his cruel satisfaction.

"Tobias!" Sebastian's voice cracked to a whisper, the anguish breaking through his rage. He could feel the weight of his loss pressing down on him, but within the pain, a burning helplessness began to overcome him.

Sebastian's muscles coiled with tension, his mind racing with plans for retribution but scattered and devoid of merit. The devastation around him was not just a testament to his enemy's power but a catalyst for his own transformation.

As Tobias disappeared into the distance, Sebastian vowed this was not the end. He would rise from the ashes stronger, more relentless, and he would hunt Tobias down with a verve that could not be quenched.

Sebastian stood amidst the wreckage, his body trembling with the intensity of his emotions. The air was thick with smoke and the scent of burning, but he breathed deeply, taking it all in. This moment of profound loss was also the birth of his unyielding quest for justice.

The battle between them was far from over. Tobias had ignited a fire within Sebastian, a relentless drive that would see him through the darkest of times unless it consumed him altogether.

As he stared into the distance, Sebastian knew with absolute certainty: he would stop at nothing to bring Tobias Teague to his knees.

Surrounded by the explosion's devastation, Sebastian stood, battered and unbroken staring at the broken body of Adriana Mercer. The flames consumed the remnants of his former life, their heat a cruel reminder of what he had lost. The image of her lifeless body haunted him, a constant ache fueling his grief and rage.

Tears no longer blurred his vision; instead, a cold clarity took their place. Tobias Teague had stolen his serenity. The sorrow weighing on his heart became the steel in his spine, driving him forward with a single-minded purpose.

Sebastian eased her body gently to the floor and stood up slowly watching her. He finally turned away and moved through the wreckage, each step was a testament to his transformation. The man who had once hoped for love and understanding was now a vessel of vengeance and sorrow. The world around him was a blur of shadows and fire.

Sebastian Storm had been irrevocably changed. His heart was heavy with loss, but it was this very pain that would guide him as it had before. The hunt had begun, and though the journey ahead was steeped in darkness, he would press on. The memory of what he had lost would be his constant companion, a sad but powerful reminder of why he could never turn back.

Sebastian Storm . . . . . would never be the same.

BOOK SUMMARY

Growing up in the spacious hills of West Virginia, Sebastian Storm's destiny was mapped out at an early age. Tragically losing both of his parents while in his early teens, Sebastian's fate was sealed, and a new path now lay before him. Through the destined guidance of a remarkable mentor, Sebastian learned the ways of military combat. It was quickly realized Sebastian possessed the gifts necessary to become a soldier elite. The United States government honed his skills further and, in the process, crafted a super soldier.

Storm was called in when all others had failed. Channeling his turbulent childhood anger, Sebastian concentrated his focus on those who wronged others, his vengeance swift and calculated, a virtual modern-day champion for those who couldn't defend themselves. A new breed of terrorism enters the global arena just as Storm's self-reflection of his own vulnerability is realized, but when he learns the leader of this auspicious group has set his focus on Storm specifically, he has no other choice but to meet it head-on. The leader of this group, Tobias Teague, and Sebastian Storm have long been rival entities bred by the same training early in their careers, with a bitter tragedy defining their emergent animosity for each other. For over a decade, they have avoided each other, but now Teague has planned a horrific terrorist event that will warrant the fear of the world, giving him the respect he commands.

The odd chance of meeting an intricate and unique woman puts Sebastian into a tailspin of emotions he has never experienced and forces him to reevaluate his priorities and future. Duty being paramount, Storm is Teague's only obstacle, and he will stop at nothing to achieve his goal. Their bond strong, defined by hate, by history, and by their lethal decree.

PROFESSIONAL SUMMARY

Diving into the vibrant tapestry of literary and professional distinction, Dr. Smallwood emerges as a trailblazing luminary celebrated for his unparalleled excellence. His global stature radiates, casting a spell over the dental community with his groundbreaking insights and mesmerizing fictional tales.

Dr. Smallwood's influence is boundless, captivating audiences worldwide with his profound knowledge and innovative strategies. He is a virtuoso across various domains, from the intricate art of comprehensive rehabilitation to the cutting-edge realm of Clear Aligner Therapy. He leads immersive educational programs that offer invaluable perspectives and techniques, empowering dental professionals to elevate their practices to unprecedented heights of success. His prowess now extends into the realm of fiction, broadening his literary horizons and amplifying his global acclaim.

In the academic sphere, his contributions are monumental. His numerous articles in prestigious peer-reviewed journals stand as a testament to his enduring brilliance, cementing his position among the elite TOP 100 speakers in dentistry for over two decades.

Lethal Storm

The Second Book of the Sebastian Storm Series

Estimated Release a Date: January 2023

After a terrorist plot is circumvented in Berlin, Germany, Sebastian Storm's life is plunged into turmoil as his past finally catches up with him. His greatest adversary, Tobias Teague, takes from Sebastian the only thing he has ever adored, sending him into a spiral of uncertainty and self-doubt.

Tobias sets out to manipulate every aspect of Sebastian's life, and those closest to him have now become Tobias's primary focus. However, key events have turned the tables, and certain perceptions are not as they seem. Information comes to light that will change everything and set Sebastian on a course of which there will be no return, unleashing the full destructive potential of Sebastian Storm and all he is capable of.

Realizing the depths that Tobias Teague will take and escalating his terrorist activities, Sebastian will stop at nothing to wreak havoc on Tobias and his organization. Tobias unleashes a new breed of supersoldier never before witnessed or tested that will help hip tip the scales in his favor.

Sebastian will have his revenge for taking Adriana Mercer from him, the only woman to elicit a human spark deep within Sebastian Storm's core. His retribution is calculated and poignant in its focus and execution.

Tobias orchestrates a new twist as his terrorizing continues, but the ultimate surprise occurs when Sebastian realizes Adriana's true fate, sending him into a profound sense of darkness. He will stop at nothing to make Teague fully realize Sebastian's truest sense of self, his conviction in seeing Teague finally suffer and witness Sebastian's full Lethal Storm . . . . unleashed.

THE REIGN COMETH

THE THIRD BOOK OF THE SEBASTIAN STORM SERIES

ESTIMATED RELEASE A DATE: SEPTEMBER 2024

With domestic anarchy weighing heavy on the balance and the current and antiquated political system failing, its ultimate implosion is imminent. Yet, a new luminary emerges from the midst of chaos. Born from a long line of staunch conservative Senators, Damian West has become the chosen hero to lead the new political faction. . . . the Unified Party.

As the established order and political system teeters on the brink of collapse, the people's champion, a neoteric face of optimism, emerges. Damian West arises as a beacon of hope amidst the crumbling political landscape. His charismatic leadership and strategic vision resonate with disillusioned leaders and American citizens seeking redemption. With a fresh perspective and a commitment to unity, he aims to bridge the divide that has plagued the nation for decades. His rallying cry echoes through the hearts of many, promising a new era of collaboration, effective governance, and equitable policies.

As the world watches with bated breath, Damian West emerges as a transformative energy, challenging the old guard and offering an alternative progressive path. The Unified Party becomes a formidable contender, drawing support from diverse circles and promising a government that prioritizes the needs and aspirations of the people as a whole. . . as a nation. Only time will tell if Damian West's leadership can reshape the political landscape and steer the country toward a brighter future.

The Unified Party, led by a determined and passionate group of key synergistic individuals, emerges as a viable alternative to the antiquated bipartisan system. With a focus on innovation and a fresh perspective, they aim to bring about positive change and efficiency in governance.

Handpicked by Damian West and his father, Senator Sam West, a team of dedicated and loyal supporters embark on a mission to redefine the values and aspirations of the United States, aiming to restore its position as a global superpower. Their unwavering dedication seeks to revive the nation's former glory and bring a new era of prosperity and influence.

Facing resistance from the Republican and Democratic parties alike, the Unified Party stands strong with its streamlined efficiency and unwavering commitment to principles of unity, racial autonomy, and a rejection of entrenched ambiguity in American democracy. Unfortunately, in modern times, the traditional parties find themselves ill-equipped to match the Unified Party's resolute stance and cohesive vision for the future.

Despite Damian West's illumination and progressive vision, hidden saboteurs lurk in the shadows, threatening his leadership and aspirations. Sebastian Storm, a dedicated ally of West, finds himself at the forefront of the battle, determined to protect and uphold the new ideals and believing in the man behind them. However, the opposing factions run deep and pose a formidable challenge to the Unified Party's agenda and evolution. The struggle for power and the nation's future intensifies as these opposing forces clash.

Damian West's dream is honed and focused; nothing will stop him or his political perspicuity, and he is determined to become the youngest candidate to hold the office of President of the United

States. His optimistic and influential core group garnered unyielding potential, and Damian West will not allow anyone or anything to stand in his way. Above all, he wishes to restore the integrity and uniformity of this great nation, but it won't come without significant cost to him, his beliefs, and the sacrifices it took to get him there.

Sebastian Storm weathers the political tempest standing at West's side, but not even Storm can imagine the depth of betrayal West must endure. Sebastian Storm, a figure shrouded in darkness, emerges as a silent guardian, vigilantly observing and safeguarding the United States' future through one man's vision. Within his unwavering presence, he is resolute in fulfilling Damian West's ambitions, meticulously paving the way for West's impending reign.

Sebastian navigates the intricate web of challenges with steadfast dedication, securing a clear path to realize West's aspirations. His unfaltering loyalty and commitment are the foundation for their shared vision, poised to shape the destiny ahead.

However, within the shadows lurk new and old enemies who threaten the sanctity of the administration. Sebastian's watchful gaze pierces through the veils of uncertainty, ever vigilant and prepared to navigate the trials that lie in wait. With quiet strength and determination, he stands as a pillar of support, tirelessly working towards realizing their common purpose.

Together, they forge ahead, united in pursuing a future crafted by West's hand and the Alternative Consortium supporting him. Sebastian's resolute presence remains an unyielding force, ensuring that the path remains clear, allowing the inevitable arrival of West's ascendancy.